This book belongs to

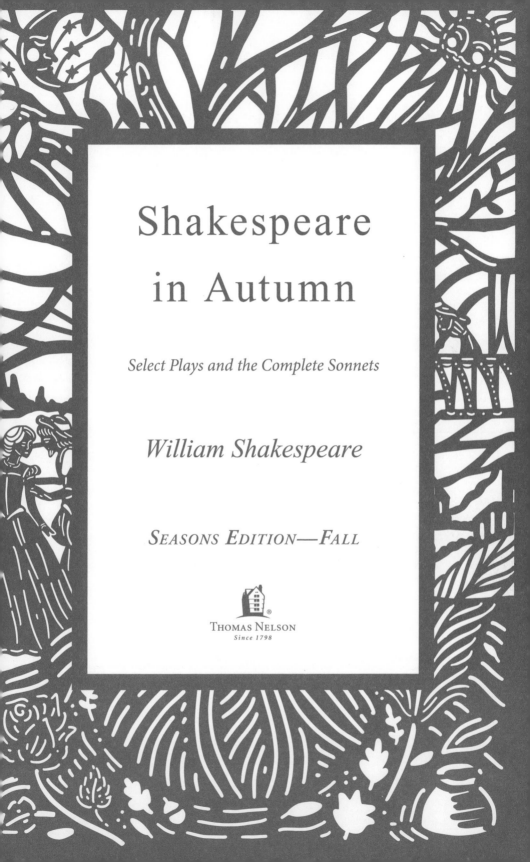

Shakespeare in Autumn

Select Plays and the Complete Sonnets

William Shakespeare

SEASONS EDITION—FALL

THOMAS NELSON
Since 1798

Produced by Thomas Nelson. Thomas Nelson is a registered trademark of HarperCollins Christian Publishing, Inc.

The Taming of the Shrew was composed 1590–94 and published in 1594.

The Tragedy of Romeo and Juliet was composed 1594–96 and published in 1597.

A Midsummer Night's Dream was composed 1595–96 and published in 1600.

As You Like It was composed 1598–1600 and published in 1623.

Twelfth Night was composed 1600–1602 and published in 1623.

The Sonnets were first published in 1609.

ISBN: 978-0-7852-5302-0 (hardcover)
ISBN: 978-0-7852-5313-6 (e-book)
ISBN: 978-0-7852-5315-0 (audio download)

Printed in China

21 22 23 24 25 DSC 5 4 3 2 1

CONTENTS

THE TAMING OF

THE SHREW

CONTENTS

ACT V

DRAMATIS PERSONÆ

PERSONS IN THE INDUCTION
A LORD
CHRISTOPHER SLY, a tinker
HOSTESS
PAGE
PLAYERS
HUNTSMEN
SERVANTS
BAPTISTA MINOLA, a rich gentleman of Padua
VINCENTIO, an old gentleman of Pisa
LUCENTIO, son to Vincentio; in love with Bianca
PETRUCHIO, a gentleman of Verona; suitor to Katherina

SUITORS TO BIANCA
GREMIO
HORTENSIO

SERVANTS TO LUCENTIO
TRANIO
BIONDELLO

SERVANTS TO PETRUCHIO
GRUMIO

CURTIS

PEDANT, set up to personate Vincentio

DAUGHTERS TO BAPTISTA

KATHERINA, the shrew

BIANCA

WIDOW

Tailor, Haberdasher, and Servants attending on Baptista and Petruchio

**SCENE: Sometimes in Padua, and sometimes
in PETRUCHIO'S house in the country.**

INDUCTION

SCENE I. Before an alehouse on a heath.

Enter HOSTESS and SLY.

SLY

I'll pheeze you, in faith.

HOSTESS

A pair of stocks, you rogue!

SLY

Y'are a baggage; the Slys are no rogues; look in the chronicles: we
came in with Richard Conqueror. Therefore, *paucas pallabris*; let the
world slide. Sessa!

HOSTESS

You will not pay for the glasses you have burst?

SLY

No, not a denier. Go by, Saint Jeronimy, go to thy cold bed and
warm thee.

HOSTESS

I know my remedy; I must go fetch the third-borough.
[Exit.]

SLY

Third, or fourth, or fifth borough, I'll answer him by law. I'll not
budge an inch, boy: let him come, and kindly.

[Lies down on the ground, and falls asleep.]
Horns winded. Enter a LORD from hunting, with HUNTSMEN
and SERVANTS.

LORD

Huntsman, I charge thee, tender well my hounds;
Brach Merriman, the poor cur is emboss'd,
And couple Clowder with the deep-mouth'd brach.
Saw'st thou not, boy, how Silver made it good
At the hedge-corner, in the coldest fault?
I would not lose the dog for twenty pound.

FIRST HUNTSMAN

Why, Bellman is as good as he, my lord;
He cried upon it at the merest loss,
And twice today pick'd out the dullest scent;
Trust me, I take him for the better dog.

LORD

Thou art a fool: if Echo were as fleet,
I would esteem him worth a dozen such.
But sup them well, and look unto them all;
Tomorrow I intend to hunt again.

FIRST HUNTSMAN

I will, my lord.

LORD

[Sees Sly.]
What's here? One dead, or drunk?
See, doth he breathe?

SECOND HUNTSMAN

He breathes, my lord. Were he not warm'd with ale,
This were a bed but cold to sleep so soundly.

LORD

O monstrous beast! how like a swine he lies!
Grim death, how foul and loathsome is thine image!
Sirs, I will practise on this drunken man.
What think you, if he were convey'd to bed,
Wrapp'd in sweet clothes, rings put upon his fingers,

A most delicious banquet by his bed,
And brave attendants near him when he wakes,
Would not the beggar then forget himself?

FIRST HUNTSMAN

Believe me, lord, I think he cannot choose.

SECOND HUNTSMAN

It would seem strange unto him when he wak'd.

LORD

Even as a flattering dream or worthless fancy.
Then take him up, and manage well the jest.
Carry him gently to my fairest chamber,
And hang it round with all my wanton pictures;
Balm his foul head in warm distilled waters,
And burn sweet wood to make the lodging sweet.
Procure me music ready when he wakes,
To make a dulcet and a heavenly sound;
And if he chance to speak, be ready straight,
And with a low submissive reverence
Say 'What is it your honour will command?'
Let one attend him with a silver basin
Full of rose-water and bestrew'd with flowers;
Another bear the ewer, the third a diaper,
And say 'Will't please your lordship cool your hands?'
Someone be ready with a costly suit,
And ask him what apparel he will wear;
Another tell him of his hounds and horse,
And that his lady mourns at his disease.
Persuade him that he hath been lunatic;
And, when he says he is—say that he dreams,
For he is nothing but a mighty lord.
This do, and do it kindly, gentle sirs;
It will be pastime passing excellent,
If it be husbanded with modesty.

FIRST HUNTSMAN

My lord, I warrant you we will play our part,
As he shall think by our true diligence,
He is no less than what we say he is.

LORD

Take him up gently, and to bed with him,
And each one to his office when he wakes.
                [SLY is bourne out. A trumpet sounds.]
Sirrah, go see what trumpet 'tis that sounds:
                [Exit SERVANT.]
Belike some noble gentleman that means,
Travelling some journey, to repose him here.
                Re-enter SERVANT.
How now! who is it?

SERVANT

An, it please your honour, players
That offer service to your lordship.

LORD

Bid them come near.
                Enter PLAYERS.
Now, fellows, you are welcome.

PLAYERS

We thank your honour.

LORD

Do you intend to stay with me tonight?

PLAYER

So please your lordship to accept our duty.

LORD

With all my heart. This fellow I remember
Since once he play'd a farmer's eldest son;
'Twas where you woo'd the gentlewoman so well.
I have forgot your name; but, sure, that part
Was aptly fitted and naturally perform'd.

PLAYER

I think 'twas Soto that your honour means.

LORD

'Tis very true; thou didst it excellent.
Well, you are come to me in happy time,

The rather for I have some sport in hand
Wherein your cunning can assist me much.
There is a lord will hear you play tonight;
But I am doubtful of your modesties,
Lest, over-eying of his odd behaviour,—
For yet his honour never heard a play,—
You break into some merry passion
And so offend him; for I tell you, sirs,
If you should smile, he grows impatient.

PLAYER

Fear not, my lord; we can contain ourselves,
Were he the veriest antick in the world.

LORD

Go, sirrah, take them to the buttery,
And give them friendly welcome everyone:
Let them want nothing that my house affords.
[Exit one with the PLAYERS.]
Sirrah, go you to Barthol'mew my page,
And see him dress'd in all suits like a lady;
That done, conduct him to the drunkard's chamber,
And call him 'madam,' do him obeisance.
Tell him from me—as he will win my love,—
He bear himself with honourable action,
Such as he hath observ'd in noble ladies
Unto their lords, by them accomplished;
Such duty to the drunkard let him do,
With soft low tongue and lowly courtesy,
And say 'What is't your honour will command,
Wherein your lady and your humble wife
May show her duty and make known her love?'
And then with kind embracements, tempting kisses,
And with declining head into his bosom,
Bid him shed tears, as being overjoy'd
To see her noble lord restor'd to health,
Who for this seven years hath esteemed him
No better than a poor and loathsome beggar.
And if the boy have not a woman's gift

To rain a shower of commanded tears,
An onion will do well for such a shift,
Which, in a napkin being close convey'd,
Shall in despite enforce a watery eye.
See this dispatch'd with all the haste thou canst;
Anon I'll give thee more instructions.

[Exit SERVANT.]

I know the boy will well usurp the grace,
Voice, gait, and action of a gentlewoman;
I long to hear him call the drunkard husband;
And how my men will stay themselves from laughter
When they do homage to this simple peasant.
I'll in to counsel them; haply my presence
May well abate the over-merry spleen,
Which otherwise would grow into extremes.

[Exeunt.]

SCENE II. A bedchamber in the LORD'S house.

SLY is discovered in a rich nightgown, with
ATTENDANTS: some with apparel, basin, ewer, and other
appurtenances; and LORD, dressed like a servant.

SLY

For God's sake! a pot of small ale.

FIRST SERVANT

Will't please your lordship drink a cup of sack?

SECOND SERVANT

Will't please your honour taste of these conserves?

THIRD SERVANT

What raiment will your honour wear today?

SLY

I am Christophero Sly; call not me honour nor lordship. I ne'er drank sack in my life; and if you give me any conserves, give me conserves of beef. Ne'er ask me what raiment I'll wear, for I have no more doublets than backs, no more stockings than legs, nor no more shoes than feet: nay, sometime more feet than shoes, or such shoes as my toes look through the over-leather.

LORD

Heaven cease this idle humour in your honour!
O, that a mighty man of such descent,
Of such possessions, and so high esteem,
Should be infused with so foul a spirit!

SLY

What! would you make me mad? Am not I Christopher Sly, old Sly's son of Burton-heath; by birth a pedlar, by education a cardmaker, by transmutation a bear-herd, and now by present profession a tinker? Ask Marian Hacket, the fat ale-wife of Wincot, if she know me not: if she say I am not fourteen pence on the score for sheer ale, score me up for the lyingest knave in Christendom. What! I am not bestraught. Here's—

THIRD SERVANT

O! this it is that makes your lady mourn.

SECOND SERVANT

O! this is it that makes your servants droop.

LORD

Hence comes it that your kindred shuns your house,
As beaten hence by your strange lunacy.
O noble lord, bethink thee of thy birth,
Call home thy ancient thoughts from banishment,
And banish hence these abject lowly dreams.
Look how thy servants do attend on thee,
Each in his office ready at thy beck:
Wilt thou have music? Hark! Apollo plays,
    [Music.]
And twenty caged nightingales do sing:
Or wilt thou sleep? We'll have thee to a couch
Softer and sweeter than the lustful bed
On purpose trimm'd up for Semiramis.
Say thou wilt walk: we will bestrew the ground:
Or wilt thou ride? Thy horses shall be trapp'd,

Their harness studded all with gold and pearl.
Dost thou love hawking? Thou hast hawks will soar
Above the morning lark: or wilt thou hunt?
Thy hounds shall make the welkin answer them
And fetch shrill echoes from the hollow earth.

FIRST SERVANT

Say thou wilt course; thy greyhounds are as swift
As breathed stags; ay, fleeter than the roe.

SECOND SERVANT

Dost thou love pictures? We will fetch thee straight
Adonis painted by a running brook,
And Cytherea all in sedges hid,
Which seem to move and wanton with her breath
Even as the waving sedges play with wind.

LORD

We'll show thee Io as she was a maid
And how she was beguiled and surpris'd,
As lively painted as the deed was done.

THIRD SERVANT

Or Daphne roaming through a thorny wood,
Scratching her legs, that one shall swear she bleeds
And at that sight shall sad Apollo weep,
So workmanly the blood and tears are drawn.

LORD

Thou art a lord, and nothing but a lord:
Thou hast a lady far more beautiful
Than any woman in this waning age.

FIRST SERVANT

And, till the tears that she hath shed for thee
Like envious floods o'er-run her lovely face,
She was the fairest creature in the world;
And yet she is inferior to none.

SLY

Am I a lord? and have I such a lady?
Or do I dream? Or have I dream'd till now?

I do not sleep: I see, I hear, I speak;
I smell sweet savours, and I feel soft things:
Upon my life, I am a lord indeed;
And not a tinker, nor Christophero Sly.
Well, bring our lady hither to our sight;
And once again, a pot o' the smallest ale.

SECOND SERVANT

Will't please your mightiness to wash your hands?
                    [Servants present a ewer, basin and napkin.]
O, how we joy to see your wit restor'd!
O, that once more you knew but what you are!
These fifteen years you have been in a dream,
Or, when you wak'd, so wak'd as if you slept.

SLY

These fifteen years! by my fay, a goodly nap.
But did I never speak of all that time?

FIRST SERVANT

O! yes, my lord, but very idle words;
For though you lay here in this goodly chamber,
Yet would you say ye were beaten out of door,
And rail upon the hostess of the house,
And say you would present her at the leet,
Because she brought stone jugs and no seal'd quarts.
Sometimes you would call out for Cicely Hacket.

SLY

Ay, the woman's maid of the house.

THIRD SERVANT

Why, sir, you know no house nor no such maid,
Nor no such men as you have reckon'd up,
As Stephen Sly, and old John Naps of Greece,
And Peter Turph, and Henry Pimpernell;
And twenty more such names and men as these,
Which never were, nor no man ever saw.

SLY

Now, Lord be thanked for my good amends!

ALL

Amen.

Enter the PAGE, as a lady, with ATTENDANTS.

SLY

I thank thee; thou shalt not lose by it.

PAGE

How fares my noble lord?

SLY

Marry, I fare well; for here is cheer enough.
Where is my wife?

PAGE

Here, noble lord: what is thy will with her?

SLY

Are you my wife, and will not call me husband?
My men should call me lord: I am your goodman.

PAGE

My husband and my lord, my lord and husband;
I am your wife in all obedience.

SLY

I know it well. What must I call her?

LORD

Madam.

SLY

Alice madam, or Joan madam?

LORD

Madam, and nothing else; so lords call ladies.

SLY

Madam wife, they say that I have dream'd
And slept above some fifteen year or more.

PAGE

Ay, and the time seems thirty unto me,
Being all this time abandon'd from your bed.

SLY

> 'Tis much. Servants, leave me and her alone.
> Madam, undress you, and come now to bed.

PAGE

> Thrice noble lord, let me entreat of you
> To pardon me yet for a night or two;
> Or, if not so, until the sun be set:
> For your physicians have expressly charg'd,
> In peril to incur your former malady,
> That I should yet absent me from your bed:
> I hope this reason stands for my excuse.

SLY

> Ay, it stands so that I may hardly tarry so long; but I would be loath
> to fall into my dreams again: I will therefore tarry in despite of the flesh
> and the blood.

> *Enter a* MESSENGER.

MESSENGER

> Your honour's players, hearing your amendment,
> Are come to play a pleasant comedy;
> For so your doctors hold it very meet,
> Seeing too much sadness hath congeal'd your blood,
> And melancholy is the nurse of frenzy:
> Therefore they thought it good you hear a play,
> And frame your mind to mirth and merriment,
> Which bars a thousand harms and lengthens life.

SLY

> Marry, I will; let them play it. Is not a commonty a Christmas gam-
> bold or a tumbling-trick?

PAGE

> No, my good lord; it is more pleasing stuff.

SLY

> What! household stuff?

PAGE

It is a kind of history.

SLY

Well, we'll see't. Come, madam wife, sit by my side and let the world slip: we shall ne'er be younger.

ACT I

SCENE I. Padua. A public place.

Flourish. Enter LUCENTIO and TRANIO.

LUCENTIO

Tranio, since for the great desire I had
To see fair Padua, nursery of arts,
I am arriv'd for fruitful Lombardy,
The pleasant garden of great Italy,
And by my father's love and leave am arm'd
With his good will and thy good company,
My trusty servant well approv'd in all,
Here let us breathe, and haply institute
A course of learning and ingenious studies.
Pisa, renowned for grave citizens,
Gave me my being and my father first,
A merchant of great traffic through the world,
Vincentio, come of the Bentivolii.
Vincentio's son, brought up in Florence,
It shall become to serve all hopes conceiv'd,
To deck his fortune with his virtuous deeds:
And therefore, Tranio, for the time I study,
Virtue and that part of philosophy
Will I apply that treats of happiness
By virtue specially to be achiev'd.
Tell me thy mind; for I have Pisa left

And am to Padua come as he that leaves
A shallow plash to plunge him in the deep,
And with satiety seeks to quench his thirst.

TRANIO

Mi perdonato, gentle master mine;
I am in all affected as yourself;
Glad that you thus continue your resolve
To suck the sweets of sweet philosophy.
Only, good master, while we do admire
This virtue and this moral discipline,
Let's be no stoics nor no stocks, I pray;
Or so devote to Aristotle's checks
As Ovid be an outcast quite abjur'd.
Balk logic with acquaintance that you have,
And practise rhetoric in your common talk;
Music and poesy use to quicken you;
The mathematics and the metaphysics,
Fall to them as you find your stomach serves you:
No profit grows where is no pleasure ta'en;
In brief, sir, study what you most affect.

LUCENTIO

Gramercies, Tranio, well dost thou advise.
If, Biondello, thou wert come ashore,
We could at once put us in readiness,
And take a lodging fit to entertain
Such friends as time in Padua shall beget.
But stay awhile; what company is this?

TRANIO

Master, some show to welcome us to town.
        [LUCENTIO and TRANIO stand aside.]
        Enter BAPTISTA, KATHERINA, BIANCA, GREMIO and HORTENSIO.

BAPTISTA

Gentlemen, importune me no farther,
For how I firmly am resolv'd you know;
That is, not to bestow my youngest daughter
Before I have a husband for the elder.

If either of you both love Katherina,
Because I know you well and love you well,
Leave shall you have to court her at your pleasure.

GREMIO

To cart her rather: she's too rough for me.
There, there, Hortensio, will you any wife?

KATHERINA

[To Baptista.]
I pray you, sir, is it your will
To make a stale of me amongst these mates?

HORTENSIO

Mates, maid! How mean you that? No mates for you,
Unless you were of gentler, milder mould.

KATHERINA

I' faith, sir, you shall never need to fear;
I wis it is not half way to her heart;
But if it were, doubt not her care should be
To comb your noddle with a three-legg'd stool,
And paint your face, and use you like a fool.

HORTENSIO

From all such devils, good Lord deliver us!

GREMIO

And me, too, good Lord!

TRANIO

Husht, master! Here's some good pastime toward:
That wench is stark mad or wonderful froward.

LUCENTIO

But in the other's silence do I see
Maid's mild behaviour and sobriety.
Peace, Tranio!

TRANIO

Well said, master; mum! and gaze your fill.

BAPTISTA

Gentlemen, that I may soon make good
What I have said,—Bianca, get you in:
And let it not displease thee, good Bianca,
For I will love thee ne'er the less, my girl.

KATHERINA

A pretty peat! it is best put finger in the eye, and she knew why.

BIANCA

Sister, content you in my discontent.
Sir, to your pleasure humbly I subscribe:
My books and instruments shall be my company,
On them to look, and practise by myself.

LUCENTIO

Hark, Tranio! thou mayst hear Minerva speak.

HORTENSIO

Signior Baptista, will you be so strange?
Sorry am I that our good will effects
Bianca's grief.

GREMIO

Why will you mew her up,
Signior Baptista, for this fiend of hell,
And make her bear the penance of her tongue?

BAPTISTA

Gentlemen, content ye; I am resolv'd.
Go in, Bianca.
      [Exit BIANCA.]
And for I know she taketh most delight
In music, instruments, and poetry,
Schoolmasters will I keep within my house
Fit to instruct her youth. If you, Hortensio,
Or, Signior Gremio, you, know any such,
Prefer them hither; for to cunning men
I will be very kind, and liberal
To mine own children in good bringing up;

And so, farewell. Katherina, you may stay;
For I have more to commune with Bianca.
    [Exit.]

KATHERINA

Why, and I trust I may go too, may I not? What! shall I be appointed hours, as though, belike, I knew not what to take and what to leave? Ha!
    [Exit.]

GREMIO

You may go to the devil's dam: your gifts are so good here's none will hold you. Their love is not so great, Hortensio, but we may blow our nails together, and fast it fairly out; our cake's dough on both sides. Farewell: yet, for the love I bear my sweet Bianca, if I can by any means light on a fit man to teach her that wherein she delights, I will wish him to her father.

HORTENSIO

So will I, Signior Gremio: but a word, I pray. Though the nature of our quarrel yet never brooked parle, know now, upon advice, it toucheth us both,—that we may yet again have access to our fair mistress, and be happy rivals in Bianca's love,—to labour and effect one thing specially.

GREMIO

What's that, I pray?

HORTENSIO

Marry, sir, to get a husband for her sister.

GREMIO

A husband! a devil.

HORTENSIO

I say, a husband.

GREMIO

I say, a devil. Thinkest thou, Hortensio, though her father be very rich, any man is so very a fool to be married to hell?

HORTENSIO

Tush, Gremio! Though it pass your patience and mine to endure her loud alarums, why, man, there be good fellows in the world, and a man could light on them, would take her with all faults, and money enough.

GREMIO

I cannot tell; but I had as lief take her dowry with this condition: to be whipp'd at the high cross every morning.

HORTENSIO

Faith, as you say, there's small choice in rotten apples. But come; since this bar in law makes us friends, it shall be so far forth friendly maintained, till by helping Baptista's eldest daughter to a husband, we set his youngest free for a husband, and then have to't afresh. Sweet Bianca! Happy man be his dole! He that runs fastest gets the ring. How say you, Signior Gremio?

GREMIO

I am agreed; and would I had given him the best horse in Padua to begin his wooing, that would thoroughly woo her, wed her, and bed her, and rid the house of her. Come on.

[Exeunt GREMIO and HORTENSIO.]

TRANIO

I pray, sir, tell me, is it possible
That love should of a sudden take such hold?

LUCENTIO

O Tranio! till I found it to be true,
I never thought it possible or likely;
But see, while idly I stood looking on,
I found the effect of love in idleness;
And now in plainness do confess to thee,
That art to me as secret and as dear
As Anna to the Queen of Carthage was,
Tranio, I burn, I pine, I perish, Tranio,
If I achieve not this young modest girl.
Counsel me, Tranio, for I know thou canst:
Assist me, Tranio, for I know thou wilt.

TRANIO

Master, it is no time to chide you now;
Affection is not rated from the heart:
If love have touch'd you, nought remains but so:
Redime te captum quam queas minimo.

LUCENTIO

Gramercies, lad; go forward; this contents;
The rest will comfort, for thy counsel's sound.

TRANIO

Master, you look'd so longly on the maid.
Perhaps you mark'd not what's the pith of all.

LUCENTIO

O, yes, I saw sweet beauty in her face,
Such as the daughter of Agenor had,
That made great Jove to humble him to her hand,
When with his knees he kiss'd the Cretan strand.

TRANIO

Saw you no more? mark'd you not how her sister
Began to scold and raise up such a storm
That mortal ears might hardly endure the din?

LUCENTIO

Tranio, I saw her coral lips to move,
And with her breath she did perfume the air;
Sacred and sweet was all I saw in her.

TRANIO

Nay, then, 'tis time to stir him from his trance.
I pray, awake, sir: if you love the maid,
Bend thoughts and wits to achieve her. Thus it stands:
Her elder sister is so curst and shrewd,
That till the father rid his hands of her,
Master, your love must live a maid at home;
And therefore has he closely mew'd her up,
Because she will not be annoy'd with suitors.

LUCENTIO

Ah, Tranio, what a cruel father's he!
But art thou not advis'd he took some care
To get her cunning schoolmasters to instruct her?

TRANIO

Ay, marry, am I, sir, and now 'tis plotted.

LUCENTIO

I have it, Tranio.

TRANIO

Master, for my hand,
Both our inventions meet and jump in one.

LUCENTIO

Tell me thine first.

TRANIO

You will be schoolmaster,
And undertake the teaching of the maid:
That's your device.

LUCENTIO

It is: may it be done?

TRANIO

Not possible; for who shall bear your part
And be in Padua here Vincentio's son;
Keep house and ply his book, welcome his friends;
Visit his countrymen, and banquet them?

LUCENTIO

Basta, content thee, for I have it full.
We have not yet been seen in any house,
Nor can we be distinguish'd by our faces
For man or master: then it follows thus:
Thou shalt be master, Tranio, in my stead,
Keep house and port and servants, as I should;
I will some other be; some Florentine,
Some Neapolitan, or meaner man of Pisa.
'Tis hatch'd, and shall be so: Tranio, at once
Uncase thee; take my colour'd hat and cloak.
When Biondello comes, he waits on thee;
But I will charm him first to keep his tongue.
        [They exchange habits.]

TRANIO

So had you need.

In brief, sir, sith it your pleasure is,
And I am tied to be obedient;
For so your father charg'd me at our parting,
'Be serviceable to my son,' quoth he,
Although I think 'twas in another sense:
I am content to be Lucentio,
Because so well I love Lucentio.

LUCENTIO

Tranio, be so, because Lucentio loves;
And let me be a slave, to achieve that maid
Whose sudden sight hath thrall'd my wounded eye.
   Enter BIONDELLO.
Here comes the rogue. Sirrah, where have you been?

BIONDELLO

Where have I been? Nay, how now! where are you?
Master, has my fellow Tranio stol'n your clothes?
Or you stol'n his? or both? Pray, what's the news?

LUCENTIO

Sirrah, come hither: 'tis no time to jest,
And therefore frame your manners to the time.
Your fellow Tranio here, to save my life,
Puts my apparel and my count'nance on,
And I for my escape have put on his;
For in a quarrel since I came ashore
I kill'd a man, and fear I was descried.
Wait you on him, I charge you, as becomes,
While I make way from hence to save my life.
You understand me?

BIONDELLO

I, sir! Ne'er a whit.

LUCENTIO

And not a jot of Tranio in your mouth:
Tranio is changed to Lucentio.

BIONDELLO

The better for him: would I were so too!

TRANIO

So could I, faith, boy, to have the next wish after,
That Lucentio indeed had Baptista's youngest daughter.
But, sirrah, not for my sake but your master's, I advise
You use your manners discreetly in all kind of companies:
When I am alone, why, then I am Tranio;
But in all places else your master, Lucentio.

LUCENTIO

Tranio, let's go.
One thing more rests, that thyself execute,
To make one among these wooers: if thou ask me why,
Sufficeth my reasons are both good and weighty.
		[Exeunt.]
		[The Presenters above speak.]

FIRST SERVANT

My lord, you nod; you do not mind the play.

SLY

Yes, by Saint Anne, I do. A good matter, surely: comes there any more of it?

PAGE

My lord, 'tis but begun.

SLY

'Tis a very excellent piece of work, madam lady: would 'twere done!
		[They sit and mark.]

SCENE II. Padua. Before HORTENSIO'S house.

Enter PETRUCHIO and his man GRUMIO.

PETRUCHIO

Verona, for a while I take my leave,
To see my friends in Padua; but of all
My best beloved and approved friend,
Hortensio; and I trow this is his house.
Here, sirrah Grumio, knock, I say.

GRUMIO

Knock, sir? Whom should I knock? Is there any man has rebused your worship?

PETRUCHIO

Villain, I say, knock me here soundly.

GRUMIO

Knock you here, sir? Why, sir, what am I, sir, that I should knock you here, sir?

PETRUCHIO

Villain, I say, knock me at this gate;
And rap me well, or I'll knock your knave's pate.

GRUMIO

My master is grown quarrelsome. I should knock you first,
And then I know after who comes by the worst.

PETRUCHIO

Will it not be?
Faith, sirrah, and you'll not knock, I'll ring it;
I'll try how you can sol, fa, and sing it.
            [He wrings Grumio by the ears.]

GRUMIO

Help, masters, help! my master is mad.

PETRUCHIO

Now, knock when I bid you, sirrah villain!
            Enter HORTENSIO.

HORTENSIO

How now! what's the matter? My old friend Grumio! and my good friend Petruchio! How do you all at Verona?

PETRUCHIO

Signior Hortensio, come you to part the fray?
Con tutto il cuore ben trovato, may I say.

HORTENSIO

Alla nostra casa ben venuto; molto honorato signor mio Petruchio.
Rise, Grumio, rise: we will compound this quarrel.

GRUMIO

Nay, 'tis no matter, sir, what he 'leges in Latin. If this be not a lawful cause for me to leave his service, look you, sir, he bid me knock him and rap him soundly, sir: well, was it fit for a servant to use his master so; being, perhaps, for aught I see, two-and-thirty, a pip out? Whom would to God I had well knock'd at first, then had not Grumio come by the worst.

PETRUCHIO

A senseless villain! Good Hortensio,
I bade the rascal knock upon your gate,
And could not get him for my heart to do it.

GRUMIO

Knock at the gate! O heavens! Spake you not these words plain: 'Sirrah knock me here, rap me here, knock me well, and knock me soundly'? And come you now with 'knocking at the gate'?

PETRUCHIO

Sirrah, be gone, or talk not, I advise you.

HORTENSIO

Petruchio, patience; I am Grumio's pledge;
Why, this's a heavy chance 'twixt him and you,
Your ancient, trusty, pleasant servant Grumio.
And tell me now, sweet friend, what happy gale
Blows you to Padua here from old Verona?

PETRUCHIO

Such wind as scatters young men through the world
To seek their fortunes farther than at home,
Where small experience grows. But in a few,
Signior Hortensio, thus it stands with me:
Antonio, my father, is deceas'd,
And I have thrust myself into this maze,
Haply to wive and thrive as best I may;
Crowns in my purse I have, and goods at home,
And so am come abroad to see the world.

HORTENSIO

Petruchio, shall I then come roundly to thee
And wish thee to a shrewd ill-favour'd wife?

Thou'dst thank me but a little for my counsel;
And yet I'll promise thee she shall be rich,
And very rich: but th'art too much my friend,
And I'll not wish thee to her.

PETRUCHIO

Signior Hortensio, 'twixt such friends as we
Few words suffice; and therefore, if thou know
One rich enough to be Petruchio's wife,
As wealth is burden of my wooing dance,
Be she as foul as was Florentius' love,
As old as Sibyl, and as curst and shrewd
As Socrates' Xanthippe or a worse,
She moves me not, or not removes, at least,
Affection's edge in me, were she as rough
As are the swelling Adriatic seas:
I come to wive it wealthily in Padua;
If wealthily, then happily in Padua.

GRUMIO

Nay, look you, sir, he tells you flatly what his mind is: why, give him
gold enough and marry him to a puppet or an aglet-baby; or an old trot
with ne'er a tooth in her head, though she have as many diseases as two-
and-fifty horses: why, nothing comes amiss, so money comes withal.

HORTENSIO

Petruchio, since we are stepp'd thus far in,
I will continue that I broach'd in jest.
I can, Petruchio, help thee to a wife
With wealth enough, and young and beauteous;
Brought up as best becomes a gentlewoman:
Her only fault,—and that is faults enough,—
Is, that she is intolerable curst,
And shrewd and froward, so beyond all measure,
That, were my state far worser than it is,
I would not wed her for a mine of gold.

PETRUCHIO

Hortensio, peace! thou know'st not gold's effect:
Tell me her father's name, and 'tis enough;

For I will board her, though she chide as loud
As thunder when the clouds in autumn crack.

HORTENSIO

Her father is Baptista Minola,
An affable and courteous gentleman;
Her name is Katherina Minola,
Renown'd in Padua for her scolding tongue.

PETRUCHIO

I know her father, though I know not her;
And he knew my deceased father well.
I will not sleep, Hortensio, till I see her;
And therefore let me be thus bold with you,
To give you over at this first encounter,
Unless you will accompany me thither.

GRUMIO

I pray you, sir, let him go while the humour lasts. O' my word, and she knew him as well as I do, she would think scolding would do little good upon him. She may perhaps call him half a score knaves or so; why, that's nothing; and he begin once, he'll rail in his rope-tricks. I'll tell you what, sir, and she stand him but a little, he will throw a figure in her face, and so disfigure her with it that she shall have no more eyes to see withal than a cat. You know him not, sir.

HORTENSIO

Tarry, Petruchio, I must go with thee,
For in Baptista's keep my treasure is:
He hath the jewel of my life in hold,
His youngest daughter, beautiful Bianca,
And her withholds from me and other more,
Suitors to her and rivals in my love;
Supposing it a thing impossible,
For those defects I have before rehears'd,
That ever Katherina will be woo'd:
Therefore this order hath Baptista ta'en,
That none shall have access unto Bianca
Till Katherine the curst have got a husband.

GRUMIO

>Katherine the curst!
>A title for a maid of all titles the worst.

HORTENSIO

>Now shall my friend Petruchio do me grace,
>And offer me disguis'd in sober robes,
>To old Baptista as a schoolmaster
>Well seen in music, to instruct Bianca;
>That so I may, by this device at least
>Have leave and leisure to make love to her,
>And unsuspected court her by herself.

GRUMIO

>Here's no knavery! See, to beguile the old folks, how the young folks
>lay their heads together!
>>*Enter GREMIO and LUCENTIO disguised, with books under his arm.*
>Master, master, look about you: who goes there, ha?

HORTENSIO

>Peace, Grumio! It is the rival of my love. Petruchio, stand by awhile.

GRUMIO

>A proper stripling, and an amorous!

GREMIO

>O! very well; I have perus'd the note.
>Hark you, sir; I'll have them very fairly bound:
>All books of love, see that at any hand,
>And see you read no other lectures to her.
>You understand me. Over and beside
>Signior Baptista's liberality,
>I'll mend it with a largess. Take your papers too,
>And let me have them very well perfum'd;
>For she is sweeter than perfume itself
>To whom they go to. What will you read to her?

LUCENTIO

>Whate'er I read to her, I'll plead for you,
>As for my patron, stand you so assur'd,

As firmly as yourself were still in place;
Yea, and perhaps with more successful words
Than you, unless you were a scholar, sir.

GREMIO

O! this learning, what a thing it is.

GRUMIO

O! this woodcock, what an ass it is.

PETRUCHIO

Peace, sirrah!

HORTENSIO

Grumio, mum! God save you, Signior Gremio!

GREMIO

And you are well met, Signior Hortensio.
Trow you whither I am going? To Baptista Minola.
I promis'd to enquire carefully
About a schoolmaster for the fair Bianca;
And by good fortune I have lighted well
On this young man; for learning and behaviour
Fit for her turn, well read in poetry
And other books, good ones, I warrant ye.

HORTENSIO

'Tis well; and I have met a gentleman
Hath promis'd me to help me to another,
A fine musician to instruct our mistress:
So shall I no whit be behind in duty
To fair Bianca, so belov'd of me.

GREMIO

Belov'd of me, and that my deeds shall prove.

GRUMIO

   [Aside.]
And that his bags shall prove.

HORTENSIO

Gremio, 'tis now no time to vent our love:

Listen to me, and if you speak me fair,
I'll tell you news indifferent good for either.
Here is a gentleman whom by chance I met,
Upon agreement from us to his liking,
Will undertake to woo curst Katherine;
Yea, and to marry her, if her dowry please.

GREMIO

So said, so done, is well.
Hortensio, have you told him all her faults?

PETRUCHIO

I know she is an irksome brawling scold;
If that be all, masters, I hear no harm.

GREMIO

No, say'st me so, friend? What countryman?

PETRUCHIO

Born in Verona, old Antonio's son.
My father dead, my fortune lives for me;
And I do hope good days and long to see.

GREMIO

O sir, such a life, with such a wife, were strange!
But if you have a stomach, to't a God's name;
You shall have me assisting you in all.
But will you woo this wild-cat?

PETRUCHIO

Will I live?

GRUMIO

Will he woo her? Ay, or I'll hang her.

PETRUCHIO

Why came I hither but to that intent?
Think you a little din can daunt mine ears?
Have I not in my time heard lions roar?
Have I not heard the sea, puff'd up with winds,
Rage like an angry boar chafed with sweat?

Have I not heard great ordnance in the field,
And heaven's artillery thunder in the skies?
Have I not in a pitched battle heard
Loud 'larums, neighing steeds, and trumpets' clang?
And do you tell me of a woman's tongue,
That gives not half so great a blow to hear
As will a chestnut in a farmer's fire?
Tush, tush! fear boys with bugs.

GRUMIO

[Aside.]
For he fears none.

GREMIO

Hortensio, hark:
This gentleman is happily arriv'd,
My mind presumes, for his own good and yours.

HORTENSIO

I promis'd we would be contributors,
And bear his charge of wooing, whatsoe'er.

GREMIO

And so we will, provided that he win her.

GRUMIO

I would I were as sure of a good dinner.
Enter TRANIO brave, and BIONDELLO.

TRANIO

Gentlemen, God save you! If I may be bold,
Tell me, I beseech you, which is the readiest way
To the house of Signior Baptista Minola?

BIONDELLO

He that has the two fair daughters; is't he you mean?

TRANIO

Even he, Biondello!

GREMIO

Hark you, sir, you mean not her to—

TRANIO

Perhaps him and her, sir; what have you to do?

PETRUCHIO

Not her that chides, sir, at any hand, I pray.

TRANIO

I love no chiders, sir. Biondello, let's away.

LUCENTIO

[Aside.]
Well begun, Tranio.

HORTENSIO

Sir, a word ere you go.
Are you a suitor to the maid you talk of, yea or no?

TRANIO

And if I be, sir, is it any offence?

GREMIO

No; if without more words you will get you hence.

TRANIO

Why, sir, I pray, are not the streets as free
For me as for you?

GREMIO

But so is not she.

TRANIO

For what reason, I beseech you?

GREMIO

For this reason, if you'll know,
That she's the choice love of Signior Gremio.

HORTENSIO

That she's the chosen of Signior Hortensio.

TRANIO

Softly, my masters! If you be gentlemen,
Do me this right; hear me with patience.

Baptista is a noble gentleman,
To whom my father is not all unknown;
And were his daughter fairer than she is,
She may more suitors have, and me for one.
Fair Leda's daughter had a thousand wooers;
Then well one more may fair Bianca have;
And so she shall: Lucentio shall make one,
Though Paris came in hope to speed alone.

GREMIO

What, this gentleman will out-talk us all.

LUCENTIO

Sir, give him head; I know he'll prove a jade.

PETRUCHIO

Hortensio, to what end are all these words?

HORTENSIO

Sir, let me be so bold as ask you,
Did you yet ever see Baptista's daughter?

TRANIO

No, sir, but hear I do that he hath two,
The one as famous for a scolding tongue
As is the other for beauteous modesty.

PETRUCHIO

Sir, sir, the first's for me; let her go by.

GREMIO

Yea, leave that labour to great Hercules,
And let it be more than Alcides' twelve.

PETRUCHIO

Sir, understand you this of me, in sooth:
The youngest daughter, whom you hearken for,
Her father keeps from all access of suitors,
And will not promise her to any man
Until the elder sister first be wed;
The younger then is free, and not before.

TRANIO

> If it be so, sir, that you are the man
> Must stead us all, and me amongst the rest;
> And if you break the ice, and do this feat,
> Achieve the elder, set the younger free
> For our access, whose hap shall be to have her
> Will not so graceless be to be ingrate.

HORTENSIO

> Sir, you say well, and well you do conceive;
> And since you do profess to be a suitor,
> You must, as we do, gratify this gentleman,
> To whom we all rest generally beholding.

TRANIO

> Sir, I shall not be slack; in sign whereof,
> Please ye we may contrive this afternoon,
> And quaff carouses to our mistress' health;
> And do as adversaries do in law,
> Strive mightily, but eat and drink as friends.

GRUMIO, BIONDELLO

> O excellent motion! Fellows, let's be gone.

HORTENSIO

> The motion's good indeed, and be it so:—
> Petruchio, I shall be your *ben venuto.*
>> *[Exeunt.]*

ACT II

SCENE I. Padua. A room in BAPTISTA'S house.

Enter KATHERINA and BIANCA.

BIANCA

    Good sister, wrong me not, nor wrong yourself,
    To make a bondmaid and a slave of me;
    That I disdain; but for these other gawds,
    Unbind my hands, I'll pull them off myself,
    Yea, all my raiment, to my petticoat;
    Or what you will command me will I do,
    So well I know my duty to my elders.

KATHERINA

    Of all thy suitors here I charge thee tell
    Whom thou lov'st best: see thou dissemble not.

BIANCA

    Believe me, sister, of all the men alive
    I never yet beheld that special face
    Which I could fancy more than any other.

KATHERINA

    Minion, thou liest. Is't not Hortensio?

BIANCA

    If you affect him, sister, here I swear
    I'll plead for you myself but you shall have him.

KATHERINA

O! then, belike, you fancy riches more:
You will have Gremio to keep you fair.

BIANCA

Is it for him you do envy me so?
Nay, then you jest; and now I well perceive
You have but jested with me all this while:
I prithee, sister Kate, untie my hands.

KATHERINA

If that be jest, then all the rest was so.
    [Strikes her.]
    Enter BAPTISTA.

BAPTISTA

Why, how now, dame! Whence grows this insolence?
Bianca, stand aside. Poor girl! she weeps.
Go ply thy needle; meddle not with her.
For shame, thou hilding of a devilish spirit,
Why dost thou wrong her that did ne'er wrong thee?
When did she cross thee with a bitter word?

KATHERINA

Her silence flouts me, and I'll be reveng'd.
    [Flies after BIANCA.]

BAPTISTA

What! in my sight? Bianca, get thee in.
    [Exit Bianca.]

KATHERINA

What! will you not suffer me? Nay, now I see
She is your treasure, she must have a husband;
I must dance bare-foot on her wedding-day,
And, for your love to her, lead apes in hell.
Talk not to me: I will go sit and weep
Till I can find occasion of revenge.
    [Exit.]

BAPTISTA

Was ever gentleman thus griev'd as I?
But who comes here?
>Enter GREMIO, *with* LUCENTIO *in the habit of a mean man;*
>   PETRUCHIO, *with* HORTENSIO *as a musician; and* TRANIO,
>   *with* BIONDELLO *bearing a lute and books.*

GREMIO

Good morrow, neighbour Baptista.

BAPTISTA

Good morrow, neighbour Gremio. God save you, gentlemen!

PETRUCHIO

And you, good sir! Pray, have you not a daughter
Call'd Katherina, fair and virtuous?

BAPTISTA

I have a daughter, sir, call'd Katherina.

GREMIO

You are too blunt: go to it orderly.

PETRUCHIO

You wrong me, Signior Gremio: give me leave.
I am a gentleman of Verona, sir,
That, hearing of her beauty and her wit,
Her affability and bashful modesty,
Her wondrous qualities and mild behaviour,
Am bold to show myself a forward guest
Within your house, to make mine eye the witness
Of that report which I so oft have heard.
And, for an entrance to my entertainment,
I do present you with a man of mine,
>   *[Presenting* HORTENSIO.*]*
Cunning in music and the mathematics,
To instruct her fully in those sciences,
Whereof I know she is not ignorant.
Accept of him, or else you do me wrong:
His name is Licio, born in Mantua.

BAPTISTA

> Y'are welcome, sir, and he for your good sake;
> But for my daughter Katherine, this I know,
> She is not for your turn, the more my grief.

PETRUCHIO

> I see you do not mean to part with her;
> Or else you like not of my company.

BAPTISTA

> Mistake me not; I speak but as I find.
> Whence are you, sir? What may I call your name?

PETRUCHIO

> Petruchio is my name, Antonio's son;
> A man well known throughout all Italy.

BAPTISTA

> I know him well: you are welcome for his sake.

GREMIO

> Saving your tale, Petruchio, I pray,
> Let us, that are poor petitioners, speak too.
> Backare! you are marvellous forward.

PETRUCHIO

> O, pardon me, Signior Gremio; I would fain be doing.

GREMIO

> I doubt it not, sir; but you will curse your wooing. Neighbour, this
> is a gift very grateful, I am sure of it. To express the like kindness,
> myself, that have been more kindly beholding to you than any, freely
> give unto you this young scholar,
>> *[Presenting LUCENTIO.]*
> that has been long studying at Rheims; as cunning in Greek, Latin,
> and other languages, as the other in music and mathematics. His name
> is Cambio; pray accept his service.

BAPTISTA

> A thousand thanks, Signior Gremio; welcome, good Cambio.
>> *[To TRANIO.]*
> But, gentle sir, methinks you walk like a stranger. May I be so bold to
> know the cause of your coming?

TRANIO

> Pardon me, sir, the boldness is mine own,
> That, being a stranger in this city here,
> Do make myself a suitor to your daughter,
> Unto Bianca, fair and virtuous.
> Nor is your firm resolve unknown to me,
> In the preferment of the eldest sister.
> This liberty is all that I request,
> That, upon knowledge of my parentage,
> I may have welcome 'mongst the rest that woo,
> And free access and favour as the rest:
> And, toward the education of your daughters,
> I here bestow a simple instrument,
> And this small packet of Greek and Latin books:
> If you accept them, then their worth is great.

BAPTISTA

> Lucentio is your name, of whence, I pray?

TRANIO

> Of Pisa, sir; son to Vincentio.

BAPTISTA

> A mighty man of Pisa: by report
> I know him well: you are very welcome, sir.
>> *[To HORTENSIO.]*
> Take you the lute,
>> *[To LUCENTIO.]*
> and you the set of books;
> You shall go see your pupils presently.
> Holla, within!
>> *Enter a SERVANT.*
> Sirrah, lead these gentlemen
> To my daughters, and tell them both
> These are their tutors: bid them use them well.
>> *[Exeunt SERVANT with HORTENSIO, LUCENTIO and BIONDELLO.]*
> We will go walk a little in the orchard,
> And then to dinner. You are passing welcome,
> And so I pray you all to think yourselves.

PETRUCHIO

Signior Baptista, my business asketh haste,
And every day I cannot come to woo.
You knew my father well, and in him me,
Left solely heir to all his lands and goods,
Which I have bettered rather than decreas'd:
Then tell me, if I get your daughter's love,
What dowry shall I have with her to wife?

BAPTISTA

After my death, the one half of my lands,
And in possession twenty thousand crowns.

PETRUCHIO

And, for that dowry, I'll assure her of
Her widowhood, be it that she survive me,
In all my lands and leases whatsoever.
Let specialities be therefore drawn between us,
That covenants may be kept on either hand.

BAPTISTA

Ay, when the special thing is well obtain'd,
That is, her love; for that is all in all.

PETRUCHIO

Why, that is nothing; for I tell you, father,
I am as peremptory as she proud-minded;
And where two raging fires meet together,
They do consume the thing that feeds their fury:
Though little fire grows great with little wind,
Yet extreme gusts will blow out fire and all;
So I to her, and so she yields to me;
For I am rough and woo not like a babe.

BAPTISTA

Well mayst thou woo, and happy be thy speed!
But be thou arm'd for some unhappy words.

PETRUCHIO

Ay, to the proof, as mountains are for winds,

That shake not though they blow perpetually.
Re-enter HORTENSIO, *with his head broke.*

BAPTISTA

How now, my friend! Why dost thou look so pale?

HORTENSIO

For fear, I promise you, if I look pale.

BAPTISTA

What, will my daughter prove a good musician?

HORTENSIO

I think she'll sooner prove a soldier:
Iron may hold with her, but never lutes.

BAPTISTA

Why, then thou canst not break her to the lute?

HORTENSIO

Why, no; for she hath broke the lute to me.
I did but tell her she mistook her frets,
And bow'd her hand to teach her fingering;
When, with a most impatient devilish spirit,
'Frets, call you these?' quoth she. 'I'll fume with them';
And with that word she struck me on the head,
And through the instrument my pate made way;
And there I stood amazed for a while,
As on a pillory, looking through the lute;
While she did call me rascal fiddler,
And twangling Jack, with twenty such vile terms,
As had she studied to misuse me so.

PETRUCHIO

Now, by the world, it is a lusty wench!
I love her ten times more than e'er I did:
O! how I long to have some chat with her!

BAPTISTA

[To HORTENSIO.*]*
Well, go with me, and be not so discomfited;
Proceed in practice with my younger daughter;

She's apt to learn, and thankful for good turns.
Signior Petruchio, will you go with us,
Or shall I send my daughter Kate to you?

PETRUCHIO

I pray you do.
[Exeunt BAPTISTA, GREMIO, TRANIO and HORTENSIO.]
I will attend her here,
And woo her with some spirit when she comes.
Say that she rail; why, then I'll tell her plain
She sings as sweetly as a nightingale:
Say that she frown; I'll say she looks as clear
As morning roses newly wash'd with dew:
Say she be mute, and will not speak a word;
Then I'll commend her volubility,
And say she uttereth piercing eloquence:
If she do bid me pack, I'll give her thanks,
As though she bid me stay by her a week:
If she deny to wed, I'll crave the day
When I shall ask the banns, and when be married.
But here she comes; and now, Petruchio, speak.
Enter KATHERINA.
Good morrow, Kate; for that's your name, I hear.

KATHERINA

Well have you heard, but something hard of hearing:
They call me Katherine that do talk of me.

PETRUCHIO

You lie, in faith, for you are call'd plain Kate,
And bonny Kate, and sometimes Kate the curst;
But, Kate, the prettiest Kate in Christendom,
Kate of Kate Hall, my super-dainty Kate,
For dainties are all Kates, and therefore, Kate,
Take this of me, Kate of my consolation;
Hearing thy mildness prais'd in every town,
Thy virtues spoke of, and thy beauty sounded,—
Yet not so deeply as to thee belongs,—
Myself am mov'd to woo thee for my wife.

KATHERINA

> Mov'd! in good time: let him that mov'd you hither
> Remove you hence. I knew you at the first,
> You were a moveable.

PETRUCHIO

> Why, what's a moveable?

KATHERINA

> A joint-stool.

PETRUCHIO

> Thou hast hit it: come, sit on me.

KATHERINA

> Asses are made to bear, and so are you.

PETRUCHIO

> Women are made to bear, and so are you.

KATHERINA

> No such jade as bear you, if me you mean.

PETRUCHIO

> Alas! good Kate, I will not burden thee;
> For, knowing thee to be but young and light,—

KATHERINA

> Too light for such a swain as you to catch;
> And yet as heavy as my weight should be.

PETRUCHIO

> Should be! should buz!

KATHERINA

> Well ta'en, and like a buzzard.

PETRUCHIO

> O, slow-wing'd turtle! shall a buzzard take thee?

KATHERINA

> Ay, for a turtle, as he takes a buzzard.

PETRUCHIO

Come, come, you wasp; i' faith, you are too angry.

KATHERINA

If I be waspish, best beware my sting.

PETRUCHIO

My remedy is then to pluck it out.

KATHERINA

Ay, if the fool could find it where it lies.

PETRUCHIO

Who knows not where a wasp does wear his sting?
In his tail.

KATHERINA

In his tongue.

PETRUCHIO

Whose tongue?

KATHERINA

Yours, if you talk of tales; and so farewell.

PETRUCHIO

What! with my tongue in your tail? Nay, come again,
Good Kate; I am a gentleman.

KATHERINA

That I'll try.
        [Striking him.]

PETRUCHIO

I swear I'll cuff you if you strike again.

KATHERINA

So may you lose your arms:
If you strike me, you are no gentleman;
And if no gentleman, why then no arms.

PETRUCHIO

A herald, Kate? O! put me in thy books.

KATHERINA

What is your crest? a coxcomb?

PETRUCHIO

A combless cock, so Kate will be my hen.

KATHERINA

No cock of mine; you crow too like a craven.

PETRUCHIO

Nay, come, Kate, come; you must not look so sour.

KATHERINA

It is my fashion when I see a crab.

PETRUCHIO

Why, here's no crab, and therefore look not sour.

KATHERINA

There is, there is.

PETRUCHIO

Then show it me.

KATHERINA

Had I a glass I would.

PETRUCHIO

What, you mean my face?

KATHERINA

Well aim'd of such a young one.

PETRUCHIO

Now, by Saint George, I am too young for you.

KATHERINA

Yet you are wither'd.

PETRUCHIO

'Tis with cares.

KATHERINA

I care not.

No, not a whit; I find you passing gentle.
'Twas told me you were rough, and coy, and sullen,
And now I find report a very liar;
For thou art pleasant, gamesome, passing courteous,
But slow in speech, yet sweet as spring-time flowers.
Thou canst not frown, thou canst not look askance,
Nor bite the lip, as angry wenches will,
Nor hast thou pleasure to be cross in talk;
But thou with mildness entertain'st thy wooers;
With gentle conference, soft and affable.
Why does the world report that Kate doth limp?
O sland'rous world! Kate like the hazel-twig
Is straight and slender, and as brown in hue
As hazel-nuts, and sweeter than the kernels.
O! let me see thee walk: thou dost not halt.

—Petruchio, *The Taming of the Shrew*

PETRUCHIO

Nay, hear you, Kate: in sooth, you 'scape not so.

KATHERINA

I chafe you, if I tarry; let me go.

PETRUCHIO

No, not a whit; I find you passing gentle.
'Twas told me you were rough, and coy, and sullen,
And now I find report a very liar;
For thou art pleasant, gamesome, passing courteous,
But slow in speech, yet sweet as spring-time flowers.
Thou canst not frown, thou canst not look askance,
Nor bite the lip, as angry wenches will,
Nor hast thou pleasure to be cross in talk;
But thou with mildness entertain'st thy wooers;
With gentle conference, soft and affable.
Why does the world report that Kate doth limp?
O sland'rous world! Kate like the hazel-twig
Is straight and slender, and as brown in hue
As hazel-nuts, and sweeter than the kernels.
O! let me see thee walk: thou dost not halt.

KATHERINA

Go, fool, and whom thou keep'st command.

PETRUCHIO

Did ever Dian so become a grove
As Kate this chamber with her princely gait?
O! be thou Dian, and let her be Kate,
And then let Kate be chaste, and Dian sportful!

KATHERINA

Where did you study all this goodly speech?

PETRUCHIO

It is extempore, from my mother-wit.

KATHERINA

A witty mother! witless else her son.

PETRUCHIO

> Am I not wise?

KATHERINA

> Yes; keep you warm.

PETRUCHIO

> Marry, so I mean, sweet Katherine, in thy bed;
> And therefore, setting all this chat aside,
> Thus in plain terms: your father hath consented
> That you shall be my wife your dowry 'greed on;
> And will you, nill you, I will marry you.
> Now, Kate, I am a husband for your turn;
> For, by this light, whereby I see thy beauty,—
> Thy beauty that doth make me like thee well,—
> Thou must be married to no man but me;
> For I am he am born to tame you, Kate,
> And bring you from a wild Kate to a Kate
> Conformable as other household Kates.
> > *Re-enter BAPTISTA, GREMIO and TRANIO.*
> Here comes your father. Never make denial;
> I must and will have Katherine to my wife.

BAPTISTA

> Now, Signior Petruchio, how speed you with my daughter?

PETRUCHIO

> How but well, sir? how but well?
> It were impossible I should speed amiss.

BAPTISTA

> Why, how now, daughter Katherine, in your dumps?

KATHERINA

> Call you me daughter? Now I promise you
> You have show'd a tender fatherly regard
> To wish me wed to one half lunatic,
> A mad-cap ruffian and a swearing Jack,
> That thinks with oaths to face the matter out.

PETRUCHIO

> Father, 'tis thus: yourself and all the world

That talk'd of her have talk'd amiss of her:
If she be curst, it is for policy,
For she's not froward, but modest as the dove;
She is not hot, but temperate as the morn;
For patience she will prove a second Grissel,
And Roman Lucrece for her chastity;
And to conclude, we have 'greed so well together
That upon Sunday is the wedding-day.

KATHERINA

I'll see thee hang'd on Sunday first.

GREMIO

Hark, Petruchio; she says she'll see thee hang'd first.

TRANIO

Is this your speeding? Nay, then good-night our part!

PETRUCHIO

Be patient, gentlemen. I choose her for myself;
If she and I be pleas'd, what's that to you?
'Tis bargain'd 'twixt us twain, being alone,
That she shall still be curst in company.
I tell you, 'tis incredible to believe
How much she loves me: O! the kindest Kate
She hung about my neck, and kiss on kiss
She vied so fast, protesting oath on oath,
That in a twink she won me to her love.
O! you are novices: 'tis a world to see,
How tame, when men and women are alone,
A meacock wretch can make the curstest shrew.
Give me thy hand, Kate; I will unto Venice,
To buy apparel 'gainst the wedding-day.
Provide the feast, father, and bid the guests;
I will be sure my Katherine shall be fine.

BAPTISTA

I know not what to say; but give me your hands.
God send you joy, Petruchio! 'Tis a match.

GREMIO, TRANIO

Amen, say we; we will be witnesses.

PETRUCHIO

Father, and wife, and gentlemen, adieu.
I will to Venice; Sunday comes apace;
We will have rings and things, and fine array;
And kiss me, Kate; we will be married o' Sunday.
[Exeunt PETRUCHIO and KATHERINA, severally.]

GREMIO

Was ever match clapp'd up so suddenly?

BAPTISTA

Faith, gentlemen, now I play a merchant's part,
And venture madly on a desperate mart.

TRANIO

'Twas a commodity lay fretting by you;
'Twill bring you gain, or perish on the seas.

BAPTISTA

The gain I seek is, quiet in the match.

GREMIO

No doubt but he hath got a quiet catch.
But now, Baptista, to your younger daughter:
Now is the day we long have looked for;
I am your neighbour, and was suitor first.

TRANIO

And I am one that love Bianca more
Than words can witness or your thoughts can guess.

GREMIO

Youngling, thou canst not love so dear as I.

TRANIO

Greybeard, thy love doth freeze.

GREMIO

But thine doth fry.
Skipper, stand back; 'tis age that nourisheth.

TRANIO

But youth in ladies' eyes that flourisheth.

BAPTISTA

Content you, gentlemen; I'll compound this strife:
'Tis deeds must win the prize, and he of both
That can assure my daughter greatest dower
Shall have my Bianca's love.
Say, Signior Gremio, what can you assure her?

GREMIO

First, as you know, my house within the city
Is richly furnished with plate and gold:
Basins and ewers to lave her dainty hands;
My hangings all of Tyrian tapestry;
In ivory coffers I have stuff'd my crowns;
In cypress chests my arras counterpoints,
Costly apparel, tents, and canopies,
Fine linen, Turkey cushions boss'd with pearl,
Valance of Venice gold in needlework;
Pewter and brass, and all things that belong
To house or housekeeping: then, at my farm
I have a hundred milch-kine to the pail,
Six score fat oxen standing in my stalls,
And all things answerable to this portion.
Myself am struck in years, I must confess;
And if I die tomorrow this is hers,
If whilst I live she will be only mine.

TRANIO

That 'only' came well in. Sir, list to me:
I am my father's heir and only son;
If I may have your daughter to my wife,
I'll leave her houses three or four as good
Within rich Pisa's walls as anyone
Old Signior Gremio has in Padua;
Besides two thousand ducats by the year
Of fruitful land, all which shall be her jointure.
What, have I pinch'd you, Signior Gremio?

GREMIO

> Two thousand ducats by the year of land!
> My land amounts not to so much in all:
> That she shall have, besides an argosy
> That now is lying in Marseilles' road.
> What, have I chok'd you with an argosy?

TRANIO

> Gremio, 'tis known my father hath no less
> Than three great argosies, besides two galliasses,
> And twelve tight galleys; these I will assure her,
> And twice as much, whate'er thou offer'st next.

GREMIO

> Nay, I have offer'd all; I have no more;
> And she can have no more than all I have;
> If you like me, she shall have me and mine.

TRANIO

> Why, then the maid is mine from all the world,
> By your firm promise; Gremio is out-vied.

BAPTISTA

> I must confess your offer is the best;
> And let your father make her the assurance,
> She is your own; else, you must pardon me;
> If you should die before him, where's her dower?

TRANIO

> That's but a cavil; he is old, I young.

GREMIO

> And may not young men die as well as old?

BAPTISTA

> Well, gentlemen,
> I am thus resolv'd. On Sunday next, you know,
> My daughter Katherine is to be married;
> Now, on the Sunday following, shall Bianca
> Be bride to you, if you make this assurance;
> If not, to Signior Gremio.
> And so I take my leave, and thank you both.

GREMIO

Adieu, good neighbour.
    [Exit BAPTISTA.]
Now, I fear thee not:
Sirrah young gamester, your father were a fool
To give thee all, and in his waning age
Set foot under thy table. Tut! a toy!
An old Italian fox is not so kind, my boy.
    [Exit.]

TRANIO

A vengeance on your crafty wither'd hide!
Yet I have fac'd it with a card of ten.
'Tis in my head to do my master good:
I see no reason but suppos'd Lucentio
Must get a father, call'd suppos'd Vincentio;
And that's a wonder: fathers commonly
Do get their children; but in this case of wooing
A child shall get a sire, if I fail not of my cunning.
    [Exit.]

ACT III

SCENE I. Padua. A room in BAPTISTA'S house.

Enter LUCENTIO, HORTENSIO and BIANCA.

LUCENTIO

Fiddler, forbear; you grow too forward, sir.
Have you so soon forgot the entertainment
Her sister Katherine welcome'd you withal?

HORTENSIO

But, wrangling pedant, this is
The patroness of heavenly harmony:
Then give me leave to have prerogative;
And when in music we have spent an hour,
Your lecture shall have leisure for as much.

LUCENTIO

Preposterous ass, that never read so far
To know the cause why music was ordain'd!
Was it not to refresh the mind of man
After his studies or his usual pain?
Then give me leave to read philosophy,
And while I pause serve in your harmony.

HORTENSIO

Sirrah, I will not bear these braves of thine.

BIANCA

Why, gentlemen, you do me double wrong,

To strive for that which resteth in my choice.
I am no breeching scholar in the schools,
I'll not be tied to hours nor 'pointed times,
But learn my lessons as I please myself.
And, to cut off all strife, here sit we down;
Take you your instrument, play you the whiles;
His lecture will be done ere you have tun'd.

HORTENSIO

You'll leave his lecture when I am in tune?
        [Retires.]

LUCENTIO

That will be never: tune your instrument.

BIANCA

Where left we last?

LUCENTIO

Here, madam:—
Hic ibat Simois; hic est Sigeia tellus;
Hic steterat Priami regia celsa senis.

BIANCA

Construe them.

LUCENTIO

Hic ibat, as I told you before, *Simois*, I am Lucentio, *hic est*, son unto
Vincentio of Pisa, *Sigeia tellus*, disguised thus to get your love, *Hic steterat*,
and that Lucentio that comes a-wooing, *Priami*, is my man Tranio, *regia*,
bearing my port, *celsa senis*, that we might beguile the old pantaloon.

HORTENSIO

        [Returning.]
Madam, my instrument's in tune.

BIANCA

Let's hear.—
        [HORTENSIO plays.]
O fie! the treble jars.

LUCENTIO

Spit in the hole, man, and tune again.

BIANCA

Now let me see if I can construe it: *Hic ibat Simois*, I know you not; *hic est Sigeia tellus*, I trust you not; *Hic steterat Priami*, take heed he hear us not; *regia*, presume not; *celsa senis*, despair not.

HORTENSIO

Madam, 'tis now in tune.

LUCENTIO

All but the base.

HORTENSIO

The base is right; 'tis the base knave that jars.
        [Aside.]
How fiery and forward our pedant is!
Now, for my life, the knave doth court my love:
Pedascule, I'll watch you better yet.

BIANCA

In time I may believe, yet I mistrust.

LUCENTIO

Mistrust it not; for sure, Æacides
Was Ajax, call'd so from his grandfather.

BIANCA

I must believe my master; else, I promise you,
I should be arguing still upon that doubt;
But let it rest. Now, Licio, to you.
Good master, take it not unkindly, pray,
That I have been thus pleasant with you both.

HORTENSIO

        [To Lucentio.]
You may go walk and give me leave a while;
My lessons make no music in three parts.

LUCENTIO

Are you so formal, sir? Well, I must wait,
        [Aside.]
And watch withal; for, but I be deceiv'd,
Our fine musician groweth amorous.

HORTENSIO

Madam, before you touch the instrument,
To learn the order of my fingering,
I must begin with rudiments of art;
To teach you gamut in a briefer sort,
More pleasant, pithy, and effectual,
Than hath been taught by any of my trade:
And there it is in writing, fairly drawn.

BIANCA

Why, I am past my gamut long ago.

HORTENSIO

Yet read the gamut of Hortensio.

BIANCA

Gamut I am, the ground of all accord,
A re, to plead Hortensio's passion;
B mi, Bianca, take him for thy lord,
C fa ut, that loves with all affection:
D sol re, one clef, two notes have I
E la mi, show pity or I die.
Call you this gamut? Tut, I like it not:
Old fashions please me best; I am not so nice,
To change true rules for odd inventions.
                    Enter a SERVANT.

SERVANT

Mistress, your father prays you leave your books,
And help to dress your sister's chamber up:
You know tomorrow is the wedding-day.

BIANCA

Farewell, sweet masters, both: I must be gone.
                    [Exeunt BIANCA and SERVANT.]

LUCENTIO

Faith, mistress, then I have no cause to stay.
                    [Exit.]

HORTENSIO

But I have cause to pry into this pedant:
Methinks he looks as though he were in love.
Yet if thy thoughts, Bianca, be so humble
To cast thy wand'ring eyes on every stale,
Seize thee that list: if once I find thee ranging,
Hortensio will be quit with thee by changing.

    [Exit.]

SCENE II. The same. Before BAPTISTA'S house.

*Enter BAPTISTA, GREMIO, TRANIO, KATHERINA, BIANCA,
LUCENTIO and ATTENDANTS.*

BAPTISTA

    [To TRANIO.]

Signior Lucentio, this is the 'pointed day
That Katherine and Petruchio should be married,
And yet we hear not of our son-in-law.
What will be said? What mockery will it be
To want the bridegroom when the priest attends
To speak the ceremonial rites of marriage!
What says Lucentio to this shame of ours?

KATHERINA

No shame but mine; I must, forsooth, be forc'd
To give my hand, oppos'd against my heart,
Unto a mad-brain rudesby, full of spleen;
Who woo'd in haste and means to wed at leisure.
I told you, I, he was a frantic fool,
Hiding his bitter jests in blunt behaviour;
And to be noted for a merry man,
He'll woo a thousand, 'point the day of marriage,
Make friends, invite, and proclaim the banns;
Yet never means to wed where he hath woo'd.
Now must the world point at poor Katherine,
And say 'Lo! there is mad Petruchio's wife,
If it would please him come and marry her.'

TRANIO

> Patience, good Katherine, and Baptista too.
> Upon my life, Petruchio means but well,
> Whatever fortune stays him from his word:
> Though he be blunt, I know him passing wise;
> Though he be merry, yet withal he's honest.

KATHERINA

> Would Katherine had never seen him though!
> *[Exit weeping, followed by BIANCA and others.]*

BAPTISTA

> Go, girl, I cannot blame thee now to weep,
> For such an injury would vex a very saint;
> Much more a shrew of thy impatient humour.
> *Enter BIONDELLO.*
> Master, master! News! old news, and such news as you never heard of!

BAPTISTA

> Is it new and old too? How may that be?

BIONDELLO

> Why, is it not news to hear of Petruchio's coming?

BAPTISTA

> Is he come?

BIONDELLO

> Why, no, sir.

BAPTISTA

> What then?

BIONDELLO

> He is coming.

BAPTISTA

> When will he be here?

BIONDELLO

> When he stands where I am and sees you there.

TRANIO

But say, what to thine old news?

BIONDELLO

Why, Petruchio is coming, in a new hat and an old jerkin; a pair of old breeches thrice turned; a pair of boots that have been candle-cases, one buckled, another laced; an old rusty sword ta'en out of the town armoury, with a broken hilt, and chapeless; with two broken points: his horse hipped with an old mothy saddle and stirrups of no kindred; besides, possessed with the glanders and like to mose in the chine; troubled with the lampass, infected with the fashions, full of windgalls, sped with spavins, rayed with the yellows, past cure of the fives, stark spoiled with the staggers, begnawn with the bots, swayed in the back and shoulder-shotten; near-legged before, and with a half-checked bit, and a head-stall of sheep's leather, which, being restrained to keep him from stumbling, hath been often burst, and now repaired with knots; one girth six times pieced, and a woman's crupper of velure, which hath two letters for her name fairly set down in studs, and here and there pieced with pack-thread.

BAPTISTA

Who comes with him?

BIONDELLO

O, sir! his lackey, for all the world caparisoned like the horse; with a linen stock on one leg and a kersey boot-hose on the other, gartered with a red and blue list; an old hat, and the humour of forty fancies prick'd in't for a feather: a monster, a very monster in apparel, and not like a Christian footboy or a gentleman's lackey.

TRANIO

'Tis some odd humour pricks him to this fashion;
Yet oftentimes lie goes but mean-apparell'd.

BAPTISTA

I am glad he's come, howsoe'er he comes.

BIONDELLO

Why, sir, he comes not.

BAPTISTA

Didst thou not say he comes?

BIONDELLO

Who? that Petruchio came?

BAPTISTA

Ay, that Petruchio came.

BIONDELLO

No, sir; I say his horse comes, with him on his back.

BAPTISTA

Why, that's all one.

BIONDELLO

Nay, by Saint Jamy,
I hold you a penny,
A horse and a man
Is more than one,
And yet not many.

Enter PETRUCHIO and GRUMIO.

PETRUCHIO

Come, where be these gallants? Who is at home?

BAPTISTA

You are welcome, sir.

PETRUCHIO

And yet I come not well.

BAPTISTA

And yet you halt not.

TRANIO

Not so well apparell'd as I wish you were.

PETRUCHIO

Were it better, I should rush in thus.
But where is Kate? Where is my lovely bride?
How does my father? Gentles, methinks you frown;
And wherefore gaze this goodly company,
As if they saw some wondrous monument,
Some comet or unusual prodigy?

BAPTISTA

    Why, sir, you know this is your wedding-day:
    First were we sad, fearing you would not come;
    Now sadder, that you come so unprovided.
    Fie! doff this habit, shame to your estate,
    An eye-sore to our solemn festival.

TRANIO

    And tell us what occasion of import
    Hath all so long detain'd you from your wife,
    And sent you hither so unlike yourself?

PETRUCHIO

    Tedious it were to tell, and harsh to hear;
    Sufficeth I am come to keep my word,
    Though in some part enforced to digress;
    Which at more leisure I will so excuse
    As you shall well be satisfied withal.
    But where is Kate? I stay too long from her;
    The morning wears, 'tis time we were at church.

TRANIO

    See not your bride in these unreverent robes;
    Go to my chamber, put on clothes of mine.

PETRUCHIO

    Not I, believe me: thus I'll visit her.

BAPTISTA

    But thus, I trust, you will not marry her.

PETRUCHIO

    Good sooth, even thus; therefore ha' done with words;
    To me she's married, not unto my clothes.
    Could I repair what she will wear in me
    As I can change these poor accoutrements,
    'Twere well for Kate and better for myself.
    But what a fool am I to chat with you
    When I should bid good morrow to my bride,
    And seal the title with a lovely kiss!
        [Exeunt PETRUCHIO, GRUMIO and BIONDELLO.]

TRANIO

>He hath some meaning in his mad attire.
>We will persuade him, be it possible,
>To put on better ere he go to church.

BAPTISTA

>I'll after him and see the event of this.
>> *[Exeunt BAPTISTA, GREMIO and ATTENDANTS.]*

TRANIO

>But, sir, to love concerneth us to add
>Her father's liking; which to bring to pass,
>As I before imparted to your worship,
>I am to get a man,—whate'er he be
>It skills not much; we'll fit him to our turn,—
>And he shall be Vincentio of Pisa,
>And make assurance here in Padua,
>Of greater sums than I have promised.
>So shall you quietly enjoy your hope,
>And marry sweet Bianca with consent.

LUCENTIO

>Were it not that my fellow schoolmaster
>Doth watch Bianca's steps so narrowly,
>'Twere good, methinks, to steal our marriage;
>Which once perform'd, let all the world say no,
>I'll keep mine own despite of all the world.

TRANIO

>That by degrees we mean to look into,
>And watch our vantage in this business.
>We'll over-reach the greybeard, Gremio,
>The narrow-prying father, Minola,
>The quaint musician, amorous Licio;
>All for my master's sake, Lucentio.
>> *Re-enter GREMIO.*
>Signior Gremio, came you from the church?

GREMIO

>As willingly as e'er I came from school.

TRANIO

And is the bride and bridegroom coming home?

GREMIO

A bridegroom, say you? 'Tis a groom indeed,
A grumbling groom, and that the girl shall find.

TRANIO

Curster than she? Why, 'tis impossible.

GREMIO

Why, he's a devil, a devil, a very fiend.

TRANIO

Why, she's a devil, a devil, the devil's dam.

GREMIO

Tut! she's a lamb, a dove, a fool, to him.
I'll tell you, Sir Lucentio: when the priest
Should ask if Katherine should be his wife,
'Ay, by gogs-wouns,' quoth he, and swore so loud
That, all amaz'd, the priest let fall the book;
And as he stoop'd again to take it up,
The mad-brain'd bridegroom took him such a cuff
That down fell priest and book, and book and priest:
'Now take them up,' quoth he, 'if any list.'

TRANIO

What said the wench, when he rose again?

GREMIO

Trembled and shook, for why, he stamp'd and swore
As if the vicar meant to cozen him.
But after many ceremonies done,
He calls for wine: 'A health!' quoth he, as if
He had been abroad, carousing to his mates
After a storm; quaff'd off the muscadel,
And threw the sops all in the sexton's face,
Having no other reason
But that his beard grew thin and hungerly
And seem'd to ask him sops as he was drinking.

This done, he took the bride about the neck,
And kiss'd her lips with such a clamorous smack
That at the parting all the church did echo.
And I, seeing this, came thence for very shame;
And after me, I know, the rout is coming.
Such a mad marriage never was before.
Hark, hark! I hear the minstrels play.

> *[Music plays.]*
> Enter PETRUCIO, KATHERINA, BIANCA, BAPTISTA, HORTENSIO,
> GRUMIO *and Train.*

PETRUCHIO

Gentlemen and friends, I thank you for your pains:
I know you think to dine with me today,
And have prepar'd great store of wedding cheer
But so it is, my haste doth call me hence,
And therefore here I mean to take my leave.

BAPTISTA

Is't possible you will away tonight?

PETRUCHIO

I must away today before night come.
Make it no wonder: if you knew my business,
You would entreat me rather go than stay.
And, honest company, I thank you all,
That have beheld me give away myself
To this most patient, sweet, and virtuous wife.
Dine with my father, drink a health to me.
For I must hence; and farewell to you all.

TRANIO

Let us entreat you stay till after dinner.

PETRUCHIO

It may not be.

GREMIO

Let me entreat you.

PETRUCHIO

It cannot be.

KATHERINA

Let me entreat you.

PETRUCHIO

I am content.

KATHERINA

Are you content to stay?

PETRUCHIO

I am content you shall entreat me stay;
But yet not stay, entreat me how you can.

KATHERINA

Now, if you love me, stay.

PETRUCHIO

Grumio, my horse!

GRUMIO

Ay, sir, they be ready; the oats have eaten the horses.

KATHERINA

Nay, then,
Do what thou canst, I will not go today;
No, nor tomorrow, not till I please myself.
The door is open, sir; there lies your way;
You may be jogging whiles your boots are green;
For me, I'll not be gone till I please myself.
'Tis like you'll prove a jolly surly groom
That take it on you at the first so roundly.

PETRUCHIO

O Kate! content thee: prithee be not angry.

KATHERINA

I will be angry: what hast thou to do?
Father, be quiet; he shall stay my leisure.

GREMIO

Ay, marry, sir, now it begins to work.

KATHERINA

Gentlemen, forward to the bridal dinner:

I see a woman may be made a fool,
If she had not a spirit to resist.

PETRUCHIO

They shall go forward, Kate, at thy command.
Obey the bride, you that attend on her;
Go to the feast, revel and domineer,
Carouse full measure to her maidenhead,
Be mad and merry, or go hang yourselves:
But for my bonny Kate, she must with me.
Nay, look not big, nor stamp, nor stare, nor fret;
I will be master of what is mine own.
She is my goods, my chattels; she is my house,
My household stuff, my field, my barn,
My horse, my ox, my ass, my anything;
And here she stands, touch her whoever dare;
I'll bring mine action on the proudest he
That stops my way in Padua. Grumio,
Draw forth thy weapon; we are beset with thieves;
Rescue thy mistress, if thou be a man.
Fear not, sweet wench; they shall not touch thee, Kate;
I'll buckler thee against a million.
        [Exeunt PETRUCIO, KATHERINA and GRUMIO.]

BAPTISTA

Nay, let them go, a couple of quiet ones.

GREMIO

Went they not quickly, I should die with laughing.

TRANIO

Of all mad matches, never was the like.

LUCENTIO

Mistress, what's your opinion of your sister?

BIANCA

That, being mad herself, she's madly mated.

GREMIO

I warrant him, Petruchio is Kated.

BAPTISTA

> Neighbours and friends, though bride and bridegroom wants
> For to supply the places at the table,
> You know there wants no junkets at the feast.
> Lucentio, you shall supply the bridegroom's place;
> And let Bianca take her sister's room.

TRANIO

> Shall sweet Bianca practise how to bride it?

BAPTISTA

> She shall, Lucentio. Come, gentlemen, let's go.
> *[Exeunt.]*

ACT IV

SCENE I. A hall in PETRUCHIO'S country house.

Enter GRUMIO.

GRUMIO

Fie, fie on all tired jades, on all mad masters, and all foul ways! Was ever man so beaten? Was ever man so ray'd? Was ever man so weary? I am sent before to make a fire, and they are coming after to warm them. Now, were not I a little pot and soon hot, my very lips might freeze to my teeth, my tongue to the roof of my mouth, my heart in my belly, ere I should come by a fire to thaw me. But I with blowing the fire shall warm myself; for, considering the weather, a taller man than I will take cold. Holla, ho! Curtis!

Enter CURTIS.

CURTIS

Who is that calls so coldly?

GRUMIO

A piece of ice: if thou doubt it, thou mayst slide from my shoulder to my heel with no greater a run but my head and my neck. A fire, good Curtis.

CURTIS

Is my master and his wife coming, Grumio?

GRUMIO

O, ay! Curtis, ay; and therefore fire, fire; cast on no water.

CURTIS

Is she so hot a shrew as she's reported?

GRUMIO

She was, good Curtis, before this frost; but thou knowest winter tames man, woman, and beast; for it hath tamed my old master, and my new mistress, and myself, fellow Curtis.

CURTIS

Away, you three-inch fool! I am no beast.

GRUMIO

Am I but three inches? Why, thy horn is a foot; and so long am I at the least. But wilt thou make a fire, or shall I complain on thee to our mistress, whose hand,—she being now at hand,—thou shalt soon feel, to thy cold comfort, for being slow in thy hot office?

CURTIS

I prithee, good Grumio, tell me, how goes the world?

GRUMIO

A cold world, Curtis, in every office but thine; and therefore fire. Do thy duty, and have thy duty, for my master and mistress are almost frozen to death.

CURTIS

There's fire ready; and therefore, good Grumio, the news.

GRUMIO

Why, 'Jack boy! ho, boy!' and as much news as wilt thou.

CURTIS

Come, you are so full of cony-catching.

GRUMIO

Why, therefore, fire; for I have caught extreme cold. Where's the cook? Is supper ready, the house trimmed, rushes strewed, cobwebs swept, the servingmen in their new fustian, their white stockings, and every officer his wedding-garment on? Be the Jacks fair within, the Jills fair without, and carpets laid, and everything in order?

CURTIS

All ready; and therefore, I pray thee, news.

GRUMIO

First, know my horse is tired; my master and mistress fallen out.

CURTIS

How?

GRUMIO

Out of their saddles into the dirt; and thereby hangs a tale.

CURTIS

Let's ha't, good Grumio.

GRUMIO

Lend thine ear.

CURTIS

Here.

GRUMIO

[Striking him.]

There.

CURTIS

This 'tis to feel a tale, not to hear a tale.

GRUMIO

And therefore 'tis called a sensible tale; and this cuff was but to knock at your ear and beseech listening. Now I begin: *Imprimis*, we came down a foul hill, my master riding behind my mistress,—

CURTIS

Both of one horse?

GRUMIO

What's that to thee?

CURTIS

Why, a horse.

GRUMIO

Tell thou the tale: but hadst thou not crossed me, thou shouldst have heard how her horse fell, and she under her horse; thou shouldst have heard in how miry a place, how she was bemoiled; how he left her with the horse upon her; how he beat me because her horse stumbled;

how she waded through the dirt to pluck him off me: how he swore; how she prayed, that never prayed before; how I cried; how the horses ran away; how her bridle was burst; how I lost my crupper; with many things of worthy memory, which now shall die in oblivion, and thou return unexperienced to thy grave.

CURTIS

By this reckoning he is more shrew than she.

GRUMIO

Ay; and that thou and the proudest of you all shall find when he comes home. But what talk I of this? Call forth Nathaniel, Joseph, Nicholas, Philip, Walter, Sugarsop, and the rest; let their heads be sleekly combed, their blue coats brush'd and their garters of an indifferent knit; let them curtsy with their left legs, and not presume to touch a hair of my master's horse-tail till they kiss their hands. Are they all ready?

CURTIS

They are.

GRUMIO

Call them forth.

CURTIS

Do you hear? ho! You must meet my master to countenance my mistress.

GRUMIO

Why, she hath a face of her own.

CURTIS

Who knows not that?

GRUMIO

Thou, it seems, that calls for company to countenance her.

CURTIS

I call them forth to credit her.

GRUMIO

Why, she comes to borrow nothing of them.
Enter four or five SERVANTS.

NATHANIEL

Welcome home, Grumio!

PHILIP

How now, Grumio!

JOSEPH

What, Grumio!

NICHOLAS

Fellow Grumio!

NATHANIEL

How now, old lad!

GRUMIO

Welcome, you; how now, you; what, you; fellow, you; and thus much for greeting. Now, my spruce companions, is all ready, and all things neat?

NATHANIEL

All things is ready. How near is our master?

GRUMIO

E'en at hand, alighted by this; and therefore be not,—
Cock's passion, silence! I hear my master.
Enter PETRUCIO and KATHERINA.

PETRUCHIO

Where be these knaves? What! no man at door
To hold my stirrup nor to take my horse?
Where is Nathaniel, Gregory, Philip?—

ALL SERVANTS

Here, here, sir; here, sir.

PETRUCHIO

Here, sir! here, sir! here, sir! here, sir!
You logger-headed and unpolish'd grooms!
What, no attendance? no regard? no duty?
Where is the foolish knave I sent before?

GRUMIO

Here, sir; as foolish as I was before.

PETRUCHIO

You peasant swain! you whoreson malt-horse drudge!
Did I not bid thee meet me in the park,
And bring along these rascal knaves with thee?

GRUMIO

Nathaniel's coat, sir, was not fully made,
And Gabriel's pumps were all unpink'd i' the heel;
There was no link to colour Peter's hat,
And Walter's dagger was not come from sheathing;
There was none fine but Adam, Ralph, and Gregory;
The rest were ragged, old, and beggarly;
Yet, as they are, here are they come to meet you.

PETRUCHIO

Go, rascals, go and fetch my supper in.
　　　[Exeunt some of the SERVANTS.]
Where is the life that late I led?
Where are those—? Sit down, Kate, and welcome.
Food, food, food, food!
　　　Re-enter SERVANTS with supper.
Why, when, I say?—Nay, good sweet Kate, be merry.—
Off with my boots, you rogues! you villains! when?
It was the friar of orders grey,
As he forth walked on his way:
Out, you rogue! you pluck my foot awry:
　　　[Strikes him.]
Take that, and mend the plucking off the other.
Be merry, Kate. Some water, here; what, ho!
Where's my spaniel Troilus? Sirrah, get you hence
And bid my cousin Ferdinand come hither:
　　　[Exit SERVANT.]
One, Kate, that you must kiss and be acquainted with.
Where are my slippers? Shall I have some water?
Come, Kate, and wash, and welcome heartily.—
　　　[SERVANT lets the ewer fall. PETRUCHIO strikes him.]
You whoreson villain! will you let it fall?

KATHERINA

Patience, I pray you; 'twas a fault unwilling.

PETRUCHIO

A whoreson, beetle-headed, flap-ear'd knave!
Come, Kate, sit down; I know you have a stomach.
Will you give thanks, sweet Kate, or else shall I?—
What's this? Mutton?

FIRST SERVANT

Ay.

PETRUCHIO

Who brought it?

PETER

I.

PETRUCHIO

'Tis burnt; and so is all the meat.
What dogs are these! Where is the rascal cook?
How durst you, villains, bring it from the dresser,
And serve it thus to me that love it not?
        [Throws the meat, etc., at them.]
There, take it to you, trenchers, cups, and all.
You heedless joltheads and unmanner'd slaves!
What! do you grumble? I'll be with you straight.

KATHERINA

I pray you, husband, be not so disquiet;
The meat was well, if you were so contented.

PETRUCHIO

I tell thee, Kate, 'twas burnt and dried away,
And I expressly am forbid to touch it;
For it engenders choler, planteth anger;
And better 'twere that both of us did fast,
Since, of ourselves, ourselves are choleric,
Than feed it with such over-roasted flesh.
Be patient; tomorrow 't shall be mended.
And for this night we'll fast for company:
Come, I will bring thee to thy bridal chamber.
        [Exeunt PETRUCHIO, KATHERINA and CURTIS.]

NATHANIEL

    Peter, didst ever see the like?

PETER

    He kills her in her own humour.
        Re-enter CURTIS.

GRUMIO

    Where is he?

CURTIS

    In her chamber, making a sermon of continency to her;
    And rails, and swears, and rates, that she, poor soul,
    Knows not which way to stand, to look, to speak,
    And sits as one new risen from a dream.
    Away, away! for he is coming hither.
        [Exeunt.]
        Re-enter PETRUCHIO.

PETRUCHIO

    Thus have I politicly begun my reign,
    And 'tis my hope to end successfully.
    My falcon now is sharp and passing empty.
    And till she stoop she must not be full-gorg'd,
    For then she never looks upon her lure.
    Another way I have to man my haggard,
    To make her come, and know her keeper's call,
    That is, to watch her, as we watch these kites
    That bate and beat, and will not be obedient.
    She eat no meat today, nor none shall eat;
    Last night she slept not, nor tonight she shall not;
    As with the meat, some undeserved fault
    I'll find about the making of the bed;
    And here I'll fling the pillow, there the bolster,
    This way the coverlet, another way the sheets;
    Ay, and amid this hurly I intend
    That all is done in reverend care of her;
    And, in conclusion, she shall watch all night:
    And if she chance to nod I'll rail and brawl,
    And with the clamour keep her still awake.

This is a way to kill a wife with kindness;
And thus I'll curb her mad and headstrong humour.
He that knows better how to tame a shrew,
Now let him speak; 'tis charity to show.
    [Exit.]

SCENE II. Padua. Before BAPTISTA'S house.

Enter TRANIO and HORTENSIO.

TRANIO

Is 't possible, friend Licio, that Mistress Bianca
Doth fancy any other but Lucentio?
I tell you, sir, she bears me fair in hand.

HORTENSIO

Sir, to satisfy you in what I have said,
Stand by and mark the manner of his teaching.
    [They stand aside.]
    Enter BIANCA and LUCENTIO.

LUCENTIO

Now, mistress, profit you in what you read?

BIANCA

What, master, read you? First resolve me that.

LUCENTIO

I read that I profess, *The Art to Love.*

BIANCA

And may you prove, sir, master of your art!

LUCENTIO

While you, sweet dear, prove mistress of my heart.
    [They retire.]

HORTENSIO

Quick proceeders, marry! Now tell me, I pray,
You that durst swear that your Mistress Bianca
Lov'd none in the world so well as Lucentio.

TRANIO

O despiteful love! unconstant womankind!
I tell thee, Licio, this is wonderful.

HORTENSIO

Mistake no more; I am not Licio.
Nor a musician as I seem to be;
But one that scorn to live in this disguise
For such a one as leaves a gentleman
And makes a god of such a cullion:
Know, sir, that I am call'd Hortensio.

TRANIO

Signior Hortensio, I have often heard
Of your entire affection to Bianca;
And since mine eyes are witness of her lightness,
I will with you, if you be so contented,
Forswear Bianca and her love for ever.

HORTENSIO

See, how they kiss and court! Signior Lucentio,
Here is my hand, and here I firmly vow
Never to woo her more, but do forswear her,
As one unworthy all the former favours
That I have fondly flatter'd her withal.

TRANIO

And here I take the like unfeigned oath,
Never to marry with her though she would entreat;
Fie on her! See how beastly she doth court him!

HORTENSIO

Would all the world but he had quite forsworn!
For me, that I may surely keep mine oath,
I will be married to a wealthy widow
Ere three days pass, which hath as long lov'd me
As I have lov'd this proud disdainful haggard.
And so farewell, Signior Lucentio.
Kindness in women, not their beauteous looks,
Shall win my love; and so I take my leave,

In resolution as I swore before.

[Exit Hortensio. Lucentio and Bianca advance.]

TRANIO

Mistress Bianca, bless you with such grace
As 'longeth to a lover's blessed case!
Nay, I have ta'en you napping, gentle love,
And have forsworn you with Hortensio.

BIANCA

Tranio, you jest; but have you both forsworn me?

TRANIO

Mistress, we have.

LUCENTIO

Then we are rid of Licio.

TRANIO

I' faith, he'll have a lusty widow now,
That shall be woo'd and wedded in a day.

BIANCA

God give him joy!

TRANIO

Ay, and he'll tame her.

BIANCA

He says so, Tranio.

TRANIO

Faith, he is gone unto the taming-school.

BIANCA

The taming-school! What, is there such a place?

TRANIO

Ay, mistress; and Petruchio is the master,
That teacheth tricks eleven and twenty long,
To tame a shrew and charm her chattering tongue.

Enter Biondello, running.

BIONDELLO

O master, master! I have watch'd so long
That I am dog-weary; but at last I spied
An ancient angel coming down the hill
Will serve the turn.

TRANIO

What is he, Biondello?

BIONDELLO

Master, a mercatante or a pedant,
I know not what; but formal in apparel,
In gait and countenance surely like a father.

LUCENTIO

And what of him, Tranio?

TRANIO

If he be credulous and trust my tale,
I'll make him glad to seem Vincentio,
And give assurance to Baptista Minola,
As if he were the right Vincentio.
Take in your love, and then let me alone.
[Exeunt LUCENTIO and BIANCA.]
Enter a PEDANT.

PEDANT

God save you, sir!

TRANIO

And you, sir! you are welcome.
Travel you far on, or are you at the farthest?

PEDANT

Sir, at the farthest for a week or two;
But then up farther, and as far as Rome;
And so to Tripoli, if God lend me life.

TRANIO

What countryman, I pray?

PEDANT

Of Mantua.

TRANIO

Of Mantua, sir? Marry, God forbid,
And come to Padua, careless of your life!

PEDANT

My life, sir! How, I pray? for that goes hard.

TRANIO

'Tis death for anyone in Mantua
To come to Padua. Know you not the cause?
Your ships are stay'd at Venice; and the Duke,—
For private quarrel 'twixt your Duke and him,—
Hath publish'd and proclaim'd it openly.
'Tis marvel, but that you are but newly come
You might have heard it else proclaim'd about.

PEDANT

Alas, sir! it is worse for me than so;
For I have bills for money by exchange
From Florence, and must here deliver them.

TRANIO

Well, sir, to do you courtesy,
This will I do, and this I will advise you:
First, tell me, have you ever been at Pisa?

PEDANT

Ay, sir, in Pisa have I often been,
Pisa renowned for grave citizens.

TRANIO

Among them know you one Vincentio?

PEDANT

I know him not, but I have heard of him,
A merchant of incomparable wealth.

TRANIO

He is my father, sir; and, sooth to say,
In countenance somewhat doth resemble you.

BIONDELLO

    [Aside.]

    As much as an apple doth an oyster, and all one.

TRANIO

    To save your life in this extremity,

    This favour will I do you for his sake;

    And think it not the worst of all your fortunes

    That you are like to Sir Vincentio.

    His name and credit shall you undertake,

    And in my house you shall be friendly lodg'd;

    Look that you take upon you as you should!

    You understand me, sir; so shall you stay

    Till you have done your business in the city.

    If this be courtesy, sir, accept of it.

PEDANT

    O, sir, I do; and will repute you ever

    The patron of my life and liberty.

TRANIO

    Then go with me to make the matter good.

    This, by the way, I let you understand:

    My father is here look'd for every day

    To pass assurance of a dower in marriage

    'Twixt me and one Baptista's daughter here:

    In all these circumstances I'll instruct you.

    Go with me to clothe you as becomes you.

    [Exeunt.]

SCENE III. A room in PETRUCHIO'S house.

Enter KATHERINA and GRUMIO.

GRUMIO

    No, no, forsooth; I dare not for my life.

KATHERINA

    The more my wrong, the more his spite appears.

    What, did he marry me to famish me?

Beggars that come unto my father's door
Upon entreaty have a present alms;
If not, elsewhere they meet with charity;
But I, who never knew how to entreat,
Nor never needed that I should entreat,
Am starv'd for meat, giddy for lack of sleep;
With oaths kept waking, and with brawling fed.
And that which spites me more than all these wants,
He does it under name of perfect love;
As who should say, if I should sleep or eat
'Twere deadly sickness, or else present death.
I prithee go and get me some repast;
I care not what, so it be wholesome food.

GRUMIO

What say you to a neat's foot?

KATHERINA

'Tis passing good; I prithee let me have it.

GRUMIO

I fear it is too choleric a meat.
How say you to a fat tripe finely broil'd?

KATHERINA

I like it well; good Grumio, fetch it me.

GRUMIO

I cannot tell; I fear 'tis choleric.
What say you to a piece of beef and mustard?

KATHERINA

A dish that I do love to feed upon.

GRUMIO

Ay, but the mustard is too hot a little.

KATHERINA

Why then the beef, and let the mustard rest.

GRUMIO

Nay, then I will not: you shall have the mustard,
Or else you get no beef of Grumio.

KATHERINA

Then both, or one, or anything thou wilt.

GRUMIO

Why then the mustard without the beef.

KATHERINA

Go, get thee gone, thou false deluding slave,
    [Beats him.]
That feed'st me with the very name of meat.
Sorrow on thee and all the pack of you
That triumph thus upon my misery!
Go, get thee gone, I say.
    Enter PETRUCHIO *with a dish of meat; and* HORTENSIO.

PETRUCHIO

How fares my Kate? What, sweeting, all amort?

HORTENSIO

Mistress, what cheer?

KATHERINA

Faith, as cold as can be.

PETRUCHIO

Pluck up thy spirits; look cheerfully upon me.
Here, love; thou seest how diligent I am,
To dress thy meat myself, and bring it thee:
    [Sets the dish on a table.]
I am sure, sweet Kate, this kindness merits thanks.
What! not a word? Nay, then thou lov'st it not,
And all my pains is sorted to no proof.
Here, take away this dish.

KATHERINA

I pray you, let it stand.

PETRUCHIO

The poorest service is repaid with thanks;
And so shall mine, before you touch the meat.

KATHERINA

I thank you, sir.

HORTENSIO

    Signior Petruchio, fie! you are to blame.
    Come, Mistress Kate, I'll bear you company.

PETRUCHIO

        [Aside.]

    Eat it up all, Hortensio, if thou lovest me.
    Much good do it unto thy gentle heart!
    Kate, eat apace: and now, my honey love,
    Will we return unto thy father's house
    And revel it as bravely as the best,
    With silken coats and caps, and golden rings,
    With ruffs and cuffs and farthingales and things;
    With scarfs and fans and double change of bravery,
    With amber bracelets, beads, and all this knavery.
    What! hast thou din'd? The tailor stays thy leisure,
    To deck thy body with his ruffling treasure.
        Enter TAILOR.
    Come, tailor, let us see these ornaments;
    Lay forth the gown.—
        Enter HABERDASHER.
    What news with you, sir?

HABERDASHER

    Here is the cap your worship did bespeak.

PETRUCHIO

    Why, this was moulded on a porringer;
    A velvet dish: fie, fie! 'tis lewd and filthy:
    Why, 'tis a cockle or a walnut-shell,
    A knack, a toy, a trick, a baby's cap:
    Away with it! come, let me have a bigger.

KATHERINA

    I'll have no bigger; this doth fit the time,
    And gentlewomen wear such caps as these.

PETRUCHIO

    When you are gentle, you shall have one too,
    And not till then.

HORTENSIO

[Aside.]

That will not be in haste.

KATHERINA

Why, sir, I trust I may have leave to speak;
And speak I will. I am no child, no babe.
Your betters have endur'd me say my mind,
And if you cannot, best you stop your ears.
My tongue will tell the anger of my heart,
Or else my heart, concealing it, will break;
And rather than it shall, I will be free
Even to the uttermost, as I please, in words.

PETRUCHIO

Why, thou say'st true; it is a paltry cap,
A custard-coffin, a bauble, a silken pie;
I love thee well in that thou lik'st it not.

KATHERINA

Love me or love me not, I like the cap;
And it I will have, or I will have none.

[Exit HABERDASHER.]

PETRUCHIO

Thy gown? Why, ay: come, tailor, let us see't.
O mercy, God! what masquing stuff is here?
What's this? A sleeve? 'Tis like a demi-cannon.
What, up and down, carv'd like an apple tart?
Here's snip and nip and cut and slish and slash,
Like to a censer in a barber's shop.
Why, what i' devil's name, tailor, call'st thou this?

HORTENSIO

[Aside.]

I see she's like to have neither cap nor gown.

TAILOR

You bid me make it orderly and well,
According to the fashion and the time.

PETRUCHIO

    Marry, and did; but if you be remember'd,
    I did not bid you mar it to the time.
    Go, hop me over every kennel home,
    For you shall hop without my custom, sir.
    I'll none of it: hence! make your best of it.

KATHERINA

    I never saw a better fashion'd gown,
    More quaint, more pleasing, nor more commendable;
    Belike you mean to make a puppet of me.

PETRUCHIO

    Why, true; he means to make a puppet of thee.

TAILOR

    She says your worship means to make a puppet of her.

PETRUCHIO

    O monstrous arrogance! Thou liest, thou thread,
    Thou thimble,
    Thou yard, three-quarters, half-yard, quarter, nail!
    Thou flea, thou nit, thou winter-cricket thou!
    Brav'd in mine own house with a skein of thread!
    Away! thou rag, thou quantity, thou remnant,
    Or I shall so be-mete thee with thy yard
    As thou shalt think on prating whilst thou liv'st!
    I tell thee, I, that thou hast marr'd her gown.

TAILOR

    Your worship is deceiv'd: the gown is made
    Just as my master had direction.
    Grumio gave order how it should be done.

GRUMIO

    I gave him no order; I gave him the stuff.

TAILOR

    But how did you desire it should be made?

GRUMIO

    Marry, sir, with needle and thread.

TAILOR

But did you not request to have it cut?

GRUMIO ·

Thou hast faced many things.

TAILOR

I have.

GRUMIO

Face not me. Thou hast braved many men; brave not me: I will neither be fac'd nor brav'd. I say unto thee, I bid thy master cut out the gown; but I did not bid him cut it to pieces: ergo, thou liest.

TAILOR

Why, here is the note of the fashion to testify.

PETRUCHIO

Read it.

GRUMIO

The note lies in 's throat, if he say I said so.

TAILOR

'Imprimis, a loose-bodied gown.'

GRUMIO

Master, if ever I said loose-bodied gown, sew me in the skirts of it and beat me to death with a bottom of brown thread; I said, a gown.

PETRUCHIO

Proceed.

TAILOR

'With a small compassed cape.'

GRUMIO

I confess the cape.

TAILOR

'With a trunk sleeve.'

GRUMIO

I confess two sleeves.

TAILOR

'The sleeves curiously cut.'

PETRUCHIO

Ay, there's the villainy.

GRUMIO

Error i' the bill, sir; error i' the bill. I commanded the sleeves should be cut out, and sew'd up again; and that I'll prove upon thee, though thy little finger be armed in a thimble.

TAILOR

This is true that I say; and I had thee in place where thou shouldst know it.

GRUMIO

I am for thee straight; take thou the bill, give me thy mete-yard, and spare not me.

HORTENSIO

God-a-mercy, Grumio! Then he shall have no odds.

PETRUCHIO

Well, sir, in brief, the gown is not for me.

GRUMIO

You are i' the right, sir; 'tis for my mistress.

PETRUCHIO

Go, take it up unto thy master's use.

GRUMIO

Villain, not for thy life! Take up my mistress' gown for thy master's use!

PETRUCHIO

Why, sir, what's your conceit in that?

GRUMIO

O, sir, the conceit is deeper than you think for.
Take up my mistress' gown to his master's use!
O fie, fie, fie!

PETRUCHIO

> *[Aside.]*
> Hortensio, say thou wilt see the tailor paid.
> *[To TAILOR.]*
> Go take it hence; be gone, and say no more.

HORTENSIO

> *[Aside to TAILOR.]*
> Tailor, I'll pay thee for thy gown tomorrow;
> Take no unkindness of his hasty words.
> Away, I say! commend me to thy master.
> *[Exit TAILOR.]*

PETRUCHIO

> Well, come, my Kate; we will unto your father's
> Even in these honest mean habiliments.
> Our purses shall be proud, our garments poor
> For 'tis the mind that makes the body rich;
> And as the sun breaks through the darkest clouds,
> So honour peereth in the meanest habit.
> What, is the jay more precious than the lark
> Because his feathers are more beautiful?
> Or is the adder better than the eel
> Because his painted skin contents the eye?
> O no, good Kate; neither art thou the worse
> For this poor furniture and mean array.
> If thou account'st it shame, lay it on me;
> And therefore frolic; we will hence forthwith,
> To feast and sport us at thy father's house.
> Go call my men, and let us straight to him;
> And bring our horses unto Long-lane end;
> There will we mount, and thither walk on foot.
> Let's see; I think 'tis now some seven o'clock,
> And well we may come there by dinner-time.

KATHERINA

> I dare assure you, sir, 'tis almost two,
> And 'twill be supper-time ere you come there.

PETRUCHIO

> It shall be seven ere I go to horse.
> Look what I speak, or do, or think to do,
> You are still crossing it. Sirs, let 't alone:
> I will not go today; and ere I do,
> It shall be what o'clock I say it is.

HORTENSIO

> Why, so this gallant will command the sun.
>> *[Exeunt.]*

SCENE IV. Padua. Before BAPTISTA'S house.

Enter TRANIO and the PEDANT dressed like Vincentio.

TRANIO

> Sir, this is the house; please it you that I call?

PEDANT

> Ay, what else? and, but I be deceived,
> Signior Baptista may remember me,
> Near twenty years ago in Genoa,
> Where we were lodgers at the Pegasus.

TRANIO

> 'Tis well; and hold your own, in any case,
> With such austerity as 'longeth to a father.

PEDANT

> I warrant you. But, sir, here comes your boy;
> 'Twere good he were school'd.
>> *Enter BIONDELLO.*

TRANIO

> Fear you not him. Sirrah Biondello,
> Now do your duty throughly, I advise you.
> Imagine 'twere the right Vincentio.

BIONDELLO

> Tut! fear not me.

TRANIO

But hast thou done thy errand to Baptista?

BIONDELLO

I told him that your father was at Venice,
And that you look'd for him this day in Padua.

TRANIO

Th'art a tall fellow; hold thee that to drink.
Here comes Baptista. Set your countenance, sir.
            Enter BAPTISTA and LUCENTIO.
Signior Baptista, you are happily met.
            [To the PEDANT.]
Sir, this is the gentleman I told you of;
I pray you stand good father to me now;
Give me Bianca for my patrimony.

PEDANT

Soft, son!
Sir, by your leave: having come to Padua
To gather in some debts, my son Lucentio
Made me acquainted with a weighty cause
Of love between your daughter and himself:
And,—for the good report I hear of you,
And for the love he beareth to your daughter,
And she to him,—to stay him not too long,
I am content, in a good father's care,
To have him match'd; and, if you please to like
No worse than I, upon some agreement
Me shall you find ready and willing
With one consent to have her so bestow'd;
For curious I cannot be with you,
Signior Baptista, of whom I hear so well.

BAPTISTA

Sir, pardon me in what I have to say.
Your plainness and your shortness please me well.
Right true it is your son Lucentio here
Doth love my daughter, and she loveth him,

Or both dissemble deeply their affections;
And therefore, if you say no more than this,
That like a father you will deal with him,
And pass my daughter a sufficient dower,
The match is made, and all is done:
Your son shall have my daughter with consent.

TRANIO

I thank you, sir. Where then do you know best
We be affied, and such assurance ta'en
As shall with either part's agreement stand?

BAPTISTA

Not in my house, Lucentio, for you know
Pitchers have ears, and I have many servants;
Besides, old Gremio is hearkening still,
And happily we might be interrupted.

TRANIO

Then at my lodging, and it like you:
There doth my father lie; and there this night
We'll pass the business privately and well.
Send for your daughter by your servant here;
My boy shall fetch the scrivener presently.
The worst is this, that at so slender warning
You are like to have a thin and slender pittance.

BAPTISTA

It likes me well. Cambio, hie you home,
And bid Bianca make her ready straight;
And, if you will, tell what hath happened:
Lucentio's father is arriv'd in Padua,
And how she's like to be Lucentio's wife.

LUCENTIO

I pray the gods she may, with all my heart!

TRANIO

Dally not with the gods, but get thee gone.
Signior Baptista, shall I lead the way?

Welcome! One mess is like to be your cheer;
Come, sir; we will better it in Pisa.

BAPTISTA

I follow you.
[Exeunt TRANIO, PEDANT and BAPTISTA.]

BIONDELLO

Cambio!

LUCENTIO

What say'st thou, Biondello?

BIONDELLO

You saw my master wink and laugh upon you?

LUCENTIO

Biondello, what of that?

BIONDELLO

Faith, nothing; but has left me here behind to expound the meaning or moral of his signs and tokens.

LUCENTIO

I pray thee moralize them.

BIONDELLO

Then thus: Baptista is safe, talking with the deceiving father of a deceitful son.

LUCENTIO

And what of him?

BIONDELLO

His daughter is to be brought by you to the supper.

LUCENTIO

And then?

BIONDELLO

The old priest at Saint Luke's church is at your command at all hours.

LUCENTIO

And what of all this?

BIONDELLO

I cannot tell, except they are busied about a counterfeit assurance. Take your assurance of her, *cum privilegio ad imprimendum solum*; to the church! take the priest, clerk, and some sufficient honest witnesses.

If this be not that you look for, I have more to say,

But bid Bianca farewell for ever and a day.

[Going.]

LUCENTIO

Hear'st thou, Biondello?

BIONDELLO

I cannot tarry: I knew a wench married in an afternoon as she went to the garden for parsley to stuff a rabbit; and so may you, sir; and so adieu, sir. My master hath appointed me to go to Saint Luke's to bid the priest be ready to come against you come with your appendix.

[Exit.]

LUCENTIO

I may, and will, if she be so contented.

She will be pleas'd; then wherefore should I doubt?

Hap what hap may, I'll roundly go about her;

It shall go hard if Cambio go without her.

[Exit.]

SCENE V. A public road.

Enter Petruchio, Katherina, Hortensio and Servants.

PETRUCHIO

Come on, i' God's name; once more toward our father's.

Good Lord, how bright and goodly shines the moon!

KATHERINA

The moon! The sun; it is not moonlight now.

PETRUCHIO

I say it is the moon that shines so bright.

KATHERINA

I know it is the sun that shines so bright.

PETRUCHIO

> Now by my mother's son, and that's myself,
> It shall be moon, or star, or what I list,
> Or ere I journey to your father's house.
> Go on and fetch our horses back again.
> Evermore cross'd and cross'd; nothing but cross'd!

HORTENSIO

> Say as he says, or we shall never go.

KATHERINA

> Forward, I pray, since we have come so far,
> And be it moon, or sun, or what you please;
> And if you please to call it a rush-candle,
> Henceforth I vow it shall be so for me.

PETRUCHIO

> I say it is the moon.

KATHERINA

> I know it is the moon.

PETRUCHIO

> Nay, then you lie; it is the blessed sun.

KATHERINA

> Then, God be bless'd, it is the blessed sun;
> But sun it is not when you say it is not,
> And the moon changes even as your mind.
> What you will have it nam'd, even that it is,
> And so it shall be so for Katherine.

HORTENSIO

> Petruchio, go thy ways; the field is won.

PETRUCHIO

> Well, forward, forward! thus the bowl should run,
> And not unluckily against the bias.
> But, soft! Company is coming here.
> > *Enter VINCENTIO, in a travelling dress.*
> > *[To VINCENTIO.]*

Good morrow, gentle mistress; where away?
Tell me, sweet Kate, and tell me truly too,
Hast thou beheld a fresher gentlewoman?
Such war of white and red within her cheeks!
What stars do spangle heaven with such beauty
As those two eyes become that heavenly face?
Fair lovely maid, once more good day to thee.
Sweet Kate, embrace her for her beauty's sake.

HORTENSIO

A, will make the man mad, to make a woman of him.

KATHERINA

Young budding virgin, fair and fresh and sweet,
Whither away, or where is thy abode?
Happy the parents of so fair a child;
Happier the man whom favourable stars
Allot thee for his lovely bedfellow.

PETRUCHIO

Why, how now, Kate! I hope thou art not mad:
This is a man, old, wrinkled, faded, wither'd,
And not a maiden, as thou sayst he is.

KATHERINA

Pardon, old father, my mistaking eyes,
That have been so bedazzled with the sun
That everything I look on seemeth green:
Now I perceive thou art a reverend father;
Pardon, I pray thee, for my mad mistaking.

PETRUCHIO

Do, good old grandsire, and withal make known
Which way thou travellest: if along with us,
We shall be joyful of thy company.

VINCENTIO

Fair sir, and you my merry mistress,
That with your strange encounter much amaz'd me,
My name is called Vincentio; my dwelling Pisa;

And bound I am to Padua, there to visit
A son of mine, which long I have not seen.

PETRUCHIO

What is his name?

VINCENTIO

Lucentio, gentle sir.

PETRUCHIO

Happily met; the happier for thy son.
And now by law, as well as reverend age,
I may entitle thee my loving father:
The sister to my wife, this gentlewoman,
Thy son by this hath married. Wonder not,
Nor be not griev'd: she is of good esteem,
Her dowry wealthy, and of worthy birth;
Beside, so qualified as may beseem
The spouse of any noble gentleman.
Let me embrace with old Vincentio;
And wander we to see thy honest son,
Who will of thy arrival be full joyous.

VINCENTIO

But is this true? or is it else your pleasure,
Like pleasant travellers, to break a jest
Upon the company you overtake?

HORTENSIO

I do assure thee, father, so it is.

PETRUCHIO

Come, go along, and see the truth hereof;
For our first merriment hath made thee jealous.
        [Exeunt all but HORTENSIO.]

HORTENSIO

Well, Petruchio, this has put me in heart.
Have to my widow! and if she be froward,
Then hast thou taught Hortensio to be untoward.
        [Exit.]

ACT V

SCENE I. Padua. Before LUCENTIO'S house.

Enter on one side BIONDELLO, LUCENTIO and BIANCA; GREMIO walking on other side.

BIONDELLO

Softly and swiftly, sir, for the priest is ready.

LUCENTIO

I fly, Biondello; but they may chance to need thee at home, therefore leave us.

BIONDELLO

Nay, faith, I'll see the church o' your back; and then come back to my master's as soon as I can.

[Exeunt LUCENTIO, BIANCA and BIONDELLO.]

GREMIO

I marvel Cambio comes not all this while.

Enter PETRUCHIO, KATHERINA, VINCENTIO and ATTENDANTS.

PETRUCHIO

Sir, here's the door; this is Lucentio's house:
My father's bears more toward the market-place;
Thither must I, and here I leave you, sir.

VINCENTIO

You shall not choose but drink before you go.

I think I shall command your welcome here,
And by all likelihood some cheer is toward.
        [Knocks.]

GREMIO

They're busy within; you were best knock louder.
        Enter PEDANT *above, at a window.*

PEDANT

What's he that knocks as he would beat down the gate?

VINCENTIO

Is Signior Lucentio within, sir?

PEDANT

He's within, sir, but not to be spoken withal.

VINCENTIO

What if a man bring him a hundred pound or two to make merry withal?

PEDANT

Keep your hundred pounds to yourself: he shall need none so long as I live.

PETRUCHIO

Nay, I told you your son was well beloved in Padua. Do you hear, sir? To leave frivolous circumstances, I pray you tell Signior Lucentio that his father is come from Pisa, and is here at the door to speak with him.

PEDANT

Thou liest: his father is come from Padua, and here looking out at the window.

VINCENTIO

Art thou his father?

PEDANT

Ay, sir; so his mother says, if I may believe her.

PETRUCHIO

        [To VINCENTIO.*]*

Why, how now, gentleman! why, this is flat knavery to take upon you another man's name.

PEDANT

Lay hands on the villain: I believe a means to cozen somebody in this city under my countenance.

Re-enter BIONDELLO.

BIONDELLO

I have seen them in the church together: God send 'em good shipping! But who is here? Mine old master, Vincentio! Now we are undone and brought to nothing.

VINCENTIO

[Seeing BIONDELLO.]

Come hither, crack-hemp.

BIONDELLO

I hope I may choose, sir.

VINCENTIO

Come hither, you rogue. What, have you forgot me?

BIONDELLO

Forgot you! No, sir: I could not forget you, for I never saw you before in all my life.

VINCENTIO

What, you notorious villain! didst thou never see thy master's father, Vincentio?

BIONDELLO

What, my old worshipful old master? Yes, marry, sir; see where he looks out of the window.

VINCENTIO

Is't so, indeed?

[He beats BIONDELLO.]

BIONDELLO

Help, help, help! here's a madman will murder me.

[Exit.]

PEDANT

Help, son! help, Signior Baptista!
[Exit from the window.]

PETRUCHIO

Prithee, Kate, let's stand aside and see the end of this controversy.
[They retire.]
Re-enter PEDANT, *below;* BAPTISTA, TRANIO *and* SERVANTS.

TRANIO

Sir, what are you that offer to beat my servant?

VINCENTIO

What am I, sir! nay, what are you, sir? O immortal gods! O fine villain! A silken doublet, a velvet hose, a scarlet cloak, and a copatain hat! O, I am undone! I am undone! While I play the good husband at home, my son and my servant spend all at the university.

TRANIO

How now! what's the matter?

BAPTISTA

What, is the man lunatic?

TRANIO

Sir, you seem a sober ancient gentleman by your habit, but your words show you a madman. Why, sir, what 'cerns it you if I wear pearl and gold? I thank my good father, I am able to maintain it.

VINCENTIO

Thy father! O villain! he is a sailmaker in Bergamo.

BAPTISTA

You mistake, sir; you mistake, sir. Pray, what do you think is his name?

VINCENTIO

His name! As if I knew not his name! I have brought him up ever since he was three years old, and his name is Tranio.

PEDANT

Away, away, mad ass! His name is Lucentio; and he is mine only son, and heir to the lands of me, Signior Vincentio.

VINCENTIO

Lucentio! O, he hath murdered his master! Lay hold on him, I charge you, in the Duke's name. O, my son, my son! Tell me, thou villain, where is my son, Lucentio?

TRANIO

Call forth an officer.
Enter one with an OFFICER.
Carry this mad knave to the gaol. Father Baptista, I charge you see that he be forthcoming.

VINCENTIO

Carry me to the gaol!

GREMIO

Stay, officer; he shall not go to prison.

BAPTISTA

Talk not, Signior Gremio; I say he shall go to prison.

GREMIO

Take heed, Signior Baptista, lest you be cony-catched in this business; I dare swear this is the right Vincentio.

PEDANT

Swear if thou darest.

GREMIO

Nay, I dare not swear it.

TRANIO

Then thou wert best say that I am not Lucentio.

GREMIO

Yes, I know thee to be Signior Lucentio.

BAPTISTA

Away with the dotard! to the gaol with him!

VINCENTIO

Thus strangers may be haled and abus'd: O monstrous villain!
Re-enter BIONDELLO, with LUCENTIO and BIANCA.

BIONDELLO

O! we are spoiled; and yonder he is: deny him, forswear him, or else we are all undone.

LUCENTIO

[Kneeling.]
Pardon, sweet father.

VINCENTIO

Lives my sweetest son?
[BIONDELLO, TRANIO and PEDANT run out.]

BIANCA

[Kneeling.]
Pardon, dear father.

BAPTISTA

How hast thou offended?
Where is Lucentio?

LUCENTIO

Here's Lucentio,
Right son to the right Vincentio;
That have by marriage made thy daughter mine,
While counterfeit supposes blear'd thine eyne.

GREMIO

Here 's packing, with a witness, to deceive us all!

VINCENTIO

Where is that damned villain, Tranio,
That fac'd and brav'd me in this matter so?

BAPTISTA

Why, tell me, is not this my Cambio?

BIANCA

Cambio is chang'd into Lucentio.

LUCENTIO

Love wrought these miracles. Bianca's love
Made me exchange my state with Tranio,
While he did bear my countenance in the town;

And happily I have arriv'd at the last
Unto the wished haven of my bliss.
What Tranio did, myself enforc'd him to;
Then pardon him, sweet father, for my sake.

VINCENTIO

I'll slit the villain's nose that would have sent me to the gaol.

BAPTISTA

[To LUCENTIO.]

But do you hear, sir? Have you married my daughter without asking my good will?

VINCENTIO

Fear not, Baptista; we will content you, go to: but I will in, to be revenged for this villainy.

[Exit.]

BAPTISTA

And I to sound the depth of this knavery.

[Exit.]

LUCENTIO

Look not pale, Bianca; thy father will not frown.

[Exeunt LUCENTIO and BIANCA.]

GREMIO

My cake is dough, but I'll in among the rest;
Out of hope of all but my share of the feast.

[Exit.]

PETRUCHIO and KATHERINA advance.

KATHERINA

Husband, let's follow to see the end of this ado.

PETRUCHIO

First kiss me, Kate, and we will.

KATHERINA

What! in the midst of the street?

PETRUCHIO

What! art thou ashamed of me?

KATHERINA

No, sir; God forbid; but ashamed to kiss.

PETRUCHIO

Why, then, let's home again. Come, sirrah, let's away.

KATHERINA

Nay, I will give thee a kiss: now pray thee, love, stay.

PETRUCHIO

Is not this well? Come, my sweet Kate:
Better once than never, for never too late.
> *[Exeunt.]*

SCENE II. A room in LUCENTIO'S house.

*Enter BAPTISTA, VINCENTIO, GREMIO, the PEDANT, LUCENTIO,
BIANCA, PETRUCHIO, KATHERINA, HORTENSIO and WIDOW.
TRANIO, BIONDELLO and GRUMIO and OTHERS, attending.*

LUCENTIO

At last, though long, our jarring notes agree:
And time it is when raging war is done,
To smile at 'scapes and perils overblown.
My fair Bianca, bid my father welcome,
While I with self-same kindness welcome thine.
Brother Petruchio, sister Katherina,
And thou, Hortensio, with thy loving widow,
Feast with the best, and welcome to my house:
My banquet is to close our stomachs up,
After our great good cheer. Pray you, sit down;
For now we sit to chat as well as eat.
> *[They sit at table.]*

PETRUCHIO

Nothing but sit and sit, and eat and eat!

BAPTISTA

Padua affords this kindness, son Petruchio.

PETRUCHIO

Padua affords nothing but what is kind.

HORTENSIO

For both our sakes I would that word were true.

PETRUCHIO

Now, for my life, Hortensio fears his widow.

WIDOW

Then never trust me if I be afeard.

PETRUCHIO

You are very sensible, and yet you miss my sense:
I mean Hortensio is afeard of you.

WIDOW

He that is giddy thinks the world turns round.

PETRUCHIO

Roundly replied.

KATHERINA

Mistress, how mean you that?

WIDOW

Thus I conceive by him.

PETRUCHIO

Conceives by me! How likes Hortensio that?

HORTENSIO

My widow says thus she conceives her tale.

PETRUCHIO

Very well mended. Kiss him for that, good widow.

KATHERINA

'He that is giddy thinks the world turns round':
I pray you tell me what you meant by that.

WIDOW

Your husband, being troubled with a shrew,
Measures my husband's sorrow by his woe;
And now you know my meaning.

KATHERINA

A very mean meaning.

WIDOW

Right, I mean you.

KATHERINA

And I am mean, indeed, respecting you.

PETRUCHIO

To her, Kate!

HORTENSIO

To her, widow!

PETRUCHIO

A hundred marks, my Kate does put her down.

HORTENSIO

That's my office.

PETRUCHIO

Spoke like an officer: ha' to thee, lad.
[Drinks to HORTENSIO.]

BAPTISTA

How likes Gremio these quick-witted folks?

GREMIO

Believe me, sir, they butt together well.

BIANCA

Head and butt! An hasty-witted body
Would say your head and butt were head and horn.

VINCENTIO

Ay, mistress bride, hath that awaken'd you?

BIANCA

Ay, but not frighted me; therefore I'll sleep again.

PETRUCHIO

Nay, that you shall not; since you have begun,
Have at you for a bitter jest or two.

BIANCA

Am I your bird? I mean to shift my bush,
And then pursue me as you draw your bow.
You are welcome all.

[*Exeunt* BIANCA, KATHERINA *and* WIDOW.]

PETRUCHIO

She hath prevented me. Here, Signior Tranio;
This bird you aim'd at, though you hit her not:
Therefore a health to all that shot and miss'd.

TRANIO

O, sir! Lucentio slipp'd me like his greyhound,
Which runs himself, and catches for his master.

PETRUCHIO

A good swift simile, but something currish.

TRANIO

'Tis well, sir, that you hunted for yourself:
'Tis thought your deer does hold you at a bay.

BAPTISTA

O ho, Petruchio! Tranio hits you now.

LUCENTIO

I thank thee for that gird, good Tranio.

HORTENSIO

Confess, confess; hath he not hit you here?

PETRUCHIO

A has a little gall'd me, I confess;
And as the jest did glance away from me,
'Tis ten to one it maim'd you two outright.

BAPTISTA

Now, in good sadness, son Petruchio,
I think thou hast the veriest shrew of all.

PETRUCHIO

Well, I say no; and therefore, for assurance,

Let's each one send unto his wife,
And he whose wife is most obedient,
To come at first when he doth send for her,
Shall win the wager which we will propose.

HORTENSIO

Content. What's the wager?

LUCENTIO

Twenty crowns.

PETRUCHIO

Twenty crowns!
I'll venture so much of my hawk or hound,
But twenty times so much upon my wife.

LUCENTIO

A hundred then.

HORTENSIO

Content.

PETRUCHIO

A match! 'tis done.

HORTENSIO

Who shall begin?

LUCENTIO

That will I.
Go, Biondello, bid your mistress come to me.

BIONDELLO

I go.
                    [Exit.]

BAPTISTA

Son, I'll be your half, Bianca comes.

LUCENTIO

I'll have no halves; I'll bear it all myself.
                    Re-enter BIONDELLO.
How now! what news?

BIONDELLO

Sir, my mistress sends you word
That she is busy and she cannot come.

PETRUCHIO

How! She's busy, and she cannot come!
Is that an answer?

GREMIO

Ay, and a kind one too:
Pray God, sir, your wife send you not a worse.

PETRUCHIO

I hope better.

HORTENSIO

Sirrah Biondello, go and entreat my wife
To come to me forthwith.
[Exit BIONDELLO.]

PETRUCHIO

O, ho! entreat her!
Nay, then she must needs come.

HORTENSIO

I am afraid, sir,
Do what you can, yours will not be entreated.
Re-enter BIONDELLO.
Now, where's my wife?

BIONDELLO

She says you have some goodly jest in hand:
She will not come; she bids you come to her.

PETRUCHIO

Worse and worse; she will not come! O vile,
Intolerable, not to be endur'd!
Sirrah Grumio, go to your mistress,
Say I command her come to me.
[Exit GRUMIO.]

HORTENSIO

    I know her answer.

PETRUCHIO

    What?

HORTENSIO

    She will not.

PETRUCHIO

    The fouler fortune mine, and there an end.
        Re-enter KATHERINA.

BAPTISTA

    Now, by my holidame, here comes Katherina!

KATHERINA

    What is your will sir, that you send for me?

PETRUCHIO

    Where is your sister, and Hortensio's wife?

KATHERINA

    They sit conferring by the parlour fire.

PETRUCHIO

    Go fetch them hither; if they deny to come,
    Swinge me them soundly forth unto their husbands.
    Away, I say, and bring them hither straight.
        [Exit KATHERINA.]

LUCENTIO

    Here is a wonder, if you talk of a wonder.

HORTENSIO

    And so it is. I wonder what it bodes.

PETRUCHIO

    Marry, peace it bodes, and love, and quiet life,
    An awful rule, and right supremacy;
    And, to be short, what not that's sweet and happy.

BAPTISTA

Now fair befall thee, good Petruchio!
The wager thou hast won; and I will add
Unto their losses twenty thousand crowns;
Another dowry to another daughter,
For she is chang'd, as she had never been.

PETRUCHIO

Nay, I will win my wager better yet,
And show more sign of her obedience,
Her new-built virtue and obedience.
See where she comes, and brings your froward wives
As prisoners to her womanly persuasion.
    Re-enter KATHERINA with BIANCA and WIDOW.
Katherine, that cap of yours becomes you not:
Off with that bauble, throw it underfoot.
    [KATHERINA pulls off her cap and throws it down.]

WIDOW

Lord, let me never have a cause to sigh
Till I be brought to such a silly pass!

BIANCA

Fie! what a foolish duty call you this?

LUCENTIO

I would your duty were as foolish too;
The wisdom of your duty, fair Bianca,
Hath cost me a hundred crowns since supper-time!

BIANCA

The more fool you for laying on my duty.

PETRUCHIO

Katherine, I charge thee, tell these headstrong women
What duty they do owe their lords and husbands.

WIDOW

Come, come, you're mocking; we will have no telling.

PETRUCHIO

Come on, I say; and first begin with her.

WIDOW

> She shall not.

PETRUCHIO

> I say she shall: and first begin with her.

KATHERINA

> Fie, fie! unknit that threatening unkind brow,
> And dart not scornful glances from those eyes
> To wound thy lord, thy king, thy governor:
> It blots thy beauty as frosts do bite the meads,
> Confounds thy fame as whirlwinds shake fair buds,
> And in no sense is meet or amiable.
> A woman mov'd is like a fountain troubled,
> Muddy, ill-seeming, thick, bereft of beauty;
> And while it is so, none so dry or thirsty
> Will deign to sip or touch one drop of it.
> Thy husband is thy lord, thy life, thy keeper,
> Thy head, thy sovereign; one that cares for thee,
> And for thy maintenance commits his body
> To painful labour both by sea and land,
> To watch the night in storms, the day in cold,
> Whilst thou liest warm at home, secure and safe;
> And craves no other tribute at thy hands
> But love, fair looks, and true obedience;
> Too little payment for so great a debt.
> Such duty as the subject owes the prince,
> Even such a woman oweth to her husband;
> And when she is froward, peevish, sullen, sour,
> And not obedient to his honest will,
> What is she but a foul contending rebel
> And graceless traitor to her loving lord?—
> I am asham'd that women are so simple
> To offer war where they should kneel for peace,
> Or seek for rule, supremacy, and sway,
> When they are bound to serve, love, and obey.
> Why are our bodies soft and weak and smooth,
> Unapt to toil and trouble in the world,
> But that our soft conditions and our hearts

Should well agree with our external parts?
Come, come, you froward and unable worms!
My mind hath been as big as one of yours,
My heart as great, my reason haply more,
To bandy word for word and frown for frown;
But now I see our lances are but straws,
Our strength as weak, our weakness past compare,
That seeming to be most which we indeed least are.
Then vail your stomachs, for it is no boot,
And place your hands below your husband's foot:
In token of which duty, if he please,
My hand is ready; may it do him ease.

PETRUCHIO

Why, there's a wench! Come on, and kiss me, Kate.

LUCENTIO

Well, go thy ways, old lad, for thou shalt ha't.

VINCENTIO

'Tis a good hearing when children are toward.

LUCENTIO

But a harsh hearing when women are froward.

PETRUCHIO

Come, Kate, we'll to bed.
We three are married, but you two are sped.
'Twas I won the wager,
          [To LUCENTIO.]
Though you hit the white;
And being a winner, God give you good night!
          [Exeunt PETRUCIO and KATHERINA.]

HORTENSIO

Now go thy ways; thou hast tam'd a curst shrew.

LUCENTIO

'Tis a wonder, by your leave, she will be tam'd so.
          [Exeunt.]

THE TRAGEDY OF
ROMEO AND JULIET

CONTENTS

DRAMATIS PERSONÆ

ESCALUS, Prince of Verona
MERCUTIO, kinsman to the Prince, and friend to Romeo
PARIS, a young Nobleman, kinsman to the Prince
Page to Paris
MONTAGUE, head of a Veronese family at feud with the Capulets
LADY MONTAGUE, wife to Montague
ROMEO, son to Montague
BENVOLIO, nephew to Montague, and friend to Romeo
ABRAM, servant to Montague
BALTHASAR, servant to Romeo
CAPULET, head of a Veronese family at feud with the Montagues
LADY CAPULET, wife to Capulet
JULIET, daughter to Capulet
TYBALT, nephew to Lady Capulet
CAPULET'S COUSIN, an old man
NURSE to Juliet
PETER, servant to Juliet's Nurse
SAMPSON, servant to Capulet
GREGORY, servant to Capulet
Servants
FRIAR LAWRENCE, a Franciscan
FRIAR JOHN, of the same Order
An Apothecary

CHORUS
Three Musicians
An Officer
Citizens of Verona; several Men and Women, relations to both houses;
Maskers, Guards, Watchmen and Attendants

SCENE. During the greater part of the Play in Verona; once, in the Fifth Act, at Mantua.

THE PROLOGUE

Enter CHORUS.

CHORUS

Two households, both alike in dignity,
In fair Verona, where we lay our scene,
From ancient grudge break to new mutiny,
Where civil blood makes civil hands unclean.
From forth the fatal loins of these two foes
A pair of star-cross'd lovers take their life;
Whose misadventur'd piteous overthrows
Doth with their death bury their parents' strife.
The fearful passage of their death-mark'd love,
And the continuance of their parents' rage,
Which, but their children's end, nought could remove,
Is now the two hours' traffic of our stage;
The which, if you with patient ears attend,
What here shall miss, our toil shall strive to mend.
		[Exit.]

ACT I

SCENE I. A public place.

Enter SAMPSON and GREGORY armed with swords and bucklers.

SAMPSON

Gregory, on my word, we'll not carry coals.

GREGORY

No, for then we should be colliers.

SAMPSON

I mean, if we be in choler, we'll draw.

GREGORY

Ay, while you live, draw your neck out o' the collar.

SAMPSON

I strike quickly, being moved.

GREGORY

But thou art not quickly moved to strike.

SAMPSON

A dog of the house of Montague moves me.

GREGORY

To move is to stir; and to be valiant is to stand: therefore, if thou art moved, thou runn'st away.

SAMPSON

> A dog of that house shall move me to stand.
> I will take the wall of any man or maid of Montague's.

GREGORY

> That shows thee a weak slave, for the weakest goes to the wall.

SAMPSON

> True, and therefore women, being the weaker vessels, are ever thrust to the wall: therefore I will push Montague's men from the wall, and thrust his maids to the wall.

GREGORY

> The quarrel is between our masters and us their men.

SAMPSON

> 'Tis all one, I will show myself a tyrant: when I have fought with the men I will be civil with the maids, I will cut off their heads.

GREGORY

> The heads of the maids?

SAMPSON

> Ay, the heads of the maids, or their maidenheads; take it in what sense thou wilt.

GREGORY

> They must take it in sense that feel it.

SAMPSON

> Me they shall feel while I am able to stand: and 'tis known I am a pretty piece of flesh.

GREGORY

> 'Tis well thou art not fish; if thou hadst, thou hadst been poor John. Draw thy tool; here comes of the house of Montagues.
> *Enter ABRAM and BALTHASAR.*

SAMPSON

> My naked weapon is out: quarrel, I will back thee.

GREGORY

> How? Turn thy back and run?

SAMPSON

Fear me not.

GREGORY

No, marry; I fear thee!

SAMPSON

Let us take the law of our sides; let them begin.

GREGORY

I will frown as I pass by, and let them take it as they list.

SAMPSON

Nay, as they dare. I will bite my thumb at them, which is disgrace to them if they bear it.

ABRAM

Do you bite your thumb at us, sir?

SAMPSON

I do bite my thumb, sir.

ABRAM

Do you bite your thumb at us, sir?

SAMPSON

Is the law of our side if I say ay?

GREGORY

No.

SAMPSON

No sir, I do not bite my thumb at you, sir; but I bite my thumb, sir.

GREGORY

Do you quarrel, sir?

ABRAM

Quarrel, sir? No, sir.

SAMPSON

But if you do, sir, I am for you. I serve as good a man as you.

ABRAM

No better.

SAMPSON

Well, sir.

Enter BENVOLIO.

GREGORY

Say better; here comes one of my master's kinsmen.

SAMPSON

Yes, better, sir.

ABRAM

You lie.

SAMPSON

Draw, if you be men. Gregory, remember thy washing blow.

[They fight.]

BENVOLIO

Part, fools! put up your swords, you know not what you do.

[Beats down their swords.]

Enter TYBALT.

TYBALT

What, art thou drawn among these heartless hinds?
Turn thee Benvolio, look upon thy death.

BENVOLIO

I do but keep the peace, put up thy sword,
Or manage it to part these men with me.

TYBALT

What, drawn, and talk of peace? I hate the word
As I hate hell, all Montagues, and thee:
Have at thee, coward.

[They fight.]

Enter three or four CITIZENS with clubs.

FIRST CITIZEN

Clubs, bills and partisans! Strike! Beat them down!
Down with the Capulets! Down with the Montagues!

Enter CAPULET in his gown, and LADY CAPULET.

CAPULET

What noise is this? Give me my long sword, ho!

LADY CAPULET

A crutch, a crutch! Why call you for a sword?

CAPULET

My sword, I say! Old Montague is come,
And flourishes his blade in spite of me.
Enter MONTAGUE and his LADY MONTAGUE.

MONTAGUE

Thou villain Capulet! Hold me not, let me go.

LADY MONTAGUE

Thou shalt not stir one foot to seek a foe.
Enter PRINCE ESCALUS, with ATTENDANTS.

PRINCE

Rebellious subjects, enemies to peace,
Profaners of this neighbour-stained steel,—
Will they not hear? What, ho! You men, you beasts,
That quench the fire of your pernicious rage
With purple fountains issuing from your veins,
On pain of torture, from those bloody hands
Throw your mistemper'd weapons to the ground
And hear the sentence of your moved prince.
Three civil brawls, bred of an airy word,
By thee, old Capulet, and Montague,
Have thrice disturb'd the quiet of our streets,
And made Verona's ancient citizens
Cast by their grave beseeming ornaments,
To wield old partisans, in hands as old,
Canker'd with peace, to part your canker'd hate.
If ever you disturb our streets again,
Your lives shall pay the forfeit of the peace.
For this time all the rest depart away:
You, Capulet, shall go along with me,
And Montague, come you this afternoon,
To know our farther pleasure in this case,

To old Free-town, our common judgement-place.
Once more, on pain of death, all men depart.
> *[Exeunt PRINCE and ATTENDANTS; CAPULET, LADY CAPULET,*
> *TYBALT, CITIZENS and SERVANTS.]*

MONTAGUE

Who set this ancient quarrel new abroach?
Speak, nephew, were you by when it began?

BENVOLIO

Here were the servants of your adversary
And yours, close fighting ere I did approach.
I drew to part them, in the instant came
The fiery Tybalt, with his sword prepar'd,
Which, as he breath'd defiance to my ears,
He swung about his head, and cut the winds,
Who nothing hurt withal, hiss'd him in scorn.
While we were interchanging thrusts and blows
Came more and more, and fought on part and part,
Till the Prince came, who parted either part.

LADY MONTAGUE

O where is Romeo, saw you him today?
Right glad I am he was not at this fray.

BENVOLIO

Madam, an hour before the worshipp'd sun
Peer'd forth the golden window of the east,
A troubled mind drave me to walk abroad,
Where underneath the grove of sycamore
That westward rooteth from this city side,
So early walking did I see your son.
Towards him I made, but he was ware of me,
And stole into the covert of the wood.
I, measuring his affections by my own,
Which then most sought where most might not be found,
Being one too many by my weary self,
Pursu'd my humour, not pursuing his,
And gladly shunn'd who gladly fled from me.

MONTAGUE

    Many a morning hath he there been seen,
    With tears augmenting the fresh morning's dew,
    Adding to clouds more clouds with his deep sighs;
    But all so soon as the all-cheering sun
    Should in the farthest east begin to draw
    The shady curtains from Aurora's bed,
    Away from light steals home my heavy son,
    And private in his chamber pens himself,
    Shuts up his windows, locks fair daylight out
    And makes himself an artificial night.
    Black and portentous must this humour prove,
    Unless good counsel may the cause remove.

BENVOLIO

    My noble uncle, do you know the cause?

MONTAGUE

    I neither know it nor can learn of him.

BENVOLIO

    Have you importun'd him by any means?

MONTAGUE

    Both by myself and many other friends;
    But he, his own affections' counsellor,
    Is to himself—I will not say how true—
    But to himself so secret and so close,
    So far from sounding and discovery,
    As is the bud bit with an envious worm
    Ere he can spread his sweet leaves to the air,
    Or dedicate his beauty to the sun.
    Could we but learn from whence his sorrows grow,
    We would as willingly give cure as know.
        Enter ROMEO.

BENVOLIO

    See, where he comes. So please you step aside;
    I'll know his grievance or be much denied.

MONTAGUE

I would thou wert so happy by thy stay
To hear true shrift. Come, madam, let's away.
[Exeunt MONTAGUE and LADY MONTAGUE.]

BENVOLIO

Good morrow, cousin.

ROMEO

Is the day so young?

BENVOLIO

But new struck nine.

ROMEO

Ay me, sad hours seem long.
Was that my father that went hence so fast?

BENVOLIO

It was. What sadness lengthens Romeo's hours?

ROMEO

Not having that which, having, makes them short.

BENVOLIO

In love?

ROMEO

Out.

BENVOLIO

Of love?

ROMEO

Out of her favour where I am in love.

BENVOLIO

Alas that love so gentle in his view,
Should be so tyrannous and rough in proof.

ROMEO

Alas that love, whose view is muffled still,
Should, without eyes, see pathways to his will!
Where shall we dine? O me! What fray was here?

Why such is love's transgression.

Griefs of mine own lie heavy in my breast,

Which thou wilt propagate to have it prest

With more of thine. This love that thou hast shown

Doth add more grief to too much of mine own.

Love is a smoke made with the fume of sighs;

Being purg'd, a fire sparkling in lovers' eyes;

Being vex'd, a sea nourish'd with lovers' tears:

What is it else? A madness most discreet,

A choking gall, and a preserving sweet.

Farewell, my coz.

—ROMEO, THE TRAGEDY OF ROMEO AND JULIET

Yet tell me not, for I have heard it all.
Here's much to do with hate, but more with love:
Why, then, O brawling love! O loving hate!
O anything, of nothing first create!
O heavy lightness! serious vanity!
Misshapen chaos of well-seeming forms!
Feather of lead, bright smoke, cold fire, sick health!
Still-waking sleep, that is not what it is!
This love feel I, that feel no love in this.
Dost thou not laugh?

BENVOLIO

No coz, I rather weep.

ROMEO

Good heart, at what?

BENVOLIO

At thy good heart's oppression.

ROMEO

Why such is love's transgression.
Griefs of mine own lie heavy in my breast,
Which thou wilt propagate to have it prest
With more of thine. This love that thou hast shown
Doth add more grief to too much of mine own.
Love is a smoke made with the fume of sighs;
Being purg'd, a fire sparkling in lovers' eyes;
Being vex'd, a sea nourish'd with lovers' tears:
What is it else? A madness most discreet,
A choking gall, and a preserving sweet.
Farewell, my coz.
        [Going.]

BENVOLIO

Soft! I will go along:
And if you leave me so, you do me wrong.

ROMEO

Tut! I have lost myself; I am not here.
This is not Romeo, he's some other where.

BENVOLIO

Tell me in sadness who is that you love?

ROMEO

What, shall I groan and tell thee?

BENVOLIO

Groan! Why, no; but sadly tell me who.

ROMEO

Bid a sick man in sadness make his will,
A word ill urg'd to one that is so ill.
In sadness, cousin, I do love a woman.

BENVOLIO

I aim'd so near when I suppos'd you lov'd.

ROMEO

A right good markman, and she's fair I love.

BENVOLIO

A right fair mark, fair coz, is soonest hit.

ROMEO

Well, in that hit you miss: she'll not be hit
With Cupid's arrow, she hath Dian's wit;
And in strong proof of chastity well arm'd,
From love's weak childish bow she lives uncharm'd.
She will not stay the siege of loving terms
Nor bide th' encounter of assailing eyes,
Nor ope her lap to saint-seducing gold:
O she's rich in beauty, only poor
That when she dies, with beauty dies her store.

BENVOLIO

Then she hath sworn that she will still live chaste?

ROMEO

She hath, and in that sparing makes huge waste;
For beauty starv'd with her severity,
Cuts beauty off from all posterity.
She is too fair, too wise; wisely too fair,

To merit bliss by making me despair.
She hath forsworn to love, and in that vow
Do I live dead, that live to tell it now.

BENVOLIO

Be rul'd by me, forget to think of her.

ROMEO

O teach me how I should forget to think.

BENVOLIO

By giving liberty unto thine eyes;
Examine other beauties.

ROMEO

'Tis the way
To call hers, exquisite, in question more.
These happy masks that kiss fair ladies' brows,
Being black, puts us in mind they hide the fair;
He that is strucken blind cannot forget
The precious treasure of his eyesight lost.
Show me a mistress that is passing fair,
What doth her beauty serve but as a note
Where I may read who pass'd that passing fair?
Farewell, thou canst not teach me to forget.

BENVOLIO

I'll pay that doctrine, or else die in debt.
         [Exeunt.]

SCENE II. A Street.

Enter CAPULET, PARIS and SERVANT.

CAPULET

But Montague is bound as well as I,
In penalty alike; and 'tis not hard, I think,
For men so old as we to keep the peace.

PARIS

Of honourable reckoning are you both,

And pity 'tis you liv'd at odds so long.
But now my lord, what say you to my suit?

CAPULET

But saying o'er what I have said before.
My child is yet a stranger in the world,
She hath not seen the change of fourteen years;
Let two more summers wither in their pride
Ere we may think her ripe to be a bride.

PARIS

Younger than she are happy mothers made.

CAPULET

And too soon marr'd are those so early made.
The earth hath swallowed all my hopes but she,
She is the hopeful lady of my earth:
But woo her, gentle Paris, get her heart,
My will to her consent is but a part;
And she agree, within her scope of choice
Lies my consent and fair according voice.
This night I hold an old accustom'd feast,
Whereto I have invited many a guest,
Such as I love, and you among the store,
One more, most welcome, makes my number more.
At my poor house look to behold this night
Earth-treading stars that make dark heaven light:
Such comfort as do lusty young men feel
When well apparell'd April on the heel
Of limping winter treads, even such delight
Among fresh female buds shall you this night
Inherit at my house. Hear all, all see,
And like her most whose merit most shall be:
Which, on more view of many, mine, being one,
May stand in number, though in reckoning none.
Come, go with me. Go, sirrah, trudge about
Through fair Verona; find those persons out
Whose names are written there, [*gives a paper*] and to them say,
My house and welcome on their pleasure stay.
    [Exeunt CAPULET and PARIS.]

SERVANT

Find them out whose names are written here! It is written that the shoemaker should meddle with his yard and the tailor with his last, the fisher with his pencil, and the painter with his nets; but I am sent to find those persons whose names are here writ, and can never find what names the writing person hath here writ. I must to the learned. In good time!

Enter BENVOLIO and ROMEO.

BENVOLIO

Tut, man, one fire burns out another's burning,
One pain is lessen'd by another's anguish;
Turn giddy, and be holp by backward turning;
One desperate grief cures with another's languish:
Take thou some new infection to thy eye,
And the rank poison of the old will die.

ROMEO

Your plantain leaf is excellent for that.

BENVOLIO

For what, I pray thee?

ROMEO

For your broken shin.

BENVOLIO

Why, Romeo, art thou mad?

ROMEO

Not mad, but bound more than a madman is:
Shut up in prison, kept without my food,
Whipp'd and tormented and—God-den, good fellow.

SERVANT

God gi' god-den. I pray, sir, can you read?

ROMEO

Ay, mine own fortune in my misery.

SERVANT

Perhaps you have learned it without book.
But I pray, can you read anything you see?

ROMEO

Ay, If I know the letters and the language.

SERVANT

Ye say honestly, rest you merry!

ROMEO

Stay, fellow; I can read.
[He reads the letter.]

Signior Martino and his wife and daughters;
County Anselmo and his beauteous sisters;
The lady widow of Utruvio;
Signior Placentio and his lovely nieces;
Mercutio and his brother Valentine;
Mine uncle Capulet, his wife, and daughters;
My fair niece Rosaline and Livia;
Signior Valentio and his cousin Tybalt;
Lucio and the lively Helena.

A fair assembly.
[Gives back the paper.]
Whither should they come?

SERVANT

Up.

ROMEO

Whither to supper?

SERVANT

To our house.

ROMEO

Whose house?

SERVANT

My master's.

ROMEO

Indeed I should have ask'd you that before.

SERVANT

Now I'll tell you without asking. My master is the great rich Capulet, and if you be not of the house of Montagues, I pray come and crush a cup of wine. Rest you merry.

[Exit.]

BENVOLIO

At this same ancient feast of Capulet's
Sups the fair Rosaline whom thou so lov'st;
With all the admired beauties of Verona.
Go thither and with unattainted eye,
Compare her face with some that I shall show,
And I will make thee think thy swan a crow.

ROMEO

When the devout religion of mine eye
Maintains such falsehood, then turn tears to fire;
And these who, often drown'd, could never die,
Transparent heretics, be burnt for liars.
One fairer than my love? The all-seeing sun
Ne'er saw her match since first the world begun.

BENVOLIO

Tut, you saw her fair, none else being by,
Herself pois'd with herself in either eye:
But in that crystal scales let there be weigh'd
Your lady's love against some other maid
That I will show you shining at this feast,
And she shall scant show well that now shows best.

ROMEO

I'll go along, no such sight to be shown,
But to rejoice in splendour of my own.

[Exeunt.]

SCENE III. Room in Capulet's House.

Enter LADY CAPULET and NURSE.

LADY CAPULET

Nurse, where's my daughter? Call her forth to me.

NURSE

Now, by my maidenhead, at twelve year old,
I bade her come. What, lamb! What, ladybird!
God forbid! Where's this girl? What, Juliet!
Enter JULIET.

JULIET

How now, who calls?

NURSE

Your mother.

JULIET

Madam, I am here. What is your will?

LADY CAPULET

This is the matter. Nurse, give leave awhile,
We must talk in secret. Nurse, come back again,
I have remember'd me, thou's hear our counsel.
Thou knowest my daughter's of a pretty age.

NURSE

Faith, I can tell her age unto an hour.

LADY CAPULET

She's not fourteen.

NURSE

I'll lay fourteen of my teeth,
And yet, to my teen be it spoken, I have but four,
She is not fourteen. How long is it now
To Lammas-tide?

LADY CAPULET

A fortnight and odd days.

NURSE

> Even or odd, of all days in the year,
> Come Lammas Eve at night shall she be fourteen.
> Susan and she,—God rest all Christian souls!—
> Were of an age. Well, Susan is with God;
> She was too good for me. But as I said,
> On Lammas Eve at night shall she be fourteen;
> That shall she, marry; I remember it well.
> 'Tis since the earthquake now eleven years;
> And she was wean'd,—I never shall forget it—,
> Of all the days of the year, upon that day:
> For I had then laid wormwood to my dug,
> Sitting in the sun under the dovehouse wall;
> My lord and you were then at Mantua:
> Nay, I do bear a brain. But as I said,
> When it did taste the wormwood on the nipple
> Of my dug and felt it bitter, pretty fool,
> To see it tetchy, and fall out with the dug!
> Shake, quoth the dovehouse: 'twas no need, I trow,
> To bid me trudge.
> And since that time it is eleven years;
> For then she could stand alone; nay, by th'rood
> She could have run and waddled all about;
> For even the day before she broke her brow,
> And then my husband,—God be with his soul!
> A was a merry man,—took up the child:
> 'Yea,' quoth he, 'dost thou fall upon thy face?
> Thou wilt fall backward when thou hast more wit;
> Wilt thou not, Jule?' and, by my holidame,
> The pretty wretch left crying, and said 'Ay.'
> To see now how a jest shall come about.
> I warrant, and I should live a thousand years,
> I never should forget it. 'Wilt thou not, Jule?' quoth he;
> And, pretty fool, it stinted, and said 'Ay.'

LADY CAPULET

> Enough of this; I pray thee hold thy peace.

NURSE

> Yes, madam, yet I cannot choose but laugh,
> To think it should leave crying, and say 'Ay';
> And yet I warrant it had upon it's brow
> A bump as big as a young cockerel's stone;
> A perilous knock, and it cried bitterly.
> 'Yea,' quoth my husband, 'fall'st upon thy face?
> Thou wilt fall backward when thou comest to age;
> Wilt thou not, Jule?' It stinted, and said 'Ay.'

JULIET

> And stint thou too, I pray thee, Nurse, say I.

NURSE

> Peace, I have done. God mark thee to his grace
> Thou wast the prettiest babe that e'er I nurs'd:
> And I might live to see thee married once, I have my wish.

LADY CAPULET

> Marry, that marry is the very theme
> I came to talk of. Tell me, daughter Juliet,
> How stands your disposition to be married?

JULIET

> It is an honour that I dream not of.

NURSE

> An honour! Were not I thine only nurse,
> I would say thou hadst suck'd wisdom from thy teat.

LADY CAPULET

> Well, think of marriage now: younger than you,
> Here in Verona, ladies of esteem,
> Are made already mothers. By my count
> I was your mother much upon these years
> That you are now a maid. Thus, then, in brief;
> The valiant Paris seeks you for his love.

NURSE

> A man, young lady! Lady, such a man
> As all the world—why he's a man of wax.

LADY CAPULET

Verona's summer hath not such a flower.

NURSE

Nay, he's a flower, in faith a very flower.

LADY CAPULET

What say you, can you love the gentleman?
This night you shall behold him at our feast;
Read o'er the volume of young Paris' face,
And find delight writ there with beauty's pen.
Examine every married lineament,
And see how one another lends content;
And what obscur'd in this fair volume lies,
Find written in the margent of his eyes.
This precious book of love, this unbound lover,
To beautify him, only lacks a cover:
The fish lives in the sea; and 'tis much pride
For fair without the fair within to hide.
That book in many's eyes doth share the glory,
That in gold clasps locks in the golden story;
So shall you share all that he doth possess,
By having him, making yourself no less.

NURSE

No less, nay bigger. Women grow by men.

LADY CAPULET

Speak briefly, can you like of Paris' love?

JULIET

I'll look to like, if looking liking move:
But no more deep will I endart mine eye
Than your consent gives strength to make it fly.
        Enter a SERVANT.

SERVANT

Madam, the guests are come, supper served up, you called, my young
lady asked for, the Nurse cursed in the pantry, and everything in extrem-
ity. I must hence to wait, I beseech you follow straight.

LADY CAPULET

We follow thee.
[Exit SERVANT.]
Juliet, the County stays.

NURSE

Go, girl, seek happy nights to happy days.
[Exeunt.]

SCENE IV. A Street.

Enter ROMEO, MERCUTIO, BENVOLIO, with five or six
MASKERS; TORCH-BEARERS and others.

ROMEO

What, shall this speech be spoke for our excuse?
Or shall we on without apology?

BENVOLIO

The date is out of such prolixity:
We'll have no Cupid hoodwink'd with a scarf,
Bearing a Tartar's painted bow of lath,
Scaring the ladies like a crow-keeper;
Nor no without-book prologue, faintly spoke
After the prompter, for our entrance:
But let them measure us by what they will,
We'll measure them a measure, and be gone.

ROMEO

Give me a torch, I am not for this ambling;
Being but heavy I will bear the light.

MERCUTIO

Nay, gentle Romeo, we must have you dance.

ROMEO

Not I, believe me, you have dancing shoes,
With nimble soles, I have a soul of lead
So stakes me to the ground I cannot move.

MERCUTIO

> You are a lover, borrow Cupid's wings,
> And soar with them above a common bound.

ROMEO

> I am too sore enpierced with his shaft
> To soar with his light feathers, and so bound,
> I cannot bound a pitch above dull woe.
> Under love's heavy burden do I sink.

MERCUTIO

> And, to sink in it, should you burden love;
> Too great oppression for a tender thing.

ROMEO

> Is love a tender thing? It is too rough,
> Too rude, too boisterous; and it pricks like thorn.

MERCUTIO

> If love be rough with you, be rough with love;
> Prick love for pricking, and you beat love down.
> Give me a case to put my visage in:
> > *[Putting on a mask.]*
> A visor for a visor. What care I
> What curious eye doth quote deformities?
> Here are the beetle-brows shall blush for me.

BENVOLIO

> Come, knock and enter; and no sooner in
> But every man betake him to his legs.

ROMEO

> A torch for me: let wantons, light of heart,
> Tickle the senseless rushes with their heels;
> For I am proverb'd with a grandsire phrase,
> I'll be a candle-holder and look on,
> The game was ne'er so fair, and I am done.

MERCUTIO

> Tut, dun's the mouse, the constable's own word:
> If thou art dun, we'll draw thee from the mire

Or save your reverence love, wherein thou stickest
Up to the ears. Come, we burn daylight, ho.

ROMEO

Nay, that's not so.

MERCUTIO

I mean, sir, in delay
We waste our lights in vain, light lights by day.
Take our good meaning, for our judgment sits
Five times in that ere once in our five wits.

ROMEO

And we mean well in going to this mask;
But 'tis no wit to go.

MERCUTIO

Why, may one ask?

ROMEO

I dreamt a dream tonight.

MERCUTIO

And so did I.

ROMEO

Well, what was yours?

MERCUTIO

That dreamers often lie.

ROMEO

In bed asleep, while they do dream things true.

MERCUTIO

O, then, I see Queen Mab hath been with you.
She is the fairies' midwife, and she comes
In shape no bigger than an agate-stone
On the fore-finger of an alderman,
Drawn with a team of little atomies
Over men's noses as they lie asleep:
Her waggon-spokes made of long spinners' legs;
The cover, of the wings of grasshoppers;

Her traces, of the smallest spider's web;
The collars, of the moonshine's watery beams;
Her whip of cricket's bone; the lash, of film;
Her waggoner, a small grey-coated gnat,
Not half so big as a round little worm
Prick'd from the lazy finger of a maid:
Her chariot is an empty hazelnut,
Made by the joiner squirrel or old grub,
Time out o' mind the fairies' coachmakers.
And in this state she gallops night by night
Through lovers' brains, and then they dream of love;
O'er courtiers' knees, that dream on curtsies straight;
O'er lawyers' fingers, who straight dream on fees;
O'er ladies' lips, who straight on kisses dream,
Which oft the angry Mab with blisters plagues,
Because their breaths with sweetmeats tainted are:
Sometime she gallops o'er a courtier's nose,
And then dreams he of smelling out a suit;
And sometime comes she with a tithe-pig's tail,
Tickling a parson's nose as a' lies asleep,
Then dreams he of another benefice:
Sometime she driveth o'er a soldier's neck,
And then dreams he of cutting foreign throats,
Of breaches, ambuscados, Spanish blades,
Of healths five fathom deep; and then anon
Drums in his ear, at which he starts and wakes;
And, being thus frighted, swears a prayer or two,
And sleeps again. This is that very Mab
That plats the manes of horses in the night;
And bakes the elf-locks in foul sluttish hairs,
Which, once untangled, much misfortune bodes:
This is the hag, when maids lie on their backs,
That presses them, and learns them first to bear,
Making them women of good carriage:
This is she,—

ROMEO

Peace, peace, Mercutio, peace,
Thou talk'st of nothing.

MERCUTIO

> True, I talk of dreams,
> Which are the children of an idle brain,
> Begot of nothing but vain fantasy,
> Which is as thin of substance as the air,
> And more inconstant than the wind, who wooes
> Even now the frozen bosom of the north,
> And, being anger'd, puffs away from thence,
> Turning his side to the dew-dropping south.

BENVOLIO

> This wind you talk of blows us from ourselves:
> Supper is done, and we shall come too late.

ROMEO

> I fear too early: for my mind misgives
> Some consequence yet hanging in the stars,
> Shall bitterly begin his fearful date
> With this night's revels; and expire the term
> Of a despised life, clos'd in my breast
> By some vile forfeit of untimely death.
> But he that hath the steerage of my course
> Direct my suit. On, lusty gentlemen!

BENVOLIO

> Strike, drum.
> *[Exeunt.]*

SCENE V. A Hall in Capulet's House.

Musicians waiting. Enter SERVANTS.

FIRST SERVANT

> Where's Potpan, that he helps not to take away?
> He shift a trencher! He scrape a trencher!

SECOND SERVANT

> When good manners shall lie all in one or two men's hands, and
> they unwash'd too, 'tis a foul thing.

FIRST SERVANT

Away with the join-stools, remove the court-cupboard, look to the plate. Good thou, save me a piece of marchpane; and as thou loves me, let the porter let in Susan Grindstone and Nell. Antony and Potpan!

SECOND SERVANT

Ay, boy, ready.

FIRST SERVANT

You are looked for and called for, asked for and sought for, in the great chamber.

SECOND SERVANT

We cannot be here and there too. Cheerly, boys. Be brisk awhile, and the longer liver take all.

[Exeunt.]

Enter CAPULET, &c. with the Guests and Gentlewomen to the Maskers.

CAPULET

Welcome, gentlemen, ladies that have their toes
Unplagu'd with corns will have a bout with you.
Ah my mistresses, which of you all
Will now deny to dance? She that makes dainty,
She I'll swear hath corns. Am I come near ye now?
Welcome, gentlemen! I have seen the day
That I have worn a visor, and could tell
A whispering tale in a fair lady's ear,
Such as would please; 'tis gone, 'tis gone, 'tis gone,
You are welcome, gentlemen! Come, musicians, play.
A hall, a hall, give room! And foot it, girls.

[Music plays, and they dance.]

More light, you knaves; and turn the tables up,
And quench the fire, the room is grown too hot.
Ah sirrah, this unlook'd-for sport comes well.
Nay sit, nay sit, good cousin Capulet,
For you and I are past our dancing days;
How long is't now since last yourself and I
Were in a mask?

CAPULET'S COUSIN

By'r Lady, thirty years.

CAPULET

What, man, 'tis not so much, 'tis not so much:
'Tis since the nuptial of Lucentio,
Come Pentecost as quickly as it will,
Some five and twenty years; and then we mask'd.

CAPULET'S COUSIN

'Tis more, 'tis more, his son is elder, sir;
His son is thirty.

CAPULET

Will you tell me that?
His son was but a ward two years ago.

ROMEO

What lady is that, which doth enrich the hand
Of yonder knight?

SERVANT

I know not, sir.

ROMEO

O, she doth teach the torches to burn bright!
It seems she hangs upon the cheek of night
As a rich jewel in an Ethiop's ear;
Beauty too rich for use, for earth too dear!
So shows a snowy dove trooping with crows
As yonder lady o'er her fellows shows.
The measure done, I'll watch her place of stand,
And touching hers, make blessed my rude hand.
Did my heart love till now? Forswear it, sight!
For I ne'er saw true beauty till this night.

TYBALT

This by his voice, should be a Montague.
Fetch me my rapier, boy. What, dares the slave
Come hither, cover'd with an antic face,
To fleer and scorn at our solemnity?

Now by the stock and honour of my kin,
To strike him dead I hold it not a sin.

CAPULET

Why how now, kinsman!
Wherefore storm you so?

TYBALT

Uncle, this is a Montague, our foe;
A villain that is hither come in spite,
To scorn at our solemnity this night.

CAPULET

Young Romeo, is it?

TYBALT

'Tis he, that villain Romeo.

CAPULET

Content thee, gentle coz, let him alone,
A, bears him like a portly gentleman;
And, to say truth, Verona brags of him
To be a virtuous and well-govern'd youth.
I would not for the wealth of all the town
Here in my house do him disparagement.
Therefore be patient, take no note of him,
It is my will; the which if thou respect,
Show a fair presence and put off these frowns,
An ill-beseeming semblance for a feast.

TYBALT

It fits when such a villain is a guest:
I'll not endure him.

CAPULET

He shall be endur'd.
What, goodman boy! I say he shall, go to;
Am I the master here, or you? Go to.
You'll not endure him! God shall mend my soul,
You'll make a mutiny among my guests!
You will set cock-a-hoop, you'll be the man!

TYBALT

Why, uncle, 'tis a shame.

CAPULET

Go to, go to!
You are a saucy boy. Is't so, indeed?
This trick may chance to scathe you, I know what.
You must contrary me! Marry, 'tis time.
Well said, my hearts!—You are a princox; go:
Be quiet, or—More light, more light!—For shame!
I'll make you quiet. What, cheerly, my hearts.

TYBALT

Patience perforce with wilful choler meeting
Makes my flesh tremble in their different greeting.
I will withdraw: but this intrusion shall,
Now seeming sweet, convert to bitter gall.
                [Exit.]

ROMEO

                [To Juliet.]
If I profane with my unworthiest hand
This holy shrine, the gentle sin is this,
My lips, two blushing pilgrims, ready stand
To smooth that rough touch with a tender kiss.

JULIET

Good pilgrim, you do wrong your hand too much,
Which mannerly devotion shows in this;
For saints have hands that pilgrims' hands do touch,
And palm to palm is holy palmers' kiss.

ROMEO

Have not saints lips, and holy palmers too?

JULIET

Ay, pilgrim, lips that they must use in prayer.

ROMEO

O, then, dear saint, let lips do what hands do:
They pray, grant thou, lest faith turn to despair.

JULIET

    Saints do not move, though grant for prayers' sake.

ROMEO

    Then move not while my prayer's effect I take.
    Thus from my lips, by thine my sin is purg'd.
        [Kissing her.]

JULIET

    Then have my lips the sin that they have took.

ROMEO

    Sin from my lips? O trespass sweetly urg'd!
    Give me my sin again.

JULIET

    You kiss by the book.

NURSE

    Madam, your mother craves a word with you.

ROMEO

    What is her mother?

NURSE

    Marry, bachelor,
    Her mother is the lady of the house,
    And a good lady, and a wise and virtuous.
    I nurs'd her daughter that you talk'd withal.
    I tell you, he that can lay hold of her
    Shall have the chinks.

ROMEO

    Is she a Capulet?
    O dear account! My life is my foe's debt.

BENVOLIO

    Away, be gone; the sport is at the best.

ROMEO

    Ay, so I fear; the more is my unrest.

CAPULET

Nay, gentlemen, prepare not to be gone,
We have a trifling foolish banquet towards.
Is it e'en so? Why then, I thank you all;
I thank you, honest gentlemen; good night.
More torches here! Come on then, let's to bed.
Ah, sirrah, by my fay, it waxes late,
I'll to my rest.

[Exeunt all but JULIET and NURSE.]

JULIET

Come hither, Nurse. What is yond gentleman?

NURSE

The son and heir of old Tiberio.

JULIET

What's he that now is going out of door?

NURSE

Marry, that I think be young Petruchio.

JULIET

What's he that follows here, that would not dance?

NURSE

I know not.

JULIET

Go ask his name. If he be married,
My grave is like to be my wedding bed.

NURSE

His name is Romeo, and a Montague,
The only son of your great enemy.

JULIET

My only love sprung from my only hate!
Too early seen unknown, and known too late!
Prodigious birth of love it is to me,
That I must love a loathed enemy.

NURSE

What's this? What's this?

JULIET

A rhyme I learn'd even now
Of one I danc'd withal.
[One calls within, 'Juliet.']

NURSE

Anon, anon!
Come let's away, the strangers all are gone.
[Exeunt.]

ACT II

Enter CHORUS.

CHORUS
>Now old desire doth in his deathbed lie,
>And young affection gapes to be his heir;
>That fair for which love groan'd for and would die,
>With tender Juliet match'd, is now not fair.
>Now Romeo is belov'd, and loves again,
>Alike bewitched by the charm of looks;
>But to his foe suppos'd he must complain,
>And she steal love's sweet bait from fearful hooks:
>Being held a foe, he may not have access
>To breathe such vows as lovers use to swear;
>And she as much in love, her means much less
>To meet her new beloved anywhere.
>But passion lends them power, time means, to meet,
>Tempering extremities with extreme sweet.
>>*[Exit.]*

SCENE I. An open place adjoining Capulet's Garden.

Enter ROMEO.

ROMEO
>Can I go forward when my heart is here?
>Turn back, dull earth, and find thy centre out.

[He climbs the wall and leaps down within it.]
Enter BENVOLIO and MERCUTIO.

BENVOLIO

Romeo! My cousin Romeo! Romeo!

MERCUTIO

He is wise,
And on my life hath stol'n him home to bed.

BENVOLIO

He ran this way, and leap'd this orchard wall:
Call, good Mercutio.

MERCUTIO

Nay, I'll conjure too.
Romeo! Humours! Madman! Passion! Lover!
Appear thou in the likeness of a sigh,
Speak but one rhyme, and I am satisfied;
Cry but 'Ah me!' Pronounce but Love and dove;
Speak to my gossip Venus one fair word,
One nickname for her purblind son and heir,
Young Abraham Cupid, he that shot so trim
When King Cophetua lov'd the beggar-maid.
He heareth not, he stirreth not, he moveth not;
The ape is dead, and I must conjure him.
I conjure thee by Rosaline's bright eyes,
By her high forehead and her scarlet lip,
By her fine foot, straight leg, and quivering thigh,
And the demesnes that there adjacent lie,
That in thy likeness thou appear to us.

BENVOLIO

An if he hear thee, thou wilt anger him.

MERCUTIO

This cannot anger him. 'Twould anger him
To raise a spirit in his mistress' circle,
Of some strange nature, letting it there stand
Till she had laid it, and conjur'd it down;

That were some spite. My invocation
Is fair and honest, and, in his mistress' name,
I conjure only but to raise up him.

BENVOLIO

Come, he hath hid himself among these trees
To be consorted with the humorous night.
Blind is his love, and best befits the dark.

MERCUTIO

If love be blind, love cannot hit the mark.
Now will he sit under a medlar tree,
And wish his mistress were that kind of fruit
As maids call medlars when they laugh alone.
O Romeo, that she were, O that she were
An open-arse and thou a poperin pear!
Romeo, good night. I'll to my truckle-bed.
This field-bed is too cold for me to sleep.
Come, shall we go?

BENVOLIO

Go then; for 'tis in vain
To seek him here that means not to be found.
    [Exeunt.]

SCENE II. Capulet's Garden.

Enter ROMEO.

ROMEO

He jests at scars that never felt a wound.
    JULIET *appears above at a window.*
But soft, what light through yonder window breaks?
It is the east, and Juliet is the sun!
Arise fair sun and kill the envious moon,
Who is already sick and pale with grief,
That thou her maid art far more fair than she.
Be not her maid since she is envious;
Her vestal livery is but sick and green,
And none but fools do wear it; cast it off.

It is my lady, O it is my love!
O, that she knew she were!
She speaks, yet she says nothing. What of that?
Her eye discourses, I will answer it.
I am too bold, 'tis not to me she speaks.
Two of the fairest stars in all the heaven,
Having some business, do entreat her eyes
To twinkle in their spheres till they return.
What if her eyes were there, they in her head?
The brightness of her cheek would shame those stars,
As daylight doth a lamp; her eyes in heaven
Would through the airy region stream so bright
That birds would sing and think it were not night.
See how she leans her cheek upon her hand.
O that I were a glove upon that hand,
That I might touch that cheek.

JULIET

Ay me.

ROMEO

She speaks.
O speak again bright angel, for thou art
As glorious to this night, being o'er my head,
As is a winged messenger of heaven
Unto the white-upturned wondering eyes
Of mortals that fall back to gaze on him
When he bestrides the lazy-puffing clouds
And sails upon the bosom of the air.

JULIET

O Romeo, Romeo, wherefore art thou Romeo?
Deny thy father and refuse thy name.
Or if thou wilt not, be but sworn my love,
And I'll no longer be a Capulet.

ROMEO

[Aside.]
Shall I hear more, or shall I speak at this?

JULIET

'Tis but thy name that is my enemy;
Thou art thyself, though not a Montague.
What's Montague? It is nor hand nor foot,
Nor arm, nor face, nor any other part
Belonging to a man. O be some other name.
What's in a name? That which we call a rose
By any other name would smell as sweet;
So Romeo would, were he not Romeo call'd,
Retain that dear perfection which he owes
Without that title. Romeo, doff thy name,
And for thy name, which is no part of thee,
Take all myself.

ROMEO

I take thee at thy word.
Call me but love, and I'll be new baptis'd;
Henceforth I never will be Romeo.

JULIET

What man art thou that, thus bescreen'd in night
So stumblest on my counsel?

ROMEO

By a name
I know not how to tell thee who I am:
My name, dear saint, is hateful to myself,
Because it is an enemy to thee.
Had I it written, I would tear the word.

JULIET

My ears have yet not drunk a hundred words
Of thy tongue's utterance, yet I know the sound.
Art thou not Romeo, and a Montague?

ROMEO

Neither, fair maid, if either thee dislike.

JULIET

How cam'st thou hither, tell me, and wherefore?
The orchard walls are high and hard to climb,

And the place death, considering who thou art,
If any of my kinsmen find thee here.

ROMEO

With love's light wings did I o'erperch these walls,
For stony limits cannot hold love out,
And what love can do, that dares love attempt:
Therefore thy kinsmen are no stop to me.

JULIET

If they do see thee, they will murder thee.

ROMEO

Alack, there lies more peril in thine eye
Than twenty of their swords. Look thou but sweet,
And I am proof against their enmity.

JULIET

I would not for the world they saw thee here.

ROMEO

I have night's cloak to hide me from their eyes,
And but thou love me, let them find me here.
My life were better ended by their hate
Than death prorogued, wanting of thy love.

JULIET

By whose direction found'st thou out this place?

ROMEO

By love, that first did prompt me to enquire;
He lent me counsel, and I lent him eyes.
I am no pilot; yet wert thou as far
As that vast shore wash'd with the farthest sea,
I should adventure for such merchandise.

JULIET

Thou knowest the mask of night is on my face,
Else would a maiden blush bepaint my cheek
For that which thou hast heard me speak tonight.
Fain would I dwell on form, fain, fain deny
What I have spoke; but farewell compliment.

Dost thou love me? I know thou wilt say Ay,
And I will take thy word. Yet, if thou swear'st,
Thou mayst prove false. At lovers' perjuries,
They say Jove laughs. O gentle Romeo,
If thou dost love, pronounce it faithfully.
Or if thou thinkest I am too quickly won,
I'll frown and be perverse, and say thee nay,
So thou wilt woo. But else, not for the world.
In truth, fair Montague, I am too fond;
And therefore thou mayst think my 'haviour light:
But trust me, gentleman, I'll prove more true
Than those that have more cunning to be strange.
I should have been more strange, I must confess,
But that thou overheard'st, ere I was 'ware,
My true-love passion; therefore pardon me,
And not impute this yielding to light love,
Which the dark night hath so discovered.

ROMEO

Lady, by yonder blessed moon I vow,
That tips with silver all these fruit-tree tops,—

JULIET

O swear not by the moon, th' inconstant moon,
That monthly changes in her circled orb,
Lest that thy love prove likewise variable.

ROMEO

What shall I swear by?

JULIET

Do not swear at all.
Or if thou wilt, swear by thy gracious self,
Which is the god of my idolatry,
And I'll believe thee.

ROMEO

If my heart's dear love,—

JULIET

Well, do not swear. Although I joy in thee,

I have no joy of this contract tonight;
It is too rash, too unadvis'd, too sudden,
Too like the lightning, which doth cease to be
Ere one can say It lightens. Sweet, good night.
This bud of love, by summer's ripening breath,
May prove a beauteous flower when next we meet.
Good night, good night. As sweet repose and rest
Come to thy heart as that within my breast.

ROMEO

O wilt thou leave me so unsatisfied?

JULIET

What satisfaction canst thou have tonight?

ROMEO

Th' exchange of thy love's faithful vow for mine.

JULIET

I gave thee mine before thou didst request it;
And yet I would it were to give again.

ROMEO

Would'st thou withdraw it? For what purpose, love?

JULIET

But to be frank and give it thee again.
And yet I wish but for the thing I have;
My bounty is as boundless as the sea,
My love as deep; the more I give to thee,
The more I have, for both are infinite.
I hear some noise within. Dear love, adieu.
        [Nurse calls within.]
Anon, good Nurse!—Sweet Montague be true.
Stay but a little, I will come again.
        [Exit.]

ROMEO

O blessed, blessed night. I am afeard,
Being in night, all this is but a dream,
Too flattering sweet to be substantial.
        Enter JULIET above.

JULIET

Three words, dear Romeo, and good night indeed.
If that thy bent of love be honourable,
Thy purpose marriage, send me word tomorrow,
By one that I'll procure to come to thee,
Where and what time thou wilt perform the rite,
And all my fortunes at thy foot I'll lay
And follow thee my lord throughout the world.

NURSE

[Within.]
Madam.

JULIET

I come, anon.—But if thou meanest not well,
I do beseech thee,—

NURSE

[Within.]
Madam.

JULIET

By and by I come—
To cease thy strife and leave me to my grief.
Tomorrow will I send.

ROMEO

So thrive my soul,—

JULIET

A thousand times good night.
[Exit.]

ROMEO

A thousand times the worse, to want thy light.
Love goes toward love as schoolboys from their books,
But love from love, towards school with heavy looks.
[Retiring slowly.]
Re-enter JULIET, above.

JULIET

Hist! Romeo, hist! O for a falconer's voice

To lure this tassel-gentle back again.
Bondage is hoarse and may not speak aloud,
Else would I tear the cave where Echo lies,
And make her airy tongue more hoarse than mine
With repetition of my Romeo's name.

ROMEO

It is my soul that calls upon my name.
How silver-sweet sound lovers' tongues by night,
Like softest music to attending ears.

JULIET

Romeo.

ROMEO

My nyas?

JULIET

What o'clock tomorrow
Shall I send to thee?

ROMEO

By the hour of nine.

JULIET

I will not fail. 'Tis twenty years till then.
I have forgot why I did call thee back.

ROMEO

Let me stand here till thou remember it.

JULIET

I shall forget, to have thee still stand there,
Remembering how I love thy company.

ROMEO

And I'll still stay, to have thee still forget,
Forgetting any other home but this.

JULIET

'Tis almost morning; I would have thee gone,
And yet no farther than a wanton's bird,

That lets it hop a little from her hand,
Like a poor prisoner in his twisted gyves,
And with a silk thread plucks it back again,
So loving-jealous of his liberty.

ROMEO

I would I were thy bird.

JULIET

Sweet, so would I:
Yet I should kill thee with much cherishing.
Good night, good night. Parting is such sweet sorrow
That I shall say good night till it be morrow.
        [Exit.]

ROMEO

Sleep dwell upon thine eyes, peace in thy breast.
Would I were sleep and peace, so sweet to rest.
The grey-ey'd morn smiles on the frowning night,
Chequering the eastern clouds with streaks of light;
And darkness fleckled like a drunkard reels
From forth day's pathway, made by Titan's wheels
Hence will I to my ghostly Sire's cell,
His help to crave and my dear hap to tell.
        [Exit.]

SCENE III. Friar Lawrence's Cell.

Enter FRIAR LAWRENCE with a basket.

FRIAR LAWRENCE

Now, ere the sun advance his burning eye,
The day to cheer, and night's dank dew to dry,
I must upfill this osier cage of ours
With baleful weeds and precious-juiced flowers.
The earth that's nature's mother, is her tomb;
What is her burying grave, that is her womb:
And from her womb children of divers kind
We sucking on her natural bosom find.
Many for many virtues excellent,

None but for some, and yet all different.
O, mickle is the powerful grace that lies
In plants, herbs, stones, and their true qualities.
For naught so vile that on the earth doth live
But to the earth some special good doth give;
Nor aught so good but, strain'd from that fair use,
Revolts from true birth, stumbling on abuse.
Virtue itself turns vice being misapplied,
And vice sometime's by action dignified.
  Enter ROMEO.
Within the infant rind of this weak flower
Poison hath residence, and medicine power:
For this, being smelt, with that part cheers each part;
Being tasted, slays all senses with the heart.
Two such opposed kings encamp them still
In man as well as herbs,—grace and rude will;
And where the worser is predominant,
Full soon the canker death eats up that plant.

ROMEO

 Good morrow, father.

FRIAR LAWRENCE

 Benedicite!
What early tongue so sweet saluteth me?
Young son, it argues a distemper'd head
So soon to bid good morrow to thy bed.
Care keeps his watch in every old man's eye,
And where care lodges sleep will never lie;
But where unbruised youth with unstuff'd brain
Doth couch his limbs, there golden sleep doth reign.
Therefore thy earliness doth me assure
Thou art uprous'd with some distemperature;
Or if not so, then here I hit it right,
Our Romeo hath not been in bed tonight.

ROMEO

 That last is true; the sweeter rest was mine.

FRIAR LAWRENCE

God pardon sin. Wast thou with Rosaline?

ROMEO

With Rosaline, my ghostly father? No.
I have forgot that name, and that name's woe.

FRIAR LAWRENCE

That's my good son. But where hast thou been then?

ROMEO

I'll tell thee ere thou ask it me again.
I have been feasting with mine enemy,
Where on a sudden one hath wounded me
That's by me wounded. Both our remedies
Within thy help and holy physic lies.
I bear no hatred, blessed man; for lo,
My intercession likewise steads my foe.

FRIAR LAWRENCE

Be plain, good son, and homely in thy drift;
Riddling confession finds but riddling shrift.

ROMEO

Then plainly know my heart's dear love is set
On the fair daughter of rich Capulet.
As mine on hers, so hers is set on mine;
And all combin'd, save what thou must combine
By holy marriage. When, and where, and how
We met, we woo'd, and made exchange of vow,
I'll tell thee as we pass; but this I pray,
That thou consent to marry us today.

FRIAR LAWRENCE

Holy Saint Francis! What a change is here!
Is Rosaline, that thou didst love so dear,
So soon forsaken? Young men's love then lies
Not truly in their hearts, but in their eyes.
Jesu Maria, what a deal of brine
Hath wash'd thy sallow cheeks for Rosaline!
How much salt water thrown away in waste,

To season love, that of it doth not taste.
The sun not yet thy sighs from heaven clears,
Thy old groans yet ring in mine ancient ears.
Lo here upon thy cheek the stain doth sit
Of an old tear that is not wash'd off yet.
If ere thou wast thyself, and these woes thine,
Thou and these woes were all for Rosaline,
And art thou chang'd? Pronounce this sentence then,
Women may fall, when there's no strength in men.

ROMEO
Thou chidd'st me oft for loving Rosaline.

FRIAR LAWRENCE
For doting, not for loving, pupil mine.

ROMEO
And bad'st me bury love.

FRIAR LAWRENCE
Not in a grave
To lay one in, another out to have.

ROMEO
I pray thee chide me not, her I love now
Doth grace for grace and love for love allow.
The other did not so.

FRIAR LAWRENCE
O, she knew well
Thy love did read by rote, that could not spell.
But come young waverer, come go with me,
In one respect I'll thy assistant be;
For this alliance may so happy prove,
To turn your households' rancour to pure love.

ROMEO
O let us hence; I stand on sudden haste.

FRIAR LAWRENCE
Wisely and slow; they stumble that run fast.
[Exeunt.]

SCENE IV. A Street.

Enter BENVOLIO and MERCUTIO.

MERCUTIO

Where the devil should this Romeo be? Came he not home tonight?

BENVOLIO

Not to his father's; I spoke with his man.

MERCUTIO

Why, that same pale hard-hearted wench, that Rosaline, torments him so that he will sure run mad.

BENVOLIO

Tybalt, the kinsman to old Capulet, hath sent a letter to his father's house.

MERCUTIO

A challenge, on my life.

BENVOLIO

Romeo will answer it.

MERCUTIO

Any man that can write may answer a letter.

BENVOLIO

Nay, he will answer the letter's master, how he dares, being dared.

MERCUTIO

Alas poor Romeo, he is already dead, stabbed with a white wench's black eye; run through the ear with a love song, the very pin of his heart cleft with the blind bow-boy's butt-shaft. And is he a man to encounter Tybalt?

BENVOLIO

Why, what is Tybalt?

MERCUTIO

More than Prince of cats. O, he's the courageous captain of compliments. He fights as you sing prick-song, keeps time, distance, and proportion. He rests his minim rest, one, two, and the third in your bosom:

the very butcher of a silk button, a duellist, a duellist; a gentleman of the very first house, of the first and second cause. Ah, the immortal passado, the punto reverso, the hay.

BENVOLIO

The what?

MERCUTIO

The pox of such antic lisping, affecting phantasies; these new tuners of accent. By Jesu, a very good blade, a very tall man, a very good whore. Why, is not this a lamentable thing, grandsire, that we should be thus afflicted with these strange flies, these fashion-mongers, these pardon-me's, who stand so much on the new form that they cannot sit at ease on the old bench? O their bones, their bones!

Enter ROMEO.

BENVOLIO

Here comes Romeo, here comes Romeo!

MERCUTIO

Without his roe, like a dried herring. O flesh, flesh, how art thou fishified! Now is he for the numbers that Petrarch flowed in. Laura, to his lady, was but a kitchen wench,—marry, she had a better love to berhyme her: Dido a dowdy; Cleopatra a gypsy; Helen and Hero hildings and harlots; Thisbe a grey eye or so, but not to the purpose. Signior Romeo, bonjour! There's a French salutation to your French slop. You gave us the counterfeit fairly last night.

ROMEO

Good morrow to you both. What counterfeit did I give you?

MERCUTIO

The slip sir, the slip; can you not conceive?

ROMEO

Pardon, good Mercutio, my business was great, and in such a case as mine a man may strain courtesy.

MERCUTIO

That's as much as to say, such a case as yours constrains a man to bow in the hams.

ROMEO

Meaning, to curtsy.

MERCUTIO

Thou hast most kindly hit it.

ROMEO

A most courteous exposition.

MERCUTIO

Nay, I am the very pink of courtesy.

ROMEO

Pink for flower.

MERCUTIO

Right.

ROMEO

Why, then is my pump well flowered.

MERCUTIO

Sure wit, follow me this jest now, till thou hast worn out thy pump, that when the single sole of it is worn, the jest may remain after the wearing, solely singular.

ROMEO

O single-soled jest, solely singular for the singleness!

MERCUTIO

Come between us, good Benvolio; my wits faint.

ROMEO

Swits and spurs, swits and spurs; or I'll cry a match.

MERCUTIO

Nay, if thy wits run the wild-goose chase, I am done. For thou hast more of the wild-goose in one of thy wits, than I am sure, I have in my whole five. Was I with you there for the goose?

ROMEO

Thou wast never with me for anything, when thou wast not there for the goose.

MERCUTIO

I will bite thee by the ear for that jest.

ROMEO

Nay, good goose, bite not.

MERCUTIO

Thy wit is a very bitter sweeting, it is a most sharp sauce.

ROMEO

And is it not then well served in to a sweet goose?

MERCUTIO

O here's a wit of cheveril, that stretches from an inch narrow to an ell broad.

ROMEO

I stretch it out for that word broad, which added to the goose, proves thee far and wide a broad goose.

MERCUTIO

Why, is not this better now than groaning for love? Now art thou sociable, now art thou Romeo; not art thou what thou art, by art as well as by nature. For this drivelling love is like a great natural, that runs lolling up and down to hide his bauble in a hole.

BENVOLIO

Stop there, stop there.

MERCUTIO

Thou desirest me to stop in my tale against the hair.

BENVOLIO

Thou wouldst else have made thy tale large.

MERCUTIO

O, thou art deceived; I would have made it short, for I was come to the whole depth of my tale, and meant indeed to occupy the argument no longer.

Enter NURSE and PETER.

ROMEO

Here's goodly gear!
A sail, a sail!

MERCUTIO

Two, two; a shirt and a smock.

NURSE

Peter!

PETER

Anon.

NURSE

My fan, Peter.

MERCUTIO

Good Peter, to hide her face; for her fan's the fairer face.

NURSE

God ye good morrow, gentlemen.

MERCUTIO

God ye good-den, fair gentlewoman.

NURSE

Is it good-den?

MERCUTIO

'Tis no less, I tell ye; for the bawdy hand of the dial is now upon the prick of noon.

NURSE

Out upon you! What a man are you?

ROMEO

One, gentlewoman, that God hath made for himself to mar.

NURSE

By my troth, it is well said; for himself to mar, quoth a'? Gentlemen, can any of you tell me where I may find the young Romeo?

ROMEO

I can tell you: but young Romeo will be older when you have found him than he was when you sought him. I am the youngest of that name, for fault of a worse.

NURSE

You say well.

MERCUTIO

Yea, is the worst well? Very well took, i' faith; wisely, wisely.

NURSE

If you be he, sir, I desire some confidence with you.

BENVOLIO

She will endite him to some supper.

MERCUTIO

A bawd, a bawd, a bawd! So ho!

ROMEO

What hast thou found?

MERCUTIO

No hare, sir; unless a hare, sir, in a lenten pie, that is something stale and hoar ere it be spent.
> *[Sings.]*
> An old hare hoar,
> And an old hare hoar,
> Is very good meat in Lent;
> But a hare that is hoar
> Is too much for a score
> When it hoars ere it be spent.
Romeo, will you come to your father's? We'll to dinner thither.

ROMEO

I will follow you.

MERCUTIO

Farewell, ancient lady; farewell, lady, lady, lady.
> *[Exeunt MERCUTIO and BENVOLIO.]*

NURSE

I pray you, sir, what saucy merchant was this that was so full of his ropery?

ROMEO

A gentleman, Nurse, that loves to hear himself talk, and will speak more in a minute than he will stand to in a month.

NURSE

And a' speak anything against me, I'll take him down, and a' were lustier than he is, and twenty such Jacks. And if I cannot, I'll find those that shall. Scurvy knave! I am none of his flirt-gills; I am none of his skains-mates.—And thou must stand by too and suffer every knave to use me at his pleasure!

PETER

I saw no man use you at his pleasure; if I had, my weapon should quickly have been out. I warrant you, I dare draw as soon as another man, if I see occasion in a good quarrel, and the law on my side.

NURSE

Now, afore God, I am so vexed that every part about me quivers. Scurvy knave. Pray you, sir, a word: and as I told you, my young lady bid me enquire you out; what she bade me say, I will keep to myself. But first let me tell ye, if ye should lead her in a fool's paradise, as they say, it were a very gross kind of behaviour, as they say; for the gentlewoman is young. And therefore, if you should deal double with her, truly it were an ill thing to be offered to any gentlewoman, and very weak dealing.

ROMEO

Nurse, commend me to thy lady and mistress. I protest unto thee,—

NURSE

Good heart, and i' faith I will tell her as much. Lord, Lord, she will be a joyful woman.

ROMEO

What wilt thou tell her, Nurse? Thou dost not mark me.

NURSE

I will tell her, sir, that you do protest, which, as I take it, is a gentle-manlike offer.

ROMEO

Bid her devise
Some means to come to shrift this afternoon,

And there she shall at Friar Lawrence' cell
Be shriv'd and married. Here is for thy pains.

NURSE

No truly, sir; not a penny.

ROMEO

Go to; I say you shall.

NURSE

This afternoon, sir? Well, she shall be there.

ROMEO

And stay, good Nurse, behind the abbey wall.
Within this hour my man shall be with thee,
And bring thee cords made like a tackled stair,
Which to the high topgallant of my joy
Must be my convoy in the secret night.
Farewell, be trusty, and I'll quit thy pains;
Farewell; commend me to thy mistress.

NURSE

Now God in heaven bless thee. Hark you, sir.

ROMEO

What say'st thou, my dear Nurse?

NURSE

Is your man secret? Did you ne'er hear say,
Two may keep counsel, putting one away?

ROMEO

I warrant thee my man's as true as steel.

NURSE

Well, sir, my mistress is the sweetest lady. Lord, Lord! When 'twas
a little prating thing,—O, there is a nobleman in town, one Paris, that
would fain lay knife aboard; but she, good soul, had as lief see a toad,
a very toad, as see him. I anger her sometimes, and tell her that Paris is
the properer man, but I'll warrant you, when I say so, she looks as pale
as any clout in the versal world. Doth not rosemary and Romeo begin
both with a letter?

ROMEO

Ay, Nurse; what of that? Both with an R.

NURSE

Ah, mocker! That's the dog's name. R is for the—no, I know it begins with some other letter, and she hath the prettiest sententious of it, of you and rosemary, that it would do you good to hear it.

ROMEO

Commend me to thy lady.

NURSE

Ay, a thousand times. Peter!
> *[Exit ROMEO.]*

PETER

Anon.

NURSE

Before and apace.
> *[Exeunt.]*

SCENE V. Capulet's Garden.

Enter JULIET.

JULIET

The clock struck nine when I did send the Nurse,
In half an hour she promised to return.
Perchance she cannot meet him. That's not so.
O, she is lame. Love's heralds should be thoughts,
Which ten times faster glides than the sun's beams,
Driving back shadows over lowering hills:
Therefore do nimble-pinion'd doves draw love,
And therefore hath the wind-swift Cupid wings.
Now is the sun upon the highmost hill
Of this day's journey, and from nine till twelve
Is three long hours, yet she is not come.
Had she affections and warm youthful blood,
She'd be as swift in motion as a ball;
My words would bandy her to my sweet love,

And his to me.
But old folks, many feign as they were dead;
Unwieldy, slow, heavy and pale as lead.
            Enter NURSE *and* PETER.
O God, she comes. O honey Nurse, what news?
Hast thou met with him? Send thy man away.

NURSE

Peter, stay at the gate.
            [Exit PETER.*]*

JULIET

Now, good sweet Nurse,—O Lord, why look'st thou sad?
Though news be sad, yet tell them merrily;
If good, thou sham'st the music of sweet news
By playing it to me with so sour a face.

NURSE

I am aweary, give me leave awhile;
Fie, how my bones ache! What a jaunt have I had!

JULIET

I would thou hadst my bones, and I thy news:
Nay come, I pray thee speak; good, good Nurse, speak.

NURSE

Jesu, what haste? Can you not stay a while? Do you not see that I
am out of breath?

JULIET

How art thou out of breath, when thou hast breath
To say to me that thou art out of breath?
The excuse that thou dost make in this delay
Is longer than the tale thou dost excuse.
Is thy news good or bad? Answer to that;
Say either, and I'll stay the circumstance.
Let me be satisfied, is't good or bad?

NURSE

Well, you have made a simple choice; you know not how to choose
a man. Romeo? No, not he. Though his face be better than any man's,

yet his leg excels all men's, and for a hand and a foot, and a body, though they be not to be talked on, yet they are past compare. He is not the flower of courtesy, but I'll warrant him as gentle as a lamb. Go thy ways, wench, serve God. What, have you dined at home?

JULIET

No, no. But all this did I know before.
What says he of our marriage? What of that?

NURSE

Lord, how my head aches! What a head have I!
It beats as it would fall in twenty pieces.
My back o' t' other side,—O my back, my back!
Beshrew your heart for sending me about
To catch my death with jaucing up and down.

JULIET

I' faith, I am sorry that thou art not well.
Sweet, sweet, sweet Nurse, tell me, what says my love?

NURSE

Your love says, like an honest gentleman,
And a courteous, and a kind, and a handsome,
And I warrant a virtuous,—Where is your mother?

JULIET

Where is my mother? Why, she is within.
Where should she be? How oddly thou repliest.
"Your love says, like an honest gentleman,
'Where is your mother?'"

NURSE

O God's lady dear,
Are you so hot? Marry, come up, I trow.
Is this the poultice for my aching bones?
Henceforward do your messages yourself.

JULIET

Here's such a coil. Come, what says Romeo?

NURSE

Have you got leave to go to shrift today?

JULIET

I have.

NURSE

Then hie you hence to Friar Lawrence' cell;
There stays a husband to make you a wife.
Now comes the wanton blood up in your cheeks,
They'll be in scarlet straight at any news.
Hie you to church. I must another way,
To fetch a ladder by the which your love
Must climb a bird's nest soon when it is dark.
I am the drudge, and toil in your delight;
But you shall bear the burden soon at night.
Go. I'll to dinner; hie you to the cell.

JULIET

Hie to high fortune! Honest Nurse, farewell.
[Exeunt.]

SCENE VI. Friar Lawrence's Cell.

Enter FRIAR LAWRENCE and ROMEO.

FRIAR LAWRENCE

So smile the heavens upon this holy act
That after-hours with sorrow chide us not.

ROMEO

Amen, amen, but come what sorrow can,
It cannot countervail the exchange of joy
That one short minute gives me in her sight.
Do thou but close our hands with holy words,
Then love-devouring death do what he dare,
It is enough I may but call her mine.

FRIAR LAWRENCE

These violent delights have violent ends,
And in their triumph die; like fire and powder,
Which as they kiss consume. The sweetest honey
Is loathsome in his own deliciousness,

And in the taste confounds the appetite.
Therefore love moderately: long love doth so;
Too swift arrives as tardy as too slow.
    Enter JULIET.
Here comes the lady. O, so light a foot
Will ne'er wear out the everlasting flint.
A lover may bestride the gossamers
That idles in the wanton summer air
And yet not fall; so light is vanity.

JULIET

Good even to my ghostly confessor.

FRIAR LAWRENCE

Romeo shall thank thee, daughter, for us both.

JULIET

As much to him, else is his thanks too much.

ROMEO

Ah, Juliet, if the measure of thy joy
Be heap'd like mine, and that thy skill be more
To blazon it, then sweeten with thy breath
This neighbour air, and let rich music's tongue
Unfold the imagin'd happiness that both
Receive in either by this dear encounter.

JULIET

Conceit more rich in matter than in words,
Brags of his substance, not of ornament.
They are but beggars that can count their worth;
But my true love is grown to such excess,
I cannot sum up sum of half my wealth.

FRIAR LAWRENCE

Come, come with me, and we will make short work,
For, by your leaves, you shall not stay alone
Till holy church incorporate two in one.
    [Exeunt.]

ACT III

SCENE I. A public place.

Enter MERCUTIO, BENVOLIO, PAGE and SERVANTS.

BENVOLIO

> I pray thee, good Mercutio, let's retire:
> The day is hot, the Capulets abroad,
> And if we meet, we shall not 'scape a brawl,
> For now these hot days, is the mad blood stirring.

MERCUTIO

> Thou art like one of these fellows that, when he enters the confines
> of a tavern, claps me his sword upon the table, and says 'God send me
> no need of thee!' and by the operation of the second cup draws him on
> the drawer, when indeed there is no need.

BENVOLIO

> Am I like such a fellow?

MERCUTIO

> Come, come, thou art as hot a Jack in thy mood as any in Italy; and
> as soon moved to be moody, and as soon moody to be moved.

BENVOLIO

> And what to?

MERCUTIO

> Nay, an there were two such, we should have none shortly, for one
> would kill the other. Thou? Why, thou wilt quarrel with a man that

hath a hair more or a hair less in his beard than thou hast. Thou wilt quarrel with a man for cracking nuts, having no other reason but because thou hast hazel eyes. What eye but such an eye would spy out such a quarrel? Thy head is as full of quarrels as an egg is full of meat, and yet thy head hath been beaten as addle as an egg for quarrelling. Thou hast quarrelled with a man for coughing in the street, because he hath wakened thy dog that hath lain asleep in the sun. Didst thou not fall out with a tailor for wearing his new doublet before Easter? with another for tying his new shoes with an old riband? And yet thou wilt tutor me from quarrelling!

BENVOLIO

And I were so apt to quarrel as thou art, any man should buy the fee simple of my life for an hour and a quarter.

MERCUTIO

The fee simple! O simple!
Enter TYBALT and others.

BENVOLIO

By my head, here comes the Capulets.

MERCUTIO

By my heel, I care not.

TYBALT

Follow me close, for I will speak to them.
Gentlemen, good-den: a word with one of you.

MERCUTIO

And but one word with one of us? Couple it with something; make it a word and a blow.

TYBALT

You shall find me apt enough to that, sir, and you will give me occasion.

MERCUTIO

Could you not take some occasion without giving?

TYBALT

Mercutio, thou consortest with Romeo.

MERCUTIO

Consort? What, dost thou make us minstrels? And thou make minstrels of us, look to hear nothing but discords. Here's my fiddlestick, here's that shall make you dance. Zounds, consort!

BENVOLIO

We talk here in the public haunt of men.
Either withdraw unto some private place,
And reason coldly of your grievances,
Or else depart; here all eyes gaze on us.

MERCUTIO

Men's eyes were made to look, and let them gaze.
I will not budge for no man's pleasure, I.
    Enter ROMEO.

TYBALT

Well, peace be with you, sir, here comes my man.

MERCUTIO

But I'll be hanged, sir, if he wear your livery.
Marry, go before to field, he'll be your follower;
Your worship in that sense may call him man.

TYBALT

Romeo, the love I bear thee can afford
No better term than this: Thou art a villain.

ROMEO

Tybalt, the reason that I have to love thee
Doth much excuse the appertaining rage
To such a greeting. Villain am I none;
Therefore farewell; I see thou know'st me not.

TYBALT

Boy, this shall not excuse the injuries
That thou hast done me, therefore turn and draw.

ROMEO

I do protest I never injur'd thee,
But love thee better than thou canst devise

Till thou shalt know the reason of my love.
And so good Capulet, which name I tender
As dearly as mine own, be satisfied.

MERCUTIO

O calm, dishonourable, vile submission!
[Draws.]
Alla stoccata carries it away.
Tybalt, you rat-catcher, will you walk?

TYBALT

What wouldst thou have with me?

MERCUTIO

Good King of Cats, nothing but one of your nine lives; that I mean to make bold withal, and, as you shall use me hereafter, dry-beat the rest of the eight. Will you pluck your sword out of his pilcher by the ears? Make haste, lest mine be about your ears ere it be out.

TYBALT

[Drawing.]
I am for you.

ROMEO.

Gentle Mercutio, put thy rapier up.

MERCUTIO

Come, sir, your passado.
[They fight.]

ROMEO

Draw, Benvolio; beat down their weapons.
Gentlemen, for shame, forbear this outrage,
Tybalt, Mercutio, the Prince expressly hath
Forbid this bandying in Verona streets.
Hold, Tybalt! Good Mercutio!
[Exeunt TYBALT with his Partizans.]

MERCUTIO

I am hurt.
A plague o' both your houses. I am sped.
Is he gone, and hath nothing?

BENVOLIO

What, art thou hurt?

MERCUTIO

Ay, ay, a scratch, a scratch. Marry, 'tis enough.
Where is my page? Go villain, fetch a surgeon.
[Exit PAGE.]

ROMEO

Courage, man; the hurt cannot be much.

MERCUTIO

No, 'tis not so deep as a well, nor so wide as a church door, but 'tis enough, 'twill serve. Ask for me tomorrow, and you shall find me a grave man. I am peppered, I warrant, for this world. A plague o' both your houses. Zounds, a dog, a rat, a mouse, a cat, to scratch a man to death. A braggart, a rogue, a villain, that fights by the book of arithmetic!—Why the devil came you between us? I was hurt under your arm.

ROMEO

I thought all for the best.

MERCUTIO

Help me into some house, Benvolio,
Or I shall faint. A plague o' both your houses.
They have made worms' meat of me.
I have it, and soundly too. Your houses!
[Exeunt MERCUTIO and BENVOLIO.]

ROMEO

This gentleman, the Prince's near ally,
My very friend, hath got his mortal hurt
In my behalf; my reputation stain'd
With Tybalt's slander,—Tybalt, that an hour
Hath been my cousin. O sweet Juliet,
Thy beauty hath made me effeminate
And in my temper soften'd valour's steel.
Re-enter BENVOLIO.

BENVOLIO

O Romeo, Romeo, brave Mercutio's dead,

That gallant spirit hath aspir'd the clouds,
Which too untimely here did scorn the earth.

ROMEO

This day's black fate on more days doth depend;
This but begins the woe others must end.
Re-enter TYBALT.

BENVOLIO

Here comes the furious Tybalt back again.

ROMEO

Again in triumph, and Mercutio slain?
Away to heaven respective lenity,
And fire-ey'd fury be my conduct now!
Now, Tybalt, take the 'villain' back again
That late thou gav'st me, for Mercutio's soul
Is but a little way above our heads,
Staying for thine to keep him company.
Either thou or I, or both, must go with him.

TYBALT

Thou wretched boy, that didst consort him here,
Shalt with him hence.

ROMEO

This shall determine that.
[They fight; TYBALT falls.]

BENVOLIO

Romeo, away, be gone!
The citizens are up, and Tybalt slain.
Stand not amaz'd. The Prince will doom thee death
If thou art taken. Hence, be gone, away!

ROMEO

O, I am fortune's fool!

BENVOLIO

Why dost thou stay?
[Exit ROMEO.]
Enter CITIZENS.

FIRST CITIZEN

Which way ran he that kill'd Mercutio?
Tybalt, that murderer, which way ran he?

BENVOLIO

There lies that Tybalt.

FIRST CITIZEN

Up, sir, go with me.
I charge thee in the Prince's name obey.

*Enter PRINCE, attended; MONTAGUE, CAPULET, their WIVES
and others.*

PRINCE

Where are the vile beginners of this fray?

BENVOLIO

O noble Prince, I can discover all
The unlucky manage of this fatal brawl.
There lies the man, slain by young Romeo,
That slew thy kinsman, brave Mercutio.

LADY CAPULET

Tybalt, my cousin! O my brother's child!
O Prince! O husband! O, the blood is spill'd
Of my dear kinsman! Prince, as thou art true,
For blood of ours shed blood of Montague.
O cousin, cousin.

PRINCE

Benvolio, who began this bloody fray?

BENVOLIO

Tybalt, here slain, whom Romeo's hand did slay;
Romeo, that spoke him fair, bid him bethink
How nice the quarrel was, and urg'd withal
Your high displeasure. All this uttered
With gentle breath, calm look, knees humbly bow'd
Could not take truce with the unruly spleen
Of Tybalt, deaf to peace, but that he tilts
With piercing steel at bold Mercutio's breast,

Who, all as hot, turns deadly point to point,
And, with a martial scorn, with one hand beats
Cold death aside, and with the other sends
It back to Tybalt, whose dexterity
Retorts it. Romeo he cries aloud,
'Hold, friends! Friends, part!' and swifter than his tongue,
His agile arm beats down their fatal points,
And 'twixt them rushes; underneath whose arm
An envious thrust from Tybalt hit the life
Of stout Mercutio, and then Tybalt fled.
But by and by comes back to Romeo,
Who had but newly entertain'd revenge,
And to't they go like lightning; for, ere I
Could draw to part them was stout Tybalt slain;
And as he fell did Romeo turn and fly.
This is the truth, or let Benvolio die.

LADY CAPULET

He is a kinsman to the Montague.
Affection makes him false, he speaks not true.
Some twenty of them fought in this black strife,
And all those twenty could but kill one life.
I beg for justice, which thou, Prince, must give;
Romeo slew Tybalt, Romeo must not live.

PRINCE

Romeo slew him, he slew Mercutio.
Who now the price of his dear blood doth owe?

MONTAGUE

Not Romeo, Prince, he was Mercutio's friend;
His fault concludes but what the law should end,
The life of Tybalt.

PRINCE

And for that offence
Immediately we do exile him hence.
I have an interest in your hate's proceeding,
My blood for your rude brawls doth lie a-bleeding.
But I'll amerce you with so strong a fine

That you shall all repent the loss of mine.
I will be deaf to pleading and excuses;
Nor tears nor prayers shall purchase out abuses.
Therefore use none. Let Romeo hence in haste,
Else, when he is found, that hour is his last.
Bear hence this body, and attend our will.
Mercy but murders, pardoning those that kill.

    [Exeunt.]

SCENE II. A Room in Capulet's House.

Enter JULIET.

JULIET

Gallop apace, you fiery-footed steeds,
Towards Phoebus' lodging. Such a waggoner
As Phaeton would whip you to the west
And bring in cloudy night immediately.
Spread thy close curtain, love-performing night,
That runaway's eyes may wink, and Romeo
Leap to these arms, untalk'd of and unseen.
Lovers can see to do their amorous rites
By their own beauties: or, if love be blind,
It best agrees with night. Come, civil night,
Thou sober-suited matron, all in black,
And learn me how to lose a winning match,
Play'd for a pair of stainless maidenhoods.
Hood my unmann'd blood, bating in my cheeks,
With thy black mantle, till strange love, grow bold,
Think true love acted simple modesty.
Come, night, come, Romeo; come, thou day in night;
For thou wilt lie upon the wings of night
Whiter than new snow upon a raven's back.
Come gentle night, come loving black-brow'd night,
Give me my Romeo, and when I shall die,
Take him and cut him out in little stars,
And he will make the face of heaven so fine
That all the world will be in love with night,

And pay no worship to the garish sun.
O, I have bought the mansion of a love,
But not possess'd it; and though I am sold,
Not yet enjoy'd. So tedious is this day
As is the night before some festival
To an impatient child that hath new robes
And may not wear them. O, here comes my Nurse,
And she brings news, and every tongue that speaks
But Romeo's name speaks heavenly eloquence.
　　　　Enter NURSE, with cords.
Now, Nurse, what news? What hast thou there?
The cords that Romeo bid thee fetch?

NURSE

Ay, ay, the cords.
　　　　[Throws them down.]

JULIET

Ay me, what news? Why dost thou wring thy hands?

NURSE

Ah, well-a-day, he's dead, he's dead, he's dead!
We are undone, lady, we are undone.
Alack the day, he's gone, he's kill'd, he's dead.

JULIET

Can heaven be so envious?

NURSE

Romeo can,
Though heaven cannot. O Romeo, Romeo.
Who ever would have thought it? Romeo!

JULIET

What devil art thou, that dost torment me thus?
This torture should be roar'd in dismal hell.
Hath Romeo slain himself? Say thou but Ay,
And that bare vowel I shall poison more
Than the death-darting eye of cockatrice.
I am not I if there be such an I;
Or those eyes shut that make thee answer Ay.

If he be slain, say Ay; or if not, No.
Brief sounds determine of my weal or woe.

NURSE

I saw the wound, I saw it with mine eyes,
God save the mark!—here on his manly breast.
A piteous corse, a bloody piteous corse;
Pale, pale as ashes, all bedaub'd in blood,
All in gore-blood. I swounded at the sight.

JULIET

O, break, my heart. Poor bankrout, break at once.
To prison, eyes; ne'er look on liberty.
Vile earth to earth resign; end motion here,
And thou and Romeo press one heavy bier.

NURSE

O Tybalt, Tybalt, the best friend I had.
O courteous Tybalt, honest gentleman!
That ever I should live to see thee dead.

JULIET

What storm is this that blows so contrary?
Is Romeo slaughter'd and is Tybalt dead?
My dearest cousin, and my dearer lord?
Then dreadful trumpet sound the general doom,
For who is living, if those two are gone?

NURSE

Tybalt is gone, and Romeo banished,
Romeo that kill'd him, he is banished.

JULIET

O God! Did Romeo's hand shed Tybalt's blood?

NURSE

It did, it did; alas the day, it did.

JULIET

O serpent heart, hid with a flowering face!
Did ever dragon keep so fair a cave?
Beautiful tyrant, fiend angelical,

Dove-feather'd raven, wolvish-ravening lamb!
Despised substance of divinest show!
Just opposite to what thou justly seem'st,
A damned saint, an honourable villain!
O nature, what hadst thou to do in hell
When thou didst bower the spirit of a fiend
In mortal paradise of such sweet flesh?
Was ever book containing such vile matter
So fairly bound? O, that deceit should dwell
In such a gorgeous palace.

NURSE

There's no trust,
No faith, no honesty in men. All perjur'd,
All forsworn, all naught, all dissemblers.
Ah, where's my man? Give me some aqua vitae.
These griefs, these woes, these sorrows make me old.
Shame come to Romeo.

JULIET

Blister'd be thy tongue
For such a wish! He was not born to shame.
Upon his brow shame is asham'd to sit;
For 'tis a throne where honour may be crown'd
Sole monarch of the universal earth.
O, what a beast was I to chide at him!

NURSE

Will you speak well of him that kill'd your cousin?

JULIET

Shall I speak ill of him that is my husband?
Ah, poor my lord, what tongue shall smooth thy name,
When I thy three-hours' wife have mangled it?
But wherefore, villain, didst thou kill my cousin?
That villain cousin would have kill'd my husband.
Back, foolish tears, back to your native spring,
Your tributary drops belong to woe,
Which you mistaking offer up to joy.
My husband lives, that Tybalt would have slain,

And Tybalt's dead, that would have slain my husband.
All this is comfort; wherefore weep I then?
Some word there was, worser than Tybalt's death,
That murder'd me. I would forget it fain,
But O, it presses to my memory
Like damned guilty deeds to sinners' minds.
Tybalt is dead, and Romeo banished.
That 'banished,' that one word 'banished,'
Hath slain ten thousand Tybalts. Tybalt's death
Was woe enough, if it had ended there.
Or if sour woe delights in fellowship,
And needly will be rank'd with other griefs,
Why follow'd not, when she said Tybalt's dead,
Thy father or thy mother, nay or both,
Which modern lamentation might have mov'd?
But with a rear-ward following Tybalt's death,
'Romeo is banished'—to speak that word
Is father, mother, Tybalt, Romeo, Juliet,
All slain, all dead. Romeo is banished,
There is no end, no limit, measure, bound,
In that word's death, no words can that woe sound.
Where is my father and my mother, Nurse?

NURSE

Weeping and wailing over Tybalt's corse.
Will you go to them? I will bring you thither.

JULIET

Wash they his wounds with tears. Mine shall be spent,
When theirs are dry, for Romeo's banishment.
Take up those cords. Poor ropes, you are beguil'd,
Both you and I; for Romeo is exil'd.
He made you for a highway to my bed,
But I, a maid, die maiden-widowed.
Come cords, come Nurse, I'll to my wedding bed,
And death, not Romeo, take my maidenhead.

NURSE

Hie to your chamber. I'll find Romeo

To comfort you. I wot well where he is.
Hark ye, your Romeo will be here at night.
I'll to him, he is hid at Lawrence' cell.

JULIET

O find him, give this ring to my true knight,
And bid him come to take his last farewell.
    [Exeunt.]

SCENE III. Friar Lawrence's Cell.

Enter FRIAR LAWRENCE.

FRIAR LAWRENCE

Romeo, come forth; come forth, thou fearful man.
Affliction is enanmour'd of thy parts
And thou art wedded to calamity.
    Enter ROMEO.

ROMEO

Father, what news? What is the Prince's doom?
What sorrow craves acquaintance at my hand,
That I yet know not?

FRIAR LAWRENCE

Too familiar
Is my dear son with such sour company.
I bring thee tidings of the Prince's doom.

ROMEO

What less than doomsday is the Prince's doom?

FRIAR LAWRENCE

A gentler judgment vanish'd from his lips,
Not body's death, but body's banishment.

ROMEO

Ha, banishment? Be merciful, say death;
For exile hath more terror in his look,
Much more than death. Do not say banishment.

FRIAR LAWRENCE

> Hence from Verona art thou banished.
> Be patient, for the world is broad and wide.

ROMEO

> There is no world without Verona walls,
> But purgatory, torture, hell itself.
> Hence banished is banish'd from the world,
> And world's exile is death. Then banished
> Is death misterm'd. Calling death banished,
> Thou cutt'st my head off with a golden axe,
> And smilest upon the stroke that murders me.

FRIAR LAWRENCE

> O deadly sin, O rude unthankfulness!
> Thy fault our law calls death, but the kind Prince,
> Taking thy part, hath brush'd aside the law,
> And turn'd that black word death to banishment.
> This is dear mercy, and thou see'st it not.

ROMEO

> 'Tis torture, and not mercy. Heaven is here
> Where Juliet lives, and every cat and dog,
> And little mouse, every unworthy thing,
> Live here in heaven and may look on her,
> But Romeo may not. More validity,
> More honourable state, more courtship lives
> In carrion flies than Romeo. They may seize
> On the white wonder of dear Juliet's hand,
> And steal immortal blessing from her lips,
> Who, even in pure and vestal modesty
> Still blush, as thinking their own kisses sin.
> But Romeo may not, he is banished.
> This may flies do, when I from this must fly.
> They are free men but I am banished.
> And say'st thou yet that exile is not death?
> Hadst thou no poison mix'd, no sharp-ground knife,
> No sudden mean of death, though ne'er so mean,
> But banished to kill me? Banished?

O Friar, the damned use that word in hell.
Howlings attends it. How hast thou the heart,
Being a divine, a ghostly confessor,
A sin-absolver, and my friend profess'd,
To mangle me with that word banished?

FRIAR LAWRENCE

Thou fond madman, hear me speak a little.

ROMEO

O, thou wilt speak again of banishment.

FRIAR LAWRENCE

I'll give thee armour to keep off that word,
Adversity's sweet milk, philosophy,
To comfort thee, though thou art banished.

ROMEO

Yet banished? Hang up philosophy.
Unless philosophy can make a Juliet,
Displant a town, reverse a Prince's doom,
It helps not, it prevails not, talk no more.

FRIAR LAWRENCE

O, then I see that mad men have no ears.

ROMEO

How should they, when that wise men have no eyes?

FRIAR LAWRENCE

Let me dispute with thee of thy estate.

ROMEO

Thou canst not speak of that thou dost not feel.
Wert thou as young as I, Juliet thy love,
An hour but married, Tybalt murdered,
Doting like me, and like me banished,
Then mightst thou speak, then mightst thou tear thy hair,
And fall upon the ground as I do now,
Taking the measure of an unmade grave.
    [Knocking within.]

FRIAR LAWRENCE

Arise; one knocks. Good Romeo, hide thyself.

ROMEO

Not I, unless the breath of heartsick groans
Mist-like infold me from the search of eyes.
> *[Knocking.]*

FRIAR LAWRENCE

Hark, how they knock!—Who's there?—Romeo, arise,
Thou wilt be taken.—Stay awhile.—Stand up.
> *[Knocking.]*

Run to my study.—By-and-by.—God's will,
What simpleness is this.—I come, I come.
> *[Knocking.]*

Who knocks so hard? Whence come you, what's your will?

NURSE

> *[Within.]*

Let me come in, and you shall know my errand.
I come from Lady Juliet.

FRIAR LAWRENCE

Welcome then.
> *Enter NURSE.*

NURSE

O holy Friar, O, tell me, holy Friar,
Where is my lady's lord, where's Romeo?

FRIAR LAWRENCE

There on the ground, with his own tears made drunk.

NURSE

O, he is even in my mistress' case.
Just in her case! O woeful sympathy!
Piteous predicament. Even so lies she,
Blubbering and weeping, weeping and blubbering.
Stand up, stand up; stand, and you be a man.
For Juliet's sake, for her sake, rise and stand.
Why should you fall into so deep an O?

ROMEO

Nurse.

NURSE

Ah sir, ah sir, death's the end of all.

ROMEO

Spakest thou of Juliet? How is it with her?
Doth not she think me an old murderer,
Now I have stain'd the childhood of our joy
With blood remov'd but little from her own?
Where is she? And how doth she? And what says
My conceal'd lady to our cancell'd love?

NURSE

O, she says nothing, sir, but weeps and weeps;
And now falls on her bed, and then starts up,
And Tybalt calls, and then on Romeo cries,
And then down falls again.

ROMEO

As if that name,
Shot from the deadly level of a gun,
Did murder her, as that name's cursed hand
Murder'd her kinsman. O, tell me, Friar, tell me,
In what vile part of this anatomy
Doth my name lodge? Tell me, that I may sack
The hateful mansion.
        [Drawing his sword.]

FRIAR LAWRENCE

Hold thy desperate hand.
Art thou a man? Thy form cries out thou art.
Thy tears are womanish, thy wild acts denote
The unreasonable fury of a beast.
Unseemly woman in a seeming man,
And ill-beseeming beast in seeming both!
Thou hast amaz'd me. By my holy order,
I thought thy disposition better temper'd.
Hast thou slain Tybalt? Wilt thou slay thyself?

And slay thy lady, that in thy life lives,
By doing damned hate upon thyself?
Why rail'st thou on thy birth, the heaven and earth?
Since birth, and heaven and earth, all three do meet
In thee at once; which thou at once wouldst lose.
Fie, fie, thou sham'st thy shape, thy love, thy wit,
Which, like a usurer, abound'st in all,
And usest none in that true use indeed
Which should bedeck thy shape, thy love, thy wit.
Thy noble shape is but a form of wax,
Digressing from the valour of a man;
Thy dear love sworn but hollow perjury,
Killing that love which thou hast vow'd to cherish;
Thy wit, that ornament to shape and love,
Misshapen in the conduct of them both,
Like powder in a skilless soldier's flask,
Is set afire by thine own ignorance,
And thou dismember'd with thine own defence.
What, rouse thee, man. Thy Juliet is alive,
For whose dear sake thou wast but lately dead.
There art thou happy. Tybalt would kill thee,
But thou slew'st Tybalt; there art thou happy.
The law that threaten'd death becomes thy friend,
And turns it to exile; there art thou happy.
A pack of blessings light upon thy back;
Happiness courts thee in her best array;
But like a misshaped and sullen wench,
Thou putt'st up thy Fortune and thy love.
Take heed, take heed, for such die miserable.
Go, get thee to thy love as was decreed,
Ascend her chamber, hence and comfort her.
But look thou stay not till the watch be set,
For then thou canst not pass to Mantua;
Where thou shalt live till we can find a time
To blaze your marriage, reconcile your friends,
Beg pardon of the Prince, and call thee back
With twenty hundred thousand times more joy
Than thou went'st forth in lamentation.

Go before, Nurse. Commend me to thy lady,
And bid her hasten all the house to bed,
Which heavy sorrow makes them apt unto.
Romeo is coming.

NURSE

O Lord, I could have stay'd here all the night
To hear good counsel. O, what learning is!
My lord, I'll tell my lady you will come.

ROMEO

Do so, and bid my sweet prepare to chide.

NURSE

Here sir, a ring she bid me give you, sir.
Hie you, make haste, for it grows very late.
        [Exit.]

ROMEO

How well my comfort is reviv'd by this.

FRIAR LAWRENCE

Go hence, good night, and here stands all your state:
Either be gone before the watch be set,
Or by the break of day disguis'd from hence.
Sojourn in Mantua. I'll find out your man,
And he shall signify from time to time
Every good hap to you that chances here.
Give me thy hand; 'tis late; farewell; good night.

ROMEO

But that a joy past joy calls out on me,
It were a grief so brief to part with thee.
Farewell.
        [Exeunt.]

SCENE IV. A Room in Capulet's House.

Enter CAPULET, LADY CAPULET and PARIS.

CAPULET

Things have fallen out, sir, so unluckily

That we have had no time to move our daughter.
Look you, she lov'd her kinsman Tybalt dearly,
And so did I. Well, we were born to die.
'Tis very late; she'll not come down tonight.
I promise you, but for your company,
I would have been abed an hour ago.

PARIS

These times of woe afford no tune to woo.
Madam, good night. Commend me to your daughter.

LADY CAPULET

I will, and know her mind early tomorrow;
Tonight she's mew'd up to her heaviness.

CAPULET

Sir Paris, I will make a desperate tender
Of my child's love. I think she will be rul'd
In all respects by me; nay more, I doubt it not.
Wife, go you to her ere you go to bed,
Acquaint her here of my son Paris' love,
And bid her, mark you me, on Wednesday next,
But, soft, what day is this?

PARIS

Monday, my lord.

CAPULET

Monday! Ha, ha! Well, Wednesday is too soon,
A Thursday let it be; a Thursday, tell her,
She shall be married to this noble earl.
Will you be ready? Do you like this haste?
We'll keep no great ado,—a friend or two,
For, hark you, Tybalt being slain so late,
It may be thought we held him carelessly,
Being our kinsman, if we revel much.
Therefore we'll have some half a dozen friends,
And there an end. But what say you to Thursday?

PARIS

My lord, I would that Thursday were tomorrow.

CAPULET

> Well, get you gone. A Thursday be it then.
> Go you to Juliet ere you go to bed,
> Prepare her, wife, against this wedding day.
> Farewell, my lord.—Light to my chamber, ho!
> Afore me, it is so very very late that we
> May call it early by and by. Good night.
>
> > *[Exeunt.]*

SCENE V. An open Gallery to Juliet's Chamber, overlooking the Garden.

Enter ROMEO and JULIET.

JULIET

> Wilt thou be gone? It is not yet near day.
> It was the nightingale, and not the lark,
> That pierc'd the fearful hollow of thine ear;
> Nightly she sings on yond pomegranate tree.
> Believe me, love, it was the nightingale.

ROMEO

> It was the lark, the herald of the morn,
> No nightingale. Look, love, what envious streaks
> Do lace the severing clouds in yonder east.
> Night's candles are burnt out, and jocund day
> Stands tiptoe on the misty mountain tops.
> I must be gone and live, or stay and die.

JULIET

> Yond light is not daylight, I know it, I.
> It is some meteor that the sun exhales
> To be to thee this night a torchbearer
> And light thee on thy way to Mantua.
> Therefore stay yet, thou need'st not to be gone.

ROMEO

> Let me be ta'en, let me be put to death,
> I am content, so thou wilt have it so.
> I'll say yon grey is not the morning's eye,

'Tis but the pale reflex of Cynthia's brow.
Nor that is not the lark whose notes do beat
The vaulty heaven so high above our heads.
I have more care to stay than will to go.
Come, death, and welcome. Juliet wills it so.
How is't, my soul? Let's talk. It is not day.

JULIET

It is, it is! Hie hence, be gone, away.
It is the lark that sings so out of tune,
Straining harsh discords and unpleasing sharps.
Some say the lark makes sweet division;
This doth not so, for she divideth us.
Some say the lark and loathed toad change eyes.
O, now I would they had chang'd voices too,
Since arm from arm that voice doth us affray,
Hunting thee hence with hunt's-up to the day.
O now be gone, more light and light it grows.

ROMEO

More light and light, more dark and dark our woes.
Enter NURSE.

NURSE

Madam.

JULIET

Nurse?

NURSE

Your lady mother is coming to your chamber.
The day is broke, be wary, look about.
[Exit.]

JULIET

Then, window, let day in, and let life out.

ROMEO

Farewell, farewell, one kiss, and I'll descend.
[Descends.]

JULIET

Art thou gone so? Love, lord, ay husband, friend,

I must hear from thee every day in the hour,
For in a minute there are many days.
O, by this count I shall be much in years
Ere I again behold my Romeo.

ROMEO

Farewell!
I will omit no opportunity
That may convey my greetings, love, to thee.

JULIET

O thinkest thou we shall ever meet again?

ROMEO

I doubt it not, and all these woes shall serve
For sweet discourses in our time to come.

JULIET

O God! I have an ill-divining soul!
Methinks I see thee, now thou art so low,
As one dead in the bottom of a tomb.
Either my eyesight fails, or thou look'st pale.

ROMEO

And trust me, love, in my eye so do you.
Dry sorrow drinks our blood. Adieu, adieu.
　　　[Exit below.]

JULIET

O Fortune, Fortune! All men call thee fickle,
If thou art fickle, what dost thou with him
That is renown'd for faith? Be fickle, Fortune;
For then, I hope thou wilt not keep him long
But send him back.

LADY CAPULET

　　　[Within.]
Ho, daughter, are you up?

JULIET

Who is't that calls? Is it my lady mother?

Is she not down so late, or up so early?
What unaccustom'd cause procures her hither?
Enter LADY CAPULET.

LADY CAPULET
Why, how now, Juliet?

JULIET
Madam, I am not well.

LADY CAPULET
Evermore weeping for your cousin's death?
What, wilt thou wash him from his grave with tears?
And if thou couldst, thou couldst not make him live.
Therefore have done: some grief shows much of love,
But much of grief shows still some want of wit.

JULIET
Yet let me weep for such a feeling loss.

LADY CAPULET
So shall you feel the loss, but not the friend
Which you weep for.

JULIET
Feeling so the loss,
I cannot choose but ever weep the friend.

LADY CAPULET
Well, girl, thou weep'st not so much for his death
As that the villain lives which slaughter'd him.

JULIET
What villain, madam?

LADY CAPULET
That same villain Romeo.

JULIET
Villain and he be many miles asunder.
God pardon him. I do, with all my heart.
And yet no man like he doth grieve my heart.

LADY CAPULET

That is because the traitor murderer lives.

JULIET

Ay madam, from the reach of these my hands.
Would none but I might venge my cousin's death.

LADY CAPULET

We will have vengeance for it, fear thou not.
Then weep no more. I'll send to one in Mantua,
Where that same banish'd runagate doth live,
Shall give him such an unaccustom'd dram
That he shall soon keep Tybalt company:
And then I hope thou wilt be satisfied.

JULIET

Indeed I never shall be satisfied
With Romeo till I behold him—dead—
Is my poor heart so for a kinsman vex'd.
Madam, if you could find out but a man
To bear a poison, I would temper it,
That Romeo should upon receipt thereof,
Soon sleep in quiet. O, how my heart abhors
To hear him nam'd, and cannot come to him,
To wreak the love I bore my cousin
Upon his body that hath slaughter'd him.

LADY CAPULET

Find thou the means, and I'll find such a man.
But now I'll tell thee joyful tidings, girl.

JULIET

And joy comes well in such a needy time.
What are they, I beseech your ladyship?

LADY CAPULET

Well, well, thou hast a careful father, child;
One who to put thee from thy heaviness,
Hath sorted out a sudden day of joy,
That thou expects not, nor I look'd not for.

JULIET

Madam, in happy time, what day is that?

LADY CAPULET

Marry, my child, early next Thursday morn
The gallant, young, and noble gentleman,
The County Paris, at Saint Peter's Church,
Shall happily make thee there a joyful bride.

JULIET

Now by Saint Peter's Church, and Peter too,
He shall not make me there a joyful bride.
I wonder at this haste, that I must wed
Ere he that should be husband comes to woo.
I pray you tell my lord and father, madam,
I will not marry yet; and when I do, I swear
It shall be Romeo, whom you know I hate,
Rather than Paris. These are news indeed.

LADY CAPULET

Here comes your father, tell him so yourself,
And see how he will take it at your hands.
                    Enter CAPULET and NURSE.

CAPULET

When the sun sets, the air doth drizzle dew;
But for the sunset of my brother's son
It rains downright.
How now? A conduit, girl? What, still in tears?
Evermore showering? In one little body
Thou counterfeits a bark, a sea, a wind.
For still thy eyes, which I may call the sea,
Do ebb and flow with tears; the bark thy body is,
Sailing in this salt flood, the winds, thy sighs,
Who raging with thy tears and they with them,
Without a sudden calm will overset
Thy tempest-tossed body. How now, wife?
Have you deliver'd to her our decree?

LADY CAPULET

    Ay, sir; but she will none, she gives you thanks.

    I would the fool were married to her grave.

CAPULET

    Soft. Take me with you, take me with you, wife.

    How, will she none? Doth she not give us thanks?

    Is she not proud? Doth she not count her blest,

    Unworthy as she is, that we have wrought

    So worthy a gentleman to be her bridegroom?

JULIET

    Not proud you have, but thankful that you have.

    Proud can I never be of what I hate;

    But thankful even for hate that is meant love.

CAPULET

    How now, how now, chopp'd logic? What is this?

    Proud, and, I thank you, and I thank you not;

    And yet not proud. Mistress minion you,

    Thank me no thankings, nor proud me no prouds,

    But fettle your fine joints 'gainst Thursday next

    To go with Paris to Saint Peter's Church,

    Or I will drag thee on a hurdle thither.

    Out, you green-sickness carrion! Out, you baggage!

    You tallow-face!

LADY CAPULET

    Fie, fie! What, are you mad?

JULIET

    Good father, I beseech you on my knees,

    Hear me with patience but to speak a word.

CAPULET

    Hang thee young baggage, disobedient wretch!

    I tell thee what,—get thee to church a Thursday,

    Or never after look me in the face.

    Speak not, reply not, do not answer me.

    My fingers itch. Wife, we scarce thought us blest

    That God had lent us but this only child;

But now I see this one is one too much,
And that we have a curse in having her.
Out on her, hilding.

NURSE

God in heaven bless her.
You are to blame, my lord, to rate her so.

CAPULET

And why, my lady wisdom? Hold your tongue,
Good prudence; smatter with your gossips, go.

NURSE

I speak no treason.

CAPULET

O God ye good-en!

NURSE

May not one speak?

CAPULET

Peace, you mumbling fool!
Utter your gravity o'er a gossip's bowl,
For here we need it not.

LADY CAPULET

You are too hot.

CAPULET

God's bread, it makes me mad!
Day, night, hour, ride, time, work, play,
Alone, in company, still my care hath been
To have her match'd, and having now provided
A gentleman of noble parentage,
Of fair demesnes, youthful, and nobly allied,
Stuff'd, as they say, with honourable parts,
Proportion'd as one's thought would wish a man,
And then to have a wretched puling fool,
A whining mammet, in her fortune's tender,
To answer, 'I'll not wed, I cannot love,

I am too young, I pray you pardon me.'
But, and you will not wed, I'll pardon you.
Graze where you will, you shall not house with me.
Look to't, think on't, I do not use to jest.
Thursday is near; lay hand on heart, advise.
And you be mine, I'll give you to my friend;
And you be not, hang, beg, starve, die in the streets,
For by my soul, I'll ne'er acknowledge thee,
Nor what is mine shall never do thee good.
Trust to't, bethink you, I'll not be forsworn.
          [Exit.]

JULIET

Is there no pity sitting in the clouds,
That sees into the bottom of my grief?
O sweet my mother, cast me not away,
Delay this marriage for a month, a week,
Or, if you do not, make the bridal bed
In that dim monument where Tybalt lies.

LADY CAPULET

Talk not to me, for I'll not speak a word.
Do as thou wilt, for I have done with thee.
          [Exit.]

JULIET

O God! O Nurse, how shall this be prevented?
My husband is on earth, my faith in heaven.
How shall that faith return again to earth,
Unless that husband send it me from heaven
By leaving earth? Comfort me, counsel me.
Alack, alack, that heaven should practise stratagems
Upon so soft a subject as myself.
What say'st thou? Hast thou not a word of joy?
Some comfort, Nurse.

NURSE

Faith, here it is.
Romeo is banished; and all the world to nothing

That he dares ne'er come back to challenge you.
Or if he do, it needs must be by stealth.
Then, since the case so stands as now it doth,
I think it best you married with the County.
O, he's a lovely gentleman.
Romeo's a dishclout to him. An eagle, madam,
Hath not so green, so quick, so fair an eye
As Paris hath. Beshrew my very heart,
I think you are happy in this second match,
For it excels your first: or if it did not,
Your first is dead, or 'twere as good he were,
As living here and you no use of him.

JULIET

Speakest thou from thy heart?

NURSE

And from my soul too,
Or else beshrew them both.

JULIET

Amen.

NURSE

What?

JULIET

Well, thou hast comforted me marvellous much.
Go in, and tell my lady I am gone,
Having displeas'd my father, to Lawrence' cell,
To make confession and to be absolv'd.

NURSE

Marry, I will; and this is wisely done.
          [Exit.]

JULIET

Ancient damnation! O most wicked fiend!
Is it more sin to wish me thus forsworn,
Or to dispraise my lord with that same tongue
Which she hath prais'd him with above compare

So many thousand times? Go, counsellor.
Thou and my bosom henceforth shall be twain.
I'll to the Friar to know his remedy.
If all else fail, myself have power to die.

    [Exit.]

ACT IV

SCENE I. Friar Lawrence's Cell.

Enter FRIAR LAWRENCE and PARIS.

FRIAR LAWRENCE
On Thursday, sir? The time is very short.

PARIS
My father Capulet will have it so;
And I am nothing slow to slack his haste.

FRIAR LAWRENCE
You say you do not know the lady's mind.
Uneven is the course; I like it not.

PARIS
Immoderately she weeps for Tybalt's death,
And therefore have I little talk'd of love;
For Venus smiles not in a house of tears.
Now, sir, her father counts it dangerous
That she do give her sorrow so much sway;
And in his wisdom, hastes our marriage,
To stop the inundation of her tears,
Which, too much minded by herself alone,
May be put from her by society.
Now do you know the reason of this haste.

FRIAR LAWRENCE
[Aside.]

219

I would I knew not why it should be slow'd.—
Look, sir, here comes the lady toward my cell.
        Enter JULIET.

PARIS

Happily met, my lady and my wife!

JULIET

That may be, sir, when I may be a wife.

PARIS

That may be, must be, love, on Thursday next.

JULIET

What must be shall be.

FRIAR LAWRENCE

That's a certain text.

PARIS

Come you to make confession to this father?

JULIET

To answer that, I should confess to you.

PARIS

Do not deny to him that you love me.

JULIET

I will confess to you that I love him.

PARIS

So will ye, I am sure, that you love me.

JULIET

If I do so, it will be of more price,
Being spoke behind your back than to your face.

PARIS

Poor soul, thy face is much abus'd with tears.

JULIET

The tears have got small victory by that;
For it was bad enough before their spite.

PARIS

> Thou wrong'st it more than tears with that report.

JULIET

> That is no slander, sir, which is a truth,
> And what I spake, I spake it to my face.

PARIS

> Thy face is mine, and thou hast slander'd it.

JULIET

> It may be so, for it is not mine own.
> Are you at leisure, holy father, now,
> Or shall I come to you at evening mass?

FRIAR LAWRENCE

> My leisure serves me, pensive daughter, now.—
> My lord, we must entreat the time alone.

PARIS

> God shield I should disturb devotion!—
> Juliet, on Thursday early will I rouse ye,
> Till then, adieu; and keep this holy kiss.
>> *[Exit.]*

JULIET

> O shut the door, and when thou hast done so,
> Come weep with me, past hope, past cure, past help!

FRIAR LAWRENCE

> O Juliet, I already know thy grief;
> It strains me past the compass of my wits.
> I hear thou must, and nothing may prorogue it,
> On Thursday next be married to this County.

JULIET

> Tell me not, Friar, that thou hear'st of this,
> Unless thou tell me how I may prevent it.
> If in thy wisdom, thou canst give no help,
> Do thou but call my resolution wise,
> And with this knife I'll help it presently.
> God join'd my heart and Romeo's, thou our hands;

And ere this hand, by thee to Romeo's seal'd,
Shall be the label to another deed,
Or my true heart with treacherous revolt
Turn to another, this shall slay them both.
Therefore, out of thy long-experienc'd time,
Give me some present counsel, or behold
'Twixt my extremes and me this bloody knife
Shall play the empire, arbitrating that
Which the commission of thy years and art
Could to no issue of true honour bring.
Be not so long to speak. I long to die,
If what thou speak'st speak not of remedy.

FRIAR LAWRENCE

Hold, daughter. I do spy a kind of hope,
Which craves as desperate an execution
As that is desperate which we would prevent.
If, rather than to marry County Paris
Thou hast the strength of will to slay thyself,
Then is it likely thou wilt undertake
A thing like death to chide away this shame,
That cop'st with death himself to 'scape from it.
And if thou dar'st, I'll give thee remedy.

JULIET

O, bid me leap, rather than marry Paris,
From off the battlements of yonder tower,
Or walk in thievish ways, or bid me lurk
Where serpents are. Chain me with roaring bears;
Or hide me nightly in a charnel-house,
O'er-cover'd quite with dead men's rattling bones,
With reeky shanks and yellow chapless skulls.
Or bid me go into a new-made grave,
And hide me with a dead man in his shroud;
Things that, to hear them told, have made me tremble,
And I will do it without fear or doubt,
To live an unstain'd wife to my sweet love.

FRIAR LAWRENCE

Hold then. Go home, be merry, give consent

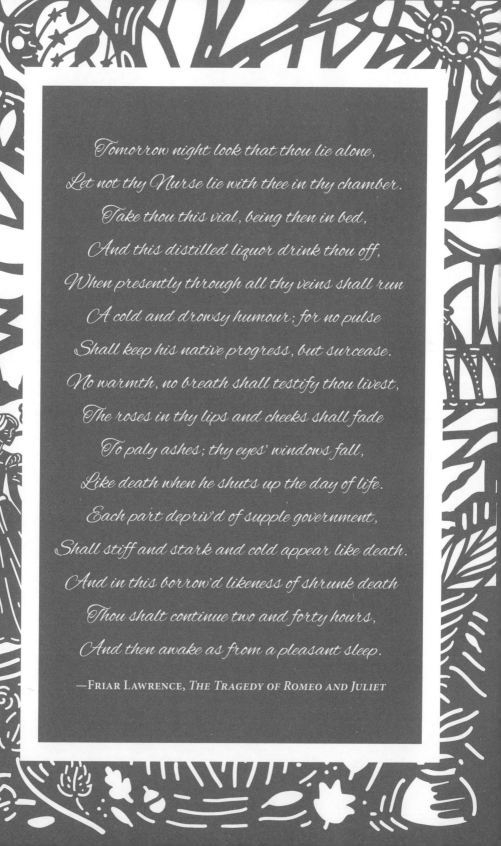

Tomorrow night look that thou lie alone,

Let not thy Nurse lie with thee in thy chamber.

Take thou this vial, being then in bed,

And this distilled liquor drink thou off,

When presently through all thy veins shall run

A cold and drowsy humour; for no pulse

Shall keep his native progress, but surcease.

No warmth, no breath shall testify thou livest,

The roses in thy lips and cheeks shall fade

To paly ashes; thy eyes' windows fall,

Like death when he shuts up the day of life.

Each part depriv'd of supple government,

Shall stiff and stark and cold appear like death.

And in this borrow'd likeness of shrunk death

Thou shalt continue two and forty hours,

And then awake as from a pleasant sleep.

—FRIAR LAWRENCE, THE TRAGEDY OF ROMEO AND JULIET

To marry Paris. Wednesday is tomorrow;
Tomorrow night look that thou lie alone,
Let not thy Nurse lie with thee in thy chamber.
Take thou this vial, being then in bed,
And this distilled liquor drink thou off,
When presently through all thy veins shall run
A cold and drowsy humour; for no pulse
Shall keep his native progress, but surcease.
No warmth, no breath shall testify thou livest,
The roses in thy lips and cheeks shall fade
To paly ashes; thy eyes' windows fall,
Like death when he shuts up the day of life.
Each part depriv'd of supple government,
Shall stiff and stark and cold appear like death.
And in this borrow'd likeness of shrunk death
Thou shalt continue two and forty hours,
And then awake as from a pleasant sleep.
Now when the bridegroom in the morning comes
To rouse thee from thy bed, there art thou dead.
Then as the manner of our country is,
In thy best robes, uncover'd, on the bier,
Thou shalt be borne to that same ancient vault
Where all the kindred of the Capulets lie.
In the meantime, against thou shalt awake,
Shall Romeo by my letters know our drift,
And hither shall he come, and he and I
Will watch thy waking, and that very night
Shall Romeo bear thee hence to Mantua.
And this shall free thee from this present shame,
If no inconstant toy nor womanish fear
Abate thy valour in the acting it.

JULIET

Give me, give me! O tell not me of fear!

FRIAR LAWRENCE

Hold; get you gone, be strong and prosperous
In this resolve. I'll send a friar with speed
To Mantua, with my letters to thy lord.

JULIET

Love give me strength, and strength shall help afford.
Farewell, dear father.
[*Exeunt.*]

SCENE II. Hall in Capulet's House.

Enter CAPULET, LADY CAPULET, NURSE and SERVANTS.

CAPULET

So many guests invite as here are writ.
[*Exit FIRST SERVANT.*]
Sirrah, go hire me twenty cunning cooks.

SECOND SERVANT

You shall have none ill, sir; for I'll try if they can lick their fingers.

CAPULET

How canst thou try them so?

SECOND SERVANT

Marry, sir, 'tis an ill cook that cannot lick his own fingers; therefore
he that cannot lick his fingers goes not with me.

CAPULET

Go, begone.
[*Exit SECOND SERVANT.*]
We shall be much unfurnish'd for this time.
What, is my daughter gone to Friar Lawrence?

NURSE

Ay, forsooth.

CAPULET

Well, he may chance to do some good on her.
A peevish self-will'd harlotry it is.
Enter JULIET.

NURSE

See where she comes from shrift with merry look.

CAPULET

How now, my headstrong. Where have you been gadding?

JULIET

> Where I have learnt me to repent the sin
> Of disobedient opposition
> To you and your behests; and am enjoin'd
> By holy Lawrence to fall prostrate here,
> To beg your pardon. Pardon, I beseech you.
> Henceforward I am ever rul'd by you.

CAPULET

> Send for the County, go tell him of this.
> I'll have this knot knit up tomorrow morning.

JULIET

> I met the youthful lord at Lawrence' cell,
> And gave him what becomed love I might,
> Not stepping o'er the bounds of modesty.

CAPULET

> Why, I am glad on't. This is well. Stand up.
> This is as't should be. Let me see the County.
> Ay, marry. Go, I say, and fetch him hither.
> Now afore God, this reverend holy Friar,
> All our whole city is much bound to him.

JULIET

> Nurse, will you go with me into my closet,
> To help me sort such needful ornaments
> As you think fit to furnish me tomorrow?

LADY CAPULET

> No, not till Thursday. There is time enough.

CAPULET

> Go, Nurse, go with her. We'll to church tomorrow.
> *[Exeunt JULIET and NURSE.]*

LADY CAPULET

> We shall be short in our provision,
> 'Tis now near night.

CAPULET

> Tush, I will stir about,

And all things shall be well, I warrant thee, wife.
Go thou to Juliet, help to deck up her.
I'll not to bed tonight, let me alone.
I'll play the housewife for this once.—What, ho!—
They are all forth: well, I will walk myself
To County Paris, to prepare him up
Against tomorrow. My heart is wondrous light
Since this same wayward girl is so reclaim'd.
          [Exeunt.]

SCENE III. Juliet's Chamber.

Enter JULIET and NURSE.

JULIET

Ay, those attires are best. But, gentle Nurse,
I pray thee leave me to myself tonight;
For I have need of many orisons
To move the heavens to smile upon my state,
Which, well thou know'st, is cross and full of sin.
          Enter LADY CAPULET.

LADY CAPULET

What, are you busy, ho? Need you my help?

JULIET

No, madam; we have cull'd such necessaries
As are behoveful for our state tomorrow.
So please you, let me now be left alone,
And let the nurse this night sit up with you,
For I am sure you have your hands full all
In this so sudden business.

LADY CAPULET

Good night.
Get thee to bed and rest, for thou hast need.
          [Exeunt LADY CAPULET and NURSE.]

JULIET

Farewell. God knows when we shall meet again.

I have a faint cold fear thrills through my veins
That almost freezes up the heat of life.
I'll call them back again to comfort me.
Nurse!—What should she do here?
My dismal scene I needs must act alone.
Come, vial.
What if this mixture do not work at all?
Shall I be married then tomorrow morning?
No, No! This shall forbid it. Lie thou there.
      [Laying down her dagger.]
What if it be a poison, which the Friar
Subtly hath minister'd to have me dead,
Lest in this marriage he should be dishonour'd,
Because he married me before to Romeo?
I fear it is. And yet methinks it should not,
For he hath still been tried a holy man.
How if, when I am laid into the tomb,
I wake before the time that Romeo
Come to redeem me? There's a fearful point!
Shall I not then be stifled in the vault,
To whose foul mouth no healthsome air breathes in,
And there die strangled ere my Romeo comes?
Or, if I live, is it not very like,
The horrible conceit of death and night,
Together with the terror of the place,
As in a vault, an ancient receptacle,
Where for this many hundred years the bones
Of all my buried ancestors are pack'd,
Where bloody Tybalt, yet but green in earth,
Lies festering in his shroud; where, as they say,
At some hours in the night spirits resort—
Alack, alack, is it not like that I,
So early waking, what with loathsome smells,
And shrieks like mandrakes torn out of the earth,
That living mortals, hearing them, run mad.
O, if I wake, shall I not be distraught,
Environed with all these hideous fears,
And madly play with my forefathers' joints?

And pluck the mangled Tybalt from his shroud?
And, in this rage, with some great kinsman's bone,
As with a club, dash out my desperate brains?
O look, methinks I see my cousin's ghost
Seeking out Romeo that did spit his body
Upon a rapier's point. Stay, Tybalt, stay!
Romeo, Romeo, Romeo, here's drink! I drink to thee.
    [Throws herself on the bed.]

SCENE IV. Hall in Capulet's House.

Enter LADY CAPULET and NURSE.

LADY CAPULET

Hold, take these keys and fetch more spices, Nurse.

NURSE

They call for dates and quinces in the pastry.
    Enter CAPULET.

CAPULET

Come, stir, stir, stir! The second cock hath crow'd,
The curfew bell hath rung, 'tis three o'clock.
Look to the bak'd meats, good Angelica;
Spare not for cost.

NURSE

Go, you cot-quean, go,
Get you to bed; faith, you'll be sick tomorrow
For this night's watching.

CAPULET

No, not a whit. What! I have watch'd ere now
All night for lesser cause, and ne'er been sick.

LADY CAPULET

Ay, you have been a mouse-hunt in your time;
But I will watch you from such watching now.
    [Exeunt LADY CAPULET and NURSE.]

CAPULET

A jealous-hood, a jealous-hood!

Enter SERVANTS, with spits, logs and baskets.

Now, fellow, what's there?

FIRST SERVANT

Things for the cook, sir; but I know not what.

CAPULET

Make haste, make haste.

[Exit FIRST SERVANT.]

—Sirrah, fetch drier logs.

Call Peter, he will show thee where they are.

SECOND SERVANT

I have a head, sir, that will find out logs

And never trouble Peter for the matter.

[Exit.]

CAPULET

Mass and well said; a merry whoreson, ha.

Thou shalt be loggerhead.—Good faith, 'tis day.

The County will be here with music straight,

For so he said he would. I hear him near.

[Play music.]

Nurse! Wife! What, ho! What, Nurse, I say!

Re-enter NURSE.

Go waken Juliet, go and trim her up.

I'll go and chat with Paris. Hie, make haste,

Make haste; the bridegroom he is come already.

Make haste I say.

[Exeunt.]

SCENE V. Juliet's Chamber; Juliet on the bed.

Enter NURSE.

NURSE

Mistress! What, mistress! Juliet! Fast, I warrant her, she.

Why, lamb, why, lady, fie, you slug-abed!

Why, love, I say! Madam! Sweetheart! Why, bride!
What, not a word? You take your pennyworths now.
Sleep for a week; for the next night, I warrant,
The County Paris hath set up his rest
That you shall rest but little. God forgive me!
Marry and amen. How sound is she asleep!
I needs must wake her. Madam, madam, madam!
Ay, let the County take you in your bed,
He'll fright you up, i' faith. Will it not be?
What, dress'd, and in your clothes, and down again?
I must needs wake you. Lady! Lady! Lady!
Alas, alas! Help, help! My lady's dead!
O, well-a-day that ever I was born.
Some aqua vitae, ho! My lord! My lady!
    Enter LADY CAPULET.

LADY CAPULET

What noise is here?

NURSE

O lamentable day!

LADY CAPULET

What is the matter?

NURSE

Look, look! O heavy day!

LADY CAPULET

O me, O me! My child, my only life.
Revive, look up, or I will die with thee.
Help, help! Call help.
    Enter CAPULET.

CAPULET

For shame, bring Juliet forth, her lord is come.

NURSE

She's dead, deceas'd, she's dead; alack the day!

LADY CAPULET

Alack the day, she's dead, she's dead, she's dead!

CAPULET

Ha! Let me see her. Out alas! She's cold,
Her blood is settled and her joints are stiff.
Life and these lips have long been separated.
Death lies on her like an untimely frost
Upon the sweetest flower of all the field.

NURSE

O lamentable day!

LADY CAPULET

O woful time!

CAPULET

Death, that hath ta'en her hence to make me wail,
Ties up my tongue and will not let me speak.
Enter FRIAR LAWRENCE and PARIS with Musicians.

FRIAR LAWRENCE

Come, is the bride ready to go to church?

CAPULET

Ready to go, but never to return.
O son, the night before thy wedding day
Hath death lain with thy bride. There she lies,
Flower as she was, deflowered by him.
Death is my son-in-law, death is my heir;
My daughter he hath wedded. I will die.
And leave him all; life, living, all is death's.

PARIS

Have I thought long to see this morning's face,
And doth it give me such a sight as this?

LADY CAPULET

Accurs'd, unhappy, wretched, hateful day.
Most miserable hour that e'er time saw
In lasting labour of his pilgrimage.
But one, poor one, one poor and loving child,
But one thing to rejoice and solace in,
And cruel death hath catch'd it from my sight.

NURSE

> O woe! O woeful, woeful, woeful day.
> Most lamentable day, most woeful day
> That ever, ever, I did yet behold!
> O day, O day, O day, O hateful day.
> Never was seen so black a day as this.
> O woeful day, O woeful day.

PARIS

> Beguil'd, divorced, wronged, spited, slain.
> Most detestable death, by thee beguil'd,
> By cruel, cruel thee quite overthrown.
> O love! O life! Not life, but love in death!

CAPULET

> Despis'd, distressed, hated, martyr'd, kill'd.
> Uncomfortable time, why cam'st thou now
> To murder, murder our solemnity?
> O child! O child! My soul, and not my child,
> Dead art thou. Alack, my child is dead,
> And with my child my joys are buried.

FRIAR LAWRENCE

> Peace, ho, for shame. Confusion's cure lives not
> In these confusions. Heaven and yourself
> Had part in this fair maid, now heaven hath all,
> And all the better is it for the maid.
> Your part in her you could not keep from death,
> But heaven keeps his part in eternal life.
> The most you sought was her promotion,
> For 'twas your heaven she should be advanc'd,
> And weep ye now, seeing she is advanc'd
> Above the clouds, as high as heaven itself?
> O, in this love, you love your child so ill
> That you run mad, seeing that she is well.
> She's not well married that lives married long,
> But she's best married that dies married young.
> Dry up your tears, and stick your rosemary
> On this fair corse, and, as the custom is,
> And in her best array bear her to church;

For though fond nature bids us all lament,
Yet nature's tears are reason's merriment.

CAPULET

All things that we ordained festival
Turn from their office to black funeral:
Our instruments to melancholy bells,
Our wedding cheer to a sad burial feast;
Our solemn hymns to sullen dirges change;
Our bridal flowers serve for a buried corse,
And all things change them to the contrary.

FRIAR LAWRENCE

Sir, go you in, and, madam, go with him,
And go, Sir Paris, everyone prepare
To follow this fair corse unto her grave.
The heavens do lower upon you for some ill;
Move them no more by crossing their high will.
    [Exeunt CAPULET, LADY CAPULET, PARIS and FRIAR.]

FIRST MUSICIAN

Faith, we may put up our pipes and be gone.

NURSE

Honest good fellows, ah, put up, put up,
For well you know this is a pitiful case.

FIRST MUSICIAN

Ay, by my troth, the case may be amended.
    [Exit NURSE.]
    Enter PETER.

PETER

Musicians, O, musicians, 'Heart's ease,' 'Heart's ease,' O, and you
will have me live, play 'Heart's ease.'

FIRST MUSICIAN

Why 'Heart's ease'?

PETER

O musicians, because my heart itself plays 'My heart is full.' O play
me some merry dump to comfort me.

FIRST MUSICIAN

Not a dump we, 'tis no time to play now.

PETER

You will not then?

FIRST MUSICIAN

No.

PETER

I will then give it you soundly.

FIRST MUSICIAN

What will you give us?

PETER

No money, on my faith, but the gleek! I will give you the minstrel.

FIRST MUSICIAN

Then will I give you the serving-creature.

PETER

Then will I lay the serving-creature's dagger on your pate. I will carry no crotchets. I'll re you, I'll fa you. Do you note me?

FIRST MUSICIAN

And you re us and fa us, you note us.

SECOND MUSICIAN

Pray you put up your dagger, and put out your wit.

PETER

Then have at you with my wit. I will dry-beat you with an iron wit, and put up my iron dagger. Answer me like men.
'When griping griefs the heart doth wound,
And doleful dumps the mind oppress,
Then music with her silver sound'—
Why 'silver sound'? Why 'music with her silver sound'? What say you, Simon Catling?

FIRST MUSICIAN

Marry, sir, because silver hath a sweet sound.

PETER

Prates. What say you, Hugh Rebeck?

SECOND MUSICIAN

I say 'silver sound' because musicians sound for silver.

PETER

Prates too! What say you, James Soundpost?

THIRD MUSICIAN

Faith, I know not what to say.

PETER

O, I cry you mercy, you are the singer. I will say for you. It is 'music with her silver sound' because musicians have no gold for sounding.
'Then music with her silver sound
With speedy help doth lend redress.'
  [Exit.]

FIRST MUSICIAN

What a pestilent knave is this same!

SECOND MUSICIAN

Hang him, Jack. Come, we'll in here, tarry for the mourners, and stay dinner.
  [Exeunt.]

ACT V

SCENE I. Mantua. A Street.

Enter ROMEO.

ROMEO

If I may trust the flattering eye of sleep,
My dreams presage some joyful news at hand.
My bosom's lord sits lightly in his throne;
And all this day an unaccustom'd spirit
Lifts me above the ground with cheerful thoughts.
I dreamt my lady came and found me dead,—
Strange dream, that gives a dead man leave to think!—
And breath'd such life with kisses in my lips,
That I reviv'd, and was an emperor.
Ah me, how sweet is love itself possess'd,
When but love's shadows are so rich in joy.
       Enter BALTHASAR.
News from Verona! How now, Balthasar?
Dost thou not bring me letters from the Friar?
How doth my lady? Is my father well?
How fares my Juliet? That I ask again;
For nothing can be ill if she be well.

BALTHASAR

Then she is well, and nothing can be ill.
Her body sleeps in Capel's monument,
And her immortal part with angels lives.

I saw her laid low in her kindred's vault,
And presently took post to tell it you.
O pardon me for bringing these ill news,
Since you did leave it for my office, sir.

ROMEO

Is it even so? Then I defy you, stars!
Thou know'st my lodging. Get me ink and paper,
And hire post-horses. I will hence tonight.

BALTHASAR

I do beseech you, sir, have patience.
Your looks are pale and wild, and do import
Some misadventure.

ROMEO

Tush, thou art deceiv'd.
Leave me, and do the thing I bid thee do.
Hast thou no letters to me from the Friar?

BALTHASAR

No, my good lord.

ROMEO

No matter. Get thee gone,
And hire those horses. I'll be with thee straight.
        [*Exit* BALTHASAR.]
Well, Juliet, I will lie with thee tonight.
Let's see for means. O mischief thou art swift
To enter in the thoughts of desperate men.
I do remember an apothecary,—
And hereabouts he dwells,—which late I noted
In tatter'd weeds, with overwhelming brows,
Culling of simples, meagre were his looks,
Sharp misery had worn him to the bones;
And in his needy shop a tortoise hung,
An alligator stuff'd, and other skins
Of ill-shaped fishes; and about his shelves
A beggarly account of empty boxes,
Green earthen pots, bladders, and musty seeds,

Remnants of packthread, and old cakes of roses
Were thinly scatter'd, to make up a show.
Noting this penury, to myself I said,
And if a man did need a poison now,
Whose sale is present death in Mantua,
Here lives a caitiff wretch would sell it him.
O, this same thought did but forerun my need,
And this same needy man must sell it me.
As I remember, this should be the house.
Being holiday, the beggar's shop is shut.
What, ho! Apothecary!
        Enter APOTHECARY.

APOTHECARY

Who calls so loud?

ROMEO

Come hither, man. I see that thou art poor.
Hold, there is forty ducats. Let me have
A dram of poison, such soon-speeding gear
As will disperse itself through all the veins,
That the life-weary taker may fall dead,
And that the trunk may be discharg'd of breath
As violently as hasty powder fir'd
Doth hurry from the fatal cannon's womb.

APOTHECARY

Such mortal drugs I have, but Mantua's law
Is death to any he that utters them.

ROMEO

Art thou so bare and full of wretchedness,
And fear'st to die? Famine is in thy cheeks,
Need and oppression starveth in thine eyes,
Contempt and beggary hangs upon thy back.
The world is not thy friend, nor the world's law;
The world affords no law to make thee rich;
Then be not poor, but break it and take this.

APOTHECARY

My poverty, but not my will consents.

ROMEO

I pay thy poverty, and not thy will.

APOTHECARY

Put this in any liquid thing you will
And drink it off; and, if you had the strength
Of twenty men, it would despatch you straight.

ROMEO

There is thy gold, worse poison to men's souls,
Doing more murder in this loathsome world
Than these poor compounds that thou mayst not sell.
I sell thee poison, thou hast sold me none.
Farewell, buy food, and get thyself in flesh.
Come, cordial and not poison, go with me
To Juliet's grave, for there must I use thee.
    [Exeunt.]

SCENE II. Friar Lawrence's Cell.

Enter FRIAR JOHN.

FRIAR JOHN

Holy Franciscan Friar! Brother, ho!
    Enter FRIAR LAWRENCE.

FRIAR LAWRENCE

This same should be the voice of Friar John.
Welcome from Mantua. What says Romeo?
Or, if his mind be writ, give me his letter.

FRIAR JOHN

Going to find a barefoot brother out,
One of our order, to associate me,
Here in this city visiting the sick,
And finding him, the searchers of the town,
Suspecting that we both were in a house
Where the infectious pestilence did reign,
Seal'd up the doors, and would not let us forth,
So that my speed to Mantua there was stay'd.

FRIAR LAWRENCE

Who bare my letter then to Romeo?

FRIAR JOHN

I could not send it,—here it is again,—
Nor get a messenger to bring it thee,
So fearful were they of infection.

FRIAR LAWRENCE

Unhappy fortune! By my brotherhood,
The letter was not nice, but full of charge,
Of dear import, and the neglecting it
May do much danger. Friar John, go hence,
Get me an iron crow and bring it straight
Unto my cell.

FRIAR JOHN

Brother, I'll go and bring it thee.
[Exit.]

FRIAR LAWRENCE

Now must I to the monument alone.
Within this three hours will fair Juliet wake.
She will beshrew me much that Romeo
Hath had no notice of these accidents;
But I will write again to Mantua,
And keep her at my cell till Romeo come.
Poor living corse, clos'd in a dead man's tomb.
[Exit.]

SCENE III. A churchyard; in it a Monument belonging to the Capulets.

Enter PARIS, and his PAGE bearing flowers and a torch.

PARIS

Give me thy torch, boy. Hence and stand aloof.
Yet put it out, for I would not be seen.
Under yond yew tree lay thee all along,
Holding thy ear close to the hollow ground;
So shall no foot upon the churchyard tread,

Being loose, unfirm, with digging up of graves,
But thou shalt hear it. Whistle then to me,
As signal that thou hear'st something approach.
Give me those flowers. Do as I bid thee, go.

PAGE

  [Aside.]
I am almost afraid to stand alone
Here in the churchyard; yet I will adventure.
  [Retires.]

PARIS

Sweet flower, with flowers thy bridal bed I strew.
O woe, thy canopy is dust and stones,
Which with sweet water nightly I will dew,
Or wanting that, with tears distill'd by moans.
The obsequies that I for thee will keep,
Nightly shall be to strew thy grave and weep.
  [The PAGE whistles.]
The boy gives warning something doth approach.
What cursed foot wanders this way tonight,
To cross my obsequies and true love's rite?
What, with a torch! Muffle me, night, awhile.
  [Retires.]
  Enter ROMEO and BALTHASAR with a torch, mattock, &c.

ROMEO

Give me that mattock and the wrenching iron.
Hold, take this letter; early in the morning
See thou deliver it to my lord and father.
Give me the light; upon thy life I charge thee,
Whate'er thou hear'st or seest, stand all aloof
And do not interrupt me in my course.
Why I descend into this bed of death
Is partly to behold my lady's face,
But chiefly to take thence from her dead finger
A precious ring, a ring that I must use
In dear employment. Therefore hence, be gone.
But if thou jealous dost return to pry
In what I further shall intend to do,

By heaven I will tear thee joint by joint,
And strew this hungry churchyard with thy limbs.
The time and my intents are savage-wild;
More fierce and more inexorable far
Than empty tigers or the roaring sea.

BALTHASAR

I will be gone, sir, and not trouble you.

ROMEO

So shalt thou show me friendship. Take thou that.
Live, and be prosperous, and farewell, good fellow.

BALTHASAR

For all this same, I'll hide me hereabout.
His looks I fear, and his intents I doubt.
[Retires.]

ROMEO

Thou detestable maw, thou womb of death,
Gorg'd with the dearest morsel of the earth,
Thus I enforce thy rotten jaws to open,
[Breaking open the door of the monument.]
And in despite, I'll cram thee with more food.

PARIS

This is that banish'd haughty Montague
That murder'd my love's cousin,—with which grief,
It is supposed, the fair creature died,—
And here is come to do some villanous shame
To the dead bodies. I will apprehend him.
[Advances.]
Stop thy unhallow'd toil, vile Montague.
Can vengeance be pursu'd further than death?
Condemned villain, I do apprehend thee.
Obey, and go with me, for thou must die.

ROMEO

I must indeed; and therefore came I hither.
Good gentle youth, tempt not a desperate man.
Fly hence and leave me. Think upon these gone;

Let them affright thee. I beseech thee, youth,
Put not another sin upon my head
By urging me to fury. O be gone.
By heaven I love thee better than myself;
For I come hither arm'd against myself.
Stay not, be gone, live, and hereafter say,
A madman's mercy bid thee run away.

PARIS

I do defy thy conjuration,
And apprehend thee for a felon here.

ROMEO

Wilt thou provoke me? Then have at thee, boy!
[They fight.]

PAGE

O lord, they fight! I will go call the watch.
[Exit.]

PARIS

O, I am slain!
[Falls.]
If thou be merciful,
Open the tomb, lay me with Juliet.
[Dies.]

ROMEO

In faith, I will. Let me peruse this face.
Mercutio's kinsman, noble County Paris!
What said my man, when my betossed soul
Did not attend him as we rode? I think
He told me Paris should have married Juliet.
Said he not so? Or did I dream it so?
Or am I mad, hearing him talk of Juliet,
To think it was so? O, give me thy hand,
One writ with me in sour misfortune's book.
I'll bury thee in a triumphant grave.
A grave? O no, a lantern, slaught'red youth,
For here lies Juliet, and her beauty makes
This vault a feasting presence full of light.

Death, lie thou there, by a dead man interr'd.
    [Laying PARIS in the monument.]
How oft when men are at the point of death
Have they been merry! Which their keepers call
A lightning before death. O, how may I
Call this a lightning? O my love, my wife,
Death that hath suck'd the honey of thy breath,
Hath had no power yet upon thy beauty.
Thou art not conquer'd. Beauty's ensign yet
Is crimson in thy lips and in thy cheeks,
And death's pale flag is not advanced there.
Tybalt, liest thou there in thy bloody sheet?
O, what more favour can I do to thee
Than with that hand that cut thy youth in twain
To sunder his that was thine enemy?
Forgive me, cousin. Ah, dear Juliet,
Why art thou yet so fair? Shall I believe
That unsubstantial death is amorous;
And that the lean abhorred monster keeps
Thee here in dark to be his paramour?
For fear of that I still will stay with thee,
And never from this palace of dim night
Depart again. Here, here will I remain
With worms that are thy chambermaids. O, here
Will I set up my everlasting rest;
And shake the yoke of inauspicious stars
From this world-wearied flesh. Eyes, look your last.
Arms, take your last embrace! And, lips, O you
The doors of breath, seal with a righteous kiss
A dateless bargain to engrossing death.
Come, bitter conduct, come, unsavoury guide.
Thou desperate pilot, now at once run on
The dashing rocks thy sea-sick weary bark.
Here's to my love! *[Drinks.]* O true apothecary!
Thy drugs are quick. Thus with a kiss I die.
    [Dies.]
    Enter, at the other end of the Churchyard, FRIAR LAWRENCE,
      with a lantern, crow and spade.

FRIAR LAWRENCE

Saint Francis be my speed. How oft tonight
Have my old feet stumbled at graves? Who's there?
Who is it that consorts, so late, the dead?

BALTHASAR

Here's one, a friend, and one that knows you well.

FRIAR LAWRENCE

Bliss be upon you. Tell me, good my friend,
What torch is yond that vainly lends his light
To grubs and eyeless skulls? As I discern,
It burneth in the Capels' monument.

BALTHASAR

It doth so, holy sir, and there's my master,
One that you love.

FRIAR LAWRENCE

Who is it?

BALTHASAR

Romeo.

FRIAR LAWRENCE

How long hath he been there?

BALTHASAR

Full half an hour.

FRIAR LAWRENCE

Go with me to the vault.

BALTHASAR

I dare not, sir;
My master knows not but I am gone hence,
And fearfully did menace me with death
If I did stay to look on his intents.

FRIAR LAWRENCE

Stay then, I'll go alone. Fear comes upon me.
O, much I fear some ill unlucky thing.

BALTHASAR

    As I did sleep under this yew tree here,
    I dreamt my master and another fought,
    And that my master slew him.

FRIAR LAWRENCE

    Romeo!
        [Advances.]
    Alack, alack, what blood is this which stains
    The stony entrance of this sepulchre?
    What mean these masterless and gory swords
    To lie discolour'd by this place of peace?
        [Enters the monument.]
    Romeo! O, pale! Who else? What, Paris too?
    And steep'd in blood? Ah what an unkind hour
    Is guilty of this lamentable chance?
    The lady stirs.
        [JULIET wakes and stirs.]

JULIET

    O comfortable Friar, where is my lord?
    I do remember well where I should be,
    And there I am. Where is my Romeo?
        [Noise within.]

FRIAR LAWRENCE

    I hear some noise. Lady, come from that nest
    Of death, contagion, and unnatural sleep.
    A greater power than we can contradict
    Hath thwarted our intents. Come, come away.
    Thy husband in thy bosom there lies dead;
    And Paris too. Come, I'll dispose of thee
    Among a sisterhood of holy nuns.
    Stay not to question, for the watch is coming.
    Come, go, good Juliet. I dare no longer stay.

JULIET

    Go, get thee hence, for I will not away.
        [Exit FRIAR LAWRENCE.]

What's here? A cup clos'd in my true love's hand?
Poison, I see, hath been his timeless end.
O churl. Drink all, and left no friendly drop
To help me after? I will kiss thy lips.
Haply some poison yet doth hang on them,
To make me die with a restorative.
  [Kisses him.]
Thy lips are warm!

FIRST WATCH
  [Within.]
Lead, boy. Which way?

JULIET
  Yea, noise? Then I'll be brief. O happy dagger.
  [Snatching ROMEO's dagger.]
This is thy sheath.
  [Stabs herself.]
There rest, and let me die.
  [Falls on ROMEO's body and dies.]
  Enter WATCH with the PAGE of PARIS.

PAGE
  This is the place. There, where the torch doth burn.

FIRST WATCH
  The ground is bloody. Search about the churchyard.
Go, some of you, whoe'er you find attach.
  [Exeunt some of the WATCH.]
Pitiful sight! Here lies the County slain,
And Juliet bleeding, warm, and newly dead,
Who here hath lain this two days buried.
Go tell the Prince; run to the Capulets.
Raise up the Montagues, some others search.
  [Exeunt others of the WATCH.]
We see the ground whereon these woes do lie,
But the true ground of all these piteous woes
We cannot without circumstance descry.
  Re-enter some of the WATCH with BALTHASAR.

SECOND WATCH

Here's Romeo's man. We found him in the churchyard.

FIRST WATCH

Hold him in safety till the Prince come hither.
Re-enter others of the WATCH with FRIAR LAWRENCE.

THIRD WATCH

Here is a Friar that trembles, sighs, and weeps.
We took this mattock and this spade from him
As he was coming from this churchyard side.

FIRST WATCH

A great suspicion. Stay the Friar too.
Enter the PRINCE and ATTENDANTS.

PRINCE

What misadventure is so early up,
That calls our person from our morning's rest?
Enter CAPULET, LADY CAPULET and others.

CAPULET

What should it be that they so shriek abroad?

LADY CAPULET

O the people in the street cry Romeo,
Some Juliet, and some Paris, and all run
With open outcry toward our monument.

PRINCE

What fear is this which startles in our ears?

FIRST WATCH

Sovereign, here lies the County Paris slain,
And Romeo dead, and Juliet, dead before,
Warm and new kill'd.

PRINCE

Search, seek, and know how this foul murder comes.

FIRST WATCH

Here is a Friar, and slaughter'd Romeo's man,
With instruments upon them fit to open
These dead men's tombs.

CAPULET

>O heaven! O wife, look how our daughter bleeds!
>This dagger hath mista'en, for lo, his house
>Is empty on the back of Montague,
>And it mis-sheathed in my daughter's bosom.

LADY CAPULET

>O me! This sight of death is as a bell
>That warns my old age to a sepulchre.
>>*Enter* MONTAGUE *and others.*

PRINCE

>Come, Montague, for thou art early up,
>To see thy son and heir more early down.

MONTAGUE

>Alas, my liege, my wife is dead tonight.
>Grief of my son's exile hath stopp'd her breath.
>What further woe conspires against mine age?

PRINCE

>Look, and thou shalt see.

MONTAGUE

>O thou untaught! What manners is in this,
>To press before thy father to a grave?

PRINCE

>Seal up the mouth of outrage for a while,
>Till we can clear these ambiguities,
>And know their spring, their head, their true descent,
>And then will I be general of your woes,
>And lead you even to death. Meantime forbear,
>And let mischance be slave to patience.
>Bring forth the parties of suspicion.

FRIAR LAWRENCE

>I am the greatest, able to do least,
>Yet most suspected, as the time and place
>Doth make against me, of this direful murder.
>And here I stand, both to impeach and purge
>Myself condemned and myself excus'd.

PRINCE

    Then say at once what thou dost know in this.

FRIAR LAWRENCE

    I will be brief, for my short date of breath
    Is not so long as is a tedious tale.
    Romeo, there dead, was husband to that Juliet,
    And she, there dead, that Romeo's faithful wife.
    I married them; and their stol'n marriage day
    Was Tybalt's doomsday, whose untimely death
    Banish'd the new-made bridegroom from this city;
    For whom, and not for Tybalt, Juliet pin'd.
    You, to remove that siege of grief from her,
    Betroth'd, and would have married her perforce
    To County Paris. Then comes she to me,
    And with wild looks, bid me devise some means
    To rid her from this second marriage,
    Or in my cell there would she kill herself.
    Then gave I her, so tutored by my art,
    A sleeping potion, which so took effect
    As I intended, for it wrought on her
    The form of death. Meantime I writ to Romeo
    That he should hither come as this dire night
    To help to take her from her borrow'd grave,
    Being the time the potion's force should cease.
    But he which bore my letter, Friar John,
    Was stay'd by accident; and yesternight
    Return'd my letter back. Then all alone
    At the prefixed hour of her waking
    Came I to take her from her kindred's vault,
    Meaning to keep her closely at my cell
    Till I conveniently could send to Romeo.
    But when I came, some minute ere the time
    Of her awaking, here untimely lay
    The noble Paris and true Romeo dead.
    She wakes; and I entreated her come forth
    And bear this work of heaven with patience.
    But then a noise did scare me from the tomb;

And she, too desperate, would not go with me,
But, as it seems, did violence on herself.
All this I know; and to the marriage
Her Nurse is privy. And if ought in this
Miscarried by my fault, let my old life
Be sacrific'd, some hour before his time,
Unto the rigour of severest law.

PRINCE

We still have known thee for a holy man.
Where's Romeo's man? What can he say to this?

BALTHASAR

I brought my master news of Juliet's death,
And then in post he came from Mantua
To this same place, to this same monument.
This letter he early bid me give his father,
And threaten'd me with death, going in the vault,
If I departed not, and left him there.

PRINCE

Give me the letter, I will look on it.
Where is the County's Page that rais'd the watch?
Sirrah, what made your master in this place?

PAGE

He came with flowers to strew his lady's grave,
And bid me stand aloof, and so I did.
Anon comes one with light to ope the tomb,
And by and by my master drew on him,
And then I ran away to call the watch.

PRINCE

This letter doth make good the Friar's words,
Their course of love, the tidings of her death.
And here he writes that he did buy a poison
Of a poor 'pothecary, and therewithal
Came to this vault to die, and lie with Juliet.
Where be these enemies? Capulet, Montague,
See what a scourge is laid upon your hate,

That heaven finds means to kill your joys with love!
And I, for winking at your discords too,
Have lost a brace of kinsmen. All are punish'd.

CAPULET

O brother Montague, give me thy hand.
This is my daughter's jointure, for no more
Can I demand.

MONTAGUE

But I can give thee more,
For I will raise her statue in pure gold,
That whiles Verona by that name is known,
There shall no figure at such rate be set
As that of true and faithful Juliet.

CAPULET

As rich shall Romeo's by his lady's lie,
Poor sacrifices of our enmity.

PRINCE

A glooming peace this morning with it brings;
The sun for sorrow will not show his head.
Go hence, to have more talk of these sad things.
Some shall be pardon'd, and some punished,
For never was a story of more woe
Than this of Juliet and her Romeo.
    [Exeunt.]

A MIDSUMMER
NIGHT'S DREAM

CONTENTS

DRAMATIS PERSONÆ

THESEUS, Duke of Athens
HIPPOLYTA, Queen of the Amazons, bethrothed to Theseus
EGEUS, Father to Hermia
HERMIA, daughter to Egeus, in love with Lysander
HELENA, in love with Demetrius
LYSANDER, in love with Hermia
DEMETRIUS, in love with Hermia
PHILOSTRATE, Master of the Revels to Theseus
QUINCE, the Carpenter
SNUG, the Joiner
BOTTOM, the Weaver
FLUTE, the Bellows-mender
SNOUT, the Tinker
STARVELING, the Tailor
OBERON, King of the Fairies
TITANIA, Queen of the Fairies
PUCK, or ROBIN GOODFELLOW, a Fairy
PEASEBLOSSOM, Fairy
COBWEB, Fairy
MOTH, Fairy
MUSTARDSEED, Fairy

PYRAMUS, THISBE, WALL, MOONSHINE, LION; Characters in
the Interlude performed by the Clowns
Other Fairies attending their King and Queen
Attendants on Theseus and Hippolyta

SCENE: Athens, and a wood not far from it.

ACT I

SCENE I. Athens. A room in the Palace of Theseus.

Enter THESEUS, HIPPOLYTA, PHILOSTRATE and ATTENDANTS.

THESEUS

Now, fair Hippolyta, our nuptial hour
Draws on apace; four happy days bring in
Another moon; but oh, methinks, how slow
This old moon wanes! She lingers my desires,
Like to a step-dame or a dowager,
Long withering out a young man's revenue.

HIPPOLYTA

Four days will quickly steep themselves in night;
Four nights will quickly dream away the time;
And then the moon, like to a silver bow
New bent in heaven, shall behold the night
Of our solemnities.

THESEUS

Go, Philostrate,
Stir up the Athenian youth to merriments;
Awake the pert and nimble spirit of mirth;
Turn melancholy forth to funerals;
The pale companion is not for our pomp.
    [Exit PHILOSTRATE.]
Hippolyta, I woo'd thee with my sword,

And won thy love doing thee injuries;
But I will wed thee in another key,
With pomp, with triumph, and with revelling.

Enter EGEUS, HERMIA, LYSANDER and DEMETRIUS.

EGEUS

Happy be Theseus, our renownèd Duke!

THESEUS

Thanks, good Egeus. What's the news with thee?

EGEUS

Full of vexation come I, with complaint
Against my child, my daughter Hermia.
Stand forth, Demetrius. My noble lord,
This man hath my consent to marry her.
Stand forth, Lysander. And, my gracious Duke,
This man hath bewitch'd the bosom of my child.
Thou, thou, Lysander, thou hast given her rhymes,
And interchang'd love-tokens with my child.
Thou hast by moonlight at her window sung,
With feigning voice, verses of feigning love;
And stol'n the impression of her fantasy
With bracelets of thy hair, rings, gauds, conceits,
Knacks, trifles, nosegays, sweetmeats (messengers
Of strong prevailment in unharden'd youth)
With cunning hast thou filch'd my daughter's heart,
Turn'd her obedience (which is due to me)
To stubborn harshness. And, my gracious Duke,
Be it so she will not here before your grace
Consent to marry with Demetrius,
I beg the ancient privilege of Athens:
As she is mine I may dispose of her;
Which shall be either to this gentleman
Or to her death, according to our law
Immediately provided in that case.

THESEUS

What say you, Hermia? Be advis'd, fair maid.
To you your father should be as a god;

One that compos'd your beauties, yea, and one
To whom you are but as a form in wax
By him imprinted, and within his power
To leave the figure, or disfigure it.
Demetrius is a worthy gentleman.

HERMIA
So is Lysander.

THESEUS
In himself he is.
But in this kind, wanting your father's voice,
The other must be held the worthier.

HERMIA
I would my father look'd but with my eyes.

THESEUS
Rather your eyes must with his judgment look.

HERMIA
I do entreat your Grace to pardon me.
I know not by what power I am made bold,
Nor how it may concern my modesty
In such a presence here to plead my thoughts:
But I beseech your Grace that I may know
The worst that may befall me in this case,
If I refuse to wed Demetrius.

THESEUS
Either to die the death, or to abjure
For ever the society of men.
Therefore, fair Hermia, question your desires,
Know of your youth, examine well your blood,
Whether, if you yield not to your father's choice,
You can endure the livery of a nun,
For aye to be in shady cloister mew'd,
To live a barren sister all your life,
Chanting faint hymns to the cold fruitless moon.
Thrice-blessèd they that master so their blood
To undergo such maiden pilgrimage,

But earthlier happy is the rose distill'd
Than that which, withering on the virgin thorn,
Grows, lives, and dies, in single blessedness.

HERMIA

So will I grow, so live, so die, my lord,
Ere I will yield my virgin patent up
Unto his lordship, whose unwishèd yoke
My soul consents not to give sovereignty.

THESEUS

Take time to pause; and by the next new moon
The sealing-day betwixt my love and me
For everlasting bond of fellowship,
Upon that day either prepare to die
For disobedience to your father's will,
Or else to wed Demetrius, as he would,
Or on Diana's altar to protest
For aye austerity and single life.

DEMETRIUS

Relent, sweet Hermia; and, Lysander, yield
Thy crazèd title to my certain right.

LYSANDER

You have her father's love, Demetrius.
Let me have Hermia's. Do you marry him.

EGEUS

Scornful Lysander, true, he hath my love;
And what is mine my love shall render him;
And she is mine, and all my right of her
I do estate unto Demetrius.

LYSANDER

I am, my lord, as well deriv'd as he,
As well possess'd; my love is more than his;
My fortunes every way as fairly rank'd,
If not with vantage, as Demetrius';
And, which is more than all these boasts can be,
I am belov'd of beauteous Hermia.

Why should not I then prosecute my right?
Demetrius, I'll avouch it to his head,
Made love to Nedar's daughter, Helena,
And won her soul; and she, sweet lady, dotes,
Devoutly dotes, dotes in idolatry,
Upon this spotted and inconstant man.

THESEUS

I must confess that I have heard so much,
And with Demetrius thought to have spoke thereof;
But, being over-full of self-affairs,
My mind did lose it.—But, Demetrius, come,
And come, Egeus; you shall go with me.
I have some private schooling for you both.—
For you, fair Hermia, look you arm yourself
To fit your fancies to your father's will,
Or else the law of Athens yields you up
(Which by no means we may extenuate)
To death, or to a vow of single life.
Come, my Hippolyta. What cheer, my love?
Demetrius and Egeus, go along;
I must employ you in some business
Against our nuptial, and confer with you
Of something nearly that concerns yourselves.

EGEUS

With duty and desire we follow you.
[Exeunt all but LYSANDER and HERMIA.]

LYSANDER

How now, my love? Why is your cheek so pale?
How chance the roses there do fade so fast?

HERMIA

Belike for want of rain, which I could well
Beteem them from the tempest of my eyes.

LYSANDER

Ay me! For aught that I could ever read,
Could ever hear by tale or history,

The course of true love never did run smooth.
But either it was different in blood—

HERMIA

O cross! Too high to be enthrall'd to low.

LYSANDER.

Or else misgraffèd in respect of years—

HERMIA

O spite! Too old to be engag'd to young.

LYSANDER

Or else it stood upon the choice of friends—

HERMIA

O hell! to choose love by another's eyes!

LYSANDER

Or, if there were a sympathy in choice,
War, death, or sickness did lay siege to it,
Making it momentany as a sound,
Swift as a shadow, short as any dream,
Brief as the lightning in the collied night
That, in a spleen, unfolds both heaven and earth,
And, ere a man hath power to say, 'Behold!'
The jaws of darkness do devour it up:
So quick bright things come to confusion.

HERMIA

If then true lovers have ever cross'd,
It stands as an edict in destiny.
Then let us teach our trial patience,
Because it is a customary cross,
As due to love as thoughts and dreams and sighs,
Wishes and tears, poor fancy's followers.

LYSANDER

A good persuasion; therefore, hear me, Hermia.
I have a widow aunt, a dowager
Of great revenue, and she hath no child.
From Athens is her house remote seven leagues,

And she respects me as her only son.
There, gentle Hermia, may I marry thee,
And to that place the sharp Athenian law
Cannot pursue us. If thou lovest me then,
Steal forth thy father's house tomorrow night;
And in the wood, a league without the town
(Where I did meet thee once with Helena
To do observance to a morn of May),
There will I stay for thee.

HERMIA

My good Lysander!
I swear to thee by Cupid's strongest bow,
By his best arrow with the golden head,
By the simplicity of Venus' doves,
By that which knitteth souls and prospers loves,
And by that fire which burn'd the Carthage queen
When the false Trojan under sail was seen,
By all the vows that ever men have broke
(In number more than ever women spoke),
In that same place thou hast appointed me,
Tomorrow truly will I meet with thee.

LYSANDER

Keep promise, love. Look, here comes Helena.
Enter HELENA.

HERMIA

God speed fair Helena! Whither away?

HELENA

Call you me fair? That fair again unsay.
Demetrius loves your fair. O happy fair!
Your eyes are lode-stars and your tongue's sweet air
More tuneable than lark to shepherd's ear,
When wheat is green, when hawthorn buds appear.
Sickness is catching. O were favour so,
Yours would I catch, fair Hermia, ere I go.
My ear should catch your voice, my eye your eye,

My tongue should catch your tongue's sweet melody.
Were the world mine, Demetrius being bated,
The rest I'd give to be to you translated.
O, teach me how you look, and with what art
You sway the motion of Demetrius' heart!

HERMIA

I frown upon him, yet he loves me still.

HELENA

O that your frowns would teach my smiles such skill!

HERMIA

I give him curses, yet he gives me love.

HELENA

O that my prayers could such affection move!

HERMIA

The more I hate, the more he follows me.

HELENA

The more I love, the more he hateth me.

HERMIA

His folly, Helena, is no fault of mine.

HELENA

None but your beauty; would that fault were mine!

HERMIA

Take comfort: he no more shall see my face;
Lysander and myself will fly this place.
Before the time I did Lysander see,
Seem'd Athens as a paradise to me.
O, then, what graces in my love do dwell,
That he hath turn'd a heaven into hell!

LYSANDER

Helen, to you our minds we will unfold:
Tomorrow night, when Phoebe doth behold
Her silver visage in the watery glass,

Decking with liquid pearl the bladed grass
(A time that lovers' flights doth still conceal),
Through Athens' gates have we devis'd to steal.

HERMIA

And in the wood where often you and I
Upon faint primrose beds were wont to lie,
Emptying our bosoms of their counsel sweet,
There my Lysander and myself shall meet,
And thence from Athens turn away our eyes,
To seek new friends and stranger companies.
Farewell, sweet playfellow. Pray thou for us,
And good luck grant thee thy Demetrius!
Keep word, Lysander. We must starve our sight
From lovers' food, till morrow deep midnight.

LYSANDER

I will, my Hermia.
        [Exit HERMIA.]
Helena, adieu.
As you on him, Demetrius dote on you!
        [Exit LYSANDER.]

HELENA

How happy some o'er other some can be!
Through Athens I am thought as fair as she.
But what of that? Demetrius thinks not so;
He will not know what all but he do know.
And as he errs, doting on Hermia's eyes,
So I, admiring of his qualities.
Things base and vile, holding no quantity,
Love can transpose to form and dignity.
Love looks not with the eyes, but with the mind;
And therefore is wing'd Cupid painted blind.
Nor hath love's mind of any judgment taste.
Wings, and no eyes, figure unheedy haste.
And therefore is love said to be a child,
Because in choice he is so oft beguil'd.
As waggish boys in game themselves forswear,

So the boy Love is perjur'd everywhere.
For, ere Demetrius look'd on Hermia's eyne,
He hail'd down oaths that he was only mine;
And when this hail some heat from Hermia felt,
So he dissolv'd, and showers of oaths did melt.
I will go tell him of fair Hermia's flight.
Then to the wood will he tomorrow night
Pursue her; and for this intelligence
If I have thanks, it is a dear expense.
But herein mean I to enrich my pain,
To have his sight thither and back again.
        [Exit HELENA.]

SCENE II. The Same. A Room in a Cottage.

Enter QUINCE, SNUG, BOTTOM, FLUTE, SNOUT and STARVELING.

QUINCE
Is all our company here?

BOTTOM
You were best to call them generally, man by man, according to the scrip.

QUINCE
Here is the scroll of every man's name, which is thought fit through all Athens, to play in our interlude before the Duke and Duchess, on his wedding-day at night.

BOTTOM
First, good Peter Quince, say what the play treats on; then read the names of the actors; and so grow to a point.

QUINCE
Marry, our play is *The most lamentable comedy and most cruel death of Pyramus and Thisbe.*

BOTTOM
A very good piece of work, I assure you, and a merry. Now, good Peter Quince, call forth your actors by the scroll. Masters, spread yourselves.

QUINCE

Answer, as I call you. Nick Bottom, the weaver.

BOTTOM

Ready. Name what part I am for, and proceed.

QUINCE

You, Nick Bottom, are set down for Pyramus.

BOTTOM

What is Pyramus—a lover, or a tyrant?

QUINCE

A lover, that kills himself most gallantly for love.

BOTTOM

That will ask some tears in the true performing of it. If I do it, let the audience look to their eyes. I will move storms; I will condole in some measure. To the rest—yet my chief humour is for a tyrant. I could play Ercles rarely, or a part to tear a cat in, to make all split.

The raging rocks
And shivering shocks
Shall break the locks
Of prison gates,
And Phibbus' car
Shall shine from far,
And make and mar
The foolish Fates.

This was lofty. Now name the rest of the players. This is Ercles' vein, a tyrant's vein; a lover is more condoling.

QUINCE

Francis Flute, the bellows-mender.

FLUTE

Here, Peter Quince.

QUINCE

Flute, you must take Thisbe on you.

FLUTE

What is Thisbe? A wandering knight?

QUINCE

It is the lady that Pyramus must love.

FLUTE

Nay, faith, let not me play a woman. I have a beard coming.

QUINCE

That's all one. You shall play it in a mask, and you may speak as small as you will.

BOTTOM

And I may hide my face, let me play Thisbe too. I'll speak in a monstrous little voice; 'Thisne, Thisne!'—'Ah, Pyramus, my lover dear! thy Thisbe dear! and lady dear!'

QUINCE

No, no, you must play Pyramus; and, Flute, you Thisbe.

BOTTOM

Well, proceed.

QUINCE

Robin Starveling, the tailor.

STARVELING

Here, Peter Quince.

QUINCE

Robin Starveling, you must play Thisbe's mother.
Tom Snout, the tinker.

SNOUT

Here, Peter Quince.

QUINCE

You, Pyramus' father; myself, Thisbe's father;
Snug, the joiner, you, the lion's part. And, I hope here is a play fitted.

SNUG

Have you the lion's part written? Pray you, if it be, give it me, for I am slow of study.

QUINCE

You may do it extempore, for it is nothing but roaring.

BOTTOM

Let me play the lion too. I will roar that I will do any man's heart good to hear me. I will roar that I will make the Duke say 'Let him roar again, let him roar again.'

QUINCE

If you should do it too terribly, you would fright the Duchess and the ladies, that they would shriek; and that were enough to hang us all.

ALL

That would hang us every mother's son.

BOTTOM

I grant you, friends, if you should fright the ladies out of their wits, they would have no more discretion but to hang us. But I will aggravate my voice so, that I will roar you as gently as any sucking dove; I will roar you an 'twere any nightingale.

QUINCE

You can play no part but Pyramus, for Pyramus is a sweet-faced man; a proper man as one shall see in a summer's day; a most lovely gentleman-like man. Therefore you must needs play Pyramus.

BOTTOM

Well, I will undertake it. What beard were I best to play it in?

QUINCE

Why, what you will.

BOTTOM

I will discharge it in either your straw-colour beard, your orange-tawny beard, your purple-in-grain beard, or your French-crown-colour beard, your perfect yellow.

QUINCE

Some of your French crowns have no hair at all, and then you will play bare-faced. But, masters, here are your parts, and I am to entreat you, request you, and desire you, to con them by tomorrow night; and meet me in the palace wood, a mile without the town, by moonlight;

there will we rehearse, for if we meet in the city, we shall be dogg'd with company, and our devices known. In the meantime I will draw a bill of properties, such as our play wants. I pray you fail me not.

BOTTOM

We will meet, and there we may rehearse most obscenely and courageously. Take pains, be perfect; adieu.

QUINCE

At the Duke's oak we meet.

BOTTOM

Enough. Hold, or cut bow-strings.
[Exeunt.]

ACT II

SCENE I. A wood near Athens.

Enter a FAIRY at one door, and PUCK at another.

PUCK

    How now, spirit! Whither wander you?

FAIRY

    Over hill, over dale,
    Thorough bush, thorough brier,
    Over park, over pale,
    Thorough flood, thorough fire,
    I do wander everywhere,
    Swifter than the moon's sphere;
    And I serve the Fairy Queen,
    To dew her orbs upon the green.
    The cowslips tall her pensioners be,
    In their gold coats spots you see;
    Those be rubies, fairy favours,
    In those freckles live their savours.
    I must go seek some dew-drops here,
    And hang a pearl in every cowslip's ear.
    Farewell, thou lob of spirits; I'll be gone.
    Our Queen and all her elves come here anon.

PUCK

    The King doth keep his revels here tonight;

Take heed the Queen come not within his sight,
For Oberon is passing fell and wrath,
Because that she, as her attendant, hath
A lovely boy, stol'n from an Indian king;
She never had so sweet a changeling.
And jealous Oberon would have the child
Knight of his train, to trace the forests wild:
But she perforce withholds the lovèd boy,
Crowns him with flowers, and makes him all her joy.
And now they never meet in grove or green,
By fountain clear, or spangled starlight sheen,
But they do square; that all their elves for fear
Creep into acorn cups, and hide them there.

FAIRY

Either I mistake your shape and making quite,
Or else you are that shrewd and knavish sprite
Call'd Robin Goodfellow. Are not you he
That frights the maidens of the villagery,
Skim milk, and sometimes labour in the quern,
And bootless make the breathless housewife churn,
And sometime make the drink to bear no barm,
Mislead night-wanderers, laughing at their harm?
Those that Hobgoblin call you, and sweet Puck,
You do their work, and they shall have good luck.
Are not you he?

PUCK

Thou speak'st aright;
I am that merry wanderer of the night.
I jest to Oberon, and make him smile,
When I a fat and bean-fed horse beguile,
Neighing in likeness of a filly foal;
And sometime lurk I in a gossip's bowl
In very likeness of a roasted crab,
And, when she drinks, against her lips I bob,
And on her withered dewlap pour the ale.
The wisest aunt, telling the saddest tale,
Sometime for three-foot stool mistaketh me;

Then slip I from her bum, down topples she,
And 'tailor' cries, and falls into a cough;
And then the whole quire hold their hips and loffe
And waxen in their mirth, and neeze, and swear
A merrier hour was never wasted there.
But room, fairy. Here comes Oberon.

FAIRY

And here my mistress. Would that he were gone!
Enter OBERON at one door, with his Train, and TITANIA at
another, with hers.

OBERON

Ill met by moonlight, proud Titania.

TITANIA

What, jealous Oberon! Fairies, skip hence;
I have forsworn his bed and company.

OBERON

Tarry, rash wanton; am not I thy lord?

TITANIA

Then I must be thy lady; but I know
When thou hast stol'n away from fairyland,
And in the shape of Corin sat all day
Playing on pipes of corn, and versing love
To amorous Phillida. Why art thou here,
Come from the farthest steep of India,
But that, forsooth, the bouncing Amazon,
Your buskin'd mistress and your warrior love,
To Theseus must be wedded; and you come
To give their bed joy and prosperity?

OBERON

How canst thou thus, for shame, Titania,
Glance at my credit with Hippolyta,
Knowing I know thy love to Theseus?
Didst not thou lead him through the glimmering night
From Perigenia, whom he ravished?

And make him with fair Aegles break his faith,
With Ariadne and Antiopa?

TITANIA

These are the forgeries of jealousy:
And never, since the middle summer's spring,
Met we on hill, in dale, forest, or mead,
By pavèd fountain, or by rushy brook,
Or on the beachèd margent of the sea,
To dance our ringlets to the whistling wind,
But with thy brawls thou hast disturb'd our sport.
Therefore the winds, piping to us in vain,
As in revenge, have suck'd up from the sea
Contagious fogs; which, falling in the land,
Hath every pelting river made so proud
That they have overborne their continents.
The ox hath therefore stretch'd his yoke in vain,
The ploughman lost his sweat, and the green corn
Hath rotted ere his youth attain'd a beard.
The fold stands empty in the drownèd field,
And crows are fatted with the murrion flock;
The nine-men's-morris is fill'd up with mud,
And the quaint mazes in the wanton green,
For lack of tread, are undistinguishable.
The human mortals want their winter here.
No night is now with hymn or carol blest.
Therefore the moon, the governess of floods,
Pale in her anger, washes all the air,
That rheumatic diseases do abound.
And thorough this distemperature we see
The seasons alter: hoary-headed frosts
Fall in the fresh lap of the crimson rose;
And on old Hiems' thin and icy crown
An odorous chaplet of sweet summer buds
Is, as in mockery, set. The spring, the summer,
The childing autumn, angry winter, change
Their wonted liveries; and the mazed world,
By their increase, now knows not which is which.

And this same progeny of evils comes
From our debate, from our dissension;
We are their parents and original.

OBERON

Do you amend it, then. It lies in you.
Why should Titania cross her Oberon?
I do but beg a little changeling boy
To be my henchman.

TITANIA

Set your heart at rest;
The fairyland buys not the child of me.
His mother was a vot'ress of my order,
And in the spicèd Indian air, by night,
Full often hath she gossip'd by my side;
And sat with me on Neptune's yellow sands,
Marking th' embarkèd traders on the flood,
When we have laugh'd to see the sails conceive,
And grow big-bellied with the wanton wind;
Which she, with pretty and with swimming gait
Following (her womb then rich with my young squire),
Would imitate, and sail upon the land,
To fetch me trifles, and return again,
As from a voyage, rich with merchandise.
But she, being mortal, of that boy did die;
And for her sake do I rear up her boy,
And for her sake I will not part with him.

OBERON

How long within this wood intend you stay?

TITANIA

Perchance till after Theseus' wedding-day.
If you will patiently dance in our round,
And see our moonlight revels, go with us;
If not, shun me, and I will spare your haunts.

OBERON

Give me that boy and I will go with thee.

TITANIA

>Not for thy fairy kingdom. Fairies, away.
>We shall chide downright if I longer stay.
>*[Exit TITANIA with her Train.]*

OBERON

>Well, go thy way. Thou shalt not from this grove
>Till I torment thee for this injury.—
>My gentle Puck, come hither. Thou rememb'rest
>Since once I sat upon a promontory,
>And heard a mermaid on a dolphin's back
>Uttering such dulcet and harmonious breath
>That the rude sea grew civil at her song
>And certain stars shot madly from their spheres
>To hear the sea-maid's music.

PUCK

>I remember.

OBERON

>That very time I saw, (but thou couldst not),
>Flying between the cold moon and the earth,
>Cupid all arm'd: a certain aim he took
>At a fair vestal, thronèd by the west,
>And loos'd his love-shaft smartly from his bow
>As it should pierce a hundred thousand hearts.
>But I might see young Cupid's fiery shaft
>Quench'd in the chaste beams of the watery moon;
>And the imperial votress passed on,
>In maiden meditation, fancy-free.
>Yet mark'd I where the bolt of Cupid fell:
>It fell upon a little western flower,
>Before milk-white, now purple with love's wound,
>And maidens call it love-in-idleness.
>Fetch me that flower, the herb I showed thee once:
>The juice of it on sleeping eyelids laid
>Will make or man or woman madly dote
>Upon the next live creature that it sees.
>Fetch me this herb, and be thou here again
>Ere the leviathan can swim a league.

PUCK

> I'll put a girdle round about the earth
> In forty minutes.
> > *[Exit PUCK.]*

OBERON

> Having once this juice,
> I'll watch Titania when she is asleep,
> And drop the liquor of it in her eyes:
> The next thing then she waking looks upon
> (Be it on lion, bear, or wolf, or bull,
> On meddling monkey, or on busy ape)
> She shall pursue it with the soul of love.
> And ere I take this charm from off her sight
> (As I can take it with another herb)
> I'll make her render up her page to me.
> But who comes here? I am invisible;
> And I will overhear their conference.
> > *Enter DEMETRIUS, HELENA following him.*

DEMETRIUS

> I love thee not, therefore pursue me not.
> Where is Lysander and fair Hermia?
> The one I'll slay, the other slayeth me.
> Thou told'st me they were stol'n into this wood,
> And here am I, and wode within this wood
> Because I cannot meet with Hermia.
> Hence, get thee gone, and follow me no more.

HELENA

> You draw me, you hard-hearted adamant,
> But yet you draw not iron, for my heart
> Is true as steel. Leave you your power to draw,
> And I shall have no power to follow you.

DEMETRIUS

> Do I entice you? Do I speak you fair?
> Or rather do I not in plainest truth
> Tell you I do not, nor I cannot love you?

HELENA

And even for that do I love you the more.
I am your spaniel; and, Demetrius,
The more you beat me, I will fawn on you.
Use me but as your spaniel, spurn me, strike me,
Neglect me, lose me; only give me leave,
Unworthy as I am, to follow you.
What worser place can I beg in your love,
(And yet a place of high respect with me)
Than to be usèd as you use your dog?

DEMETRIUS

Tempt not too much the hatred of my spirit;
For I am sick when I do look on thee.

HELENA

And I am sick when I look not on you.

DEMETRIUS

You do impeach your modesty too much
To leave the city and commit yourself
Into the hands of one that loves you not,
To trust the opportunity of night.
And the ill counsel of a desert place,
With the rich worth of your virginity.

HELENA

Your virtue is my privilege: for that.
It is not night when I do see your face,
Therefore I think I am not in the night;
Nor doth this wood lack worlds of company,
For you, in my respect, are all the world.
Then how can it be said I am alone
When all the world is here to look on me?

DEMETRIUS

I'll run from thee and hide me in the brakes,
And leave thee to the mercy of wild beasts.

HELENA

The wildest hath not such a heart as you.
Run when you will, the story shall be chang'd;
Apollo flies, and Daphne holds the chase;
The dove pursues the griffin, the mild hind
Makes speed to catch the tiger. Bootless speed,
When cowardice pursues and valour flies!

DEMETRIUS

I will not stay thy questions. Let me go,
Or if thou follow me, do not believe
But I shall do thee mischief in the wood.

HELENA

Ay, in the temple, in the town, the field,
You do me mischief. Fie, Demetrius!
Your wrongs do set a scandal on my sex.
We cannot fight for love as men may do.
We should be woo'd, and were not made to woo.
    [Exit DEMETRIUS.]
I'll follow thee, and make a heaven of hell,
To die upon the hand I love so well.
    [Exit HELENA.]

OBERON

Fare thee well, nymph. Ere he do leave this grove,
Thou shalt fly him, and he shall seek thy love.
    Enter PUCK.
Hast thou the flower there? Welcome, wanderer.

PUCK

Ay, there it is.

OBERON

I pray thee give it me.
I know a bank where the wild thyme blows,
Where oxlips and the nodding violet grows,
Quite over-canopied with luscious woodbine,
With sweet musk-roses, and with eglantine.
There sleeps Titania sometime of the night,
Lull'd in these flowers with dances and delight;

And there the snake throws her enamell'd skin,
Weed wide enough to wrap a fairy in.
And with the juice of this I'll streak her eyes,
And make her full of hateful fantasies.
Take thou some of it, and seek through this grove:
A sweet Athenian lady is in love
With a disdainful youth. Anoint his eyes;
But do it when the next thing he espies
May be the lady. Thou shalt know the man
By the Athenian garments he hath on.
Effect it with some care, that he may prove
More fond on her than she upon her love:
And look thou meet me ere the first cock crow.

PUCK

Fear not, my lord, your servant shall do so.
    [Exeunt.]

SCENE II. Another part of the wood.

Enter TITANIA with her Train.

TITANIA

Come, now a roundel and a fairy song;
Then for the third part of a minute, hence;
Some to kill cankers in the musk-rose buds;
Some war with reremice for their leathern wings,
To make my small elves coats; and some keep back
The clamorous owl, that nightly hoots and wonders
At our quaint spirits. Sing me now asleep;
Then to your offices, and let me rest.
    [FAIRIES sing.]

FIRST FAIRY

You spotted snakes with double tongue,
Thorny hedgehogs, be not seen;
Newts and blind-worms do no wrong,
Come not near our Fairy Queen:

CHORUS

> Philomel, with melody,
> Sing in our sweet lullaby:
> Lulla, lulla, lullaby; lulla, lulla, lullaby.
> Never harm, nor spell, nor charm,
> Come our lovely lady nigh;
> So good night, with lullaby.

FIRST FAIRY

> Weaving spiders, come not here;
> Hence, you long-legg'd spinners, hence.
> Beetles black, approach not near;
> Worm nor snail do no offence.

CHORUS

> *[Philomel with melody, &c.]*

SECOND FAIRY

> Hence away! Now all is well.
> One aloof stand sentinel.
> > *[Exeunt FAIRIES. TITANIA sleeps.]*
> > *Enter OBERON.*

OBERON

> What thou seest when thou dost wake,
> > *[Squeezes the flower on TITANIA'S eyelids.]*
> Do it for thy true love take;
> Love and languish for his sake.
> Be it ounce, or cat, or bear,
> Pard, or boar with bristled hair,
> In thy eye that shall appear
> When thou wak'st, it is thy dear.
> Wake when some vile thing is near.
> > *[Exit.]*
> > *Enter LYSANDER and HERMIA.*

LYSANDER

> Fair love, you faint with wand'ring in the wood.
> And, to speak troth, I have forgot our way.
> We'll rest us, Hermia, if you think it good,
> And tarry for the comfort of the day.

HERMIA

> Be it so, Lysander: find you out a bed,
> For I upon this bank will rest my head.

LYSANDER

> One turf shall serve as pillow for us both;
> One heart, one bed, two bosoms, and one troth.

HERMIA

> Nay, good Lysander; for my sake, my dear,
> Lie further off yet, do not lie so near.

LYSANDER

> O take the sense, sweet, of my innocence!
> Love takes the meaning in love's conference.
> I mean that my heart unto yours is knit,
> So that but one heart we can make of it:
> Two bosoms interchainèd with an oath,
> So then two bosoms and a single troth.
> Then by your side no bed-room me deny;
> For lying so, Hermia, I do not lie.

HERMIA

> Lysander riddles very prettily.
> Now much beshrew my manners and my pride,
> If Hermia meant to say Lysander lied!
> But, gentle friend, for love and courtesy
> Lie further off, in human modesty,
> Such separation as may well be said
> Becomes a virtuous bachelor and a maid,
> So far be distant; and good night, sweet friend:
> Thy love ne'er alter till thy sweet life end!

LYSANDER

> Amen, amen, to that fair prayer say I;
> And then end life when I end loyalty!
> Here is my bed. Sleep give thee all his rest!

HERMIA

> With half that wish the wisher's eyes be pressed!

[They sleep.]
Enter PUCK.

PUCK

    Through the forest have I gone,
    But Athenian found I none,
    On whose eyes I might approve
    This flower's force in stirring love.
    Night and silence! Who is here?
    Weeds of Athens he doth wear:
    This is he, my master said,
    Despisèd the Athenian maid;
    And here the maiden, sleeping sound,
    On the dank and dirty ground.
    Pretty soul, she durst not lie
    Near this lack-love, this kill-courtesy.
    Churl, upon thy eyes I throw
    All the power this charm doth owe;
    When thou wak'st let love forbid
    Sleep his seat on thy eyelid.
    So awake when I am gone;
    For I must now to Oberon.
        [Exit.]
    Enter DEMETRIUS *and* HELENA, *running.*

HELENA

    Stay, though thou kill me, sweet Demetrius.

DEMETRIUS

    I charge thee, hence, and do not haunt me thus.

HELENA

    O, wilt thou darkling leave me? Do not so.

DEMETRIUS

    Stay, on thy peril; I alone will go.
        [Exit DEMETRIUS.*]*

HELENA

    O, I am out of breath in this fond chase!
    The more my prayer, the lesser is my grace.

Happy is Hermia, wheresoe'er she lies,
For she hath blessèd and attractive eyes.
How came her eyes so bright? Not with salt tears.
If so, my eyes are oftener wash'd than hers.
No, no, I am as ugly as a bear,
For beasts that meet me run away for fear:
Therefore no marvel though Demetrius
Do, as a monster, fly my presence thus.
What wicked and dissembling glass of mine
Made me compare with Hermia's sphery eyne?
But who is here? Lysander, on the ground!
Dead or asleep? I see no blood, no wound.
Lysander, if you live, good sir, awake.

LYSANDER

    [Waking.]
And run through fire I will for thy sweet sake.
Transparent Helena! Nature shows art,
That through thy bosom makes me see thy heart.
Where is Demetrius? O, how fit a word
Is that vile name to perish on my sword!

HELENA

Do not say so, Lysander, say not so.
What though he love your Hermia? Lord, what though?
Yet Hermia still loves you. Then be content.

LYSANDER

Content with Hermia? No, I do repent
The tedious minutes I with her have spent.
Not Hermia, but Helena I love.
Who will not change a raven for a dove?
The will of man is by his reason sway'd,
And reason says you are the worthier maid.
Things growing are not ripe until their season;
So I, being young, till now ripe not to reason;
And touching now the point of human skill,
Reason becomes the marshal to my will,
And leads me to your eyes, where I o'erlook
Love's stories, written in love's richest book.

HELENA

Wherefore was I to this keen mockery born?
When at your hands did I deserve this scorn?
Is't not enough, is't not enough, young man,
That I did never, no, nor never can
Deserve a sweet look from Demetrius' eye,
But you must flout my insufficiency?
Good troth, you do me wrong, good sooth, you do,
In such disdainful manner me to woo.
But fare you well; perforce I must confess,
I thought you lord of more true gentleness.
O, that a lady of one man refus'd,
Should of another therefore be abus'd!
　　　[Exit.]

LYSANDER

She sees not Hermia. Hermia, sleep thou there,
And never mayst thou come Lysander near!
For, as a surfeit of the sweetest things
The deepest loathing to the stomach brings;
Or as the heresies that men do leave
Are hated most of those they did deceive;
So thou, my surfeit and my heresy,
Of all be hated, but the most of me!
And, all my powers, address your love and might
To honour Helen, and to be her knight!
　　　[Exit.]

HERMIA

　　　[Starting.]
Help me, Lysander, help me! Do thy best
To pluck this crawling serpent from my breast!
Ay me, for pity! What a dream was here!
Lysander, look how I do quake with fear.
Methought a serpent eat my heart away,
And you sat smiling at his cruel prey.
Lysander! What, removed? Lysander! lord!
What, out of hearing? Gone? No sound, no word?
Alack, where are you? Speak, and if you hear;

Speak, of all loves! I swoon almost with fear.
No? Then I well perceive you are not nigh.
Either death or you I'll find immediately.
     [Exit.]

ACT III

SCENE I. The Wood.

The Queen of Fairies still lying asleep.
Enter BOTTOM, QUINCE, SNOUT, STARVELING, SNUG and FLUTE.

BOTTOM

Are we all met?

QUINCE

Pat, pat; and here's a marvellous convenient place for our rehearsal. This green plot shall be our stage, this hawthorn brake our tiring-house; and we will do it in action, as we will do it before the Duke.

BOTTOM

Peter Quince?

QUINCE

What sayest thou, bully Bottom?

BOTTOM

There are things in this comedy of Pyramus and Thisbe that will never please. First, Pyramus must draw a sword to kill himself; which the ladies cannot abide. How answer you that?

SNOUT

By'r lakin, a parlous fear.

STARVELING

I believe we must leave the killing out, when all is done.

BOTTOM

Not a whit; I have a device to make all well. Write me a prologue, and let the prologue seem to say we will do no harm with our swords, and that Pyramus is not killed indeed; and for the more better assurance, tell them that I Pyramus am not Pyramus but Bottom the weaver. This will put them out of fear.

QUINCE

Well, we will have such a prologue; and it shall be written in eight and six.

BOTTOM

No, make it two more; let it be written in eight and eight.

SNOUT

Will not the ladies be afeard of the lion?

STARVELING

I fear it, I promise you.

BOTTOM

Masters, you ought to consider with yourselves, to bring in (God shield us!) a lion among ladies is a most dreadful thing. For there is not a more fearful wild-fowl than your lion living; and we ought to look to it.

SNOUT

Therefore another prologue must tell he is not a lion.

BOTTOM

Nay, you must name his name, and half his face must be seen through the lion's neck; and he himself must speak through, saying thus, or to the same defect: 'Ladies,' or, 'Fair ladies, I would wish you,' or, 'I would request you,' or, 'I would entreat you, not to fear, not to tremble: my life for yours. If you think I come hither as a lion, it were pity of my life. No, I am no such thing; I am a man as other men are': and there, indeed, let him name his name, and tell them plainly he is Snug the joiner.

QUINCE

Well, it shall be so. But there is two hard things: that is, to bring the moonlight into a chamber, for you know, Pyramus and Thisbe meet by moonlight.

SNOUT

Doth the moon shine that night we play our play?

BOTTOM

A calendar, a calendar! Look in the almanack; find out moonshine, find out moonshine.

QUINCE

Yes, it doth shine that night.

BOTTOM

Why, then may you leave a casement of the great chamber window, where we play, open; and the moon may shine in at the casement.

QUINCE

Ay; or else one must come in with a bush of thorns and a lantern, and say he comes to disfigure or to present the person of Moonshine. Then there is another thing: we must have a wall in the great chamber; for Pyramus and Thisbe, says the story, did talk through the chink of a wall.

SNOUT

You can never bring in a wall. What say you, Bottom?

BOTTOM

Some man or other must present Wall. And let him have some plaster, or some loam, or some rough-cast about him, to signify wall; and let him hold his fingers thus, and through that cranny shall Pyramus and Thisbe whisper.

QUINCE

If that may be, then all is well. Come, sit down, every mother's son, and rehearse your parts. Pyramus, you begin: when you have spoken your speech, enter into that brake; and so everyone according to his cue.

Enter PUCK behind.

PUCK

What hempen homespuns have we swaggering here,
So near the cradle of the Fairy Queen?
What, a play toward? I'll be an auditor;
An actor too perhaps, if I see cause.

QUINCE

Speak, Pyramus.—Thisbe, stand forth.

PYRAMUS

Thisbe, the flowers of odious savours sweet

QUINCE

Odours, odours.

PYRAMUS

—odours savours sweet.
So hath thy breath, my dearest Thisbe dear.
But hark, a voice! Stay thou but here awhile,
And by and by I will to thee appear.
[Exit.]

PUCK

A stranger Pyramus than e'er played here!
[Exit.]

THISBE

Must I speak now?

QUINCE

Ay, marry, must you, For you must understand he goes but to see a noise that he heard, and is to come again.

THISBE

Most radiant Pyramus, most lily-white of hue,
Of colour like the red rose on triumphant brier,
Most brisky juvenal, and eke most lovely Jew,
As true as truest horse, that yet would never tire,
I'll meet thee, Pyramus, at Ninny's tomb.

QUINCE

Ninus' tomb, man! Why, you must not speak that yet. That you answer to Pyramus. You speak all your part at once, cues, and all.— Pyramus enter! Your cue is past; it is 'never tire.'

THISBE

O, *As true as truest horse, that yet would never tire.*
Enter PUCK *and* BOTTOM *with an ass's head.*

PYRAMUS

> *If I were fair, Thisbe, I were only thine.*

QUINCE

> O monstrous! O strange! We are haunted. Pray, masters, fly, masters! Help!
>> *[Exeunt Clowns.]*

PUCK

> I'll follow you. I'll lead you about a round,
> Through bog, through bush, through brake, through brier;
> Sometime a horse I'll be, sometime a hound,
> A hog, a headless bear, sometime a fire;
> And neigh, and bark, and grunt, and roar, and burn,
> Like horse, hound, hog, bear, fire, at every turn.
>> *[Exit.]*

BOTTOM

> Why do they run away? This is a knavery of them to make me afeard.
>> *Enter SNOUT.*

SNOUT

> O Bottom, thou art changed! What do I see on thee?

BOTTOM

> What do you see? You see an ass-head of your own, do you?
>> *[Exit SNOUT.]*
>> *Enter QUINCE.*

QUINCE

> Bless thee, Bottom! bless thee! Thou art translated.
>> *[Exit.]*

BOTTOM

> I see their knavery. This is to make an ass of me, to fright me, if they could. But I will not stir from this place, do what they can. I will walk up and down here, and I will sing, that they shall hear I am not afraid.
>> *[Sings.]*
> The ousel cock, so black of hue,
> With orange-tawny bill,

The throstle with his note so true,
The wren with little quill.

TITANIA

[Waking.]
What angel wakes me from my flowery bed?

BOTTOM

[Sings.]
The finch, the sparrow, and the lark,
The plain-song cuckoo gray,
Whose note full many a man doth mark,
And dares not answer nay.

For, indeed, who would set his wit to so foolish a bird? Who would give a bird the lie, though he cry 'cuckoo' never so?

TITANIA

I pray thee, gentle mortal, sing again.
Mine ear is much enamour'd of thy note.
So is mine eye enthrallèd to thy shape;
And thy fair virtue's force perforce doth move me,
On the first view, to say, to swear, I love thee.

BOTTOM

Methinks, mistress, you should have little reason for that. And yet, to say the truth, reason and love keep little company together nowadays. The more the pity that some honest neighbours will not make them friends. Nay, I can gleek upon occasion.

TITANIA

Thou art as wise as thou art beautiful.

BOTTOM

Not so, neither; but if I had wit enough to get out of this wood, I have enough to serve mine own turn.

TITANIA

Out of this wood do not desire to go.
Thou shalt remain here whether thou wilt or no.
I am a spirit of no common rate.
The summer still doth tend upon my state;

And I do love thee: therefore, go with me.
I'll give thee fairies to attend on thee;
And they shall fetch thee jewels from the deep,
And sing, while thou on pressèd flowers dost sleep.
And I will purge thy mortal grossness so
That thou shalt like an airy spirit go.—
Peaseblossom! Cobweb! Moth! and Mustardseed!
            Enter four FAIRIES.

PEASEBLOSSOM
    Ready.

COBWEB
    And I.

MOTH
    And I.

MUSTARDSEED
    And I.

ALL
    Where shall we go?

TITANIA
    Be kind and courteous to this gentleman;
    Hop in his walks and gambol in his eyes;
    Feed him with apricocks and dewberries,
    With purple grapes, green figs, and mulberries;
    The honey-bags steal from the humble-bees,
    And for night-tapers, crop their waxen thighs,
    And light them at the fiery glow-worm's eyes,
    To have my love to bed and to arise;
    And pluck the wings from painted butterflies,
    To fan the moonbeams from his sleeping eyes.
    Nod to him, elves, and do him courtesies.

PEASEBLOSSOM
    Hail, mortal!

COBWEB
    Hail!

MOTH

Hail!

MUSTARDSEED

Hail!

BOTTOM

I cry your worship's mercy, heartily.—I beseech your worship's name.

COBWEB

Cobweb.

BOTTOM

I shall desire you of more acquaintance, good Master Cobweb. If I cut my finger, I shall make bold with you.—Your name, honest gentleman?

PEASEBLOSSOM

Peaseblossom.

BOTTOM

I pray you, commend me to Mistress Squash, your mother, and to Master Peascod, your father. Good Master Peaseblossom, I shall desire you of more acquaintance too.—Your name, I beseech you, sir?

MUSTARDSEED

Mustardseed.

BOTTOM

Good Master Mustardseed, I know your patience well. That same cowardly giant-like ox-beef hath devoured many a gentleman of your house. I promise you, your kindred hath made my eyes water ere now. I desire you of more acquaintance, good Master Mustardseed.

TITANIA

Come, wait upon him; lead him to my bower.
The moon, methinks, looks with a watery eye,
And when she weeps, weeps every little flower,
Lamenting some enforced chastity.
Tie up my love's tongue, bring him silently.

[Exeunt.]

SCENE II. Another part of the wood.

Enter OBERON.

OBERON

    I wonder if Titania be awak'd;
    Then, what it was that next came in her eye,
    Which she must dote on in extremity.
        Enter PUCK.
    Here comes my messenger. How now, mad spirit?
    What night-rule now about this haunted grove?

PUCK

    My mistress with a monster is in love.
    Near to her close and consecrated bower,
    While she was in her dull and sleeping hour,
    A crew of patches, rude mechanicals,
    That work for bread upon Athenian stalls,
    Were met together to rehearse a play
    Intended for great Theseus' nuptial day.
    The shallowest thick-skin of that barren sort
    Who Pyramus presented in their sport,
    Forsook his scene and enter'd in a brake.
    When I did him at this advantage take,
    An ass's nole I fixed on his head.
    Anon, his Thisbe must be answerèd,
    And forth my mimic comes. When they him spy,
    As wild geese that the creeping fowler eye,
    Or russet-pated choughs, many in sort,
    Rising and cawing at the gun's report,
    Sever themselves and madly sweep the sky,
    So at his sight away his fellows fly,
    And at our stamp, here o'er and o'er one falls;
    He murder cries, and help from Athens calls.
    Their sense thus weak, lost with their fears, thus strong,
    Made senseless things begin to do them wrong;
    For briers and thorns at their apparel snatch;
    Some sleeves, some hats, from yielders all things catch.
    I led them on in this distracted fear,

And left sweet Pyramus translated there.
When in that moment, so it came to pass,
Titania wak'd, and straightway lov'd an ass.

OBERON

This falls out better than I could devise.
But hast thou yet latch'd the Athenian's eyes
With the love-juice, as I did bid thee do?

PUCK

I took him sleeping—that is finish'd too—
And the Athenian woman by his side,
That, when he wak'd, of force she must be ey'd.
Enter DEMETRIUS and HERMIA.

OBERON

Stand close. This is the same Athenian.

PUCK

This is the woman, but not this the man.

DEMETRIUS

O why rebuke you him that loves you so?
Lay breath so bitter on your bitter foe.

HERMIA

Now I but chide, but I should use thee worse,
For thou, I fear, hast given me cause to curse.
If thou hast slain Lysander in his sleep,
Being o'er shoes in blood, plunge in the deep,
And kill me too.
The sun was not so true unto the day
As he to me. Would he have stol'n away
From sleeping Hermia? I'll believe as soon
This whole earth may be bor'd, and that the moon
May through the centre creep and so displease
Her brother's noontide with th' Antipodes.
It cannot be but thou hast murder'd him.
So should a murderer look, so dead, so grim.

DEMETRIUS

> So should the murder'd look, and so should I,
> Pierc'd through the heart with your stern cruelty.
> Yet you, the murderer, look as bright, as clear,
> As yonder Venus in her glimmering sphere.

HERMIA

> What's this to my Lysander? Where is he?
> Ah, good Demetrius, wilt thou give him me?

DEMETRIUS

> I had rather give his carcass to my hounds.

HERMIA

> Out, dog! Out, cur! Thou driv'st me past the bounds
> Of maiden's patience. Hast thou slain him, then?
> Henceforth be never number'd among men!
> O once tell true; tell true, even for my sake!
> Durst thou have look'd upon him, being awake,
> And hast thou kill'd him sleeping? O brave touch!
> Could not a worm, an adder, do so much?
> An adder did it; for with doubler tongue
> Than thine, thou serpent, never adder stung.

DEMETRIUS

> You spend your passion on a mispris'd mood:
> I am not guilty of Lysander's blood;
> Nor is he dead, for aught that I can tell.

HERMIA

> I pray thee, tell me then that he is well.

DEMETRIUS

> And if I could, what should I get therefore?

HERMIA

> A privilege never to see me more.
> And from thy hated presence part I so:
> See me no more, whether he be dead or no.
> > *[Exit.]*

DEMETRIUS

There is no following her in this fierce vein.
Here, therefore, for a while I will remain.
So sorrow's heaviness doth heavier grow
For debt that bankrupt sleep doth sorrow owe;
Which now in some slight measure it will pay,
If for his tender here I make some stay.
[Lies down.]

OBERON

What hast thou done? Thou hast mistaken quite,
And laid the love-juice on some true-love's sight.
Of thy misprision must perforce ensue
Some true love turn'd, and not a false turn'd true.

PUCK

Then fate o'er-rules, that, one man holding troth,
A million fail, confounding oath on oath.

OBERON

About the wood go swifter than the wind,
And Helena of Athens look thou find.
All fancy-sick she is, and pale of cheer
With sighs of love, that costs the fresh blood dear.
By some illusion see thou bring her here;
I'll charm his eyes against she do appear.

PUCK

I go, I go; look how I go,
Swifter than arrow from the Tartar's bow.
[Exit.]

OBERON

Flower of this purple dye,
Hit with Cupid's archery,
Sink in apple of his eye.
When his love he doth espy,
Let her shine as gloriously
As the Venus of the sky.—

When thou wak'st, if she be by,
Beg of her for remedy.
Enter PUCK.

PUCK

Captain of our fairy band,
Helena is here at hand,
And the youth mistook by me,
Pleading for a lover's fee.
Shall we their fond pageant see?
Lord, what fools these mortals be!

OBERON

Stand aside. The noise they make
Will cause Demetrius to awake.

PUCK

Then will two at once woo one.
That must needs be sport alone;
And those things do best please me
That befall prepost'rously.
Enter LYSANDER and HELENA.

LYSANDER

Why should you think that I should woo in scorn?
Scorn and derision never come in tears.
Look when I vow, I weep; and vows so born,
In their nativity all truth appears.
How can these things in me seem scorn to you,
Bearing the badge of faith, to prove them true?

HELENA

You do advance your cunning more and more.
When truth kills truth, O devilish-holy fray!
These vows are Hermia's: will you give her o'er?
Weigh oath with oath, and you will nothing weigh:
Your vows to her and me, put in two scales,
Will even weigh; and both as light as tales.

LYSANDER

I had no judgment when to her I swore.

HELENA

Nor none, in my mind, now you give her o'er.

LYSANDER

Demetrius loves her, and he loves not you.

DEMETRIUS

[Waking.]

O Helen, goddess, nymph, perfect, divine!
To what, my love, shall I compare thine eyne?
Crystal is muddy. O how ripe in show
Thy lips, those kissing cherries, tempting grow!
That pure congealèd white, high Taurus' snow,
Fann'd with the eastern wind, turns to a crow
When thou hold'st up thy hand. O, let me kiss
This princess of pure white, this seal of bliss!

HELENA

O spite! O hell! I see you all are bent
To set against me for your merriment.
If you were civil, and knew courtesy,
You would not do me thus much injury.
Can you not hate me, as I know you do,
But you must join in souls to mock me too?
If you were men, as men you are in show,
You would not use a gentle lady so;
To vow, and swear, and superpraise my parts,
When I am sure you hate me with your hearts.
You both are rivals, and love Hermia;
And now both rivals, to mock Helena.
A trim exploit, a manly enterprise,
To conjure tears up in a poor maid's eyes
With your derision! None of noble sort
Would so offend a virgin, and extort
A poor soul's patience, all to make you sport.

LYSANDER

You are unkind, Demetrius; be not so,
For you love Hermia; this you know I know.

And here, with all good will, with all my heart,
In Hermia's love I yield you up my part;
And yours of Helena to me bequeath,
Whom I do love and will do till my death.

HELENA

Never did mockers waste more idle breath.

DEMETRIUS

Lysander, keep thy Hermia; I will none.
If e'er I lov'd her, all that love is gone.
My heart to her but as guest-wise sojourn'd;
And now to Helen is it home return'd,
There to remain.

LYSANDER

Helen, it is not so.

DEMETRIUS

Disparage not the faith thou dost not know,
Lest to thy peril thou aby it dear.
Look where thy love comes; yonder is thy dear.
        Enter HERMIA.

HERMIA

Dark night, that from the eye his function takes,
The ear more quick of apprehension makes;
Wherein it doth impair the seeing sense,
It pays the hearing double recompense.
Thou art not by mine eye, Lysander, found;
Mine ear, I thank it, brought me to thy sound.
But why unkindly didst thou leave me so?

LYSANDER

Why should he stay whom love doth press to go?

HERMIA

What love could press Lysander from my side?

LYSANDER

Lysander's love, that would not let him bide,

Fair Helena, who more engilds the night
Than all yon fiery oes and eyes of light.
Why seek'st thou me? Could not this make thee know
The hate I bare thee made me leave thee so?

HERMIA

You speak not as you think; it cannot be.

HELENA

Lo, she is one of this confederacy!
Now I perceive they have conjoin'd all three
To fashion this false sport in spite of me.
Injurious Hermia, most ungrateful maid!
Have you conspir'd, have you with these contriv'd,
To bait me with this foul derision?
Is all the counsel that we two have shar'd,
The sisters' vows, the hours that we have spent,
When we have chid the hasty-footed time
For parting us—O, is all forgot?
All school-days' friendship, childhood innocence?
We, Hermia, like two artificial gods,
Have with our needles created both one flower,
Both on one sampler, sitting on one cushion,
Both warbling of one song, both in one key,
As if our hands, our sides, voices, and minds,
Had been incorporate. So we grew together,
Like to a double cherry, seeming parted,
But yet a union in partition,
Two lovely berries moulded on one stem;
So, with two seeming bodies, but one heart;
Two of the first, like coats in heraldry,
Due but to one, and crownèd with one crest.
And will you rent our ancient love asunder,
To join with men in scorning your poor friend?
It is not friendly, 'tis not maidenly.
Our sex, as well as I, may chide you for it,
Though I alone do feel the injury.

HERMIA

I am amazèd at your passionate words:
I scorn you not; it seems that you scorn me.

HELENA

Have you not set Lysander, as in scorn,
To follow me, and praise my eyes and face?
And made your other love, Demetrius,
Who even but now did spurn me with his foot,
To call me goddess, nymph, divine and rare,
Precious, celestial? Wherefore speaks he this
To her he hates? And wherefore doth Lysander
Deny your love, so rich within his soul,
And tender me, forsooth, affection,
But by your setting on, by your consent?
What though I be not so in grace as you,
So hung upon with love, so fortunate,
But miserable most, to love unlov'd?
This you should pity rather than despise.

HERMIA

I understand not what you mean by this.

HELENA

Ay, do. Persever, counterfeit sad looks,
Make mouths upon me when I turn my back,
Wink each at other; hold the sweet jest up.
This sport, well carried, shall be chronicled.
If you have any pity, grace, or manners,
You would not make me such an argument.
But fare ye well. 'Tis partly my own fault,
Which death, or absence, soon shall remedy.

LYSANDER

Stay, gentle Helena; hear my excuse;
My love, my life, my soul, fair Helena!

HELENA

O excellent!

HERMIA

Sweet, do not scorn her so.

DEMETRIUS

If she cannot entreat, I can compel.

LYSANDER

Thou canst compel no more than she entreat;
Thy threats have no more strength than her weak prayers.
Helen, I love thee, by my life I do;
I swear by that which I will lose for thee
To prove him false that says I love thee not.

DEMETRIUS

I say I love thee more than he can do.

LYSANDER

If thou say so, withdraw, and prove it too.

DEMETRIUS

Quick, come.

HERMIA

Lysander, whereto tends all this?

LYSANDER

Away, you Ethiope!

DEMETRIUS

No, no. He will
Seem to break loose. Take on as you would follow,
But yet come not. You are a tame man, go!

LYSANDER

Hang off, thou cat, thou burr! Vile thing, let loose,
Or I will shake thee from me like a serpent.

HERMIA

Why are you grown so rude? What change is this,
Sweet love?

LYSANDER

Thy love? Out, tawny Tartar, out!
Out, loathèd medicine! O hated potion, hence!

HERMIA

Do you not jest?

HELENA

Yes, sooth, and so do you.

LYSANDER

Demetrius, I will keep my word with thee.

DEMETRIUS

I would I had your bond; for I perceive
A weak bond holds you; I'll not trust your word.

LYSANDER

What, should I hurt her, strike her, kill her dead?
Although I hate her, I'll not harm her so.

HERMIA

What, can you do me greater harm than hate?
Hate me? Wherefore? O me! what news, my love?
Am not I Hermia? Are not you Lysander?
I am as fair now as I was erewhile.
Since night you lov'd me; yet since night you left me.
Why then, you left me—O, the gods forbid!—
In earnest, shall I say?

LYSANDER

Ay, by my life;
And never did desire to see thee more.
Therefore be out of hope, of question, of doubt;
Be certain, nothing truer; 'tis no jest
That I do hate thee and love Helena.

HERMIA

O me! You juggler! You cankerblossom!
You thief of love! What! have you come by night
And stol'n my love's heart from him?

HELENA

Fine, i' faith!
Have you no modesty, no maiden shame,
No touch of bashfulness? What, will you tear

Impatient answers from my gentle tongue?
Fie, fie, you counterfeit, you puppet, you!

HERMIA

Puppet! Why so? Ay, that way goes the game.
Now I perceive that she hath made compare
Between our statures; she hath urg'd her height;
And with her personage, her tall personage,
Her height, forsooth, she hath prevail'd with him.
And are you grown so high in his esteem
Because I am so dwarfish and so low?
How low am I, thou painted maypole? Speak,
How low am I? I am not yet so low
But that my nails can reach unto thine eyes.

HELENA

I pray you, though you mock me, gentlemen,
Let her not hurt me. I was never curst;
I have no gift at all in shrewishness;
I am a right maid for my cowardice;
Let her not strike me. You perhaps may think,
Because she is something lower than myself,
That I can match her.

HERMIA

Lower! Hark, again.

HELENA

Good Hermia, do not be so bitter with me.
I evermore did love you, Hermia,
Did ever keep your counsels, never wrong'd you,
Save that, in love unto Demetrius,
I told him of your stealth unto this wood.
He follow'd you; for love I follow'd him;
But he hath chid me hence, and threaten'd me
To strike me, spurn me, nay, to kill me too:
And now, so you will let me quiet go,
To Athens will I bear my folly back,
And follow you no further. Let me go:
You see how simple and how fond I am.

HERMIA

Why, get you gone. Who is't that hinders you?

HELENA

A foolish heart that I leave here behind.

HERMIA

What! with Lysander?

HELENA

With Demetrius.

LYSANDER

Be not afraid; she shall not harm thee, Helena.

DEMETRIUS

No, sir, she shall not, though you take her part.

HELENA

O, when she's angry, she is keen and shrewd.
She was a vixen when she went to school,
And though she be but little, she is fierce.

HERMIA

Little again! Nothing but low and little?
Why will you suffer her to flout me thus?
Let me come to her.

LYSANDER

Get you gone, you dwarf;
You minimus, of hind'ring knot-grass made;
You bead, you acorn.

DEMETRIUS

You are too officious
In her behalf that scorns your services.
Let her alone. Speak not of Helena;
Take not her part; for if thou dost intend
Never so little show of love to her,
Thou shalt aby it.

LYSANDER

Now she holds me not.
Now follow, if thou dar'st, to try whose right,
Of thine or mine, is most in Helena.

DEMETRIUS

Follow! Nay, I'll go with thee, cheek by jole.
[Exeunt LYSANDER and DEMETRIUS.]

HERMIA

You, mistress, all this coil is long of you.
Nay, go not back.

HELENA

I will not trust you, I,
Nor longer stay in your curst company.
Your hands than mine are quicker for a fray.
My legs are longer though, to run away.
[Exit.]

HERMIA

I am amaz'd, and know not what to say.
[Exit, pursuing HELENA.]

OBERON

This is thy negligence: still thou mistak'st,
Or else commit'st thy knaveries willfully.

PUCK

Believe me, king of shadows, I mistook.
Did not you tell me I should know the man
By the Athenian garments he had on?
And so far blameless proves my enterprise
That I have 'nointed an Athenian's eyes:
And so far am I glad it so did sort,
As this their jangling I esteem a sport.

OBERON

Thou seest these lovers seek a place to fight.
Hie therefore, Robin, overcast the night;
The starry welkin cover thou anon

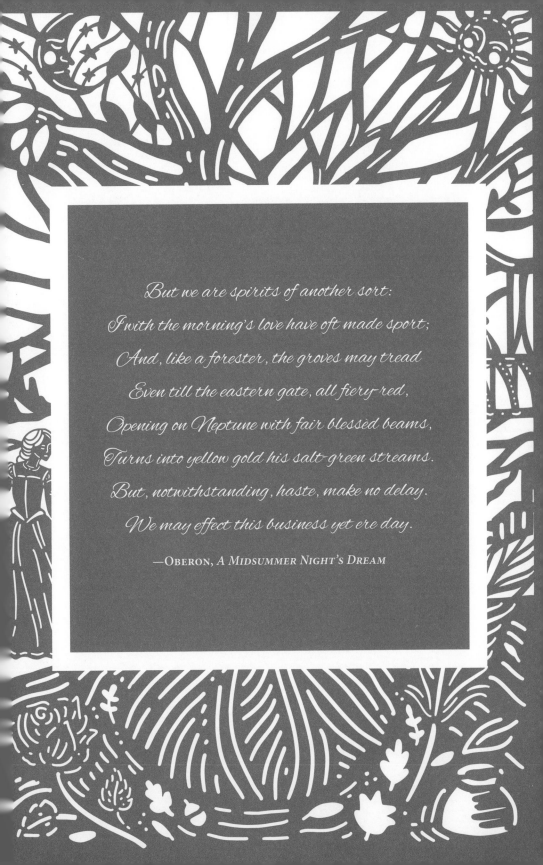

But we are spirits of another sort:
I with the morning's love have oft made sport;
And, like a forester, the groves may tread
Even till the eastern gate, all fiery-red,
Opening on Neptune with fair blessèd beams,
Turns into yellow gold his salt-green streams.
But, notwithstanding, haste, make no delay.
We may effect this business yet ere day.

—OBERON, A MIDSUMMER NIGHT'S DREAM

With drooping fog, as black as Acheron,
And lead these testy rivals so astray
As one come not within another's way.
Like to Lysander sometime frame thy tongue,
Then stir Demetrius up with bitter wrong;
And sometime rail thou like Demetrius.
And from each other look thou lead them thus,
Till o'er their brows death-counterfeiting sleep
With leaden legs and batty wings doth creep.
Then crush this herb into Lysander's eye,
Whose liquor hath this virtuous property,
To take from thence all error with his might
And make his eyeballs roll with wonted sight.
When they next wake, all this derision
Shall seem a dream and fruitless vision;
And back to Athens shall the lovers wend,
With league whose date till death shall never end.
Whiles I in this affair do thee employ,
I'll to my queen, and beg her Indian boy;
And then I will her charmèd eye release
From monster's view, and all things shall be peace.

PUCK

My fairy lord, this must be done with haste,
For night's swift dragons cut the clouds full fast;
And yonder shines Aurora's harbinger,
At whose approach, ghosts wandering here and there
Troop home to churchyards. Damnèd spirits all,
That in cross-ways and floods have burial,
Already to their wormy beds are gone;
For fear lest day should look their shames upon,
They wilfully themselves exile from light,
And must for aye consort with black-brow'd night.

OBERON

But we are spirits of another sort:
I with the morning's love have oft made sport;
And, like a forester, the groves may tread
Even till the eastern gate, all fiery-red,

Opening on Neptune with fair blessèd beams,
Turns into yellow gold his salt-green streams.
But, notwithstanding, haste, make no delay.
We may effect this business yet ere day.
    [Exit OBERON.]

PUCK

Up and down, up and down,
I will lead them up and down.
I am fear'd in field and town.
Goblin, lead them up and down.
Here comes one.
    Enter LYSANDER.

LYSANDER

Where art thou, proud Demetrius? Speak thou now.

PUCK

Here, villain, drawn and ready. Where art thou?

LYSANDER

I will be with thee straight.

PUCK

Follow me then to plainer ground.
    [Exit LYSANDER as following the voice.]
    Enter DEMETRIUS.

DEMETRIUS

Lysander, speak again.
Thou runaway, thou coward, art thou fled?
Speak. In some bush? Where dost thou hide thy head?

PUCK

Thou coward, art thou bragging to the stars,
Telling the bushes that thou look'st for wars,
And wilt not come? Come, recreant, come, thou child!
I'll whip thee with a rod. He is defil'd
That draws a sword on thee.

DEMETRIUS

Yea, art thou there?

PUCK

> Follow my voice; we'll try no manhood here.
>> *[Exeunt.]*
>> *Enter LYSANDER.*

LYSANDER

> He goes before me, and still dares me on;
> When I come where he calls, then he is gone.
> The villain is much lighter-heel'd than I:
> I follow'd fast, but faster he did fly,
> That fallen am I in dark uneven way,
> And here will rest me. Come, thou gentle day!
>> *[Lies down.]*
> For if but once thou show me thy grey light,
> I'll find Demetrius, and revenge this spite.
>> *[Sleeps.]*
>> *Enter PUCK and DEMETRIUS.*

PUCK

> Ho, ho, ho! Coward, why com'st thou not?

DEMETRIUS

> Abide me, if thou dar'st; for well I wot
> Thou runn'st before me, shifting every place,
> And dar'st not stand, nor look me in the face.
> Where art thou?

PUCK

> Come hither; I am here.

DEMETRIUS

> Nay, then, thou mock'st me. Thou shalt buy this dear
> If ever I thy face by daylight see:
> Now go thy way. Faintness constraineth me
> To measure out my length on this cold bed.
> By day's approach look to be visited.
>> *[Lies down and sleeps.]*
>> *Enter HELENA.*

HELENA

> O weary night, O long and tedious night,
> Abate thy hours! Shine, comforts, from the east,
> That I may back to Athens by daylight,
> From these that my poor company detest.
> And sleep, that sometimes shuts up sorrow's eye,
> Steal me awhile from mine own company.
>> *[Sleeps.]*

PUCK

> Yet but three? Come one more.
> Two of both kinds makes up four.
> Here she comes, curst and sad.
> Cupid is a knavish lad
> Thus to make poor females mad.
>> *Enter HERMIA.*

HERMIA

> Never so weary, never so in woe,
> Bedabbled with the dew, and torn with briers,
> I can no further crawl, no further go;
> My legs can keep no pace with my desires.
> Here will I rest me till the break of day.
> Heavens shield Lysander, if they mean a fray!
>> *[Lies down.]*

PUCK

> On the ground
> Sleep sound.
> I'll apply
> To your eye,
> Gentle lover, remedy.
>> *[Squeezing the juice on LYSANDER'S eye.]*
> When thou wak'st,
> Thou tak'st
> True delight
> In the sight
> Of thy former lady's eye.
> And the country proverb known,

That every man should take his own,
In your waking shall be shown:
Jack shall have Jill;
Nought shall go ill;
The man shall have his mare again, and all shall be well.
  [Exit Puck.]

ACT IV

SCENE I. The Wood.

*Lysander, Demetrius, Helena and Hermia still asleep.
Enter TITANIA and BOTTOM; PEASEBLOSSOM, COBWEB, MOTH,
MUSTARDSEED and other FAIRIES attending; OBERON
behind, unseen.*

TITANIA
    Come, sit thee down upon this flowery bed,
    While I thy amiable cheeks do coy,
    And stick musk-roses in thy sleek smooth head,
    And kiss thy fair large ears, my gentle joy.

BOTTOM
    Where's Peaseblossom?

PEASEBLOSSOM
    Ready.

BOTTOM
    Scratch my head, Peaseblossom. Where's Monsieur Cobweb?

COBWEB
    Ready.

BOTTOM

Monsieur Cobweb; good monsieur, get you your weapons in your hand and kill me a red-hipped humble-bee on the top of a thistle; and, good monsieur, bring me the honey-bag. Do not fret yourself too much in the action, monsieur; and, good monsieur, have a care the honey-bag break not; I would be loath to have you overflown with a honey-bag, signior. Where's Monsieur Mustardseed?

MUSTARDSEED

Ready.

BOTTOM

Give me your neaf, Monsieur Mustardseed. Pray you, leave your courtesy, good monsieur.

MUSTARDSEED

What's your will?

BOTTOM

Nothing, good monsieur, but to help Cavalery Cobweb to scratch. I must to the barber's, monsieur, for methinks I am marvellous hairy about the face; and I am such a tender ass, if my hair do but tickle me, I must scratch.

TITANIA

What, wilt thou hear some music, my sweet love?

BOTTOM

I have a reasonable good ear in music. Let us have the tongs and the bones.

TITANIA

Or say, sweet love, what thou desirest to eat.

BOTTOM

Truly, a peck of provender; I could munch your good dry oats. Methinks I have a great desire to a bottle of hay: good hay, sweet hay, hath no fellow.

TITANIA

I have a venturous fairy that shall seek
The squirrel's hoard, and fetch thee new nuts.

BOTTOM

I had rather have a handful or two of dried peas. But, I pray you, let none of your people stir me; I have an exposition of sleep come upon me.

TITANIA

Sleep thou, and I will wind thee in my arms.
Fairies, be gone, and be all ways away.
So doth the woodbine the sweet honeysuckle
Gently entwist, the female ivy so
Enrings the barky fingers of the elm.
O, how I love thee! How I dote on thee!
     [They sleep.]
     OBERON *advances. Enter* PUCK.

OBERON

Welcome, good Robin. Seest thou this sweet sight?
Her dotage now I do begin to pity.
For, meeting her of late behind the wood,
Seeking sweet favours for this hateful fool,
I did upbraid her and fall out with her:
For she his hairy temples then had rounded
With coronet of fresh and fragrant flowers;
And that same dew, which sometime on the buds
Was wont to swell like round and orient pearls,
Stood now within the pretty flouriets' eyes,
Like tears that did their own disgrace bewail.
When I had at my pleasure taunted her,
And she in mild terms begg'd my patience,
I then did ask of her her changeling child;
Which straight she gave me, and her fairy sent
To bear him to my bower in fairyland.
And now I have the boy, I will undo
This hateful imperfection of her eyes.
And, gentle Puck, take this transformèd scalp
From off the head of this Athenian swain,
That he awaking when the other do,
May all to Athens back again repair,
And think no more of this night's accidents

But as the fierce vexation of a dream.
But first I will release the Fairy Queen.
　　[Touching her eyes with an herb.]
Be as thou wast wont to be;
See as thou was wont to see.
Dian's bud o'er Cupid's flower
Hath such force and blessed power.
Now, my Titania, wake you, my sweet queen.

TITANIA

My Oberon, what visions have I seen!
Methought I was enamour'd of an ass.

OBERON

There lies your love.

TITANIA

How came these things to pass?
O, how mine eyes do loathe his visage now!

OBERON

Silence awhile.—Robin, take off this head.
Titania, music call; and strike more dead
Than common sleep, of all these five the sense.

TITANIA

Music, ho, music, such as charmeth sleep.

PUCK

Now when thou wak'st, with thine own fool's eyes peep.

OBERON

Sound, music.
　　[Still music.]
Come, my queen, take hands with me,
And rock the ground whereon these sleepers be.
Now thou and I are new in amity,
And will tomorrow midnight solemnly
Dance in Duke Theseus' house triumphantly,
And bless it to all fair prosperity:
There shall the pairs of faithful lovers be
Wedded, with Theseus, all in jollity.

PUCK

Fairy king, attend and mark.
I do hear the morning lark.

OBERON

Then, my queen, in silence sad,
Trip we after night's shade.
We the globe can compass soon,
Swifter than the wand'ring moon.

TITANIA

Come, my lord, and in our flight,
Tell me how it came this night
That I sleeping here was found
With these mortals on the ground.
                    [Exeunt. Horns sound within.]
                    Enter THESEUS, HIPPOLYTA, EGEUS and Train.

THESEUS

Go, one of you, find out the forester;
For now our observation is perform'd;
And since we have the vaward of the day,
My love shall hear the music of my hounds.
Uncouple in the western valley; let them go.
Dispatch I say, and find the forester.
                    [Exit an ATTENDANT.]
We will, fair queen, up to the mountain's top,
And mark the musical confusion
Of hounds and echo in conjunction.

HIPPOLYTA

I was with Hercules and Cadmus once,
When in a wood of Crete they bay'd the bear
With hounds of Sparta. Never did I hear
Such gallant chiding; for, besides the groves,
The skies, the fountains, every region near
Seem'd all one mutual cry. I never heard
So musical a discord, such sweet thunder.

THESEUS

My hounds are bred out of the Spartan kind,

So flew'd, so sanded; and their heads are hung
With ears that sweep away the morning dew;
Crook-knee'd and dewlap'd like Thessalian bulls;
Slow in pursuit, but match'd in mouth like bells,
Each under each. A cry more tuneable
Was never holla'd to, nor cheer'd with horn,
In Crete, in Sparta, nor in Thessaly.
Judge when you hear.—But, soft, what nymphs are these?

EGEUS

My lord, this is my daughter here asleep,
And this Lysander; this Demetrius is;
This Helena, old Nedar's Helena:
I wonder of their being here together.

THESEUS

No doubt they rose up early to observe
The rite of May; and, hearing our intent,
Came here in grace of our solemnity.
But speak, Egeus; is not this the day
That Hermia should give answer of her choice?

EGEUS

It is, my lord.

THESEUS

Go, bid the huntsmen wake them with their horns.
*[Horns, and shout within. DEMETRIUS, LYSANDER, HERMIA
and HELENA wake and start up.]*
Good morrow, friends. Saint Valentine is past.
Begin these wood-birds but to couple now?

LYSANDER

Pardon, my lord.
[He and the rest kneel to THESEUS.]

THESEUS

I pray you all, stand up.
I know you two are rival enemies.
How comes this gentle concord in the world,

That hatred is so far from jealousy
To sleep by hate, and fear no enmity?

LYSANDER

My lord, I shall reply amazedly,
Half sleep, half waking; but as yet, I swear,
I cannot truly say how I came here.
But, as I think (for truly would I speak)
And now I do bethink me, so it is:
I came with Hermia hither. Our intent
Was to be gone from Athens, where we might be,
Without the peril of the Athenian law.

EGEUS

Enough, enough, my lord; you have enough.
I beg the law, the law upon his head.
They would have stol'n away, they would, Demetrius,
Thereby to have defeated you and me:
You of your wife, and me of my consent,
Of my consent that she should be your wife.

DEMETRIUS

My lord, fair Helen told me of their stealth,
Of this their purpose hither to this wood;
And I in fury hither follow'd them,
Fair Helena in fancy following me.
But, my good lord, I wot not by what power,
(But by some power it is) my love to Hermia,
Melted as the snow, seems to me now
As the remembrance of an idle gaud
Which in my childhood I did dote upon;
And all the faith, the virtue of my heart,
The object and the pleasure of mine eye,
Is only Helena. To her, my lord,
Was I betroth'd ere I saw Hermia.
But like a sickness did I loathe this food.
But, as in health, come to my natural taste,
Now I do wish it, love it, long for it,
And will for evermore be true to it.

THESEUS

    Fair lovers, you are fortunately met.

    Of this discourse we more will hear anon.

    Egeus, I will overbear your will;

    For in the temple, by and by with us,

    These couples shall eternally be knit.

    And, for the morning now is something worn,

    Our purpos'd hunting shall be set aside.

    Away with us to Athens. Three and three,

    We'll hold a feast in great solemnity.

    Come, Hippolyta.

        [Exeunt THESEUS, HIPPOLYTA, EGEUS and Train.]

DEMETRIUS

    These things seem small and undistinguishable,

    Like far-off mountains turnèd into clouds.

HERMIA

    Methinks I see these things with parted eye,

    When everything seems double.

HELENA

    So methinks.

    And I have found Demetrius like a jewel,

    Mine own, and not mine own.

DEMETRIUS

    Are you sure

    That we are awake? It seems to me

    That yet we sleep, we dream. Do not you think

    The Duke was here, and bid us follow him?

HERMIA

    Yea, and my father.

HELENA

    And Hippolyta.

LYSANDER

    And he did bid us follow to the temple.

DEMETRIUS

Why, then, we are awake: let's follow him,
And by the way let us recount our dreams.

[Exeunt.]

BOTTOM

[Waking.]

When my cue comes, call me, and I will answer. My next is 'Most fair Pyramus.' Heigh-ho! Peter Quince! Flute, the bellows-mender! Snout, the tinker! Starveling! God's my life! Stol'n hence, and left me asleep! I have had a most rare vision. I have had a dream, past the wit of man to say what dream it was. Man is but an ass if he go about to expound this dream. Methought I was—there is no man can tell what. Methought I was, and methought I had—but man is but a patched fool if he will offer to say what methought I had. The eye of man hath not heard, the ear of man hath not seen, man's hand is not able to taste, his tongue to conceive, nor his heart to report, what my dream was. I will get Peter Quince to write a ballad of this dream: it shall be called 'Bottom's Dream,' because it hath no bottom; and I will sing it in the latter end of a play, before the Duke. Peradventure, to make it the more gracious, I shall sing it at her death.

[Exit.]

SCENE II. Athens. A Room in Quince's House.

Enter QUINCE, FLUTE, SNOUT and STARVELING.

QUINCE

Have you sent to Bottom's house? Is he come home yet?

STARVELING

He cannot be heard of. Out of doubt he is transported.

FLUTE

If he come not, then the play is marred. It goes not forward, doth it?

QUINCE

It is not possible. You have not a man in all Athens able to discharge Pyramus but he.

FLUTE

No, he hath simply the best wit of any handicraft man in Athens.

QUINCE

Yea, and the best person too, and he is a very paramour for a sweet voice.

FLUTE

You must say paragon. A paramour is, God bless us, a thing of naught.
Enter SNUG.

SNUG

Masters, the Duke is coming from the temple, and there is two or three lords and ladies more married. If our sport had gone forward, we had all been made men.

FLUTE

O sweet bully Bottom! Thus hath he lost sixpence a day during his life; he could not have 'scaped sixpence a day. An the Duke had not given him sixpence a day for playing Pyramus, I'll be hanged. He would have deserved it: sixpence a day in Pyramus, or nothing.
Enter BOTTOM.

BOTTOM

Where are these lads? Where are these hearts?

QUINCE

Bottom! O most courageous day! O most happy hour!

BOTTOM

Masters, I am to discourse wonders: but ask me not what; for if I tell you, I am not true Athenian. I will tell you everything, right as it fell out.

QUINCE

Let us hear, sweet Bottom.

BOTTOM

Not a word of me. All that I will tell you is, that the Duke hath dined. Get your apparel together, good strings to your beards, new ribbons to your pumps; meet presently at the palace; every man look o'er his part. For the short and the long is, our play is preferred. In any case, let Thisbe have clean linen; and let not him that plays the lion pare his nails, for they shall hang out for the lion's claws. And most dear actors, eat no onions nor garlick, for we are to utter sweet breath; and I do not doubt but to hear them say it is a sweet comedy. No more words. Away! Go, away!

[Exeunt.]

ACT V

SCENE I. Athens. An Apartment in the Palace of Theseus.

Enter THESEUS, HIPPOLYTA, PHILOSTRATE, LORDS *and*
ATTENDANTS.

HIPPOLYTA

'Tis strange, my Theseus, that these lovers speak of.

THESEUS

More strange than true. I never may believe
These antique fables, nor these fairy toys.
Lovers and madmen have such seething brains,
Such shaping fantasies, that apprehend
More than cool reason ever comprehends.
The lunatic, the lover, and the poet
Are of imagination all compact:
One sees more devils than vast hell can hold;
That is the madman: the lover, all as frantic,
Sees Helen's beauty in a brow of Egypt:
The poet's eye, in a fine frenzy rolling,
Doth glance from heaven to earth, from earth to heaven;
And as imagination bodies forth
The forms of things unknown, the poet's pen
Turns them to shapes, and gives to airy nothing
A local habitation and a name.
Such tricks hath strong imagination,

That if it would but apprehend some joy,
It comprehends some bringer of that joy.
Or in the night, imagining some fear,
How easy is a bush supposed a bear?

HIPPOLYTA

But all the story of the night told over,
And all their minds transfigur'd so together,
More witnesseth than fancy's images,
And grows to something of great constancy;
But, howsoever, strange and admirable.

Enter lovers: LYSANDER, DEMETRIUS, HERMIA *and* HELENA.

THESEUS

Here come the lovers, full of joy and mirth.
Joy, gentle friends, joy and fresh days of love
Accompany your hearts!

LYSANDER

More than to us
Wait in your royal walks, your board, your bed!

THESEUS

Come now; what masques, what dances shall we have,
To wear away this long age of three hours
Between our after-supper and bed-time?
Where is our usual manager of mirth?
What revels are in hand? Is there no play
To ease the anguish of a torturing hour?
Call Philostrate.

PHILOSTRATE

Here, mighty Theseus.

THESEUS

Say, what abridgment have you for this evening?
What masque? What music? How shall we beguile
The lazy time, if not with some delight?

PHILOSTRATE

There is a brief how many sports are ripe.
Make choice of which your Highness will see first.
[Giving a paper.]

THESEUS

[Reads.]
'The battle with the Centaurs, to be sung
By an Athenian eunuch to the harp.'
We'll none of that. That have I told my love
In glory of my kinsman Hercules.
'The riot of the tipsy Bacchanals,
Tearing the Thracian singer in their rage.'
That is an old device, and it was play'd
When I from Thebes came last a conqueror.
'The thrice three Muses mourning for the death
Of learning, late deceas'd in beggary.'
That is some satire, keen and critical,
Not sorting with a nuptial ceremony.
'A tedious brief scene of young Pyramus
And his love Thisbe; very tragical mirth.'
Merry and tragical? Tedious and brief?
That is hot ice and wondrous strange snow.
How shall we find the concord of this discord?

PHILOSTRATE

A play there is, my lord, some ten words long,
Which is as brief as I have known a play;
But by ten words, my lord, it is too long,
Which makes it tedious. For in all the play
There is not one word apt, one player fitted.
And tragical, my noble lord, it is.
For Pyramus therein doth kill himself,
Which, when I saw rehears'd, I must confess,
Made mine eyes water; but more merry tears
The passion of loud laughter never shed.

THESEUS

What are they that do play it?

PHILOSTRATE

>Hard-handed men that work in Athens here,
>Which never labour'd in their minds till now;
>And now have toil'd their unbreath'd memories
>With this same play against your nuptial.

THESEUS

>And we will hear it.

PHILOSTRATE

>No, my noble lord,
>It is not for you: I have heard it over,
>And it is nothing, nothing in the world;
>Unless you can find sport in their intents,
>Extremely stretch'd and conn'd with cruel pain
>To do you service.

THESEUS

>I will hear that play;
>For never anything can be amiss
>When simpleness and duty tender it.
>Go, bring them in: and take your places, ladies.
>>*[Exit PHILOSTRATE.]*

HIPPOLYTA

>I love not to see wretchedness o'ercharged,
>And duty in his service perishing.

THESEUS

>Why, gentle sweet, you shall see no such thing.

HIPPOLYTA

>He says they can do nothing in this kind.

THESEUS

>The kinder we, to give them thanks for nothing.
>Our sport shall be to take what they mistake:
>And what poor duty cannot do, noble respect
>Takes it in might, not merit.
>Where I have come, great clerks have purposed
>To greet me with premeditated welcomes;

Where I have seen them shiver and look pale,
Make periods in the midst of sentences,
Throttle their practis'd accent in their fears,
And, in conclusion, dumbly have broke off,
Not paying me a welcome. Trust me, sweet,
Out of this silence yet I pick'd a welcome;
And in the modesty of fearful duty
I read as much as from the rattling tongue
Of saucy and audacious eloquence.
Love, therefore, and tongue-tied simplicity
In least speak most to my capacity.
            Enter PHILOSTRATE.

PHILOSTRATE

So please your grace, the Prologue is address'd.

THESEUS

Let him approach.
            Flourish of trumpets. Enter the PROLOGUE.

PROLOGUE

If we offend, it is with our good will.
That you should think, we come not to offend,
But with good will. To show our simple skill,
That is the true beginning of our end.
Consider then, we come but in despite.
We do not come, as minding to content you,
Our true intent is. All for your delight
We are not here. That you should here repent you,
The actors are at hand, and, by their show,
You shall know all that you are like to know.

THESEUS

This fellow doth not stand upon points.

LYSANDER

He hath rid his prologue like a rough colt; he knows not the stop.
A good moral, my lord: it is not enough to speak, but to speak true.

HIPPOLYTA

Indeed he hath played on this prologue like a child on a recorder; a sound, but not in government.

THESEUS

His speech was like a tangled chain; nothing impaired, but all disordered. Who is next?

Enter PYRAMUS *and* THISBE, WALL, MOONSHINE *and* LION *as in dumb show.*

PROLOGUE

Gentles, perchance you wonder at this show;
But wonder on, till truth make all things plain.
This man is Pyramus, if you would know;
This beauteous lady Thisbe is certain.
This man, with lime and rough-cast, doth present
Wall, that vile wall which did these lovers sunder;
And through Wall's chink, poor souls, they are content
To whisper, at the which let no man wonder.
This man, with lanthern, dog, and bush of thorn,
Presenteth Moonshine, for, if you will know,
By moonshine did these lovers think no scorn
To meet at Ninus' tomb, there, there to woo.
This grisly beast (which Lion hight by name)
The trusty Thisbe, coming first by night,
Did scare away, or rather did affright;
And as she fled, her mantle she did fall;
Which Lion vile with bloody mouth did stain.
Anon comes Pyramus, sweet youth, and tall,
And finds his trusty Thisbe's mantle slain;
Whereat with blade, with bloody blameful blade,
He bravely broach'd his boiling bloody breast;
And Thisbe, tarrying in mulberry shade,
His dagger drew, and died. For all the rest,
Let Lion, Moonshine, Wall and lovers twain,
At large discourse while here they do remain.

[Exeunt PROLOGUE, PYRAMUS, THISBE, LION *and* MOONSHINE.]

THESEUS

I wonder if the lion be to speak.

DEMETRIUS

No wonder, my lord. One lion may, when many asses do.

WALL

In this same interlude it doth befall
That I, one Snout by name, present a wall:
And such a wall as I would have you think
That had in it a crannied hole or chink,
Through which the lovers, Pyramus and Thisbe,
Did whisper often very secretly.
This loam, this rough-cast, and this stone, doth show
That I am that same wall; the truth is so:
And this the cranny is, right and sinister,
Through which the fearful lovers are to whisper.

THESEUS

Would you desire lime and hair to speak better?

DEMETRIUS

It is the wittiest partition that ever I heard discourse, my lord.

THESEUS

Pyramus draws near the wall; silence.
                    Enter PYRAMUS.

PYRAMUS

O grim-look'd night! O night with hue so black!
O night, which ever art when day is not!
O night, O night, alack, alack, alack,
I fear my Thisbe's promise is forgot!
And thou, O wall, O sweet, O lovely wall,
That stand'st between her father's ground and mine;
Thou wall, O wall, O sweet and lovely wall,
Show me thy chink, to blink through with mine eyne.
          [WALL holds up his fingers.]
Thanks, courteous wall: Jove shield thee well for this!
But what see I? No Thisbe do I see.

333

O wicked wall, through whom I see no bliss,
Curs'd be thy stones for thus deceiving me!

THESEUS

The wall, methinks, being sensible, should curse again.

PYRAMUS

No, in truth, sir, he should not. 'Deceiving me' is Thisbe's cue: she
is to enter now, and I am to spy her through the wall. You shall see it
will fall pat as I told you. Yonder she comes.

Enter THISBE.

THISBE

O wall, full often hast thou heard my moans,
For parting my fair Pyramus and me.
My cherry lips have often kiss'd thy stones,
Thy stones with lime and hair knit up in thee.

PYRAMUS

I see a voice; now will I to the chink,
To spy an I can hear my Thisbe's face.
Thisbe?

THISBE

My love thou art, my love I think.

PYRAMUS

Think what thou wilt, I am thy lover's grace;
And like Limander am I trusty still.

THISBE

And I like Helen, till the fates me kill.

PYRAMUS

Not Shafalus to Procrus was so true.

THISBE

As Shafalus to Procrus, I to you.

PYRAMUS

O kiss me through the hole of this vile wall.

THISBE

    I kiss the wall's hole, not your lips at all.

PYRAMUS

    Wilt thou at Ninny's tomb meet me straightway?

THISBE

    'Tide life, 'tide death, I come without delay.

WALL

    Thus have I, Wall, my part discharged so;
    And, being done, thus Wall away doth go.
        [Exeunt WALL, PYRAMUS and THISBE.]

THESEUS

    Now is the mural down between the two neighbours.

DEMETRIUS

    No remedy, my lord, when walls are so wilful to hear without warning.

HIPPOLYTA

    This is the silliest stuff that ever I heard.

THESEUS

    The best in this kind are but shadows; and the worst are no worse, if imagination amend them.

HIPPOLYTA

    It must be your imagination then, and not theirs.

THESEUS

    If we imagine no worse of them than they of themselves, they may pass for excellent men. Here come two noble beasts in, a man and a lion.
        Enter LION and MOONSHINE.

LION

    You, ladies, you, whose gentle hearts do fear
    The smallest monstrous mouse that creeps on floor,
    May now, perchance, both quake and tremble here,
    When lion rough in wildest rage doth roar.
    Then know that I, one Snug the joiner, am
    A lion fell, nor else no lion's dam;

For if I should as lion come in strife
Into this place, 'twere pity on my life.

THESEUS
A very gentle beast, and of a good conscience.

DEMETRIUS
The very best at a beast, my lord, that e'er I saw.

LYSANDER
This lion is a very fox for his valour.

THESEUS
True; and a goose for his discretion.

DEMETRIUS
Not so, my lord, for his valour cannot carry his discretion, and the fox carries the goose.

THESEUS
His discretion, I am sure, cannot carry his valour; for the goose carries not the fox. It is well; leave it to his discretion, and let us listen to the moon.

MOONSHINE
This lanthorn doth the hornèd moon present.

DEMETRIUS
He should have worn the horns on his head.

THESEUS
He is no crescent, and his horns are invisible within the circumference.

MOONSHINE
This lanthorn doth the hornèd moon present;
Myself the man i' the moon do seem to be.

THESEUS
This is the greatest error of all the rest; the man should be put into the lantern. How is it else the man i' the moon?

DEMETRIUS
He dares not come there for the candle, for you see, it is already in snuff.

HIPPOLYTA

I am aweary of this moon. Would he would change!

THESEUS

It appears by his small light of discretion that he is in the wane; but yet, in courtesy, in all reason, we must stay the time.

LYSANDER

Proceed, Moon.

MOON

All that I have to say, is to tell you that the lantern is the moon; I the man i' the moon; this thorn-bush my thorn-bush; and this dog my dog.

DEMETRIUS

Why, all these should be in the lantern, for all these are in the moon. But silence; here comes Thisbe.

Enter THISBE.

THISBE

This is old Ninny's tomb. Where is my love?

LION

Oh!

[The LION roars, THISBE runs off.]

DEMETRIUS

Well roared, Lion.

THESEUS

Well run, Thisbe.

HIPPOLYTA

Well shone, Moon. Truly, the moon shines with a good grace.

[The LION tears THISBE's mantle, and exit.]

THESEUS

Well moused, Lion.

LYSANDER

And so the lion vanished.

DEMETRIUS

And then came Pyramus.

Enter PYRAMUS.

PYRAMUS

Sweet Moon, I thank thee for thy sunny beams;
I thank thee, Moon, for shining now so bright;
For, by thy gracious golden, glittering gleams,
I trust to take of truest Thisbe sight.
But stay! O spite!
But mark, poor knight,
What dreadful dole is here!
Eyes, do you see?
How can it be?
O dainty duck! O dear!
Thy mantle good,
What, stained with blood?
Approach, ye Furies fell!
O Fates, come, come;
Cut thread and thrum;
Quail, rush, conclude, and quell!

THESEUS

This passion, and the death of a dear friend, would go near to make
a man look sad.

HIPPOLYTA

Beshrew my heart, but I pity the man.

PYRAMUS

O wherefore, Nature, didst thou lions frame,
Since lion vile hath here deflower'd my dear?
Which is—no, no—which was the fairest dame
That liv'd, that lov'd, that lik'd, that look'd with cheer.
Come, tears, confound!
Out, sword, and wound
The pap of Pyramus;
Ay, that left pap,
Where heart doth hop:

Thus die I, thus, thus, thus.
Now am I dead,
Now am I fled;
My soul is in the sky.
Tongue, lose thy light!
Moon, take thy flight!
Now die, die, die, die, die.
[Dies. Exit MOONSHINE.]

DEMETRIUS

No die, but an ace, for him; for he is but one.

LYSANDER

Less than an ace, man; for he is dead, he is nothing.

THESEUS

With the help of a surgeon he might yet recover and prove an ass.

HIPPOLYTA

How chance Moonshine is gone before Thisbe comes back and finds her lover?

THESEUS

She will find him by starlight.
Enter THISBE.
Here she comes, and her passion ends the play.

HIPPOLYTA

Methinks she should not use a long one for such a Pyramus. I hope she will be brief.

DEMETRIUS

A mote will turn the balance, which Pyramus, which Thisbe, is the better: he for a man, God warrant us; she for a woman, God bless us!

LYSANDER

She hath spied him already with those sweet eyes.

DEMETRIUS

And thus she means, *videlicet*—

THISBE

Asleep, my love?
What, dead, my dove?
O Pyramus, arise,
Speak, speak. Quite dumb?
Dead, dead? A tomb
Must cover thy sweet eyes.
These lily lips,
This cherry nose,
These yellow cowslip cheeks,
Are gone, are gone!
Lovers, make moan;
His eyes were green as leeks.
O Sisters Three,
Come, come to me,
With hands as pale as milk;
Lay them in gore,
Since you have shore
With shears his thread of silk.
Tongue, not a word:
Come, trusty sword,
Come, blade, my breast imbrue;
And farewell, friends.
Thus Thisbe ends.
Adieu, adieu, adieu.
        [Dies.]

THESEUS

Moonshine and Lion are left to bury the dead.

DEMETRIUS

Ay, and Wall too.

BOTTOM

No, I assure you; the wall is down that parted their fathers. Will it please you to see the epilogue, or to hear a Bergomask dance between two of our company?

THESEUS

No epilogue, I pray you; for your play needs no excuse. Never excuse; for when the players are all dead there need none to be blamed. Marry, if he that writ it had played Pyramus, and hanged himself in Thisbe's garter, it would have been a fine tragedy; and so it is, truly; and very notably discharged. But come, your Bergomask; let your epilogue alone.

> *[Here a dance of Clowns.]*
> The iron tongue of midnight hath told twelve.
> Lovers, to bed; 'tis almost fairy time.
> I fear we shall outsleep the coming morn
> As much as we this night have overwatch'd.
> This palpable-gross play hath well beguil'd
> The heavy gait of night. Sweet friends, to bed.
> A fortnight hold we this solemnity
> In nightly revels and new jollity.
> > *[Exeunt.]*
> > *Enter PUCK.*

PUCK

> Now the hungry lion roars,
> And the wolf behowls the moon;
> Whilst the heavy ploughman snores,
> All with weary task fordone.
> Now the wasted brands do glow,
> Whilst the screech-owl, screeching loud,
> Puts the wretch that lies in woe
> In remembrance of a shroud.
> Now it is the time of night
> That the graves, all gaping wide,
> Every one lets forth his sprite,
> In the church-way paths to glide.
> And we fairies, that do run
> By the triple Hecate's team
> From the presence of the sun,
> Following darkness like a dream,
> Now are frolic; not a mouse
> Shall disturb this hallow'd house.

I am sent with broom before,
To sweep the dust behind the door.
Enter OBERON *and* TITANIA *with their Train.*

OBERON

Through the house give glimmering light,
By the dead and drowsy fire.
Every elf and fairy sprite
Hop as light as bird from brier,
And this ditty after me,
Sing and dance it trippingly.

TITANIA

First rehearse your song by rote,
To each word a warbling note;
Hand in hand, with fairy grace,
Will we sing, and bless this place.
[Song and Dance.]

OBERON

Now, until the break of day,
Through this house each fairy stray.
To the best bride-bed will we,
Which by us shall blessèd be;
And the issue there create
Ever shall be fortunate.
So shall all the couples three
Ever true in loving be;
And the blots of Nature's hand
Shall not in their issue stand:
Never mole, hare-lip, nor scar,
Nor mark prodigious, such as are
Despised in nativity,
Shall upon their children be.
With this field-dew consecrate,
Every fairy take his gait,
And each several chamber bless,
Through this palace, with sweet peace;
And the owner of it blest.

Ever shall it in safety rest,
Trip away. Make no stay;
Meet me all by break of day.
            [Exeunt OBERON, TITANIA and Train.]

PUCK

If we shadows have offended,
Think but this, and all is mended,
That you have but slumber'd here
While these visions did appear.
And this weak and idle theme,
No more yielding but a dream,
Gentles, do not reprehend.
If you pardon, we will mend.
And, as I am an honest Puck,
If we have unearnèd luck
Now to 'scape the serpent's tongue,
We will make amends ere long;
Else the Puck a liar call.
So, good night unto you all.
Give me your hands, if we be friends,
And Robin shall restore amends.
            [Exit.]

AS YOU LIKE IT

DRAMATIS PERSONÆ

DUKE, living in exile
FREDERICK, his brother, and usurper of his dominions
AMIENS, lord attending on the banished Duke
JAQUES, " " " " " "
LE BEAU, a courtier attending upon Frederick
CHARLES, wrestler to Frederick
OLIVER, son of Sir Rowland de Boys
JAQUES, " " " " " "
ORLANDO, " " " " " "
ADAM, servant to Oliver
DENNIS, " " "
TOUCHSTONE, the court jester
SIR OLIVER MARTEXT, a vicar
CORIN, shepherd
SILVIUS, "
WILLIAM, a country fellow, in love with Audrey
A person representing HYMEN
ROSALIND, daughter to the banished Duke
CELIA, daughter to Frederick
PHEBE, a shepherdess
AUDREY, a country wench
Lords, Pages, Foresters, and Attendants

CONTENTS

SCENE: OLIVER'S house; FREDERICK'S court; and the Forest of Arden.

ACT I

SCENE I. Orchard of OLIVER'S house.

Enter ORLANDO and ADAM

ORLANDO

As I remember, Adam, it was upon this fashion bequeathed me by will but poor a thousand crowns, and, as thou say'st, charged my brother, on his blessing, to breed me well; and there begins my sadness. My brother Jaques he keeps at school, and report speaks goldenly of his profit. For my part, he keeps me rustically at home, or, to speak more properly, stays me here at home unkept; for call you that keeping for a gentleman of my birth that differs not from the stalling of an ox? His horses are bred better; for, besides that they are fair with their feeding, they are taught their manage, and to that end riders dearly hir'd; but I, his brother, gain nothing under him but growth; for the which his animals on his dunghills are as much bound to him as I. Besides this nothing that he so plentifully gives me, the something that nature gave me his countenance seems to take from me. He lets me feed with his hinds, bars me the place of a brother, and as much as in him lies, mines my gentility with my education. This is it, Adam, that grieves me; and the spirit of my father, which I think is within me, begins to mutiny against this servitude. I will no longer endure it, though yet I know no wise remedy how to avoid it.

Enter OLIVER

ADAM

Yonder comes my master, your brother.

351

ORLANDO

Go apart, Adam, and thou shalt hear how he will shake me up.
[ADAM retires]

OLIVER

Now, sir! what make you here?

ORLANDO

Nothing; I am not taught to make any thing.

OLIVER

What mar you then, sir?

ORLANDO

Marry, sir, I am helping you to mar that which God made, a poor
unworthy brother of yours, with idleness.

OLIVER

Marry, sir, be better employed, and be nought awhile.

ORLANDO

Shall I keep your hogs, and eat husks with them? What prodigal
portion have I spent that I should come to such penury?

OLIVER

Know you where you are, sir?

ORLANDO

O, sir, very well; here in your orchard.

OLIVER

Know you before whom, sir?

ORLANDO

Ay, better than him I am before knows me. I know you are my
eldest brother; and in the gentle condition of blood, you should so
know me. The courtesy of nations allows you my better in that you are
the first-born; but the same tradition takes not away my blood, were
there twenty brothers betwixt us. I have as much of my father in me as
you, albeit I confess your coming before me is nearer to his reverence.

OLIVER

What, boy!
[Strikes him]

ORLANDO

Come, come, elder brother, you are too young in this.

OLIVER

Wilt thou lay hands on me, villain?

ORLANDO

I am no villain; I am the youngest son of Sir Rowland de Boys. He was my father; and he is thrice a villain that says such a father begot villains. Wert thou not my brother, I would not take this hand from thy throat till this other had pull'd out thy tongue for saying so. Thou has rail'd on thyself.

ADAM

[Coming forward]

Sweet masters, be patient; for your father's remembrance, be at accord.

OLIVER

Let me go, I say.

ORLANDO

I will not, till I please; you shall hear me. My father charg'd you in his will to give me good education: you have train'd me like a peasant, obscuring and hiding from me all gentleman-like qualities. The spirit of my father grows strong in me, and I will no longer endure it; therefore allow me such exercises as may become a gentleman, or give me the poor allottery my father left me by testament; with that I will go buy my fortunes.

OLIVER

And what wilt thou do? Beg, when that is spent? Well, sir, get you in. I will not long be troubled with you; you shall have some part of your will. I pray you leave me.

ORLANDO

I no further offend you than becomes me for my good.

OLIVER

Get you with him, you old dog.

ADAM

Is 'old dog' my reward? Most true, I have lost my teeth in your service. God be with my old master! He would not have spoke such a word.
Exeunt ORLANDO and ADAM

OLIVER

Is it even so? Begin you to grow upon me? I will physic your rankness, and yet give no thousand crowns neither. Holla, Dennis!
Enter DENNIS

DENNIS

Calls your worship?

OLIVER

Was not Charles, the Duke's wrestler, here to speak with me?

DENNIS

So please you, he is here at the door and importunes access to you.

OLIVER

Call him in.
Exit DENNIS
'Twill be a good way; and to-morrow the wrestling is.
Enter CHARLES

CHARLES

Good morrow to your worship.

OLIVER

Good Monsieur Charles! What's the new news at the new court?

CHARLES

There's no news at the court, sir, but the old news; that is, the old Duke is banished by his younger brother the new Duke; and three or four loving lords have put themselves into voluntary exile with him, whose lands and revenues enrich the new Duke; therefore he gives them good leave to wander.

OLIVER

Can you tell if Rosalind, the Duke's daughter, be banished with her father?

CHARLES

O, no; for the Duke's daughter, her cousin, so loves her, being ever from their cradles bred together, that she would have followed her exile, or have died to stay behind her. She is at the court, and no less beloved of her uncle than his own daughter; and never two ladies loved as they do.

OLIVER

Where will the old Duke live?

CHARLES

They say he is already in the Forest of Arden, and a many merry men with him; and there they live like the old Robin Hood of England. They say many young gentlemen flock to him every day, and fleet the time carelessly, as they did in the golden world.

OLIVER

What, you wrestle to-morrow before the new Duke?

CHARLES

Marry, do I, sir; and I came to acquaint you with a matter. I am given, sir, secretly to understand that your younger brother, Orlando, hath a disposition to come in disguis'd against me to try a fall. To-morrow, sir, I wrestle for my credit; and he that escapes me without some broken limb shall acquit him well. Your brother is but young and tender; and, for your love, I would be loath to foil him, as I must, for my own honour, if he come in; therefore, out of my love to you, I came hither to acquaint you withal, that either you might stay him from his intendment, or brook such disgrace well as he shall run into, in that it is thing of his own search and altogether against my will.

OLIVER

Charles, I thank thee for thy love to me, which thou shalt find I will most kindly requite. I had myself notice of my brother's purpose herein, and have by underhand means laboured to dissuade him from it; but he is resolute. I'll tell thee, Charles, it is the stubbornest young fellow of France; full of ambition, an envious emulator of every man's good parts, a secret and villainous contriver against me his natural brother. Therefore use thy discretion: I had as lief thou didst break his neck as his finger. And thou wert best look to't; for if thou dost him any slight disgrace, or if he do not mightily grace himself on thee, he will practise against thee by poison, entrap thee by some treacherous device, and never leave thee till he hath ta'en thy life by some indirect means or other; for, I assure thee, and almost with tears I speak it, there is not one so young and so villainous this day living. I speak but brotherly of him; but should I anatomize him to thee as he is, I must blush and weep, and thou must look pale and wonder.

CHARLES

I am heartily glad I came hither to you. If he come to-morrow I'll give him his payment. If ever he go alone again, I'll never wrestle for prize more. And so, God keep your worship!

Exit

OLIVER

Farewell, good Charles. Now will I stir this gamester. I hope I shall see an end of him; for my soul, yet I know not why, hates nothing more than he. Yet he's gentle; never school'd and yet learned; full of noble device; of all sorts enchantingly beloved; and, indeed, so much in the heart of the world, and especially of my own people, who best know him, that I am altogether misprised. But it shall not be so long; this wrestler shall clear all. Nothing remains but that I kindle the boy thither, which now I'll go about.

Exit

SCENE II. A lawn before the DUKE'S palace.

Enter ROSALIND and CELIA

CELIA

I pray thee, Rosalind, sweet my coz, be merry.

ROSALIND

Dear Celia, I show more mirth than I am mistress of; and would you yet I were merrier? Unless you could teach me to forget a banished father, you must not learn me how to remember any extraordinary pleasure.

CELIA

Herein I see thou lov'st me not with the full weight that I love thee. If my uncle, thy banished father, had banished thy uncle, the Duke my father, so thou hadst been still with me, I could have taught my love to take thy father for mine; so wouldst thou, if the truth of thy love to me were so righteously temper'd as mine is to thee.

ROSALIND

Well, I will forget the condition of my estate, to rejoice in yours.

CELIA

You know my father hath no child but I, nor none is like to have; and, truly, when he dies thou shalt be his heir; for what he hath taken away from thy father perforce, I will render thee again in affection. By mine honour, I will; and when I break that oath, let me turn monster; therefore, my sweet Rose, my dear Rose, be merry.

ROSALIND

From henceforth I will, coz, and devise sports. Let me see; what think you of falling in love?

CELIA

Marry, I prithee, do, to make sport withal; but love no man in good earnest, nor no further in sport neither than with safety of a pure blush thou mayst in honour come off again.

ROSALIND

What shall be our sport, then?

CELIA

Let us sit and mock the good housewife Fortune from her wheel, that her gifts may henceforth be bestowed equally.

ROSALIND

I would we could do so; for her benefits are mightily misplaced; and the bountiful blind woman doth most mistake in her gifts to women.

CELIA

'Tis true; for those that she makes fair she scarce makes honest; and those that she makes honest she makes very ill-favouredly.

ROSALIND

Nay; now thou goest from Fortune's office to Nature's: Fortune reigns in gifts of the world, not in the lineaments of Nature.

Enter TOUCHSTONE

CELIA

No; when Nature hath made a fair creature, may she not by Fortune fall into the fire? Though Nature hath given us wit to flout at Fortune, hath not Fortune sent in this fool to cut off the argument?

ROSALIND

Indeed, there is Fortune too hard for Nature, when Fortune makes Nature's natural the cutter-off of Nature's wit.

CELIA

Peradventure this is not Fortune's work neither, but Nature's, who perceiveth our natural wits too dull to reason of such goddesses, and hath sent this natural for our whetstone; for always the dullness of the fool is the whetstone of the wits. How now, wit! Whither wander you?

TOUCHSTONE

Mistress, you must come away to your father.

CELIA

Were you made the messenger?

TOUCHSTONE

No, by mine honour; but I was bid to come for you.

ROSALIND

Where learned you that oath, fool?

TOUCHSTONE

Of a certain knight that swore by his honour they were good pancakes, and swore by his honour the mustard was naught. Now I'll stand to it, the pancakes were naught and the mustard was good, and yet was not the knight forsworn.

CELIA

How prove you that, in the great heap of your knowledge?

ROSALIND

Ay, marry, now unmuzzle your wisdom.

TOUCHSTONE

Stand you both forth now: stroke your chins, and swear by your beards that I am a knave.

CELIA

By our beards, if we had them, thou art.

TOUCHSTONE

By my knavery, if I had it, then I were. But if you swear by that that not, you are not forsworn; no more was this knight, swearing by his honour, for he never had any; or if he had, he had sworn it away before ever he saw those pancackes or that mustard.

CELIA

Prithee, who is't that thou mean'st?

TOUCHSTONE

One that old Frederick, your father, loves.

CELIA

My father's love is enough to honour him. Enough, speak no more of him; you'll be whipt for taxation one of these days.

TOUCHSTONE

The more pity that fools may not speak wisely what wise men do foolishly.

CELIA

By my troth, thou sayest true; for since the little wit that fools have was silenced, the little foolery that wise men have makes a great show. Here comes Monsieur Le Beau.

Enter LE BEAU

ROSALIND

With his mouth full of news.

CELIA

Which he will put on us as pigeons feed their young.

ROSALIND

Then shall we be news-cramm'd.

CELIA

All the better; we shall be the more marketable. Bon jour, Monsieur Le Beau. What's the news?

LE BEAU

Fair Princess, you have lost much good sport.

CELIA

Sport! of what colour?

LE BEAU

What colour, madam? How shall I answer you?

ROSALIND

As wit and fortune will.

TOUCHSTONE

Or as the Destinies decree.

CELIA

Well said; that was laid on with a trowel.

TOUCHSTONE

Nay, if I keep not my rank—

ROSALIND

Thou losest thy old smell.

LE BEAU

You amaze me, ladies. I would have told you of good wrestling, which you have lost the sight of.

ROSALIND

Yet tell us the manner of the wrestling.

LE BEAU

I will tell you the beginning, and, if it please your ladyships, you may see the end; for the best is yet to do; and here, where you are, they are coming to perform it.

CELIA

Well, the beginning, that is dead and buried.

LE BEAU

There comes an old man and his three sons—

CELIA

I could match this beginning with an old tale.

LE BEAU

Three proper young men, of excellent growth and presence.

ROSALIND

With bills on their necks: 'Be it known unto all men by these presents'—

LE BEAU

The eldest of the three wrestled with Charles, the Duke's wrestler; which Charles in a moment threw him, and broke three of his ribs, that there is little hope of life in him. So he serv'd the second, and so the third. Yonder they lie; the poor old man, their father, making such pitiful dole over them that all the beholders take his part with weeping.

ROSALIND

Alas!

TOUCHSTONE

But what is the sport, monsieur, that the ladies have lost?

LE BEAU

Why, this that I speak of.

TOUCHSTONE

Thus men may grow wiser every day. It is the first time that ever I heard breaking of ribs was sport for ladies.

CELIA

Or I, I promise thee.

ROSALIND

But is there any else longs to see this broken music in his sides? Is there yet another dotes upon rib-breaking? Shall we see this wrestling, cousin?

LE BEAU

You must, if you stay here; for here is the place appointed for the wrestling, and they are ready to perform it.

CELIA

Yonder, sure, they are coming. Let us now stay and see it.
Flourish.
Enter DUKE FREDERICK, LORDS, ORLANDO,
CHARLES and ATTENDANTS

FREDERICK

Come on; since the youth will not be entreated, his own peril on his forwardness.

ROSALIND

Is yonder the man?

LE BEAU

Even he, madam.

CELIA

Alas, he is too young; yet he looks successfully.

FREDERICK

How now, daughter and cousin! Are you crept hither to see the wrestling?

ROSALIND

Ay, my liege; so please you give us leave.

FREDERICK

You will take little delight in it, I can tell you, there is such odds in the man. In pity of the challenger's youth I would fain dissuade him, but he will not be entreated. Speak to him, ladies; see if you can move him.

CELIA

Call him hither, good Monsieur Le Beau.

FREDERICK

Do so; I'll not be by.
[DUKE FREDERICK goes apart]

LE BEAU

Monsieur the Challenger, the Princess calls for you.

ORLANDO

I attend them with all respect and duty.

ROSALIND

Young man, have you challeng'd Charles the wrestler?

ORLANDO

No, fair Princess; he is the general challenger. I come but in, as others do, to try with him the strength of my youth.

CELIA

Young gentleman, your spirits are too bold for your years. You have seen cruel proof of this man's strength; if you saw yourself with your eyes, or knew yourself with your judgment, the fear of your adventure would counsel you to a more equal enterprise. We pray you, for your own sake, to embrace your own safety and give over this attempt.

ROSALIND

Do, young sir; your reputation shall not therefore be misprised: we will make it our suit to the Duke that the wrestling might not go forward.

ORLANDO

I beseech you, punish me not with your hard thoughts, wherein I confess me much guilty to deny so fair and excellent ladies any thing. But let your fair eyes and gentle wishes go with me to my trial; wherein if I be foil'd there is but one sham'd that was never gracious; if kill'd, but one dead that is willing to be so. I shall do my friends no wrong, for I have none to lament me; the world no injury, for in it I have nothing; only in the world I fill up a place, which may be better supplied when I have made it empty.

ROSALIND

The little strength that I have, I would it were with you.

CELIA

And mine to eke out hers.

ROSALIND

Fare you well. Pray heaven I be deceiv'd in you!

CELIA

Your heart's desires be with you!

CHARLES

Come, where is this young gallant that is so desirous to lie with his mother earth?

ORLANDO

Ready, sir; but his will hath in it a more modest working.

FREDERICK

You shall try but one fall.

CHARLES

No, I warrant your Grace, you shall not entreat him to a second, that have so mightily persuaded him from a first.

ORLANDO

You mean to mock me after; you should not have mock'd me before; but come your ways.

ROSALIND

Now, Hercules be thy speed, young man!

CELIA

I would I were invisible, to catch the strong fellow by the leg.
[They wrestle]

ROSALIND

O excellent young man!

CELIA

If I had a thunderbolt in mine eye, I can tell who should down.
[CHARLES is thrown. Shout]

FREDERICK

No more, no more.

ORLANDO

Yes, I beseech your Grace; I am not yet well breath'd.

FREDERICK

How dost thou, Charles?

LE BEAU

He cannot speak, my lord.

FREDERICK

Bear him away. What is thy name, young man?

ORLANDO

Orlando, my liege; the youngest son of Sir Rowland de Boys.

FREDERICK

> I would thou hadst been son to some man else.
> The world esteem'd thy father honourable,
> But I did find him still mine enemy.
> Thou shouldst have better pleas'd me with this deed,
> Hadst thou descended from another house.
> But fare thee well; thou art a gallant youth;
> I would thou hadst told me of another father.
>> *Exeunt DUKE, Train and LE BEAU*

CELIA

> Were I my father, coz, would I do this?

ORLANDO

> I am more proud to be Sir Rowland's son,
> His youngest son—and would not change that calling
> To be adopted heir to Frederick.

ROSALIND

> My father lov'd Sir Rowland as his soul,
> And all the world was of my father's mind;
> Had I before known this young man his son,
> I should have given him tears unto entreaties
> Ere he should thus have ventur'd.

CELIA

> Gentle cousin,
> Let us go thank him, and encourage him;
> My father's rough and envious disposition
> Sticks me at heart. Sir, you have well deserv'd;
> If you do keep your promises in love
> But justly as you have exceeded all promise,
> Your mistress shall be happy.

ROSALIND

> Gentleman,
>> *[Giving him a chain from her neck]*
> Wear this for me; one out of suits with fortune,
> That could give more, but that her hand lacks means.
> Shall we go, coz?

CELIA

Ay. Fare you well, fair gentleman.

ORLANDO

Can I not say 'I thank you'? My better parts
Are all thrown down; and that which here stands up
Is but a quintain, a mere lifeless block.

ROSALIND

He calls us back. My pride fell with my fortunes;
I'll ask him what he would. Did you call, sir?
Sir, you have wrestled well, and overthrown
More than your enemies.

CELIA

Will you go, coz?

ROSALIND

Have with you. Fare you well.
              Exeunt ROSALIND and CELIA

ORLANDO

What passion hangs these weights upon my tongue?
I cannot speak to her, yet she urg'd conference.
O poor Orlando, thou art overthrown!
Or Charles or something weaker masters thee.
              Re-enter LE BEAU

LE BEAU

Good sir, I do in friendship counsel you
To leave this place. Albeit you have deserv'd
High commendation, true applause, and love,
Yet such is now the Duke's condition
That he misconstrues all that you have done.
The Duke is humorous; what he is, indeed,
More suits you to conceive than I to speak of.

ORLANDO

I thank you, sir; and pray you tell me this:
Which of the two was daughter of the Duke
That here was at the wrestling?

LE BEAU

Neither his daughter, if we judge by manners;
But yet, indeed, the smaller is his daughter;
The other is daughter to the banish'd Duke,
And here detain'd by her usurping uncle,
To keep his daughter company; whose loves
Are dearer than the natural bond of sisters.
But I can tell you that of late this Duke
Hath ta'en displeasure 'gainst his gentle niece,
Grounded upon no other argument
But that the people praise her for her virtues
And pity her for her good father's sake;
And, on my life, his malice 'gainst the lady
Will suddenly break forth. Sir, fare you well.
Hereafter, in a better world than this,
I shall desire more love and knowledge of you.

ORLANDO

I rest much bounden to you; fare you well.
        Exit LE BEAU
Thus must I from the smoke into the smother;
From tyrant Duke unto a tyrant brother.
But heavenly Rosalind!
        Exit

SCENE III. The DUKE's palace.

Enter CELIA and ROSALIND

CELIA

Why, cousin! why, Rosalind! Cupid have mercy! Not a word?

ROSALIND

Not one to throw at a dog.

CELIA

No, thy words are too precious to be cast away upon curs; throw
some of them at me; come, lame me with reasons.

ROSALIND

Then there were two cousins laid up, when the one should be lam'd with reasons and the other mad without any.

CELIA

But is all this for your father?

ROSALIND

No, some of it is for my child's father. O, how full of briers is this working-day world!

CELIA

They are but burs, cousin, thrown upon thee in holiday foolery; if we walk not in the trodden paths, our very petticoats will catch them.

ROSALIND

I could shake them off my coat: these burs are in my heart.

CELIA

Hem them away.

ROSALIND

I would try, if I could cry 'hem' and have him.

CELIA

Come, come, wrestle with thy affections.

ROSALIND

O, they take the part of a better wrestler than myself.

CELIA

O, a good wish upon you! You will try in time, in despite of a fall. But, turning these jests out of service, let us talk in good earnest. Is it possible, on such a sudden, you should fall into so strong a liking with old Sir Rowland's youngest son?

ROSALIND

The Duke my father lov'd his father dearly.

CELIA

Doth it therefore ensue that you should love his son dearly? By this kind of chase I should hate him, for my father hated his father dearly; yet I hate not Orlando.

ROSALIND

No, faith, hate him not, for my sake.

CELIA

Why should I not? Doth he not deserve well?
Enter DUKE FREDERICK, with LORDS

ROSALIND

Let me love him for that; and do you love him because I do. Look, here comes the Duke.

CELIA

With his eyes full of anger.

FREDERICK

Mistress, dispatch you with your safest haste,
And get you from our court.

ROSALIND

Me, uncle?

FREDERICK

You, cousin.
Within these ten days if that thou beest found
So near our public court as twenty miles,
Thou diest for it.

ROSALIND

I do beseech your Grace,
Let me the knowledge of my fault bear with me.
If with myself I hold intelligence,
Or have acquaintance with mine own desires;
If that I do not dream, or be not frantic—
As I do trust I am not—then, dear uncle,
Never so much as in a thought unborn
Did I offend your Highness.

FREDERICK

Thus do all traitors;
If their purgation did consist in words,
They are as innocent as grace itself.
Let it suffice thee that I trust thee not.

ROSALIND

Yet your mistrust cannot make me a traitor.
Tell me whereon the likelihood depends.

FREDERICK

Thou art thy father's daughter; there's enough.

ROSALIND

So was I when your Highness took his dukedom;
So was I when your Highness banish'd him.
Treason is not inherited, my lord;
Or, if we did derive it from our friends,
What's that to me? My father was no traitor.
Then, good my liege, mistake me not so much
To think my poverty is treacherous.

CELIA

Dear sovereign, hear me speak.

FREDERICK

Ay, Celia; we stay'd her for your sake,
Else had she with her father rang'd along.

CELIA

I did not then entreat to have her stay;
It was your pleasure, and your own remorse;
I was too young that time to value her,
But now I know her. If she be a traitor,
Why so am I: we still have slept together,
Rose at an instant, learn'd, play'd, eat together;
And wheresoe'er we went, like Juno's swans,
Still we went coupled and inseparable.

FREDERICK

She is too subtle for thee; and her smoothness,
Her very silence and her patience,
Speak to the people, and they pity her.
Thou art a fool. She robs thee of thy name;
And thou wilt show more bright and seem more virtuous
When she is gone. Then open not thy lips.

Firm and irrevocable is my doom
Which I have pass'd upon her; she is banish'd.

CELIA

Pronounce that sentence, then, on me, my liege;
I cannot live out of her company.

FREDERICK

You are a fool. You, niece, provide yourself.
If you outstay the time, upon mine honour,
And in the greatness of my word, you die.
Exeunt DUKE and LORDS

CELIA

O my poor Rosalind! Whither wilt thou go?
Wilt thou change fathers? I will give thee mine.
I charge thee be not thou more griev'd than I am.

ROSALIND

I have more cause.

CELIA

Thou hast not, cousin.
Prithee be cheerful. Know'st thou not the Duke
Hath banish'd me, his daughter?

ROSALIND

That he hath not.

CELIA

No, hath not? Rosalind lacks, then, the love
Which teacheth thee that thou and I am one.
Shall we be sund'red? Shall we part, sweet girl?
No; let my father seek another heir.
Therefore devise with me how we may fly,
Whither to go, and what to bear with us;
And do not seek to take your charge upon you,
To bear your griefs yourself, and leave me out;
For, by this heaven, now at our sorrows pale,
Say what thou canst, I'll go along with thee.

ROSALIND

Why, whither shall we go?

CELIA

To seek my uncle in the Forest of Arden.

ROSALIND

Alas, what danger will it be to us,
Maids as we are, to travel forth so far!
Beauty provoketh thieves sooner than gold.

CELIA

I'll put myself in poor and mean attire,
And with a kind of umber smirch my face;
The like do you; so shall we pass along,
And never stir assailants.

ROSALIND

Were it not better,
Because that I am more than common tall,
That I did suit me all points like a man?
A gallant curtle-axe upon my thigh,
A boar spear in my hand; and—in my heart
Lie there what hidden woman's fear there will—
We'll have a swashing and a martial outside,
As many other mannish cowards have
That do outface it with their semblances.

CELIA

What shall I call thee when thou art a man?

ROSALIND

I'll have no worse a name than Jove's own page,
And therefore look you call me Ganymede.
But what will you be call'd?

CELIA

Something that hath a reference to my state:
No longer Celia, but Aliena.

ROSALIND

> But, cousin, what if we assay'd to steal
> The clownish fool out of your father's court?
> Would he not be a comfort to our travel?

CELIA

> He'll go along o'er the wide world with me;
> Leave me alone to woo him. Let's away,
> And get our jewels and our wealth together;
> Devise the fittest time and safest way
> To hide us from pursuit that will be made
> After my flight. Now go we in content
> To liberty, and not to banishment.
> > *Exeunt*

ACT II

SCENE I. The Forest of Arden.

Enter DUKE SENIOR, AMIENS and two or three LORDS,
like foresters

DUKE SENIOR
> Now, my co-mates and brothers in exile,
> Hath not old custom made this life more sweet
> Than that of painted pomp? Are not these woods
> More free from peril than the envious court?
> Here feel we not the penalty of Adam,
> The seasons' difference; as the icy fang
> And churlish chiding of the winter's wind,
> Which when it bites and blows upon my body,
> Even till I shrink with cold, I smile and say
> 'This is no flattery; these are counsellors
> That feelingly persuade me what I am.'
> Sweet are the uses of adversity,
> Which, like the toad, ugly and venomous,
> Wears yet a precious jewel in his head;
> And this our life, exempt from public haunt,
> Finds tongues in trees, books in the running brooks,
> Sermons in stones, and good in everything.
> I would not change it.

AMIENS

> Happy is your Grace,
> That can translate the stubbornness of fortune
> Into so quiet and so sweet a style.

DUKE SENIOR

> Come, shall we go and kill us venison?
> And yet it irks me the poor dappled fools,
> Being native burghers of this desert city,
> Should, in their own confines, with forked heads
> Have their round haunches gor'd.

FIRST LORD

> Indeed, my lord,
> The melancholy Jaques grieves at that;
> And, in that kind, swears you do more usurp
> Than doth your brother that hath banish'd you.
> To-day my Lord of Amiens and myself
> Did steal behind him as he lay along
> Under an oak whose antique root peeps out
> Upon the brook that brawls along this wood!
> To the which place a poor sequest'red stag,
> That from the hunter's aim had ta'en a hurt,
> Did come to languish; and, indeed, my lord,
> The wretched animal heav'd forth such groans
> That their discharge did stretch his leathern coat
> Almost to bursting; and the big round tears
> Cours'd one another down his innocent nose
> In piteous chase; and thus the hairy fool,
> Much marked of the melancholy Jaques,
> Stood on th' extremest verge of the swift brook,
> Augmenting it with tears.

DUKE SENIOR

> But what said Jaques?
> Did he not moralize this spectacle?

FIRST LORD

> O, yes, into a thousand similes.

First, for his weeping into the needless stream:
'Poor deer,' quoth he, 'thou mak'st a testament
As worldlings do, giving thy sum of more
To that which had too much.' Then, being there alone,
Left and abandoned of his velvet friends:
''Tis right'; quoth he; 'thus misery doth part
The flux of company.' Anon, a careless herd,
Full of the pasture, jumps along by him
And never stays to greet him. 'Ay,' quoth Jaques,
'Sweep on, you fat and greasy citizens;
'Tis just the fashion. Wherefore do you look
Upon that poor and broken bankrupt there?'
Thus most invectively he pierceth through
The body of the country, city, court,
Yea, and of this our life; swearing that we
Are mere usurpers, tyrants, and what's worse,
To fright the animals, and to kill them up
In their assign'd and native dwelling-place.

DUKE SENIOR

And did you leave him in this contemplation?

SECOND LORD

We did, my lord, weeping and commenting
Upon the sobbing deer.

DUKE SENIOR

Show me the place;
I love to cope him in these sullen fits,
For then he's full of matter.

FIRST LORD

I'll bring you to him straight.
Exeunt

SCENE II. The DUKE'S palace.

Enter DUKE FREDERICK with LORDS

FREDERICK

> Can it be possible that no man saw them?
> It cannot be; some villains of my court
> Are of consent and sufferance in this.

FIRST LORD

> I cannot hear of any that did see her.
> The ladies, her attendants of her chamber,
> Saw her abed, and in the morning early
> They found the bed untreasur'd of their mistress.

SECOND LORD

> My lord, the roynish clown, at whom so oft
> Your Grace was wont to laugh, is also missing.
> Hisperia, the Princess' gentlewoman,
> Confesses that she secretly o'erheard
> Your daughter and her cousin much commend
> The parts and graces of the wrestler
> That did but lately foil the sinewy Charles;
> And she believes, wherever they are gone,
> That youth is surely in their company.

FREDERICK

> Send to his brother; fetch that gallant hither.
> If he be absent, bring his brother to me;
> I'll make him find him. Do this suddenly;
> And let not search and inquisition quail
> To bring again these foolish runaways.
> > *Exeunt*

SCENE III. Before OLIVER'S house.

Enter ORLANDO and ADAM, meeting

ORLANDO

> Who's there?

ADAM

> What, my young master? O my gentle master!
> O my sweet master! O you memory

Of old Sir Rowland! Why, what make you here?
Why are you virtuous? Why do people love you?
And wherefore are you gentle, strong, and valiant?
Why would you be so fond to overcome
The bonny prizer of the humorous Duke?
Your praise is come too swiftly home before you.
Know you not, master, to some kind of men
Their graces serve them but as enemies?
No more do yours. Your virtues, gentle master,
Are sanctified and holy traitors to you.
O, what a world is this, when what is comely
Envenoms him that bears it!

ORLANDO
Why, what's the matter?

ADAM
O unhappy youth!
Come not within these doors; within this roof
The enemy of all your graces lives.
Your brother—no, no brother; yet the son—
Yet not the son; I will not call him son
Of him I was about to call his father—
Hath heard your praises; and this night he means
To burn the lodging where you use to lie,
And you within it. If he fail of that,
He will have other means to cut you off;
I overheard him and his practices.
This is no place; this house is but a butchery;
Abhor it, fear it, do not enter it.

ORLANDO
Why, whither, Adam, wouldst thou have me go?

ADAM
No matter whither, so you come not here.

ORLANDO
What, wouldst thou have me go and beg my food,
Or with a base and boist'rous sword enforce

A thievish living on the common road?
This I must do, or know not what to do;
Yet this I will not do, do how I can.
I rather will subject me to the malice
Of a diverted blood and bloody brother.

ADAM

But do not so. I have five hundred crowns,
The thrifty hire I sav'd under your father,
Which I did store to be my foster-nurse,
When service should in my old limbs lie lame,
And unregarded age in corners thrown.
Take that, and He that doth the ravens feed,
Yea, providently caters for the sparrow,
Be comfort to my age! Here is the gold;
All this I give you. Let me be your servant;
Though I look old, yet I am strong and lusty;
For in my youth I never did apply
Hot and rebellious liquors in my blood,
Nor did not with unbashful forehead woo
The means of weakness and debility;
Therefore my age is as a lusty winter,
Frosty, but kindly. Let me go with you;
I'll do the service of a younger man
In all your business and necessities.

ORLANDO

O good old man, how well in thee appears
The constant service of the antique world,
When service sweat for duty, not for meed!
Thou art not for the fashion of these times,
Where none will sweat but for promotion,
And having that do choke their service up
Even with the having; it is not so with thee.
But, poor old man, thou prun'st a rotten tree
That cannot so much as a blossom yield
In lieu of all thy pains and husbandry.
But come thy ways, we'll go along together,

And ere we have thy youthful wages spent
We'll light upon some settled low content.

ADAM

Master, go on; and I will follow thee,
To the last gasp, with truth and loyalty.
From seventeen years till now almost four-score
Here lived I, but now live here no more.
At seventeen years many their fortunes seek,
But at fourscore it is too late a week;
Yet fortune cannot recompense me better
Than to die well and not my master's debtor.

Exeunt

SCENE IV. The Forest of Arden.

*Enter ROSALIND for GANYMEDE, CELIA for ALIENA,
and CLOWN alias TOUCHSTONE*

ROSALIND

O Jupiter, how weary are my spirits!

TOUCHSTONE

I care not for my spirits, if my legs were not weary.

ROSALIND

I could find in my heart to disgrace my man's apparel, and to cry like a woman; but I must comfort the weaker vessel, as doublet and hose ought to show itself courageous to petticoat; therefore, courage, good Aliena.

CELIA

I pray you bear with me; I cannot go no further.

TOUCHSTONE

For my part, I had rather bear with you than bear you; yet I should bear no cross if I did bear you; for I think you have no money in your purse.

ROSALIND

Well this is the Forest of Arden.

TOUCHSTONE

Ay, now am I in Arden; the more fool I; when I was at home I was in a better place; but travellers must be content.

Enter CORIN and SILVIUS

ROSALIND

Ay, be so, good Touchstone. Look you, who comes here, a young man and an old in solemn talk.

CORIN

That is the way to make her scorn you still.

SILVIUS

O Corin, that thou knew'st how I do love her!

CORIN

I partly guess; for I have lov'd ere now.

SILVIUS

No, Corin, being old, thou canst not guess,
Though in thy youth thou wast as true a lover
As ever sigh'd upon a midnight pillow.
But if thy love were ever like to mine,
As sure I think did never man love so,
How many actions most ridiculous
Hast thou been drawn to by thy fantasy?

CORIN

Into a thousand that I have forgotten.

SILVIUS

O, thou didst then never love so heartily!
If thou rememb'rest not the slightest folly
That ever love did make thee run into,
Thou hast not lov'd;
Or if thou hast not sat as I do now,
Wearing thy hearer in thy mistress' praise,
Thou hast not lov'd;
Or if thou hast not broke from company
Abruptly, as my passion now makes me,
Thou hast not lov'd.
O Phebe, Phebe, Phebe!

Exit SILVIUS

ROSALIND

Alas, poor shepherd! searching of thy wound,
I have by hard adventure found mine own.

TOUCHSTONE

And I mine. I remember, when I was in love, I broke my sword
upon a stone, and bid him take that for coming a-night to Jane Smile;
and I remember the kissing of her batler, and the cow's dugs that her
pretty chopt hands had milk'd; and I remember the wooing of peas-
cod instead of her; from whom I took two cods, and giving her them
again, said with weeping tears 'Wear these for my sake.' We that are
true lovers run into strange capers; but as all is mortal in nature, so is
all nature in love mortal in folly.

ROSALIND

Thou speak'st wiser than thou art ware of.

TOUCHSTONE

Nay, I shall ne'er be ware of mine own wit till I break my shins
against it.

ROSALIND

Jove, Jove! this shepherd's passion
Is much upon my fashion.

TOUCHSTONE

And mine; but it grows something stale with me.

CELIA

I pray you, one of you question yond man
If he for gold will give us any food;
I faint almost to death.

TOUCHSTONE

Holla, you clown!

ROSALIND

Peace, fool; he's not thy Ensman.

CORIN

Who calls?

TOUCHSTONE

Your betters, sir.

CORIN

Else are they very wretched.

ROSALIND

Peace, I say. Good even to you, friend.

CORIN

And to you, gentle sir, and to you all.

ROSALIND

I prithee, shepherd, if that love or gold
Can in this desert place buy entertainment,
Bring us where we may rest ourselves and feed.
Here's a young maid with travel much oppress'd,
And faints for succour.

CORIN

Fair sir, I pity her,
And wish, for her sake more than for mine own,
My fortunes were more able to relieve her;
But I am shepherd to another man,
And do not shear the fleeces that I graze.
My master is of churlish disposition,
And little recks to find the way to heaven
By doing deeds of hospitality.
Besides, his cote, his flocks, and bounds of feed,
Are now on sale; and at our sheepcote now,
By reason of his absence, there is nothing
That you will feed on; but what is, come see,
And in my voice most welcome shall you be.

ROSALIND

What is he that shall buy his flock and pasture?

CORIN

That young swain that you saw here but erewhile,
That little cares for buying any thing.

ROSALIND

> I pray thee, if it stand with honesty,
> Buy thou the cottage, pasture, and the flock,
> And thou shalt have to pay for it of us.

CELIA

> And we will mend thy wages. I like this place,
> And willingly could waste my time in it.

CORIN

> Assuredly the thing is to be sold.
> Go with me; if you like upon report
> The soil, the profit, and this kind of life,
> I will your very faithful feeder be,
> And buy it with your gold right suddenly.
> > *Exeunt*

SCENE V. Another part of the forest.

Enter AMIENS, JAQUES and OTHERS

AMIENS

SONG

> Under the greenwood tree
> Who loves to lie with me,
> And turn his merry note
> Unto the sweet bird's throat,
> Come hither, come hither, come hither.
> Here shall he see
> No enemy
> But winter and rough weather.

JAQUES

> More, more, I prithee, more.

AMIENS

> It will make you melancholy, Monsieur Jaques.

JAQUES

> I thank it. More, I prithee, more. I can suck melancholy out of a
> song, as a weasel sucks eggs. More, I prithee, more.

AMIENS

My voice is ragged; I know I cannot please you.

JAQUES

I do not desire you to please me; I do desire you to sing.
Come, more; another stanzo. Call you 'em stanzos?

AMIENS

What you will, Monsieur Jaques.

JAQUES

Nay, I care not for their names; they owe me nothing. Will you
sing?

AMIENS

More at your request than to please myself.

JAQUES

Well then, if ever I thank any man, I'll thank you; but that they
call compliment is like th' encounter of two dog-apes; and when a man
thanks me heartily, methinks have given him a penny, and he renders
me the beggarly thanks. Come, sing; and you that will not, hold your
tongues.

AMIENS

Well, I'll end the song. Sirs, cover the while; the Duke will drink
under this tree. He hath been all this day to look you.

JAQUES

And I have been all this day to avoid him. He is to disputable for my
company. I think of as many matters as he; but I give heaven thanks,
and make no boast of them. Come, warble, come.

SONG

[All together here]

Who doth ambition shun,
And loves to live i' th' sun,
Seeking the food he eats,
And pleas'd with what he gets,
Come hither, come hither, come hither.

> Here shall he see
> No enemy
> But winter and rough weather.

JAQUES

I'll give you a verse to this note that I made yesterday in despite of my invention.

AMIENS

And I'll sing it.

JAQUES

Thus it goes:

> If it do come to pass
> That any man turn ass,
> Leaving his wealth and ease
> A stubborn will to please,
> Ducdame, ducdame, ducdame;
> Here shall he see
> Gross fools as he,
> An if he will come to me.

AMIENS

What's that 'ducdame'?

JAQUES

'Tis a Greek invocation, to call fools into a circle. I'll go sleep, if I can; if I cannot, I'll rail against all the first-born of Egypt.

AMIENS

And I'll go seek the Duke; his banquet is prepar'd.
Exeunt severally

SCENE VI. The forest.

Enter ORLANDO and ADAM

ADAM

Dear master, I can go no further. O, I die for food! Here lie I down, and measure out my grave. Farewell, kind master.

ORLANDO

Why, how now, Adam! No greater heart in thee? Live a little; comfort a little; cheer thyself a little. If this uncouth forest yield anything savage, I will either be food for it or bring it for food to thee. Thy conceit is nearer death than thy powers. For my sake be comfortable; hold death awhile at the arm's end. I will here be with the presently; and if I bring thee not something to eat, I will give thee leave to die; but if thou diest before I come, thou art a mocker of my labour. Well said! thou look'st cheerly; and I'll be with thee quickly. Yet thou liest in the bleak air. Come, I will bear thee to some shelter; and thou shalt not die for lack of a dinner, if there live anything in this desert. Cheerly, good Adam!

Exeunt

SCENE VII. The forest.

A table set out. Enter DUKE SENIOR, AMIENS and
LORDS, like outlaws

DUKE SENIOR

I think he be transform'd into a beast;
For I can nowhere find him like a man.

FIRST LORD

My lord, he is but even now gone hence;
Here was he merry, hearing of a song.

DUKE SENIOR

If he, compact of jars, grow musical,
We shall have shortly discord in the spheres.
Go seek him; tell him I would speak with him.
Enter JAQUES

FIRST LORD

He saves my labour by his own approach.

DUKE SENIOR

Why, how now, monsieur! what a life is this,
That your poor friends must woo your company?
What, you look merrily!

JAQUES

 A fool, a fool! I met a fool i' th' forest,
 A motley fool. A miserable world!
 As I do live by food, I met a fool,
 Who laid him down and bask'd him in the sun,
 And rail'd on Lady Fortune in good terms,
 In good set terms-and yet a motley fool.
 'Good morrow, fool,' quoth I; 'No, sir,' quoth he,
 'Call me not fool till heaven hath sent me fortune.'
 And then he drew a dial from his poke,
 And, looking on it with lack-lustre eye,
 Says very wisely, 'It is ten o'clock;
 Thus we may see,' quoth he, 'how the world wags;
 'Tis but an hour ago since it was nine;
 And after one hour more 'twill be eleven;
 And so, from hour to hour, we ripe and ripe,
 And then, from hour to hour, we rot and rot;
 And thereby hangs a tale.' When I did hear
 The motley fool thus moral on the time,
 My lungs began to crow like chanticleer
 That fools should be so deep contemplative;
 And I did laugh sans intermission
 An hour by his dial. O noble fool!
 A worthy fool! Motley's the only wear.

DUKE SENIOR

 What fool is this?

JAQUES

 O worthy fool! One that hath been a courtier,
 And says, if ladies be but young and fair,
 They have the gift to know it; and in his brain,
 Which is as dry as the remainder biscuit
 After a voyage, he hath strange places cramm'd
 With observation, the which he vents
 In mangled forms. O that I were a fool!
 I am ambitious for a motley coat.

DUKE SENIOR

 Thou shalt have one.

JAQUES

    It is my only suit,
    Provided that you weed your better judgments
    Of all opinion that grows rank in them
    That I am wise. I must have liberty
    Withal, as large a charter as the wind,
    To blow on whom I please, for so fools have;
    And they that are most galled with my folly,
    They most must laugh. And why, sir, must they so?
    The why is plain as way to parish church:
    He that a fool doth very wisely hit
    Doth very foolishly, although he smart,
    Not to seem senseless of the bob; if not,
    The wise man's folly is anatomiz'd
    Even by the squand'ring glances of the fool.
    Invest me in my motley; give me leave
    To speak my mind, and I will through and through
    Cleanse the foul body of th' infected world,
    If they will patiently receive my medicine.

DUKE SENIOR

    Fie on thee! I can tell what thou wouldst do.

JAQUES

    What, for a counter, would I do but good?

DUKE SENIOR

    Most Mischievous foul sin, in chiding sin;
    For thou thyself hast been a libertine,
    As sensual as the brutish sting itself;
    And all th' embossed sores and headed evils
    That thou with license of free foot hast caught
    Wouldst thou disgorge into the general world.

JAQUES

    Why, who cries out on pride
    That can therein tax any private party?
    Doth it not flow as hugely as the sea,
    Till that the wearer's very means do ebb?
    What woman in the city do I name

When that I say the city-woman bears
The cost of princes on unworthy shoulders?
Who can come in and say that I mean her,
When such a one as she such is her neighbour?
Or what is he of basest function
That says his bravery is not on my cost,
Thinking that I mean him, but therein suits
His folly to the mettle of my speech?
There then! how then? what then? Let me see wherein
My tongue hath wrong'd him: if it do him right,
Then he hath wrong'd himself; if he be free,
Why then my taxing like a wild-goose flies,
Unclaim'd of any man. But who comes here?
              Enter ORLANDO with his sword drawn

ORLANDO
Forbear, and eat no more.

JAQUES
Why, I have eat none yet.

ORLANDO
Nor shalt not, till necessity be serv'd.

JAQUES
Of what kind should this cock come of?

DUKE SENIOR
Art thou thus bolden'd, man, by thy distress?
Or else a rude despiser of good manners,
That in civility thou seem'st so empty?

ORLANDO
You touch'd my vein at first: the thorny point
Of bare distress hath ta'en from me the show
Of smooth civility; yet arn I inland bred,
And know some nurture. But forbear, I say;
He dies that touches any of this fruit
Till I and my affairs are answered.

JAQUES
An you will not be answer'd with reason, I must die.

DUKE SENIOR

> What would you have? Your gentleness shall force
> More than your force move us to gentleness.

ORLANDO

> I almost die for food, and let me have it.

DUKE SENIOR

> Sit down and feed, and welcome to our table.

ORLANDO

> Speak you so gently? Pardon me, I pray you;
> I thought that all things had been savage here,
> And therefore put I on the countenance
> Of stern commandment. But whate'er you are
> That in this desert inaccessible,
> Under the shade of melancholy boughs,
> Lose and neglect the creeping hours of time;
> If ever you have look'd on better days,
> If ever been where bells have knoll'd to church,
> If ever sat at any good man's feast,
> If ever from your eyelids wip'd a tear,
> And know what 'tis to pity and be pitied,
> Let gentleness my strong enforcement be;
> In the which hope I blush, and hide my sword.

DUKE SENIOR

> True is it that we have seen better days,
> And have with holy bell been knoll'd to church,
> And sat at good men's feasts, and wip'd our eyes
> Of drops that sacred pity hath engend'red;
> And therefore sit you down in gentleness,
> And take upon command what help we have
> That to your wanting may be minist'red.

ORLANDO

> Then but forbear your food a little while,
> Whiles, like a doe, I go to find my fawn,
> And give it food. There is an old poor man
> Who after me hath many a weary step

Limp'd in pure love; till he be first suffic'd,
Oppress'd with two weak evils, age and hunger,
I will not touch a bit.

DUKE SENIOR

Go find him out.
And we will nothing waste till you return.

ORLANDO

I thank ye; and be blest for your good comfort!
Exit

DUKE SENIOR

Thou seest we are not all alone unhappy:
This wide and universal theatre
Presents more woeful pageants than the scene
Wherein we play in.

JAQUES

All the world's a stage,
And all the men and women merely players;
They have their exits and their entrances;
And one man in his time plays many parts,
His acts being seven ages. At first the infant,
Mewling and puking in the nurse's arms;
Then the whining school-boy, with his satchel
And shining morning face, creeping like snail
Unwillingly to school. And then the lover,
Sighing like furnace, with a woeful ballad
Made to his mistress' eyebrow. Then a soldier,
Full of strange oaths, and bearded like the pard,
Jealous in honour, sudden and quick in quarrel,
Seeking the bubble reputation
Even in the cannon's mouth. And then the justice,
In fair round belly with good capon lin'd,
With eyes severe and beard of formal cut,
Full of wise saws and modern instances;
And so he plays his part. The sixth age shifts
Into the lean and slipper'd pantaloon,

With spectacles on nose and pouch on side,
His youthful hose, well sav'd, a world too wide
For his shrunk shank; and his big manly voice,
Turning again toward childish treble, pipes
And whistles in his sound. Last scene of all,
That ends this strange eventful history,
Is second childishness and mere oblivion;
Sans teeth, sans eyes, sans taste, sans every thing.
Re-enter ORLANDO with ADAM

DUKE SENIOR
Welcome. Set down your venerable burden.
And let him feed.

ORLANDO
I thank you most for him.

ADAM
So had you need;
I scarce can speak to thank you for myself.

DUKE SENIOR
Welcome; fall to. I will not trouble you
As yet to question you about your fortunes.
Give us some music; and, good cousin, sing.

SONG
Blow, blow, thou winter wind,
Thou art not so unkind
As man's ingratitude;
Thy tooth is not so keen,
Because thou art not seen,
Although thy breath be rude.
Heigh-ho! sing heigh-ho! unto the green holly.
Most friendship is feigning, most loving mere folly.
Then, heigh-ho, the holly!
This life is most jolly.
Freeze, freeze, thou bitter sky,
That dost not bite so nigh
As benefits forgot;

Though thou the waters warp,
Thy sting is not so sharp
As friend rememb'red not.
Heigh-ho! sing, &c.

DUKE SENIOR

If that you were the good Sir Rowland's son,
As you have whisper'd faithfully you were,
And as mine eye doth his effigies witness
Most truly limn'd and living in your face,
Be truly welcome hither. I am the Duke
That lov'd your father. The residue of your fortune,
Go to my cave and tell me. Good old man,
Thou art right welcome as thy master is.
Support him by the arm. Give me your hand,
And let me all your fortunes understand.

Exeunt

ACT III

SCENE I. The palace.

Enter DUKE FREDERICK, OLIVER and LORDS

FREDERICK

> Not see him since! Sir, sir, that cannot be.
> But were I not the better part made mercy,
> I should not seek an absent argument
> Of my revenge, thou present. But look to it:
> Find out thy brother wheresoe'er he is;
> Seek him with candle; bring him dead or living
> Within this twelvemonth, or turn thou no more
> To seek a living in our territory.
> Thy lands and all things that thou dost call thine
> Worth seizure do we seize into our hands,
> Till thou canst quit thee by thy brother's mouth
> Of what we think against thee.

OLIVER

> O that your Highness knew my heart in this!
> I never lov'd my brother in my life.

FREDERICK

> More villain thou. Well, push him out of doors;
> And let my officers of such a nature
> Make an extent upon his house and lands.
> Do this expediently, and turn him going.
> > *Exeunt*

SCENE II. The forest.

Enter ORLANDO, with a paper

ORLANDO

Hang there, my verse, in witness of my love;
And thou, thrice-crowned Queen of Night, survey
With thy chaste eye, from thy pale sphere above,
Thy huntress' name that my full life doth sway.
O Rosalind! these trees shall be my books,
And in their barks my thoughts I'll character,
That every eye which in this forest looks
Shall see thy virtue witness'd every where.
Run, run, Orlando; carve on every tree,
The fair, the chaste, and unexpressive she.

Exit
Enter CORIN and TOUCHSTONE

CORIN

And how like you this shepherd's life, Master Touchstone?

TOUCHSTONE

Truly, shepherd, in respect of itself, it is a good life; but in respect that it is a shepherd's life, it is nought. In respect that it is solitary, I like it very well; but in respect that it is private, it is a very vile life. Now in respect it is in the fields, it pleaseth me well; but in respect it is not in the court, it is tedious. As it is a spare life, look you, it fits my humour well; but as there is no more plenty in it, it goes much against my stomach. Hast any philosophy in thee, shepherd?

CORIN

No more but that I know the more one sickens the worse at ease he is; and that he that wants money, means, and content, is without three good friends; that the property of rain is to wet, and fire to burn; that good pasture makes fat sheep; and that a great cause of the night is lack of the sun; that he that hath learned no wit by nature nor art may complain of good breeding, or comes of a very dull kindred.

TOUCHSTONE

Such a one is a natural philosopher. Wast ever in court, shepherd?

No more but that I know the more
one sickens the worse at ease he is;
and that he that wants money,
means, and content, is without three
good friends; that the property of
rain is to wet, and fire to burn;
that good pasture makes fat sheep;
and that a great cause of the night
is lack of the sun; that he that hath
learned no wit by nature nor art
may complain of good breeding,
or comes of a very dull kindred.

—Corin, *As You Like It*

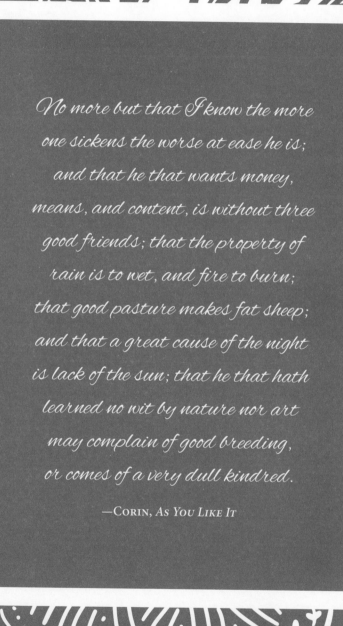

CORIN

No, truly.

TOUCHSTONE

Then thou art damn'd.

CORIN

Nay, I hope.

TOUCHSTONE

Truly, thou art damn'd, like an ill-roasted egg, all on one side.

CORIN

For not being at court? Your reason.

TOUCHSTONE

Why, if thou never wast at court thou never saw'st good manners; if thou never saw'st good manners, then thy manners must be wicked; and wickedness is sin, and sin is damnation. Thou art in a parlous state, shepherd.

CORIN

Not a whit, Touchstone. Those that are good manners at the court are as ridiculous in the country as the behaviour of the country is most mockable at the court. You told me you salute not at the court, but you kiss your hands; that courtesy would be uncleanly if courtiers were shepherds.

TOUCHSTONE

Instance, briefly; come, instance.

CORIN

Why, we are still handling our ewes; and their fells, you know, are greasy.

TOUCHSTONE

Why, do not your courtier's hands sweat? And is not the grease of a mutton as wholesome as the sweat of a man? Shallow, shallow. A better instance, I say; come.

CORIN

Besides, our hands are hard.

TOUCHSTONE

Your lips will feel them the sooner. Shallow again. A more sounder instance; come.

CORIN

And they are often tarr'd over with the surgery of our sheep; and would you have us kiss tar? The courtier's hands are perfum'd with civet.

TOUCHSTONE

Most shallow man! thou worm's meat in respect of a good piece of flesh indeed! Learn of the wise, and perpend: civet is of a baser birth than tar—the very uncleanly flux of a cat. Mend the instance, shepherd.

CORIN

You have too courtly a wit for me; I'll rest.

TOUCHSTONE

Wilt thou rest damn'd? God help thee, shallow man! God make incision in thee! thou art raw.

CORIN

Sir, I am a true labourer: I earn that I eat, get that I wear; owe no man hate, envy no man's happiness; glad of other men's good, content with my harm; and the greatest of my pride is to see my ewes graze and my lambs suck.

TOUCHSTONE

That is another simple sin in you: to bring the ewes and the rams together, and to offer to get your living by the copulation of cattle; to be bawd to a bell-wether, and to betray a she-lamb of a twelvemonth to crooked-pated, old, cuckoldly ram, out of all reasonable match. If thou beest not damn'd for this, the devil himself will have no shepherds; I cannot see else how thou shouldst 'scape.

CORIN

Here comes young Master Ganymede, my new mistress's brother.
Enter ROSALIND, reading a paper

ROSALIND

'From the east to western Inde,
No jewel is like Rosalinde.
Her worth, being mounted on the wind,

Through all the world bears Rosalinde.
All the pictures fairest lin'd
Are but black to Rosalinde.
Let no face be kept in mind
But the fair of Rosalinde.'

TOUCHSTONE

I'll rhyme you so eight years together, dinners, and suppers, and sleeping hours, excepted. It is the right butter-women's rank to market.

ROSALIND

Out, fool!

TOUCHSTONE

For a taste:

If a hart do lack a hind,
Let him seek out Rosalinde.
If the cat will after kind,
So be sure will Rosalinde.
Winter garments must be lin'd,
So must slender Rosalinde.
They that reap must sheaf and bind,
Then to cart with Rosalinde.
Sweetest nut hath sourest rind,
Such a nut is Rosalinde.
He that sweetest rose will find
Must find love's prick and Rosalinde.

This is the very false gallop of verses; why do you infect yourself with them?

ROSALIND

Peace, you dull fool! I found them on a tree.

TOUCHSTONE

Truly, the tree yields bad fruit.

ROSALIND

I'll graff it with you, and then I shall graff it with a medlar. Then it will be the earliest fruit i' th' country; for you'll be rotten ere you be half ripe, and that's the right virtue of the medlar.

TOUCHSTONE

You have said; but whether wisely or no, let the forest judge.

Enter CELIA, with a writing

ROSALIND

Peace!

Here comes my sister, reading; stand aside.

CELIA

'Why should this a desert be?

For it is unpeopled? No;

Tongues I'll hang on every tree

That shall civil sayings show.

Some, how brief the life of man

Runs his erring pilgrimage,

That the streching of a span

Buckles in his sum of age;

Some, of violated vows

'Twixt the souls of friend and friend;

But upon the fairest boughs,

Or at every sentence end,

Will I Rosalinda write,

Teaching all that read to know

The quintessence of every sprite

Heaven would in little show.

Therefore heaven Nature charg'd

That one body should be fill'd

With all graces wide-enlarg'd.

Nature presently distill'd

Helen's cheek, but not her heart,

Cleopatra's majesty,

Atalanta's better part,

Sad Lucretia's modesty.

Thus Rosalinde of many parts

By heavenly synod was devis'd,

Of many faces, eyes, and hearts,

To have the touches dearest priz'd.

Heaven would that she these gifts should have,

And I to live and die her slave.'

ROSALIND

O most gentle pulpiter! What tedious homily of love have you wearied your parishioners withal, and never cried 'Have patience, good people.'

CELIA

How now! Back, friends; shepherd, go off a little; go with him, sirrah.

TOUCHSTONE

Come, shepherd, let us make an honourable retreat; though not with bag and baggage, yet with scrip and scrippage.

Exeunt CORIN and TOUCHSTONE

CELIA

Didst thou hear these verses?

ROSALIND

O, yes, I heard them all, and more too; for some of them had in them more feet than the verses would bear.

CELIA

That's no matter; the feet might bear the verses.

ROSALIND

Ay, but the feet were lame, and could not bear themselves without the verse, and therefore stood lamely in the verse.

CELIA

But didst thou hear without wondering how thy name should be hang'd and carved upon these trees?

ROSALIND

I was seven of the nine days out of the wonder before you came; for look here what I found on a palm-tree. I was never so berhym'd since Pythagoras' time that I was an Irish rat, which I can hardly remember.

CELIA

Trow you who hath done this?

ROSALIND

Is it a man?

CELIA

And a chain, that you once wore, about his neck. Change you colour?

ROSALIND

I prithee, who?

CELIA

O Lord, Lord! it is a hard matter for friends to meet; but mountains may be remov'd with earthquakes, and so encounter.

ROSALIND

Nay, but who is it?

CELIA

Is it possible?

ROSALIND

Nay, I prithee now, with most petitionary vehemence, tell me who it is.

CELIA

O wonderful, wonderful, most wonderful wonderful, and yet again wonderful, and after that, out of all whooping!

ROSALIND

Good my complexion! dost thou think, though I am caparison'd like a man, I have a doublet and hose in my disposition? One inch of delay more is a South Sea of discovery. I prithee tell me who is it quickly, and speak apace. I would thou could'st stammer, that thou mightst pour this conceal'd man out of thy mouth, as wine comes out of narrow-mouth'd bottle—either too much at once or none at all. I prithee take the cork out of thy mouth that I may drink thy tidings.

CELIA

So you may put a man in your belly.

ROSALIND

Is he of God's making? What manner of man?
Is his head worth a hat or his chin worth a beard?

CELIA

Nay, he hath but a little beard.

ROSALIND

Why, God will send more if the man will be thankful. Let me stay the growth of his beard, if thou delay me not the knowledge of his chin.

CELIA

It is young Orlando, that tripp'd up the wrestler's heels and your heart both in an instant.

ROSALIND

Nay, but the devil take mocking! Speak sad brow and true maid.

CELIA

I' faith, coz, 'tis he.

ROSALIND

Orlando?

CELIA

Orlando.

ROSALIND

Alas the day! what shall I do with my doublet and hose? What did he when thou saw'st him? What said he? How look'd he? Wherein went he? What makes he here? Did he ask for me? Where remains he? How parted he with thee? And when shalt thou see him again? Answer me in one word.

CELIA

You must borrow me Gargantua's mouth first; 'tis a word too great for any mouth of this age's size. To say ay and no to these particulars is more than to answer in a catechism.

ROSALIND

But doth he know that I am in this forest, and in man's apparel? Looks he as freshly as he did the day he wrestled?

CELIA

It is as easy to count atomies as to resolve the propositions of a lover; but take a taste of my finding him, and relish it with good observance. I found him under a tree, like a dropp'd acorn.

ROSALIND

It may well be call'd Jove's tree, when it drops forth such fruit.

CELIA

Give me audience, good madam.

ROSALIND

Proceed.

CELIA

There lay he, stretch'd along like a wounded knight.

ROSALIND

Though it be pity to see such a sight, it well becomes the ground.

CELIA

Cry 'Holla' to thy tongue, I prithee; it curvets unseasonably. He was furnish'd like a hunter.

ROSALIND

O, ominous! he comes to kill my heart.

CELIA

I would sing my song without a burden; thou bring'st me out of tune.

ROSALIND

Do you not know I am a woman? When I think, I must speak. Sweet, say on.

CELIA

You bring me out. Soft! comes he not here?
Enter ORLANDO and JAQUES

ROSALIND

'Tis he; slink by, and note him.

JAQUES

I thank you for your company; but, good faith, I had as lief have been myself alone.

ORLANDO

And so had I; but yet, for fashion sake, I thank you too for your society.

JAQUES

God buy you; let's meet as little as we can.

ORLANDO

I do desire we may be better strangers.

JAQUES

I pray you mar no more trees with writing love songs in their barks.

ORLANDO

I pray you mar no more of my verses with reading them ill-favouredly.

JAQUES

Rosalind is your love's name?

ORLANDO

Yes, just.

JAQUES

I do not like her name.

ORLANDO

There was no thought of pleasing you when she was christen'd.

JAQUES

What stature is she of?

ORLANDO

Just as high as my heart.

JAQUES

You are full of pretty answers. Have you not been acquainted with goldsmiths' wives, and conn'd them out of rings?

ORLANDO

Not so; but I answer you right painted cloth, from whence you have studied your questions.

JAQUES

You have a nimble wit; I think 'twas made of Atalanta's heels. Will you sit down with me? and we two will rail against our mistress the world, and all our misery.

ORLANDO

I will chide no breather in the world but myself, against whom I know most faults.

JAQUES

The worst fault you have is to be in love.

ORLANDO

'Tis a fault I will not change for your best virtue. I am weary of you.

JAQUES

By my troth, I was seeking for a fool when I found you.

ORLANDO

He is drown'd in the brook; look but in, and you shall see him.

JAQUES

There I shall see mine own figure.

ORLANDO

Which I take to be either a fool or a cipher.

JAQUES

I'll tarry no longer with you; farewell, good Signior Love.

ORLANDO

I am glad of your departure; adieu, good Monsieur Melancholy.
Exit JAQUES

ROSALIND

[Aside to CELIA]
I will speak to him like a saucy lackey, and under that habit play the knave with him.—Do you hear, forester?

ORLANDO

Very well; what would you?

ROSALIND

I pray you, what is't o'clock?

ORLANDO

You should ask me what time o' day; there's no clock in the forest.

ROSALIND

Then there is no true lover in the forest, else sighing every minute and groaning every hour would detect the lazy foot of Time as well as a clock.

ORLANDO

And why not the swift foot of Time? Had not that been as proper?

ROSALIND

By no means, sir. Time travels in divers paces with divers persons. I'll tell you who Time ambles withal, who Time trots withal, who Time gallops withal, and who he stands still withal.

ORLANDO

I prithee, who doth he trot withal?

ROSALIND

Marry, he trots hard with a young maid between the contract of her marriage and the day it is solemniz'd; if the interim be but a se'nnight, Time's pace is so hard that it seems the length of seven year.

ORLANDO

Who ambles Time withal?

ROSALIND

With a priest that lacks Latin and a rich man that hath not the gout; for the one sleeps easily because he cannot study, and the other lives merrily because he feels no pain; the one lacking the burden of lean and wasteful learning, the other knowing no burden of heavy tedious penury. These Time ambles withal.

ORLANDO

Who doth he gallop withal?

ROSALIND

With a thief to the gallows; for though he go as softly as foot can fall, he thinks himself too soon there.

ORLANDO

Who stays it still withal?

ROSALIND

With lawyers in the vacation; for they sleep between term and term, and then they perceive not how Time moves.

ORLANDO

Where dwell you, pretty youth?

ROSALIND

With this shepherdess, my sister; here in the skirts of the forest, like fringe upon a petticoat.

ORLANDO

Are you native of this place?

ROSALIND

As the coney that you see dwell where she is kindled.

ORLANDO

Your accent is something finer than you could purchase in so removed a dwelling.

ROSALIND

I have been told so of many; but indeed an old religious uncle of mine taught me to speak, who was in his youth an inland man; one that knew courtship too well, for there he fell in love. I have heard him read many lectures against it; and I thank God I am not a woman, to be touch'd with so many giddy offences as he hath generally tax'd their whole sex withal.

ORLANDO

Can you remember any of the principal evils that he laid to the charge of women?

ROSALIND

There were none principal; they were all like one another as half-pence are; every one fault seeming monstrous till his fellow-fault came to match it.

ORLANDO

I prithee recount some of them.

ROSALIND

No; I will not cast away my physic but on those that are sick. There is a man haunts the forest that abuses our young plants with carving 'Rosalind' on their barks; hangs odes upon hawthorns and elegies on brambles; all, forsooth, deifying the name of Rosalind. If I could meet that fancy-monger, I would give him some good counsel, for he seems to have the quotidian of love upon him.

ORLANDO

I am he that is so love-shak'd; I pray you tell me your remedy.

ROSALIND

There is none of my uncle's marks upon you; he taught me how to know a man in love; in which cage of rushes I am sure you are not prisoner.

ORLANDO

What were his marks?

ROSALIND

A lean cheek, which you have not; a blue eye and sunken, which you have not; an unquestionable spirit, which you have not; a beard neglected, which you have not; but I pardon you for that, for simply your having in beard is a younger brother's revenue. Then your hose should be ungarter'd, your bonnet unbanded, your sleeve unbutton'd, your shoe untied, and every thing about you demonstrating a careless desolation. But you are no such man; you are rather point-device in your accoutrements, as loving yourself than seeming the lover of any other.

ORLANDO

Fair youth, I would I could make thee believe I love.

ROSALIND

Me believe it! You may as soon make her that you love believe it; which, I warrant, she is apter to do than to confess she does. That is one of the points in the which women still give the lie to their consciences. But, in good sooth, are you he that hangs the verses on the trees wherein Rosalind is so admired?

ORLANDO

I swear to thee, youth, by the white hand of Rosalind, I am that he, that unfortunate he.

ROSALIND

But are you so much in love as your rhymes speak?

ORLANDO

Neither rhyme nor reason can express how much.

ROSALIND

Love is merely a madness; and, I tell you, deserves as well a dark house and a whip as madmen do; and the reason why they are not so punish'd and cured is that the lunacy is so ordinary that the whippers are in love too. Yet I profess curing it by counsel.

ORLANDO

Did you ever cure any so?

ROSALIND

Yes, one; and in this manner. He was to imagine me his love, his mistress; and I set him every day to woo me; at which time would I, being but a moonish youth, grieve, be effeminate, changeable, longing and liking, proud, fantastical, apish, shallow, inconstant, full of tears, full of smiles; for every passion something and for no passion truly anything, as boys and women are for the most part cattle of this colour; would now like him, now loathe him; then entertain him, then forswear him; now weep for him, then spit at him; that I drave my suitor from his mad humour of love to a living humour of madness; which was, to forswear the full stream of the world and to live in a nook merely monastic. And thus I cur'd him; and this way will I take upon me to wash your liver as clean as a sound sheep's heart, that there shall not be one spot of love in 't.

ORLANDO

I would not be cured, youth.

ROSALIND

I would cure you, if you would but call me Rosalind, and come every day to my cote and woo me.

ORLANDO

Now, by the faith of my love, I will. Tell me where it is.

ROSALIND

Go with me to it, and I'll show it you; and, by the way, you shall tell me where in the forest you live. Will you go?

ORLANDO

With all my heart, good youth.

ROSALIND

Nay, you must call me Rosalind. Come, sister, will you go?
Exeunt

SCENE III. The forest.

Enter TOUCHSTONE and AUDREY; JAQUES behind

TOUCHSTONE

Come apace, good Audrey; I will fetch up your goats, Audrey. And how, Audrey, am I the man yet? Doth my simple feature content you?

AUDREY

Your features! Lord warrant us! What features?

TOUCHSTONE

I am here with thee and thy goats, as the most capricious poet, honest Ovid, was among the Goths.

JAQUES

[Aside]

O knowledge ill-inhabited, worse than Jove in a thatch'd house!

TOUCHSTONE

When a man's verses cannot be understood, nor a man's good wit seconded with the forward child understanding, it strikes a man more dead than a great reckoning in a little room. Truly, I would the gods had made thee poetical.

AUDREY

I do not know what 'poetical' is. Is it honest in deed and word? Is it a true thing?

TOUCHSTONE

No, truly; for the truest poetry is the most feigning, and lovers are given to poetry; and what they swear in poetry may be said as lovers they do feign.

AUDREY

Do you wish, then, that the gods had made me poetical?

TOUCHSTONE

I do, truly, for thou swear'st to me thou art honest; now, if thou wert a poet, I might have some hope thou didst feign.

AUDREY

Would you not have me honest?

TOUCHSTONE

No, truly, unless thou wert hard-favour'd; for honesty coupled to beauty is to have honey a sauce to sugar.

JAQUES

[Aside]
A material fool!

AUDREY

Well, I am not fair; and therefore I pray the gods make me honest.

TOUCHSTONE

Truly, and to cast away honesty upon a foul slut were to put good meat into an unclean dish.

AUDREY

I am not a slut, though I thank the gods I am foul.

TOUCHSTONE

Well, praised be the gods for thy foulness; sluttishness may come hereafter. But be it as it may be, I will marry thee; and to that end I have been with Sir Oliver Martext, the vicar of the next village, who hath promis'd to meet me in this place of the forest, and to couple us.

JAQUES

[Aside]
I would fain see this meeting.

AUDREY

Well, the gods give us joy!

TOUCHSTONE

Amen. A man may, if he were of a fearful heart, stagger in this attempt; for here we have no temple but the wood, no assembly but horn-beasts. But what though? Courage! As horns are odious, they are necessary. It is said: 'Many a man knows no end of his goods.' Right! Many a man has good horns and knows no end of them. Well, that is the dowry of his wife; 'tis none of his own getting. Horns? Even so. Poor men alone? No, no; the noblest deer hath them as huge as the rascal. Is the single man therefore blessed? No; as a wall'd town is more worthier than a village, so is the forehead of a married man more honourable than the bare brow of a bachelor; and by how much defence is better than no skill, by so much is horn more precious than to want. Here comes Sir Oliver.

Enter SIR OLIVER MARTEXT

Sir Oliver Martext, you are well met. Will you dispatch us here under this tree, or shall we go with you to your chapel?

MARTEXT

Is there none here to give the woman?

TOUCHSTONE

I will not take her on gift of any man.

MARTEXT

Truly, she must be given, or the marriage is not lawful.

JAQUES

[Discovering himself]

Proceed, proceed; I'll give her.

TOUCHSTONE

Good even, good Master What-ye-call't; how do you, sir? You are very well met. Goddild you for your last company. I am very glad to see you. Even a toy in hand here, sir. Nay; pray be cover'd.

JAQUES

Will you be married, motley?

TOUCHSTONE

As the ox hath his bow, sir, the horse his curb, and the falcon her bells, so man hath his desires; and as pigeons bill, so wedlock would be nibbling.

JAQUES

And will you, being a man of your breeding, be married under a bush, like a beggar? Get you to church and have a good priest that can tell you what marriage is; this fellow will but join you together as they join wainscot; then one of you will prove a shrunk panel, and like green timber warp, warp.

TOUCHSTONE

[Aside]

I am not in the mind but I were better to be married of him than of another; for he is not like to marry me well; and not being well married, it will be a good excuse for me hereafter to leave my wife.

JAQUES

Go thou with me, and let me counsel thee.

TOUCHSTONE

Come, sweet Audrey;
We must be married or we must live in bawdry.
Farewell, good Master Oliver. Not—
O sweet Oliver,
O brave Oliver,
Leave me not behind thee.
But—
Wind away,
Begone, I say,
I will not to wedding with thee.

Exeunt JAQUES, TOUCHSTONE and AUDREY

MARTEXT

'Tis no matter; ne'er a fantastical knave of them all shall flout me out of my calling.

Exit

SCENE IV. The forest.

Enter ROSALIND and CELIA

ROSALIND

Never talk to me; I will weep.

CELIA

Do, I prithee; but yet have the grace to consider that tears do not become a man.

ROSALIND

But have I not cause to weep?

CELIA

As good cause as one would desire; therefore weep.

ROSALIND

His very hair is of the dissembling colour.

CELIA

Something browner than Judas's. Marry, his kisses are Judas's own children.

ROSALIND

I' faith, his hair is of a good colour.

CELIA

An excellent colour: your chestnut was ever the only colour.

ROSALIND

And his kissing is as full of sanctity as the touch of holy bread.

CELIA

He hath bought a pair of cast lips of Diana. A nun of winter's sisterhood kisses not more religiously; the very ice of chastity is in them.

ROSALIND

But why did he swear he would come this morning, and comes not?

CELIA

Nay, certainly, there is no truth in him.

ROSALIND

Do you think so?

CELIA

Yes; I think he is not a pick-purse nor a horse-stealer; but for his verity in love, I do think him as concave as covered goblet or a worm-eaten nut.

ROSALIND

Not true in love?

CELIA

Yes, when he is in; but I think he is not in.

ROSALIND

You have heard him swear downright he was.

CELIA

'Was' is not 'is'; besides, the oath of a lover is no stronger than the word of a tapster; they are both the confirmer of false reckonings. He attends here in the forest on the Duke, your father.

ROSALIND

I met the Duke yesterday, and had much question with him. He asked me of what parentage I was; I told him, of as good as he; so he laugh'd and let me go. But what talk we of fathers when there is such a man as Orlando?

CELIA

O, that's a brave man! He writes brave verses, speaks brave words, swears brave oaths, and breaks them bravely, quite traverse, athwart the heart of his lover; as a puny tilter, that spurs his horse but on one side, breaks his staff like a noble goose. But all's brave that youth mounts and folly guides. Whocomes here?
Enter CORIN

CORIN

Mistress and master, you have oft enquired
After the shepherd that complain'd of love,
Who you saw sitting by me on the turf,
Praising the proud disdainful shepherdess
That was his mistress.

CELIA

Well, and what of him?

CORIN

If you will see a pageant truly play'd
Between the pale complexion of true love
And the red glow of scorn and proud disdain,
Go hence a little, and I shall conduct you,
If you will mark it.

ROSALIND

O, come, let us remove!
The sight of lovers feedeth those in love.
Bring us to this sight, and you shall say
I'll prove a busy actor in their play.
Exeunt

SCENE V. Another part of the forest.

Enter SILVIUS and PHEBE

SILVIUS

> Sweet Phebe, do not scorn me; do not, Phebe.
> Say that you love me not; but say not so
> In bitterness. The common executioner,
> Whose heart th' accustom'd sight of death makes hard,
> Falls not the axe upon the humbled neck
> But first begs pardon. Will you sterner be
> Than he that dies and lives by bloody drops?
>> *Enter ROSALIND, CELIA and CORIN, at a distance*

PHEBE

> I would not be thy executioner;
> I fly thee, for I would not injure thee.
> Thou tell'st me there is murder in mine eye.
> 'Tis pretty, sure, and very probable,
> That eyes, that are the frail'st and softest things,
> Who shut their coward gates on atomies,
> Should be call'd tyrants, butchers, murderers!
> Now I do frown on thee with all my heart;
> And if mine eyes can wound, now let them kill thee.
> Now counterfeit to swoon; why, now fall down;
> Or, if thou canst not, O, for shame, for shame,
> Lie not, to say mine eyes are murderers.
> Now show the wound mine eye hath made in thee.
> Scratch thee but with a pin, and there remains
> Some scar of it; lean upon a rush,
> The cicatrice and capable impressure
> Thy palm some moment keeps; but now mine eyes,
> Which I have darted at thee, hurt thee not;
> Nor, I am sure, there is not force in eyes
> That can do hurt.

SILVIUS

> O dear Phebe,
> If ever—as that ever may be near—
> You meet in some fresh cheek the power of fancy,
> Then shall you know the wounds invisible
> That love's keen arrows make.

PHEBE

> But till that time
> Come not thou near me; and when that time comes,
> Afflict me with thy mocks, pity me not;
> As till that time I shall not pity thee.

ROSALIND

> *[Advancing]*
> And why, I pray you? Who might be your mother,
> That you insult, exult, and all at once,
> Over the wretched? What though you have no beauty—
> As, by my faith, I see no more in you
> Than without candle may go dark to bed—
> Must you be therefore proud and pitiless?
> Why, what means this? Why do you look on me?
> I see no more in you than in the ordinary
> Of nature's sale-work. 'Od's my little life,
> I think she means to tangle my eyes too!
> No faith, proud mistress, hope not after it;
> 'Tis not your inky brows, your black silk hair,
> Your bugle eyeballs, nor your cheek of cream,
> That can entame my spirits to your worship.
> You foolish shepherd, wherefore do you follow her,
> Like foggy south, puffing with wind and rain?
> You are a thousand times a properer man
> Than she a woman. 'Tis such fools as you
> That makes the world full of ill-favour'd children.
> 'Tis not her glass, but you, that flatters her;
> And out of you she sees herself more proper
> Than any of her lineaments can show her.
> But, mistress, know yourself. Down on your knees,
> And thank heaven, fasting, for a good man's love;
> For I must tell you friendly in your ear:
> Sell when you can; you are not for all markets.
> Cry the man mercy, love him, take his offer;
> Foul is most foul, being foul to be a scoffer.
> So take her to thee, shepherd. Fare you well.

PHEBE

Sweet youth, I pray you chide a year together;
I had rather hear you chide than this man woo.

ROSALIND

He's fall'n in love with your foulness, and she'll fall in love with my anger. If it be so, as fast as she answers thee with frowning looks, I'll sauce her with bitter words. Why look you so upon me?

PHEBE

For no ill will I bear you.

ROSALIND

I pray you do not fall in love with me,
For I am falser than vows made in wine;
Besides, I like you not. If you will know my house,
'Tis at the tuft of olives here hard by.
Will you go, sister? Shepherd, ply her hard.
Come, sister. Shepherdess, look on him better,
And be not proud; though all the world could see,
None could be so abus'd in sight as he.
Come, to our flock.
                    Exeunt ROSALIND, CELIA and CORIN

PHEBE

Dead shepherd, now I find thy saw of might:
'Who ever lov'd that lov'd not at first sight?'

SILVIUS

Sweet Phebe.

PHEBE

Ha! what say'st thou, Silvius?

SILVIUS

Sweet Phebe, pity me.

PHEBE

Why, I am sorry for thee, gentle Silvius.

SILVIUS

Wherever sorrow is, relief would be.

If you do sorrow at my grief in love,
By giving love, your sorrow and my grief
Were both extermin'd.

PHEBE

Thou hast my love; is not that neighbourly?

SILVIUS

I would have you.

PHEBE

Why, that were covetousness.
Silvius, the time was that I hated thee;
And yet it is not that I bear thee love;
But since that thou canst talk of love so well,
Thy company, which erst was irksome to me,
I will endure; and I'll employ thee too.
But do not look for further recompense
Than thine own gladness that thou art employ'd.

SILVIUS

So holy and so perfect is my love,
And I in such a poverty of grace,
That I shall think it a most plenteous crop
To glean the broken ears after the man
That the main harvest reaps; loose now and then
A scatt'red smile, and that I'll live upon.

PHEBE

Know'st thou the youth that spoke to me erewhile?

SILVIUS

Not very well; but I have met him oft;
And he hath bought the cottage and the bounds
That the old carlot once was master of.

PHEBE

Think not I love him, though I ask for him;
'Tis but a peevish boy; yet he talks well.
But what care I for words? Yet words do well
When he that speaks them pleases those that hear.

It is a pretty youth—not very pretty;
But, sure, he's proud; and yet his pride becomes him.
He'll make a proper man. The best thing in him
Is his complexion; and faster than his tongue
Did make offence, his eye did heal it up.
He is not very tall; yet for his years he's tall;
His leg is but so-so; and yet 'tis well.
There was a pretty redness in his lip,
A little riper and more lusty red
Than that mix'd in his cheek; 'twas just the difference
Betwixt the constant red and mingled damask.
There be some women, Silvius, had they mark'd him
In parcels as I did, would have gone near
To fall in love with him; but, for my part,
I love him not, nor hate him not; and yet
I have more cause to hate him than to love him;
For what had he to do to chide at me?
He said mine eyes were black, and my hair black,
And, now I am remilb'red, scorn'd at me.
I marvel why I answer'd not again;
But that's all one: omittance is no quittance.
I'll write to him a very taunting letter,
And thou shalt bear it; wilt thou, Silvius?

SILVIUS

Phebe, with all my heart.

PHEBE

I'll write it straight;
The matter's in my head and in my heart;
I will be bitter with him and passing short.
Go with me, Silvius.
        Exeunt

ACT IV

SCENE I. The forest.

Enter ROSALIND, CELIA and JAQUES

JAQUES

I prithee, pretty youth, let me be better acquainted with thee.

ROSALIND

They say you are a melancholy fellow.

JAQUES

I am so; I do love it better than laughing.

ROSALIND

Those that are in extremity of either are abominable fellows, and betray themselves to every modern censure worse than drunkards.

JAQUES

Why, 'tis good to be sad and say nothing.

ROSALIND

Why then, 'tis good to be a post.

JAQUES

I have neither the scholar's melancholy, which is emulation; nor the musician's, which is fantastical; nor the courtier's, which is proud; nor the soldier's, which is ambitious; nor the lawyer's, which is politic; nor the lady's, which is nice; nor the lover's, which is all these; but it is a melancholy of mine own, compounded of many simples, extracted from many objects, and, indeed, the sundry contemplation of my travels; in which my often rumination wraps me in a most humorous sadness.

ROSALIND

A traveller! By my faith, you have great reason to be sad. I fear you have sold your own lands to see other men's; then to have seen much and to have nothing is to have rich eyes and poor hands.

JAQUES

Yes, I have gain'd my experience.

Enter ORLANDO

ROSALIND

And your experience makes you sad. I had rather have a fool to make me merry than experience to make me sad—and to travel for it too.

ORLANDO

Good day, and happiness, dear Rosalind!

JAQUES

Nay, then, God buy you, an you talk in blank verse.

ROSALIND

Farewell, Monsieur Traveller; look you lisp and wear strange suits, disable all the benefits of your own country, be out of love with your nativity, and almost chide God for making you that countenance you are; or I will scarce think you have swam in a gondola.

Exit JAQUES

Why, how now, Orlando! Where have you been all this while? You a lover! An you serve me such another trick, never come in my sight more.

ORLANDO

My fair Rosalind, I come within an hour of my promise.

ROSALIND

Break an hour's promise in love! He that will divide a minute into a thousand parts, and break but a part of the thousand part of a minute in the affairs of love, it may be said of him that Cupid hath clapp'd him o' th' shoulder, but I'll warrant him heart-whole.

ORLANDO

Pardon me, dear Rosalind.

ROSALIND

Nay, an you be so tardy, come no more in my sight. I had as lief be woo'd of a snail.

ORLANDO

Of a snail!

ROSALIND

Ay, of a snail; for though he comes slowly, he carries his house on his head—a better jointure, I think, than you make a woman; besides, he brings his destiny with him.

ORLANDO

What's that?

ROSALIND

Why, horns; which such as you are fain to be beholding to your wives for; but he comes armed in his fortune, and prevents the slander of his wife.

ORLANDO

Virtue is no horn-maker; and my Rosalind is virtuous.

ROSALIND

And I am your Rosalind.

CELIA

It pleases him to call you so; but he hath a Rosalind of a better leer than you.

ROSALIND

Come, woo me, woo me; for now I am in a holiday humour, and like enough to consent. What would you say to me now, an I were your very very Rosalind?

ORLANDO

I would kiss before I spoke.

ROSALIND

Nay, you were better speak first; and when you were gravell'd for lack of matter, you might take occasion to kiss. Very good orators, when they are out, they will spit; and for lovers lacking—God warn us!—matter, the cleanliest shift is to kiss.

ORLANDO

How if the kiss be denied?

ROSALIND

Then she puts you to entreaty, and there begins new matter.

ORLANDO

Who could be out, being before his beloved mistress?

ROSALIND

Marry, that should you, if I were your mistress; or I should think my honesty ranker than my wit.

ORLANDO

What, of my suit?

ROSALIND

Not out of your apparel, and yet out of your suit.
Am not I your Rosalind?

ORLANDO

I take some joy to say you are, because I would be talking of her.

ROSALIND

Well, in her person, I say I will not have you.

ORLANDO

Then, in mine own person, I die.

ROSALIND

No, faith, die by attorney. The poor world is almost six thousand years old, and in all this time there was not any man died in his own person, videlicet, in a love-cause. Troilus had his brains dash'd out with a Grecian club; yet he did what he could to die before, and he is one of the patterns of love. Leander, he would have liv'd many a fair year, though Hero had turn'd nun, if it had not been for a hot midsummer night; for, good youth, he went but forth to wash him in the Hellespont, and, being taken with the cramp, was drown'd; and the foolish chroniclers of that age found it was—Hero of Sestos. But these are all lies: men have died from time to time, and worms have eaten them, but not for love.

ORLANDO

I would not have my right Rosalind of this mind; for, I protest, her frown might kill me.

ROSALIND

By this hand, it will not kill a fly. But come, now I will be your Rosalind in a more coming-on disposition; and ask me what you will, I will grant it.

ORLANDO

Then love me, Rosalind.

ROSALIND

Yes, faith, will I, Fridays and Saturdays, and all.

ORLANDO

And wilt thou have me?

ROSALIND

Ay, and twenty such.

ORLANDO

What sayest thou?

ROSALIND

Are you not good?

ORLANDO

I hope so.

ROSALIND

Why then, can one desire too much of a good thing? Come, sister, you shall be the priest, and marry us. Give me your hand, Orlando. What do you say, sister?

ORLANDO

Pray thee, marry us.

CELIA

I cannot say the words.

ROSALIND

You must begin 'Will you, Orlando'—

CELIA

Go to. Will you, Orlando, have to wife this Rosalind?

ORLANDO

I will.

ROSALIND

Ay, but when?

ORLANDO

Why, now; as fast as she can marry us.

ROSALIND

Then you must say 'I take thee, Rosalind, for wife.'

ORLANDO

I take thee, Rosalind, for wife.

ROSALIND

I might ask you for your commission; but—I do take thee, Orlando, for my husband. There's a girl goes before the priest; and, certainly, a woman's thought runs before her actions.

ORLANDO

So do all thoughts; they are wing'd.

ROSALIND

Now tell me how long you would have her, after you have possess'd her.

ORLANDO

For ever and a day.

ROSALIND

Say 'a day' without the 'ever.' No, no, Orlando; men are April when they woo, December when they wed: maids are May when they are maids, but the sky changes when they are wives. I will be more jealous of thee than a Barbary cock-pigeon over his hen, more clamorous than a parrot against rain, more new-fangled than an ape, more giddy in my desires than a monkey. I will weep for nothing, like Diana in the fountain, and I will do that when you are dispos'd to be merry; I will laugh like a hyen, and that when thou are inclin'd to sleep.

ORLANDO

But will my Rosalind do so?

ROSALIND

By my life, she will do as I do.

ORLANDO

O, but she is wise.

ROSALIND

Or else she could not have the wit to do this. The wiser, the waywarder. Make the doors upon a woman's wit, and it will out at the casement; shut that, and 'twill out at the key-hole; stop that, 'twill fly with the smoke out at the chimney.

ORLANDO

A man that had a wife with such a wit, he might say 'Wit, whither wilt?'

ROSALIND

Nay, you might keep that check for it, till you met your wife's wit going to your neighbour's bed.

ORLANDO

And what wit could wit have to excuse that?

ROSALIND

Marry, to say she came to seek you there. You shall never take her without her answer, unless you take her without her tongue. O, that woman that cannot make her fault her husband's occasion, let her never nurse her child herself, for she will breed it like a fool!

ORLANDO

For these two hours, Rosalind, I will leave thee.

ROSALIND

Alas, dear love, I cannot lack thee two hours!

ORLANDO

I must attend the Duke at dinner; by two o'clock I will be with thee again.

ROSALIND

Ay, go your ways, go your ways. I knew what you would prove; my friends told me as much, and I thought no less. That flattering tongue of yours won me. 'Tis but one cast away, and so, come death! Two o'clock is your hour?

ORLANDO

Ay, sweet Rosalind.

ROSALIND

By my troth, and in good earnest, and so God mend me, and by all pretty oaths that are not dangerous, if you break one jot of your promise, or come one minute behind your hour, I will think you the most pathetical break-promise, and the most hollow lover, and the most unworthy of her you call Rosalind, that may be chosen out of the gross band of the unfaithful. Therefore beware my censure, and keep your promise.

ORLANDO

With no less religion than if thou wert indeed my Rosalind; so, adieu.

ROSALIND

Well, Time is the old justice that examines all such offenders, and let Time try. Adieu.

Exit ORLANDO

CELIA

You have simply misus'd our sex in your love-prate. We must have your doublet and hose pluck'd over your head, and show the world what the bird hath done to her own nest.

ROSALIND

O coz, coz, coz, my pretty little coz, that thou didst know how many fathom deep I am in love! But it cannot be sounded; my affection hath an unknown bottom, like the Bay of Portugal.

CELIA

Or rather, bottomless; that as fast as you pour affection in, it runs out.

ROSALIND

No; that same wicked bastard of Venus, that was begot of thought, conceiv'd of spleen, and born of madness; that blind rascally boy, that abuses every one's eyes, because his own are out—let him be judge how deep I am in love. I'll tell thee, Aliena, I cannot be out of the sight of Orlando. I'll go find a shadow, and sigh till he come.

CELIA

And I'll sleep.
Exeunt

SCENE II. The forest.

Enter JAQUES and LORDS, in the habit of foresters

JAQUES

Which is he that killed the deer?

LORD

Sir, it was I.

JAQUES

Let's present him to the Duke, like a Roman conqueror; and it would do well to set the deer's horns upon his head for a branch of victory. Have you no song, forester, for this purpose?

LORD

Yes, sir.

JAQUES

Sing it; 'tis no matter how it be in tune, so it make noise enough.

SONG

What shall he have that kill'd the deer?
His leather skin and horns to wear.

The rest shall hear this burden:

Then sing him home.
Take thou no scorn to wear the horn;
It was a crest ere thou wast born.
Thy father's father wore it;
And thy father bore it.
The horn, the horn, the lusty horn,
Is not a thing to laugh to scorn.

Exeunt

SCENE III. The forest.

Enter ROSALIND and CELIA

ROSALIND

How say you now? Is it not past two o'clock? And here much
Orlando!

CELIA

I warrant you, with pure love and troubled brain, he hath ta'en his
bow and arrows, and is gone forth—to sleep. Look, who comes here.

Enter SILVIUS

SILVIUS

My errand is to you, fair youth;
My gentle Phebe did bid me give you this.
I know not the contents; but, as I guess
By the stern brow and waspish action
Which she did use as she was writing of it,
It bears an angry tenour. Pardon me,
I am but as a guiltless messenger.

ROSALIND

Patience herself would startle at this letter,
And play the swaggerer. Bear this, bear all.
She says I am not fair, that I lack manners;
She calls me proud, and that she could not love me,
Were man as rare as Phoenix. 'Od's my will!
Her love is not the hare that I do hunt;
Why writes she so to me? Well, shepherd, well,
This is a letter of your own device.

SILVIUS

No, I protest, I know not the contents;
Phebe did write it.

ROSALIND

Come, come, you are a fool,
And turn'd into the extremity of love.
I saw her hand; she has a leathern hand,
A freestone-colour'd hand; I verily did think
That her old gloves were on, but 'twas her hands;
She has a huswife's hand—but that's no matter.
I say she never did invent this letter:
This is a man's invention, and his hand.

SILVIUS

Sure, it is hers.

ROSALIND

Why, 'tis a boisterous and a cruel style;
A style for challengers. Why, she defies me,
Like Turk to Christian. Women's gentle brain
Could not drop forth such giant-rude invention,
Such Ethiope words, blacker in their effect
Than in their countenance. Will you hear the letter?

SILVIUS

So please you, for I never heard it yet;
Yet heard too much of Phebe's cruelty.

ROSALIND

She Phebes me: mark how the tyrant writes.
    [Reads]
'Art thou god to shepherd turn'd,
That a maiden's heart hath burn'd?'
Can a woman rail thus?

SILVIUS

Call you this railing?

ROSALIND

'Why, thy godhead laid apart,

Warr'st thou with a woman's heart?'
Did you ever hear such railing?
'Whiles the eye of man did woo me,
That could do no vengeance to me.'
Meaning me a beast.
'If the scorn of your bright eyne
Have power to raise such love in mine,
Alack, in me what strange effect
Would they work in mild aspect!
Whiles you chid me, I did love;
How then might your prayers move!
He that brings this love to thee
Little knows this love in me;
And by him seal up thy mind,
Whether that thy youth and kind
Will the faithful offer take
Of me and all that I can make;
Or else by him my love deny,
And then I'll study how to die.'

SILVIUS

Call you this chiding?

CELIA

Alas, poor shepherd!

ROSALIND

Do you pity him? No, he deserves no pity. Wilt thou love such a woman? What, to make thee an instrument, and play false strains upon thee! Not to be endur'd! Well, go your way to her, for I see love hath made thee tame snake, and say this to her—that if she love me, I charge her to love thee; if she will not, I will never have her unless thou entreat for her. If you be a true lover, hence, and not a word; for here comes more company.

Exit SILVIUS
Enter OLIVER

OLIVER

Good morrow, fair ones; pray you, if you know,

Where in the purlieus of this forest stands
A sheep-cote fenc'd about with olive trees?

CELIA

West of this place, down in the neighbour bottom.
The rank of osiers by the murmuring stream
Left on your right hand brings you to the place.
But at this hour the house doth keep itself;
There's none within.

OLIVER

If that an eye may profit by a tongue,
Then should I know you by description—
Such garments, and such years: 'The boy is fair,
Of female favour, and bestows himself
Like a ripe sister; the woman low,
And browner than her brother.' Are not you
The owner of the house I did inquire for?

CELIA

It is no boast, being ask'd, to say we are.

OLIVER

Orlando doth commend him to you both;
And to that youth he calls his Rosalind
He sends this bloody napkin. Are you he?

ROSALIND

I am. What must we understand by this?

OLIVER

Some of my shame; if you will know of me
What man I am, and how, and why, and where,
This handkercher was stain'd.

CELIA

I pray you, tell it.

OLIVER

When last the young Orlando parted from you,
He left a promise to return again

Within an hour; and, pacing through the forest,
Chewing the food of sweet and bitter fancy,
Lo, what befell! He threw his eye aside,
And mark what object did present itself.
Under an oak, whose boughs were moss'd with age,
And high top bald with dry antiquity,
A wretched ragged man, o'ergrown with hair,
Lay sleeping on his back. About his neck
A green and gilded snake had wreath'd itself,
Who with her head nimble in threats approach'd
The opening of his mouth; but suddenly,
Seeing Orlando, it unlink'd itself,
And with indented glides did slip away
Into a bush; under which bush's shade
A lioness, with udders all drawn dry,
Lay couching, head on ground, with catlike watch,
When that the sleeping man should stir; for 'tis
The royal disposition of that beast
To prey on nothing that doth seem as dead.
This seen, Orlando did approach the man,
And found it was his brother, his elder brother.

CELIA

O, I have heard him speak of that same brother;
And he did render him the most unnatural
That liv'd amongst men.

OLIVER

And well he might so do,
For well I know he was unnatural.

ROSALIND

But, to Orlando: did he leave him there,
Food to the suck'd and hungry lioness?

OLIVER

Twice did he turn his back, and purpos'd so;
But kindness, nobler ever than revenge,
And nature, stronger than his just occasion,
Made him give battle to the lioness,

Who quickly fell before him; in which hurtling
From miserable slumber I awak'd.

CELIA

Are you his brother?

ROSALIND

Was't you he rescu'd?

CELIA

Was't you that did so oft contrive to kill him?

OLIVER

'Twas I; but 'tis not I. I do not shame
To tell you what I was, since my conversion
So sweetly tastes, being the thing I am.

ROSALIND

But for the bloody napkin?

OLIVER

By and by.
When from the first to last, betwixt us two,
Tears our recountments had most kindly bath'd,
As how I came into that desert place—
In brief, he led me to the gentle Duke,
Who gave me fresh array and entertainment,
Committing me unto my brother's love;
Who led me instantly unto his cave,
There stripp'd himself, and here upon his arm
The lioness had torn some flesh away,
Which all this while had bled; and now he fainted,
And cried, in fainting, upon Rosalind.
Brief, I recover'd him, bound up his wound,
And, after some small space, being strong at heart,
He sent me hither, stranger as I am,
To tell this story, that you might excuse
His broken promise, and to give this napkin,
Dy'd in his blood, unto the shepherd youth
That he in sport doth call his Rosalind.
                    [ROSALIND swoons]

436

CELIA

Why, how now, Ganymede! sweet Ganymede!

OLIVER

Many will swoon when they do look on blood.

CELIA

There is more in it. Cousin Ganymede!

OLIVER

Look, he recovers.

ROSALIND

I would I were at home.

CELIA

We'll lead you thither.
I pray you, will you take him by the arm?

OLIVER

Be of good cheer, youth. You a man!
You lack a man's heart.

ROSALIND

I do so, I confess it. Ah, sirrah, a body would think this was well counterfeited. I pray you tell your brother how well I counterfeited. Heigh-ho!

OLIVER

This was not counterfeit; there is too great testimony in your complexion that it was a passion of earnest.

ROSALIND

Counterfeit, I assure you.

OLIVER

Well then, take a good heart and counterfeit to be a man.

ROSALIND

So I do; but, i' faith, I should have been a woman by right.

CELIA

Come, you look paler and paler; pray you draw homewards.
Good sir, go with us.

OLIVER

That will I, for I must bear answer back
How you excuse my brother, Rosalind.

ROSALIND

I shall devise something; but, I pray you, commend my counterfeiting to him. Will you go?

Exeunt

ACT V

SCENE I. The forest.

Enter TOUCHSTONE and AUDREY

TOUCHSTONE
We shall find a time, Audrey; patience, gentle Audrey.

AUDREY
Faith, the priest was good enough, for all the old gentleman's saying.

TOUCHSTONE
A most wicked Sir Oliver, Audrey, a most vile Martext.
But, Audrey, there is a youth here in the forest lays claim to you.

AUDREY
Ay, I know who 'tis; he hath no interest in me in the world; here comes the man you mean.
Enter WILLIAM

TOUCHSTONE
It is meat and drink to me to see a clown. By my troth, we that have good wits have much to answer for: we shall be flouting; we cannot hold.

WILLIAM
Good ev'n, Audrey.

AUDREY
God ye good ev'n, William.

WILLIAM

And good ev'n to you, sir.

TOUCHSTONE

Good ev'n, gentle friend. Cover thy head, cover thy head; nay, prithee be cover'd. How old are you, friend?

WILLIAM

Five and twenty, sir.

TOUCHSTONE

A ripe age. Is thy name William?

WILLIAM

William, sir.

TOUCHSTONE

A fair name. Wast born i' th' forest here?

WILLIAM

Ay, sir, I thank God.

TOUCHSTONE

'Thank God.' A good answer.
Art rich?

WILLIAM

Faith, sir, so so.

TOUCHSTONE

'So so' is good, very good, very excellent good; and yet it is not; it is but so so. Art thou wise?

WILLIAM

Ay, sir, I have a pretty wit.

TOUCHSTONE

Why, thou say'st well. I do now remember a saying: 'The fool doth think he is wise, but the wise man knows himself to be a fool.' The heathen philosopher, when he had a desire to eat a grape, would open his lips when he put it into his mouth; meaning thereby that grapes were made to eat and lips to open. You do love this maid?

WILLIAM

I do, sir.

TOUCHSTONE

Give me your hand. Art thou learned?

WILLIAM

No, sir.

TOUCHSTONE

Then learn this of me: to have is to have; for it is a figure in rhetoric that drink, being pour'd out of cup into a glass, by filling the one doth empty the other; for all your writers do consent that ipse is he; now, you are not ipse, for I am he.

WILLIAM

Which he, sir?

TOUCHSTONE

He, sir, that must marry this woman. Therefore, you clown, abandon—which is in the vulgar leave—the society—which in the boorish is company—of this female—which in the common is woman—which together is: abandon the society of this female; or, clown, thou perishest; or, to thy better understanding, diest; or, to wit, I kill thee, make thee away, translate thy life into death, thy liberty into bondage. I will deal in poison with thee, or in bastinado, or in steel; I will bandy with thee in faction; will o'er-run thee with policy; I will kill thee a hundred and fifty ways; therefore tremble and depart.

AUDREY

Do, good William.

WILLIAM

God rest you merry, sir.
> *Exit*
> *Enter CORIN*

CORIN

Our master and mistress seeks you; come away, away.

TOUCHSTONE

Trip, Audrey, trip, Audrey. I attend, I attend.
> *Exeunt*

SCENE II. The forest

Enter ORLANDO and OLIVER

ORLANDO

Is't possible that on so little acquaintance you should like her? that but seeing you should love her? and loving woo? and, wooing, she should grant? and will you persever to enjoy her?

OLIVER

Neither call the giddiness of it in question, the poverty of her, the small acquaintance, my sudden wooing, nor her sudden consenting; but say with me, I love Aliena; say with her that she loves me; consent with both that we may enjoy each other. It shall be to your good; for my father's house and all the revenue that was old Sir Rowland's will I estate upon you, and here live and die a shepherd.

ORLANDO

You have my consent. Let your wedding be to-morrow. Thither will I invite the Duke and all's contented followers. Go you and prepare Aliena; for, look you, here comes my Rosalind.

Enter ROSALIND

ROSALIND

God save you, brother.

OLIVER

And you, fair sister.

Exit

ROSALIND

O, my dear Orlando, how it grieves me to see thee wear thy heart in a scarf!

ORLANDO

It is my arm.

ROSALIND

I thought thy heart had been wounded with the claws of a lion.

ORLANDO

Wounded it is, but with the eyes of a lady.

ROSALIND

Did your brother tell you how I counterfeited to swoon when he show'd me your handkercher?

ORLANDO

Ay, and greater wonders than that.

ROSALIND

O, I know where you are. Nay, 'tis true. There was never any thing so sudden but the fight of two rams and Caesar's thrasonical brag of 'I came, saw, and overcame.' For your brother and my sister no sooner met but they look'd; no sooner look'd but they lov'd; no sooner lov'd but they sigh'd; no sooner sigh'd but they ask'd one another the reason; no sooner knew the reason but they sought the remedy—and in these degrees have they made pair of stairs to marriage, which they will climb incontinent, or else be incontinent before marriage. They are in the very wrath of love, and they will together. Clubs cannot part them.

ORLANDO

They shall be married to-morrow; and I will bid the Duke to the nuptial. But, O, how bitter a thing it is to look into happiness through another man's eyes! By so much the more shall I to-morrow be at the height of heart-heaviness, by how much I shall think my brother happy in having what he wishes for.

ROSALIND

Why, then, to-morrow I cannot serve your turn for Rosalind?

ORLANDO

I can live no longer by thinking.

ROSALIND

I will weary you, then, no longer with idle talking. Know of me then—for now I speak to some purpose—that I know you are a gentleman of good conceit. I speak not this that you should bear a good opinion of my knowledge, insomuch I say I know you are; neither do I labour for a greater esteem than may in some little measure draw a belief from you, to do yourself good, and not to grace me. Believe then, if you please, that I can do strange things. I have, since I was three year old, convers'd with a magician, most profound in his art and yet not damnable. If you do love Rosalind so near the heart as your gesture cries it out, when your brother marries Aliena shall you marry her. I know into what straits of fortune she is driven; and it is not impossible to me, if it appear not inconvenient to you, to set her before your eyes to-morrow, human as she is, and without any danger.

ORLANDO

Speak'st thou in sober meanings?

ROSALIND

By my life, I do; which I tender dearly, though I say I am a magician. Therefore put you in your best array, bid your friends; for if you will be married to-morrow, you shall; and to Rosalind, if you will.

Enter SILVIUS and PHEBE

Look, here comes a lover of mine, and a lover of hers.

PHEBE

Youth, you have done me much ungentleness
To show the letter that I writ to you.

ROSALIND

I care not if I have. It is my study
To seem despiteful and ungentle to you.
You are there follow'd by a faithful shepherd;
Look upon him, love him; he worships you.

PHEBE

Good shepherd, tell this youth what 'tis to love.

SILVIUS

It is to be all made of sighs and tears;
And so am I for Phebe.

PHEBE

And I for Ganymede.

ORLANDO

And I for Rosalind.

ROSALIND

And I for no woman.

SILVIUS

It is to be all made of faith and service;
And so am I for Phebe.

PHEBE

And I for Ganymede.

ORLANDO

And I for Rosalind.

ROSALIND

And I for no woman.

SILVIUS

It is to be all made of fantasy,
All made of passion, and all made of wishes;
All adoration, duty, and observance,
All humbleness, all patience, and impatience,
All purity, all trial, all obedience;
And so am I for Phebe.

PHEBE

And so am I for Ganymede.

ORLANDO

And so am I for Rosalind.

ROSALIND

And so am I for no woman.

PHEBE

If this be so, why blame you me to love you?

SILVIUS

If this be so, why blame you me to love you?

ORLANDO

If this be so, why blame you me to love you?

ROSALIND

Why do you speak too, 'Why blame you me to love you?'

ORLANDO

To her that is not here, nor doth not hear.

ROSALIND

Pray you, no more of this; 'tis like the howling of Irish wolves against the moon.

[To SILVIUS]

I will help you if I can.

[To PHEBE]

I would love you if I could. To-morrow meet me all together.

[To PHEBE]

I will marry you if ever I marry woman, and I'll be married to-morrow.

[To ORLANDO]

I will satisfy you if ever I satisfied man, and you shall be married to-morrow.

[To SILVIUS]

I will content you if what pleases you contents you, and you shall be married to-morrow.

[To ORLANDO]

As you love Rosalind, meet.

[To SILVIUS]

As you love Phebe, meet; and as I love no woman, I'll meet. So, fare you well; I have left you commands.

SILVIUS

I'll not fail, if I live.

PHEBE

Nor I.

ORLANDO

Nor I.

Exeunt

SCENE III. The forest.

Enter TOUCHSTONE and AUDREY

TOUCHSTONE

To-morrow is the joyful day, Audrey; to-morrow will we be married.

AUDREY

I do desire it with all my heart; and I hope it is no dishonest desire to desire to be a woman of the world. Here come two of the banish'd Duke's pages.

Enter two PAGES

FIRST PAGE

Well met, honest gentleman.

TOUCHSTONE

By my troth, well met. Come sit, sit, and a song.

SECOND PAGE

We are for you; sit i' th' middle.

FIRST PAGE

Shall we clap into't roundly, without hawking, or spitting, or saying we are hoarse, which are the only prologues to a bad voice?

SECOND PAGE

I' faith, i' faith; and both in a tune, like two gipsies on a horse.

SONG

It was a lover and his lass,
With a hey, and a ho, and a hey nonino,
That o'er the green corn-field did pass
In the spring time, the only pretty ring time,
When birds do sing, hey ding a ding, ding.
Sweet lovers love the spring.
Between the acres of the rye,
With a hey, and a ho, and a hey nonino,
These pretty country folks would lie,
In the spring time, &c.
This carol they began that hour,
With a hey, and a ho, and a hey nonino,
How that a life was but a flower,
In the spring time, &c.
And therefore take the present time,
With a hey, and a ho, and a hey nonino,
For love is crowned with the prime,
In the spring time, &c.

TOUCHSTONE

Truly, young gentlemen, though there was no great matter in the ditty, yet the note was very untuneable.

FIRST PAGE

You are deceiv'd, sir; we kept time, we lost not our time.

TOUCHSTONE

By my troth, yes; I count it but time lost to hear such a foolish song. God buy you; and God mend your voices. Come, Audrey.

Exeunt

SCENE IV. The forest.

*Enter DUKE SENIOR, AMIENS, JAQUES, ORLANDO,
OLIVER and CELIA*

DUKE SENIOR

Dost thou believe, Orlando, that the boy
Can do all this that he hath promised?

ORLANDO

I sometimes do believe and sometimes do not:
As those that fear they hope, and know they fear.
Enter ROSALIND, SILVIUS and PHEBE

ROSALIND

Patience once more, whiles our compact is urg'd:
You say, if I bring in your Rosalind,
You will bestow her on Orlando here?

DUKE SENIOR

That would I, had I kingdoms to give with her.

ROSALIND

And you say you will have her when I bring her?

ORLANDO

That would I, were I of all kingdoms king.

ROSALIND

You say you'll marry me, if I be willing?

PHEBE

That will I, should I die the hour after.

ROSALIND

But if you do refuse to marry me,
You'll give yourself to this most faithful shepherd?

PHEBE

So is the bargain.

ROSALIND

You say that you'll have Phebe, if she will?

SILVIUS

Though to have her and death were both one thing.

ROSALIND

I have promis'd to make all this matter even.
Keep you your word, O Duke, to give your daughter;
You yours, Orlando, to receive his daughter;
Keep your word, Phebe, that you'll marry me,
Or else, refusing me, to wed this shepherd;
Keep your word, Silvius, that you'll marry her
If she refuse me; and from hence I go,
To make these doubts all even.
Exeunt ROSALIND and CELIA

DUKE SENIOR

I do remember in this shepherd boy
Some lively touches of my daughter's favour.

ORLANDO

My lord, the first time that I ever saw him
Methought he was a brother to your daughter.
But, my good lord, this boy is forest-born,
And hath been tutor'd in the rudiments
Of many desperate studies by his uncle,
Whom he reports to be a great magician,
Obscured in the circle of this forest.
Enter TOUCHSTONE and AUDREY

JAQUES

There is, sure, another flood toward, and these couples are coming to the ark. Here comes a pair of very strange beasts which in all tongues are call'd fools.

TOUCHSTONE

Salutation and greeting to you all!

JAQUES

Good my lord, bid him welcome. This is the motley-minded gentleman that I have so often met in the forest. He hath been a courtier, he swears.

TOUCHSTONE

If any man doubt that, let him put me to my purgation. I have trod a measure; I have flatt'red a lady; I have been politic with my friend, smooth with mine enemy; I have undone three tailors; I have had four quarrels, and like to have fought one.

JAQUES

And how was that ta'en up?

TOUCHSTONE

Faith, we met, and found the quarrel was upon the seventh cause.

JAQUES

How seventh cause? Good my lord, like this fellow.

DUKE SENIOR

I like him very well.

TOUCHSTONE

God 'ild you, sir; I desire you of the like. I press in here, sir, amongst the rest of the country copulatives, to swear and to forswear, according as marriage binds and blood breaks. A poor virgin, sir, an ill-favour'd thing, sir, but mine own; a poor humour of mine, sir, to take that that man else will. Rich honesty dwells like a miser, sir, in a poor house; as your pearl in your foul oyster.

DUKE SENIOR

By my faith, he is very swift and sententious.

TOUCHSTONE

According to the fool's bolt, sir, and such dulcet diseases.

JAQUES

But, for the seventh cause: how did you find the quarrel on the seventh cause?

TOUCHSTONE

Upon a lie seven times removed—bear your body more seeming, Audrey—as thus, sir. I did dislike the cut of a certain courtier's beard; he sent me word, if I said his beard was not cut well, he was in the mind it was. This is call'd the Retort Courteous. If I sent him word again it was not well cut, he would send me word he cut it to please himself. This is call'd the Quip Modest. If again it was not well cut, he disabled my judgment. This is call'd the Reply Churlish. If again it was not well cut, he would answer I spake not true. This is call'd the Reproof Valiant. If again it was not well cut, he would say I lie. This is call'd the Countercheck Quarrelsome. And so to the Lie Circumstantial and the Lie Direct.

JAQUES

And how oft did you say his beard was not well cut?

TOUCHSTONE

I durst go no further than the Lie Circumstantial, nor he durst not give me the Lie Direct; and so we measur'd swords and parted.

JAQUES

Can you nominate in order now the degrees of the lie?

TOUCHSTONE

O, sir, we quarrel in print by the book, as you have books for good manners. I will name you the degrees. The first, the Retort Courteous; the second, the Quip Modest; the third, the Reply Churlish; the fourth, the Reproof Valiant; the fifth, the Countercheck Quarrelsome; the sixth, the Lie with Circumstance; the seventh, the Lie Direct. All these you may avoid but the Lie Direct; and you may avoid that too with an If. I knew when seven justices could not take up a quarrel; but when the parties were met themselves, one of them thought but of an If, as: 'If you said so, then I said so.' And they shook hands, and swore brothers. Your If is the only peace-maker; much virtue in If.

JAQUES

Is not this a rare fellow, my lord?

He's as good at any thing, and yet a fool.

DUKE SENIOR

He uses his folly like a stalking-horse, and under the presentation

of that he shoots his wit:

Enter HYMEN, ROSALIND and CELIA. Still MUSIC

HYMEN

Then is there mirth in heaven,

When earthly things made even

Atone together.

Good Duke, receive thy daughter;

Hymen from heaven brought her,

Yea, brought her hither,

That thou mightst join her hand with his,

Whose heart within his bosom is.

ROSALIND

[To DUKE]

To you I give myself, for I am yours.

[To ORLANDO]

To you I give myself, for I am yours.

DUKE SENIOR

If there be truth in sight, you are my daughter.

ORLANDO

If there be truth in sight, you are my Rosalind.

PHEBE

If sight and shape be true,

Why then, my love adieu!

ROSALIND

I'll have no father, if you be not he;

I'll have no husband, if you be not he;

Nor ne'er wed woman, if you be not she.

HYMEN

    Peace, ho! I bar confusion;
    'Tis I must make conclusion
    Of these most strange events.
    Here's eight that must take hands
    To join in Hymen's bands,
    If truth holds true contents.
    You and you no cross shall part;
    You and you are heart in heart;
    You to his love must accord,
    Or have a woman to your lord;
    You and you are sure together,
    As the winter to foul weather.
    Whiles a wedlock-hymn we sing,
    Feed yourselves with questioning,
    That reason wonder may diminish,
    How thus we met, and these things finish.

SONG

    Wedding is great Juno's crown;
    O blessed bond of board and bed!
    'Tis Hymen peoples every town;
    High wedlock then be honoured.
    Honour, high honour, and renown,
    To Hymen, god of every town!

DUKE SENIOR

    O my dear niece, welcome thou art to me!
    Even daughter, welcome in no less degree.

PHEBE

    I will not eat my word, now thou art mine;
    Thy faith my fancy to thee doth combine.
        Enter JAQUES de BOYS

JAQUES de BOYS

    Let me have audience for a word or two.
    I am the second son of old Sir Rowland,
    That bring these tidings to this fair assembly.

Duke Frederick, hearing how that every day
Men of great worth resorted to this forest,
Address'd a mighty power; which were on foot,
In his own conduct, purposely to take
His brother here, and put him to the sword;
And to the skirts of this wild wood he came,
Where, meeting with an old religious man,
After some question with him, was converted
Both from his enterprise and from the world;
His crown bequeathing to his banish'd brother,
And all their lands restor'd to them again
That were with him exil'd. This to be true
I do engage my life.

DUKE SENIOR

Welcome, young man.
Thou offer'st fairly to thy brothers' wedding:
To one, his lands withheld; and to the other,
A land itself at large, a potent dukedom.
First, in this forest let us do those ends
That here were well begun and well begot;
And after, every of this happy number,
That have endur'd shrewd days and nights with us,
Shall share the good of our returned fortune,
According to the measure of their states.
Meantime, forget this new-fall'n dignity,
And fall into our rustic revelry.
Play, music; and you brides and bridegrooms all,
With measure heap'd in joy, to th' measures fall.

JAQUES

Sir, by your patience. If I heard you rightly,
The Duke hath put on a religious life,
And thrown into neglect the pompous court.

JAQUES DE BOYS

He hath.

JAQUES

To him will I. Out of these convertites

There is much matter to be heard and learn'd.
  [To DUKE]
You to your former honour I bequeath;
Your patience and your virtue well deserves it.
  [To ORLANDO]
You to a love that your true faith doth merit;
  [To OLIVER]
You to your land, and love, and great allies
  [To SILVIUS]
You to a long and well-deserved bed;
  [To TOUCHSTONE]
And you to wrangling; for thy loving voyage
Is but for two months victuall'd. So to your pleasures;
I am for other than for dancing measures.

DUKE SENIOR

Stay, Jaques, stay.

JAQUES

To see no pastime I. What you would have
I'll stay to know at your abandon'd cave.
  Exit

DUKE SENIOR

Proceed, proceed. We will begin these rites,
As we do trust they'll end, in true delights.
  [A dance]
  Exeunt

EPILOGUE

ROSALIND

It is not the fashion to see the lady the epilogue; but
it is no more unhandsome than to see the lord the prologue. If it
be true that good wine needs no bush, 'tis true that a good play
needs no epilogue. Yet to good wine they do use good bushes; and
good plays prove the better by the help of good epilogues. What a
case am I in then, that am neither a good epilogue, nor cannot
insinuate with you in the behalf of a good play! I am not
furnish'd like a beggar; therefore to beg will not become me. My
way is to conjure you; and I'll begin with the women. I charge
you, O women, for the love you bear to men, to like as much of
this play as please you; and I charge you, O men, for the love
you bear to women—as I perceive by your simp'ring none of you
hates them—that between you and the women the play may please.
If I were a woman, I would kiss as many of you as had beards that
pleas'd me, complexions that lik'd me, and breaths that I defied
not; and, I am sure, as many as have good beards, or good faces,
or sweet breaths, will, for my kind offer, when I make curtsy,
bid me farewell.

TWELFTH NIGHT:
OR, WHAT YOU WILL

CONTENTS

ACT IV

ACT V

DRAMATIS PERSONÆ

ORSINO, Duke of Illyria
VALENTINE, Gentleman attending on the Duke
CURIO, Gentleman attending on the Duke
VIOLA, in love with the Duke
SEBASTIAN, a young Gentleman, twin brother to Viola
A SEA CAPTAIN, friend to Viola
ANTONIO, a Sea Captain, friend to Sebastian
OLIVIA, a rich Countess
MARIA, Olivia's Woman
SIR TOBY BELCH, Uncle of Olivia
SIR ANDREW AGUECHEEK
MALVOLIO, Steward to Olivia
FABIAN, Servant to Olivia
CLOWN, Servant to Olivia
PRIEST
Lords, Sailors, Officers, Musicians, and other Attendants

SCENE: A City in Illyria; and the Sea-coast near it.

ACT I

SCENE I. An Apartment in the Duke's Palace.

Enter Orsino, Duke of Illyria, Curio and other Lords; Musicians attending.

DUKE

> If music be the food of love, play on,
> Give me excess of it; that, surfeiting,
> The appetite may sicken and so die.
> That strain again, it had a dying fall;
> O, it came o'er my ear like the sweet sound
> That breathes upon a bank of violets,
> Stealing and giving odour. Enough; no more;
> 'Tis not so sweet now as it was before.
> O spirit of love, how quick and fresh art thou,
> That notwithstanding thy capacity
> Receiveth as the sea, nought enters there,
> Of what validity and pitch soever,
> But falls into abatement and low price
> Even in a minute! So full of shapes is fancy,
> That it alone is high fantastical.

CURIO

> Will you go hunt, my lord?

DUKE

> What, Curio?

CURIO

The hart.

DUKE

Why so I do, the noblest that I have.
O, when mine eyes did see Olivia first,
Methought she purg'd the air of pestilence;
That instant was I turn'd into a hart,
And my desires, like fell and cruel hounds,
E'er since pursue me. How now? what news from her?
Enter VALENTINE.

VALENTINE

So please my lord, I might not be admitted,
But from her handmaid do return this answer:
The element itself, till seven years' heat,
Shall not behold her face at ample view;
But like a cloistress she will veiled walk,
And water once a day her chamber round
With eye-offending brine: all this to season
A brother's dead love, which she would keep fresh
And lasting in her sad remembrance.

DUKE

O, she that hath a heart of that fine frame
To pay this debt of love but to a brother,
How will she love, when the rich golden shaft
Hath kill'd the flock of all affections else
That live in her; when liver, brain, and heart,
These sovereign thrones, are all supplied and fill'd
Her sweet perfections with one self king!
Away before me to sweet beds of flowers,
Love-thoughts lie rich when canopied with bowers.
[Exeunt.]

SCENE II. The sea-coast.

Enter VIOLA, a CAPTAIN and Sailors.

VIOLA

What country, friends, is this?

CAPTAIN

This is Illyria, lady.

VIOLA

And what should I do in Illyria?
My brother he is in Elysium.
Perchance he is not drown'd. What think you, sailors?

CAPTAIN

It is perchance that you yourself were sav'd.

VIOLA

O my poor brother! and so perchance may he be.

CAPTAIN

True, madam; and to comfort you with chance,
Assure yourself, after our ship did split,
When you, and those poor number sav'd with you,
Hung on our driving boat, I saw your brother,
Most provident in peril, bind himself,
(Courage and hope both teaching him the practice)
To a strong mast that liv'd upon the sea;
Where, like Arion on the dolphin's back,
I saw him hold acquaintance with the waves
So long as I could see.

VIOLA

For saying so, there's gold!
Mine own escape unfoldeth to my hope,
Whereto thy speech serves for authority,
The like of him. Know'st thou this country?

CAPTAIN

Ay, madam, well, for I was bred and born
Not three hours' travel from this very place.

VIOLA

Who governs here?

CAPTAIN

> A noble duke, in nature as in name.

VIOLA

> What is his name?

CAPTAIN

> Orsino.

VIOLA

> Orsino! I have heard my father name him.
> He was a bachelor then.

CAPTAIN

> And so is now, or was so very late;
> For but a month ago I went from hence,
> And then 'twas fresh in murmur, (as, you know,
> What great ones do, the less will prattle of)
> That he did seek the love of fair Olivia.

VIOLA

> What's she?

CAPTAIN

> A virtuous maid, the daughter of a count
> That died some twelvemonth since; then leaving her
> In the protection of his son, her brother,
> Who shortly also died; for whose dear love
> They say, she hath abjur'd the company
> And sight of men.

VIOLA

> O that I served that lady,
> And might not be delivered to the world,
> Till I had made mine own occasion mellow,
> What my estate is.

CAPTAIN

> That were hard to compass,
> Because she will admit no kind of suit,
> No, not the Duke's.

VIOLA

    There is a fair behaviour in thee, Captain;
    And though that nature with a beauteous wall
    Doth oft close in pollution, yet of thee
    I will believe thou hast a mind that suits
    With this thy fair and outward character.
    I pray thee, and I'll pay thee bounteously,
    Conceal me what I am, and be my aid
    For such disguise as haply shall become
    The form of my intent. I'll serve this duke;
    Thou shalt present me as an eunuch to him.
    It may be worth thy pains; for I can sing,
    And speak to him in many sorts of music,
    That will allow me very worth his service.
    What else may hap, to time I will commit;
    Only shape thou thy silence to my wit.

CAPTAIN

    Be you his eunuch and your mute I'll be;
    When my tongue blabs, then let mine eyes not see.

VIOLA

    I thank thee. Lead me on.
      [Exeunt.]

SCENE III. A Room in Olivia's House.

Enter SIR TOBY and MARIA.

SIR TOBY

    What a plague means my niece to take the death of her brother
thus? I am sure care's an enemy to life.

MARIA

    By my troth, Sir Toby, you must come in earlier o' nights; your
cousin, my lady, takes great exceptions to your ill hours.

SIR TOBY

    Why, let her except, before excepted.

MARIA

Ay, but you must confine yourself within the modest limits of order.

SIR TOBY

Confine? I'll confine myself no finer than I am. These clothes are good enough to drink in, and so be these boots too; and they be not, let them hang themselves in their own straps.

MARIA

That quaffing and drinking will undo you: I heard my lady talk of it yesterday; and of a foolish knight that you brought in one night here to be her wooer.

SIR TOBY

Who? Sir Andrew Aguecheek?

MARIA

Ay, he.

SIR TOBY

He's as tall a man as any's in Illyria.

MARIA

What's that to th' purpose?

SIR TOBY

Why, he has three thousand ducats a year.

MARIA

Ay, but he'll have but a year in all these ducats. He's a very fool, and a prodigal.

SIR TOBY

Fie, that you'll say so! he plays o' the viol-de-gamboys, and speaks three or four languages word for word without book, and hath all the good gifts of nature.

MARIA

He hath indeed, almost natural: for, besides that he's a fool, he's a great quarreller; and, but that he hath the gift of a coward to allay the gust he hath in quarrelling, 'tis thought among the prudent he would quickly have the gift of a grave.

SIR TOBY

By this hand, they are scoundrels and substractors that say so of him. Who are they?

MARIA

They that add, moreover, he's drunk nightly in your company.

SIR TOBY

With drinking healths to my niece; I'll drink to her as long as there is a passage in my throat, and drink in Illyria. He's a coward and a coystril that will not drink to my niece till his brains turn o' the toe like a parish top. What, wench! *Castiliano vulgo*: for here comes Sir Andrew Agueface.

Enter Sir Andrew.

AGUECHEEK

Sir Toby Belch! How now, Sir Toby Belch?

SIR TOBY

Sweet Sir Andrew!

SIR ANDREW

Bless you, fair shrew.

MARIA

And you too, sir.

SIR TOBY

Accost, Sir Andrew, accost.

SIR ANDREW

What's that?

SIR TOBY

My niece's chamber-maid.

SIR ANDREW

Good Mistress Accost, I desire better acquaintance.

MARIA

My name is Mary, sir.

SIR ANDREW

Good Mistress Mary Accost,—

SIR TOBY

You mistake, knight: accost is front her, board her, woo her, assail her.

SIR ANDREW

By my troth, I would not undertake her in this company. Is that the meaning of accost?

MARIA

Fare you well, gentlemen.

SIR TOBY

And thou let part so, Sir Andrew, would thou mightst never draw sword again.

SIR ANDREW

And you part so, mistress, I would I might never draw sword again. Fair lady, do you think you have fools in hand?

MARIA

Sir, I have not you by the hand.

SIR ANDREW

Marry, but you shall have, and here's my hand.

MARIA

Now, sir, thought is free. I pray you, bring your hand to th' buttery bar and let it drink.

SIR ANDREW

Wherefore, sweetheart? What's your metaphor?

MARIA

It's dry, sir.

SIR ANDREW

Why, I think so; I am not such an ass but I can keep my hand dry. But what's your jest?

MARIA

A dry jest, sir.

SIR ANDREW

Are you full of them?

MARIA

Ay, sir, I have them at my fingers' ends: marry, now I let go your hand, I am barren.

[Exit MARIA.]

SIR TOBY

O knight, thou lack'st a cup of canary: When did I see thee so put down?

SIR ANDREW

Never in your life, I think, unless you see canary put me down. Methinks sometimes I have no more wit than a Christian or an ordinary man has; but I am a great eater of beef, and I believe that does harm to my wit.

SIR TOBY

No question.

SIR ANDREW

And I thought that, I'd forswear it. I'll ride home tomorrow, Sir Toby.

SIR TOBY

Pourquoy, my dear knight?

SIR ANDREW

What is *pourquoy*? Do, or not do? I would I had bestowed that time in the tongues that I have in fencing, dancing, and bear-baiting. O, had I but followed the arts!

SIR TOBY

Then hadst thou had an excellent head of hair.

SIR ANDREW

Why, would that have mended my hair?

SIR TOBY

Past question; for thou seest it will not curl by nature.

SIR ANDREW

But it becomes me well enough, does't not?

SIR TOBY

Excellent, it hangs like flax on a distaff; and I hope to see a houswife take thee between her legs, and spin it off.

SIR ANDREW

Faith, I'll home tomorrow, Sir Toby; your niece will not be seen, or if she be, it's four to one she'll none of me; the Count himself here hard by woos her.

SIR TOBY

She'll none o' the Count; she'll not match above her degree, neither in estate, years, nor wit; I have heard her swear't. Tut, there's life in't, man.

SIR ANDREW

I'll stay a month longer. I am a fellow o' the strangest mind i' the world; I delight in masques and revels sometimes altogether.

SIR TOBY

Art thou good at these kick-shawses, knight?

SIR ANDREW

As any man in Illyria, whatsoever he be, under the degree of my betters; and yet I will not compare with an old man.

SIR TOBY

What is thy excellence in a galliard, knight?

SIR ANDREW

Faith, I can cut a caper.

SIR TOBY

And I can cut the mutton to't.

SIR ANDREW

And I think I have the back-trick simply as strong as any man in Illyria.

SIR TOBY

Wherefore are these things hid? Wherefore have these gifts a curtain before 'em? Are they like to take dust, like Mistress Mall's picture?

Why dost thou not go to church in a galliard, and come home in a coranto? My very walk should be a jig; I would not so much as make water but in a sink-a-pace. What dost thou mean? Is it a world to hide virtues in? I did think, by the excellent constitution of thy leg, it was formed under the star of a galliard.

SIR ANDREW

Ay, 'tis strong, and it does indifferent well in a dam'd-colour'd stock. Shall we set about some revels?

SIR TOBY

What shall we do else? Were we not born under Taurus?

SIR ANDREW

Taurus? That's sides and heart.

SIR TOBY

No, sir, it is legs and thighs. Let me see thee caper. Ha, higher: ha, ha, excellent!

[Exeunt.]

SCENE IV. A Room in the Duke's Palace.

Enter VALENTINE and VIOLA in man's attire.

VALENTINE

If the duke continue these favours towards you, Cesario, you are like to be much advanced; he hath known you but three days, and already you are no stranger.

VIOLA

You either fear his humour or my negligence, that you call in question the continuance of his love. Is he inconstant, sir, in his favours?

VALENTINE

No, believe me.

Enter DUKE, CURIO and ATTENDANTS.

VIOLA

I thank you. Here comes the Count.

DUKE

> Who saw Cesario, ho?

VIOLA

> On your attendance, my lord, here.

DUKE

> Stand you awhile aloof.—Cesario,
> Thou know'st no less but all; I have unclasp'd
> To thee the book even of my secret soul.
> Therefore, good youth, address thy gait unto her,
> Be not denied access, stand at her doors,
> And tell them, there thy fixed foot shall grow
> Till thou have audience.

VIOLA

> Sure, my noble lord,
> If she be so abandon'd to her sorrow
> As it is spoke, she never will admit me.

DUKE

> Be clamorous and leap all civil bounds,
> Rather than make unprofited return.

VIOLA

> Say I do speak with her, my lord, what then?

DUKE

> O then unfold the passion of my love,
> Surprise her with discourse of my dear faith;
> It shall become thee well to act my woes;
> She will attend it better in thy youth,
> Than in a nuncio's of more grave aspect.

VIOLA

> I think not so, my lord.

DUKE

> Dear lad, believe it;
> For they shall yet belie thy happy years,
> That say thou art a man: Diana's lip

Is not more smooth and rubious; thy small pipe
Is as the maiden's organ, shrill and sound,
And all is semblative a woman's part.
I know thy constellation is right apt
For this affair. Some four or five attend him:
All, if you will; for I myself am best
When least in company. Prosper well in this,
And thou shalt live as freely as thy lord,
To call his fortunes thine.

VIOLA

I'll do my best
To woo your lady.
    [Aside.]
Yet, a barful strife!
Whoe'er I woo, myself would be his wife.
    [Exeunt.]

SCENE V. A Room in Olivia's House.

Enter MARIA and CLOWN.

MARIA

Nay; either tell me where thou hast been, or I will not open my lips so wide as a bristle may enter, in way of thy excuse: my lady will hang thee for thy absence.

CLOWN

Let her hang me: he that is well hanged in this world needs to fear no colours.

MARIA

Make that good.

CLOWN

He shall see none to fear.

MARIA

A good lenten answer. I can tell thee where that saying was born, of I fear no colours.

CLOWN

Where, good Mistress Mary?

MARIA

In the wars, and that may you be bold to say in your foolery.

CLOWN

Well, God give them wisdom that have it; and those that are fools, let them use their talents.

MARIA

Yet you will be hanged for being so long absent; or to be turned away; is not that as good as a hanging to you?

CLOWN

Many a good hanging prevents a bad marriage; and for turning away, let summer bear it out.

MARIA

You are resolute then?

CLOWN

Not so, neither, but I am resolved on two points.

MARIA

That if one break, the other will hold; or if both break, your gaskins fall.

CLOWN

Apt, in good faith, very apt! Well, go thy way; if Sir Toby would leave drinking, thou wert as witty a piece of Eve's flesh as any in Illyria.

MARIA

Peace, you rogue, no more o' that. Here comes my lady: make your excuse wisely, you were best.

[Exit.]

Enter OLIVIA with MALVOLIO.

CLOWN

Wit, and't be thy will, put me into good fooling! Those wits that think they have thee, do very oft prove fools; and I that am sure I lack thee, may pass for a wise man. For what says Quinapalus? Better a witty fool than a foolish wit. God bless thee, lady!

OLIVIA

Take the fool away.

CLOWN

Do you not hear, fellows? Take away the lady.

OLIVIA

Go to, y'are a dry fool; I'll no more of you. Besides, you grow dishonest.

CLOWN

Two faults, madonna, that drink and good counsel will amend: for give the dry fool drink, then is the fool not dry; bid the dishonest man mend himself, if he mend, he is no longer dishonest; if he cannot, let the botcher mend him. Anything that's mended is but patched; virtue that transgresses is but patched with sin, and sin that amends is but patched with virtue. If that this simple syllogism will serve, so; if it will not, what remedy? As there is no true cuckold but calamity, so beauty's a flower. The lady bade take away the fool, therefore, I say again, take her away.

OLIVIA

Sir, I bade them take away you.

CLOWN

Misprision in the highest degree! Lady, *cucullus non facit monachum*: that's as much to say, I wear not motley in my brain. Good madonna, give me leave to prove you a fool.

OLIVIA

Can you do it?

CLOWN

Dexteriously, good madonna.

OLIVIA

Make your proof.

CLOWN

I must catechize you for it, madonna. Good my mouse of virtue, answer me.

OLIVIA

Well sir, for want of other idleness, I'll 'bide your proof.

CLOWN

Good madonna, why mourn'st thou?

OLIVIA

Good fool, for my brother's death.

CLOWN

I think his soul is in hell, madonna.

OLIVIA

I know his soul is in heaven, fool.

CLOWN

The more fool you, madonna, to mourn for your brother's soul being in heaven. Take away the fool, gentlemen.

OLIVIA

What think you of this fool, Malvolio? doth he not mend?

MALVOLIO

Yes; and shall do, till the pangs of death shake him. Infirmity, that decays the wise, doth ever make the better fool.

CLOWN

God send you, sir, a speedy infirmity, for the better increasing your folly! Sir Toby will be sworn that I am no fox; but he will not pass his word for twopence that you are no fool.

OLIVIA

How say you to that, Malvolio?

MALVOLIO

I marvel your ladyship takes delight in such a barren rascal; I saw him put down the other day with an ordinary fool, that has no more brain than a stone. Look you now, he's out of his guard already; unless you laugh and minister occasion to him, he is gagged. I protest I take these wise men, that crow so at these set kind of fools, no better than the fools' zanies.

OLIVIA

O, you are sick of self-love, Malvolio, and taste with a distempered appetite. To be generous, guiltless, and of free disposition, is to take those things for bird-bolts that you deem cannon bullets. There is no slander in an allowed fool, though he do nothing but rail; nor no railing in a known discreet man, though he do nothing but reprove.

CLOWN

Now Mercury endue thee with leasing, for thou speak'st well of fools!
Enter MARIA.

MARIA

Madam, there is at the gate a young gentleman much desires to speak with you.

OLIVIA

From the Count Orsino, is it?

MARIA

I know not, madam; 'tis a fair young man, and well attended.

OLIVIA

Who of my people hold him in delay?

MARIA

Sir Toby, madam, your kinsman.

OLIVIA

Fetch him off, I pray you; he speaks nothing but madman. Fie on him!
[Exit MARIA.]
Go you, Malvolio. If it be a suit from the Count, I am sick, or not at home. What you will, to dismiss it.
[Exit MALVOLIO.]
Now you see, sir, how your fooling grows old, and people dislike it.

CLOWN

Thou hast spoke for us, madonna, as if thy eldest son should be a fool: whose skull Jove cram with brains, for here he comes, one of thy kin has a most weak *pia mater.*
Enter SIR TOBY.

OLIVIA

By mine honour, half drunk. What is he at the gate, cousin?

SIR TOBY

A gentleman.

OLIVIA

A gentleman? What gentleman?

SIR TOBY

'Tis a gentleman here. A plague o' these pickle-herrings! How now, sot?

CLOWN

Good Sir Toby.

OLIVIA

Cousin, cousin, how have you come so early by this lethargy?

SIR TOBY

Lechery! I defy lechery. There's one at the gate.

OLIVIA

Ay, marry, what is he?

SIR TOBY

Let him be the devil an he will, I care not: give me faith, say I. Well, it's all one.

   [Exit.]

OLIVIA

What's a drunken man like, fool?

CLOWN

Like a drowned man, a fool, and a madman: one draught above heat makes him a fool, the second mads him, and a third drowns him.

OLIVIA

Go thou and seek the coroner, and let him sit o' my coz; for he's in the third degree of drink; he's drowned. Go, look after him.

CLOWN

He is but mad yet, madonna; and the fool shall look to the madman.

[Exit CLOWN.]
Enter MALVOLIO.

MALVOLIO

Madam, yond young fellow swears he will speak with you. I told him you were sick; he takes on him to understand so much, and therefore comes to speak with you. I told him you were asleep; he seems to have a foreknowledge of that too, and therefore comes to speak with you. What is to be said to him, lady? He's fortified against any denial.

OLIVIA

Tell him, he shall not speak with me.

MALVOLIO

Has been told so; and he says he'll stand at your door like a sheriff's post, and be the supporter of a bench, but he'll speak with you.

OLIVIA

What kind o' man is he?

MALVOLIO

Why, of mankind.

OLIVIA

What manner of man?

MALVOLIO

Of very ill manner; he'll speak with you, will you or no.

OLIVIA

Of what personage and years is he?

MALVOLIO

Not yet old enough for a man, nor young enough for a boy; as a squash is before 'tis a peascod, or a codling, when 'tis almost an apple. 'Tis with him in standing water, between boy and man. He is very well-favoured, and he speaks very shrewishly. One would think his mother's milk were scarce out of him.

OLIVIA

Let him approach. Call in my gentlewoman.

MALVOLIO

Gentlewoman, my lady calls.
[Exit.]
Enter MARIA.

OLIVIA

Give me my veil; come, throw it o'er my face.
We'll once more hear Orsino's embassy.
Enter VIOLA.

VIOLA

The honourable lady of the house, which is she?

OLIVIA

Speak to me; I shall answer for her. Your will?

VIOLA

Most radiant, exquisite, and unmatchable beauty,—I pray you, tell me if this be the lady of the house, for I never saw her. I would be loath to cast away my speech; for besides that it is excellently well penned, I have taken great pains to con it. Good beauties, let me sustain no scorn; I am very comptible, even to the least sinister usage.

OLIVIA

Whence came you, sir?

VIOLA

I can say little more than I have studied, and that question's out of my part. Good gentle one, give me modest assurance, if you be the lady of the house, that I may proceed in my speech.

OLIVIA

Are you a comedian?

VIOLA

No, my profound heart: and yet, by the very fangs of malice I swear, I am not that I play. Are you the lady of the house?

OLIVIA

If I do not usurp myself, I am.

VIOLA

Most certain, if you are she, you do usurp yourself; for what is yours to bestow is not yours to reserve. But this is from my commission. I will on with my speech in your praise, and then show you the heart of my message.

OLIVIA

Come to what is important in't: I forgive you the praise.

VIOLA

Alas, I took great pains to study it, and 'tis poetical.

OLIVIA

It is the more like to be feigned; I pray you keep it in. I heard you were saucy at my gates; and allowed your approach, rather to wonder at you than to hear you. If you be mad, be gone; if you have reason, be brief: 'tis not that time of moon with me to make one in so skipping a dialogue.

MARIA

Will you hoist sail, sir? Here lies your way.

VIOLA

No, good swabber, I am to hull here a little longer. Some mollification for your giant, sweet lady. Tell me your mind. I am a messenger.

OLIVIA

Sure, you have some hideous matter to deliver, when the courtesy of it is so fearful. Speak your office.

VIOLA

It alone concerns your ear. I bring no overture of war, no taxation of homage; I hold the olive in my hand: my words are as full of peace as matter.

OLIVIA

Yet you began rudely. What are you? What would you?

VIOLA

The rudeness that hath appeared in me have I learned from my entertainment. What I am and what I would are as secret as maidenhead: to your ears, divinity; to any other's, profanation.

OLIVIA

Give us the place alone: we will hear this divinity.
> *[Exit MARIA.]*

Now, sir, what is your text?

VIOLA

Most sweet lady—

OLIVIA

A comfortable doctrine, and much may be said of it. Where lies your text?

VIOLA

In Orsino's bosom.

OLIVIA

In his bosom? In what chapter of his bosom?

VIOLA

To answer by the method, in the first of his heart.

OLIVIA

O, I have read it; it is heresy. Have you no more to say?

VIOLA

Good madam, let me see your face.

OLIVIA

Have you any commission from your lord to negotiate with my face? You are now out of your text: but we will draw the curtain and show you the picture. [*Unveiling.*] Look you, sir, such a one I was this present. Is't not well done?

VIOLA

Excellently done, if God did all.

OLIVIA

'Tis in grain, sir; 'twill endure wind and weather.

VIOLA

'Tis beauty truly blent, whose red and white
Nature's own sweet and cunning hand laid on.
Lady, you are the cruel'st she alive

If you will lead these graces to the grave,
And leave the world no copy.

OLIVIA

O, sir, I will not be so hard-hearted; I will give out divers schedules
of my beauty. It shall be inventoried and every particle and utensil
labelled to my will: as, item, two lips indifferent red; item, two grey
eyes with lids to them; item, one neck, one chin, and so forth. Were
you sent hither to praise me?

VIOLA

I see you what you are, you are too proud;
But, if you were the devil, you are fair.
My lord and master loves you. O, such love
Could be but recompens'd though you were crown'd
The nonpareil of beauty!

OLIVIA

How does he love me?

VIOLA

With adorations, fertile tears,
With groans that thunder love, with sighs of fire.

OLIVIA

Your lord does know my mind, I cannot love him:
Yet I suppose him virtuous, know him noble,
Of great estate, of fresh and stainless youth;
In voices well divulg'd, free, learn'd, and valiant,
And in dimension and the shape of nature,
A gracious person. But yet I cannot love him.
He might have took his answer long ago.

VIOLA

If I did love you in my master's flame,
With such a suff'ring, such a deadly life,
In your denial I would find no sense,
I would not understand it.

OLIVIA

Why, what would you?

VIOLA

> Make me a willow cabin at your gate,
> And call upon my soul within the house;
> Write loyal cantons of contemned love,
> And sing them loud even in the dead of night;
> Hallow your name to the reverberate hills,
> And make the babbling gossip of the air
> Cry out Olivia! O, you should not rest
> Between the elements of air and earth,
> But you should pity me.

OLIVIA

> You might do much.
> What is your parentage?

VIOLA

> Above my fortunes, yet my state is well:
> I am a gentleman.

OLIVIA

> Get you to your lord;
> I cannot love him: let him send no more,
> Unless, perchance, you come to me again,
> To tell me how he takes it. Fare you well:
> I thank you for your pains: spend this for me.

VIOLA

> I am no fee'd post, lady; keep your purse;
> My master, not myself, lacks recompense.
> Love make his heart of flint that you shall love,
> And let your fervour like my master's be
> Plac'd in contempt. Farewell, fair cruelty.
>> *[Exit.]*

OLIVIA

> What is your parentage?
> 'Above my fortunes, yet my state is well:
> I am a gentleman.' I'll be sworn thou art;
> Thy tongue, thy face, thy limbs, actions, and spirit,
> Do give thee five-fold blazon. Not too fast: soft, soft!

Unless the master were the man. How now?
Even so quickly may one catch the plague?
Methinks I feel this youth's perfections
With an invisible and subtle stealth
To creep in at mine eyes. Well, let it be.
What ho, Malvolio!

Enter MALVOLIO.

MALVOLIO

Here, madam, at your service.

OLIVIA

Run after that same peevish messenger
The County's man: he left this ring behind him,
Would I or not; tell him, I'll none of it.
Desire him not to flatter with his lord,
Nor hold him up with hopes; I am not for him.
If that the youth will come this way tomorrow,
I'll give him reasons for't. Hie thee, Malvolio.

MALVOLIO

Madam, I will.

[Exit.]

OLIVIA

I do I know not what, and fear to find
Mine eye too great a flatterer for my mind.
Fate, show thy force, ourselves we do not owe.
What is decreed must be; and be this so!

[Exit.]

ACT II

SCENE I. The sea-coast.

Enter ANTONIO and SEBASTIAN.

ANTONIO

Will you stay no longer? Nor will you not that I go with you?

SEBASTIAN

By your patience, no; my stars shine darkly over me; the malignancy of my fate might perhaps distemper yours; therefore I shall crave of you your leave that I may bear my evils alone. It were a bad recompense for your love, to lay any of them on you.

ANTONIO

Let me know of you whither you are bound.

SEBASTIAN

No, sooth, sir; my determinate voyage is mere extravagancy. But I perceive in you so excellent a touch of modesty, that you will not extort from me what I am willing to keep in. Therefore it charges me in manners the rather to express myself. You must know of me then, Antonio, my name is Sebastian, which I called Roderigo; my father was that Sebastian of Messaline whom I know you have heard of. He left behind him myself and a sister, both born in an hour. If the heavens had been pleased, would we had so ended! But you, sir, altered that, for some hour before you took me from the breach of the sea was my sister drowned.

ANTONIO

Alas the day!

SEBASTIAN

A lady, sir, though it was said she much resembled me, was yet of many accounted beautiful. But though I could not with such estimable wonder overfar believe that, yet thus far I will boldly publish her, she bore a mind that envy could not but call fair. She is drowned already, sir, with salt water, though I seem to drown her remembrance again with more.

ANTONIO

Pardon me, sir, your bad entertainment.

SEBASTIAN

O good Antonio, forgive me your trouble.

ANTONIO

If you will not murder me for my love, let me be your servant.

SEBASTIAN

If you will not undo what you have done, that is, kill him whom you have recovered, desire it not. Fare ye well at once; my bosom is full of kindness, and I am yet so near the manners of my mother, that upon the least occasion more, mine eyes will tell tales of me. I am bound to the Count Orsino's court: farewell.

 [Exit.]

ANTONIO

The gentleness of all the gods go with thee!
I have many enemies in Orsino's court,
Else would I very shortly see thee there:
But come what may, I do adore thee so,
That danger shall seem sport, and I will go.

 [Exit.]

SCENE II. A street.

Enter VIOLA; MALVOLIO at several doors.

MALVOLIO

Were you not even now with the Countess Olivia?

VIOLA

Even now, sir; on a moderate pace I have since arrived but hither.

MALVOLIO

She returns this ring to you, sir; you might have saved me my pains, to have taken it away yourself. She adds, moreover, that you should put your lord into a desperate assurance she will none of him. And one thing more, that you be never so hardy to come again in his affairs, unless it be to report your lord's taking of this. Receive it so.

VIOLA

She took the ring of me: I'll none of it.

MALVOLIO

Come sir, you peevishly threw it to her; and her will is it should be so returned. If it be worth stooping for, there it lies in your eye; if not, be it his that finds it.

   [Exit.]

VIOLA

I left no ring with her; what means this lady?
Fortune forbid my outside have not charm'd her!
She made good view of me, indeed, so much,
That methought her eyes had lost her tongue,
For she did speak in starts distractedly.
She loves me, sure, the cunning of her passion
Invites me in this churlish messenger.
None of my lord's ring? Why, he sent her none.
I am the man; if it be so, as 'tis,
Poor lady, she were better love a dream.
Disguise, I see thou art a wickedness
Wherein the pregnant enemy does much.
How easy is it for the proper false
In women's waxen hearts to set their forms!
Alas, our frailty is the cause, not we,
For such as we are made of, such we be.
How will this fadge? My master loves her dearly,
And I, poor monster, fond as much on him,
And she, mistaken, seems to dote on me.

What will become of this? As I am man,
My state is desperate for my master's love;
As I am woman (now alas the day!)
What thriftless sighs shall poor Olivia breathe!
O time, thou must untangle this, not I,
It is too hard a knot for me t'untie!
            [Exit.]

SCENE III. A Room in Olivia's House.

Enter Sir Toby and Sir Andrew.

SIR TOBY

Approach, Sir Andrew; not to be abed after midnight, is to be up betimes; and *diluculo surgere*, thou know'st.

SIR ANDREW

Nay, by my troth, I know not; but I know to be up late is to be up late.

SIR TOBY

A false conclusion; I hate it as an unfilled can. To be up after midnight, and to go to bed then is early: so that to go to bed after midnight is to go to bed betimes. Does not our lives consist of the four elements?

SIR ANDREW

Faith, so they say, but I think it rather consists of eating and drinking.

SIR TOBY

Th'art a scholar; let us therefore eat and drink.
Marian, I say! a stoup of wine.
            Enter Clown.

SIR ANDREW

Here comes the fool, i' faith.

CLOWN

How now, my hearts? Did you never see the picture of 'we three'?

SIR TOBY

Welcome, ass. Now let's have a catch.

SIR ANDREW

By my troth, the fool has an excellent breast. I had rather than forty shillings I had such a leg, and so sweet a breath to sing, as the fool has. In sooth, thou wast in very gracious fooling last night when thou spok'st of Pigrogromitus, of the Vapians passing the equinoctial of Queubus; 'twas very good, i' faith. I sent thee sixpence for thy leman. Hadst it?

CLOWN

I did impeticos thy gratillity; for Malvolio's nose is no whipstock. My lady has a white hand, and the Myrmidons are no bottle-ale houses.

SIR ANDREW

Excellent! Why, this is the best fooling, when all is done. Now, a song.

SIR TOBY

Come on, there is sixpence for you. Let's have a song.

SIR ANDREW

There's a testril of me too: if one knight give a—

CLOWN

Would you have a love-song, or a song of good life?

SIR TOBY

A love-song, a love-song.

SIR ANDREW

Ay, ay. I care not for good life.

CLOWN

[Sings.]

> O mistress mine, where are you roaming?
> O stay and hear, your true love's coming,
> That can sing both high and low.
> Trip no further, pretty sweeting.
> Journeys end in lovers meeting,
> Every wise man's son doth know.

SIR ANDREW

Excellent good, i' faith.

SIR TOBY

Good, good.

CLOWN

What is love? 'Tis not hereafter,
Present mirth hath present laughter.
What's to come is still unsure.
In delay there lies no plenty,
Then come kiss me, sweet and twenty.
Youth's a stuff will not endure.

SIR ANDREW

A mellifluous voice, as I am true knight.

SIR TOBY

A contagious breath.

SIR ANDREW

Very sweet and contagious, i' faith.

SIR TOBY

To hear by the nose, it is dulcet in contagion. But shall we make the welkin dance indeed? Shall we rouse the night-owl in a catch that will draw three souls out of one weaver? Shall we do that?

SIR ANDREW

And you love me, let's do't: I am dog at a catch.

CLOWN

By'r lady, sir, and some dogs will catch well.

SIR ANDREW

Most certain. Let our catch be, 'Thou knave.'

CLOWN

'Hold thy peace, thou knave' knight? I shall be constrain'd in't to call thee knave, knight.

SIR ANDREW

'Tis not the first time I have constrained one to call me knave. Begin, fool; it begins 'Hold thy peace.'

CLOWN

I shall never begin if I hold my peace.

SIR ANDREW

Good, i' faith! Come, begin.
[Catch sung.]
Enter MARIA.

MARIA

What a caterwauling do you keep here! If my lady have not called up her steward Malvolio, and bid him turn you out of doors, never trust me.

SIR TOBY

My lady's a Cataian, we are politicians, Malvolio's a Peg-a-Ramsey, and
[Sings.]

Three merry men be we.

Am not I consanguineous? Am I not of her blood? Tilly-vally! 'Lady'!

There dwelt a man in Babylon, Lady, Lady.

CLOWN

Beshrew me, the knight's in admirable fooling.

SIR ANDREW

Ay, he does well enough if he be disposed, and so do I too; he does it with a better grace, but I do it more natural.

SIR TOBY

[Sings.]

O' the twelfth day of December—

MARIA

For the love o' God, peace!
Enter MALVOLIO.

MALVOLIO

My masters, are you mad? Or what are you? Have you no wit, manners, nor honesty, but to gabble like tinkers at this time of night? Do ye make an ale-house of my lady's house, that ye squeak out your coziers' catches without any mitigation or remorse of voice? Is there no respect of place, persons, nor time, in you?

SIR TOBY

We did keep time, sir, in our catches. Sneck up!

MALVOLIO

Sir Toby, I must be round with you. My lady bade me tell you that, though she harbours you as her kinsman she's nothing allied to your disorders. If you can separate yourself and your misdemeanours, you are welcome to the house; if not, and it would please you to take leave of her, she is very willing to bid you farewell.

SIR TOBY

[Sings.]

Farewell, dear heart, since I must needs be gone.

MARIA

Nay, good Sir Toby.

CLOWN

[Sings.]

His eyes do show his days are almost done.

MALVOLIO

Is't even so?

SIR TOBY

[Sings.]

But I will never die.

CLOWN

[Sings.]

Sir Toby, there you lie.

MALVOLIO

This is much credit to you.

SIR TOBY

[Sings.]

Shall I bid him go?

CLOWN

[Sings.]

What and if you do?

SIR TOBY

[Sings.]

Shall I bid him go, and spare not?

CLOWN

[Sings.]

O, no, no, no, no, you dare not.

SIR TOBY

Out o' tune? sir, ye lie. Art any more than a steward? Dost thou think, because thou art virtuous, there shall be no more cakes and ale?

CLOWN

Yes, by Saint Anne, and ginger shall be hot i' the mouth too.

SIR TOBY

Th'art i' the right. Go, sir, rub your chain with crumbs. A stoup of wine, Maria!

MALVOLIO

Mistress Mary, if you prized my lady's favour at anything more than contempt, you would not give means for this uncivil rule; she shall know of it, by this hand.

[Exit.]

MARIA

Go shake your ears.

SIR ANDREW

'Twere as good a deed as to drink when a man's a-hungry, to challenge him the field, and then to break promise with him and make a fool of him.

SIR TOBY

Do't, knight. I'll write thee a challenge; or I'll deliver thy indignation to him by word of mouth.

MARIA

Sweet Sir Toby, be patient for tonight. Since the youth of the Count's was today with my lady, she is much out of quiet. For Monsieur Malvolio, let me alone with him. If I do not gull him into a nayword, and make him a common recreation, do not think I have wit enough to lie straight in my bed. I know I can do it.

SIR TOBY

Possess us, possess us, tell us something of him.

MARIA

Marry, sir, sometimes he is a kind of Puritan.

SIR ANDREW

O, if I thought that, I'd beat him like a dog.

SIR TOBY

What, for being a Puritan? Thy exquisite reason, dear knight?

SIR ANDREW

I have no exquisite reason for't, but I have reason good enough.

MARIA

The devil a Puritan that he is, or anything constantly but a time-pleaser, an affectioned ass that cons state without book and utters it by great swarths; the best persuaded of himself, so crammed (as he thinks) with excellencies, that it is his grounds of faith that all that look on him love him. And on that vice in him will my revenge find notable cause to work.

SIR TOBY

What wilt thou do?

MARIA

I will drop in his way some obscure epistles of love, wherein by the colour of his beard, the shape of his leg, the manner of his gait, the expressure of his eye, forehead, and complexion, he shall find himself most feelingly personated. I can write very like my lady your niece; on a forgotten matter we can hardly make distinction of our hands.

SIR TOBY

Excellent! I smell a device.

SIR ANDREW

I have't in my nose too.

SIR TOBY

He shall think, by the letters that thou wilt drop, that they come from my niece, and that she is in love with him.

MARIA

My purpose is indeed a horse of that colour.

SIR ANDREW

And your horse now would make him an ass.

MARIA

Ass, I doubt not.

SIR ANDREW

O 'twill be admirable!

MARIA

Sport royal, I warrant you. I know my physic will work with him. I will plant you two, and let the fool make a third, where he shall find the letter. Observe his construction of it. For this night, to bed, and dream on the event. Farewell.

    [Exit.]

SIR TOBY

Good night, Penthesilea.

SIR ANDREW

Before me, she's a good wench.

SIR TOBY

She's a beagle true bred, and one that adores me. What o' that?

SIR ANDREW

I was adored once too.

SIR TOBY

Let's to bed, knight. Thou hadst need send for more money.

SIR ANDREW

If I cannot recover your niece, I am a foul way out.

SIR TOBY

Send for money, knight; if thou hast her not i' th' end, call me cut.

SIR ANDREW

If I do not, never trust me, take it how you will.

SIR TOBY

Come, come, I'll go burn some sack, 'tis too late to go to bed now. Come, knight, come, knight.

[Exeunt.]

SCENE IV. A Room in the Duke's Palace.

Enter DUKE, VIOLA, CURIO and others.

DUKE

Give me some music. Now, good morrow, friends.
Now, good Cesario, but that piece of song,
That old and antique song we heard last night;
Methought it did relieve my passion much,
More than light airs and recollected terms
Of these most brisk and giddy-paced times.
Come, but one verse.

CURIO

He is not here, so please your lordship, that should sing it.

DUKE

Who was it?

CURIO

Feste, the jester, my lord, a fool that the Lady Olivia's father took much delight in. He is about the house.

DUKE

Seek him out, and play the tune the while.
[Exit CURIO. Music plays.]
Come hither, boy. If ever thou shalt love,
In the sweet pangs of it remember me:
For such as I am, all true lovers are,
Unstaid and skittish in all motions else,

Save in the constant image of the creature
That is belov'd. How dost thou like this tune?

VIOLA

It gives a very echo to the seat
Where love is throned.

DUKE

Thou dost speak masterly.
My life upon't, young though thou art, thine eye
Hath stayed upon some favour that it loves.
Hath it not, boy?

VIOLA

A little, by your favour.

DUKE

What kind of woman is't?

VIOLA

Of your complexion.

DUKE

She is not worth thee, then. What years, i' faith?

VIOLA

About your years, my lord.

DUKE

Too old, by heaven! Let still the woman take
An elder than herself; so wears she to him,
So sways she level in her husband's heart.
For, boy, however we do praise ourselves,
Our fancies are more giddy and unfirm,
More longing, wavering, sooner lost and worn,
Than women's are.

VIOLA

I think it well, my lord.

DUKE

Then let thy love be younger than thyself,
Or thy affection cannot hold the bent:

For women are as roses, whose fair flower
Being once display'd, doth fall that very hour.

VIOLA

And so they are: alas, that they are so;
To die, even when they to perfection grow!
Enter CURIO and CLOWN.

DUKE

O, fellow, come, the song we had last night.
Mark it, Cesario, it is old and plain;
The spinsters and the knitters in the sun,
And the free maids, that weave their thread with bones
Do use to chant it: it is silly sooth,
And dallies with the innocence of love
Like the old age.

CLOWN

Are you ready, sir?

DUKE

Ay; prithee, sing.
[Music.]
[The CLOWN'S song.]

Come away, come away, death.
And in sad cypress let me be laid.
Fly away, fly away, breath;
I am slain by a fair cruel maid.
My shroud of white, stuck all with yew,
O, prepare it!
My part of death no one so true
Did share it.
Not a flower, not a flower sweet,
On my black coffin let there be strown:
Not a friend, not a friend greet
My poor corpse where my bones shall be thrown:
A thousand thousand sighs to save,
Lay me, O, where
Sad true lover never find my grave,
To weep there.

DUKE

There's for thy pains.

CLOWN

No pains, sir; I take pleasure in singing, sir.

DUKE

I'll pay thy pleasure, then.

CLOWN

Truly sir, and pleasure will be paid one time or another.

DUKE

Give me now leave to leave thee.

CLOWN

Now the melancholy god protect thee, and the tailor make thy dou-
blet of changeable taffeta, for thy mind is a very opal. I would have
men of such constancy put to sea, that their business might be every-
thing, and their intent everywhere, for that's it that always makes a
good voyage of nothing. Farewell.
[Exit CLOWN.]

DUKE

Let all the rest give place.
[Exeunt CURIO and ATTENDANTS.]
Once more, Cesario,
Get thee to yond same sovereign cruelty.
Tell her my love, more noble than the world,
Prizes not quantity of dirty lands;
The parts that fortune hath bestow'd upon her,
Tell her I hold as giddily as fortune;
But 'tis that miracle and queen of gems
That nature pranks her in attracts my soul.

VIOLA

But if she cannot love you, sir?

DUKE

I cannot be so answer'd.

VIOLA

Sooth, but you must.

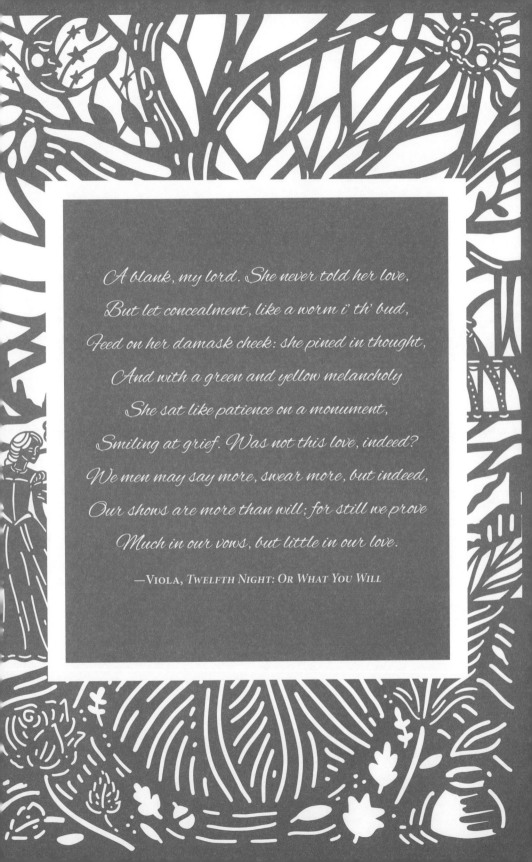

A blank, my lord. She never told her love,

But let concealment, like a worm i' th' bud,

Feed on her damask cheek: she pined in thought,

And with a green and yellow melancholy

She sat like patience on a monument,

Smiling at grief. Was not this love, indeed?

We men may say more, swear more, but indeed,

Our shows are more than will; for still we prove

Much in our vows, but little in our love.

—VIOLA, TWELFTH NIGHT: OR WHAT YOU WILL

Say that some lady, as perhaps there is,
Hath for your love as great a pang of heart
As you have for Olivia: you cannot love her;
You tell her so. Must she not then be answer'd?

DUKE

There is no woman's sides
Can bide the beating of so strong a passion
As love doth give my heart: no woman's heart
So big, to hold so much; they lack retention.
Alas, their love may be called appetite,
No motion of the liver, but the palate,
That suffer surfeit, cloyment, and revolt;
But mine is all as hungry as the sea,
And can digest as much. Make no compare
Between that love a woman can bear me
And that I owe Olivia.

VIOLA

Ay, but I know—

DUKE

What dost thou know?

VIOLA

Too well what love women to men may owe.
In faith, they are as true of heart as we.
My father had a daughter loved a man,
As it might be perhaps, were I a woman,
I should your lordship.

DUKE

And what's her history?

VIOLA

A blank, my lord. She never told her love,
But let concealment, like a worm i' th' bud,
Feed on her damask cheek: she pined in thought,
And with a green and yellow melancholy
She sat like patience on a monument,

Smiling at grief. Was not this love, indeed?
We men may say more, swear more, but indeed,
Our shows are more than will; for still we prove
Much in our vows, but little in our love.

DUKE

But died thy sister of her love, my boy?

VIOLA

I am all the daughters of my father's house,
And all the brothers too: and yet I know not.
Sir, shall I to this lady?

DUKE

Ay, that's the theme.
To her in haste. Give her this jewel; say
My love can give no place, bide no denay.
                    [Exeunt.]

SCENE V. Olivia's garden.

Enter Sir Toby, Sir Andrew and Fabian.

SIR TOBY

Come thy ways, Signior Fabian.

FABIAN

Nay, I'll come. If I lose a scruple of this sport, let me be boiled to death with melancholy.

SIR TOBY

Wouldst thou not be glad to have the niggardly rascally sheep-biter come by some notable shame?

FABIAN

I would exult, man. You know he brought me out o' favour with my lady about a bear-baiting here.

SIR TOBY

To anger him we'll have the bear again, and we will fool him black and blue, shall we not, Sir Andrew?

SIR ANDREW

And we do not, it is pity of our lives.
Enter MARIA.

SIR TOBY

Here comes the little villain. How now, my metal of India?

MARIA

Get ye all three into the box-tree. Malvolio's coming down this walk; he has been yonder i' the sun practising behaviour to his own shadow this half hour: observe him, for the love of mockery; for I know this letter will make a contemplative idiot of him. Close, in the name of jesting!
[The men hide themselves.]
Lie thou there;
[Throws down a letter.]
for here comes the trout that must be caught with tickling.
[Exit MARIA.]
Enter MALVOLIO.

MALVOLIO

'Tis but fortune, all is fortune. Maria once told me she did affect me, and I have heard herself come thus near, that should she fancy, it should be one of my complexion. Besides, she uses me with a more exalted respect than anyone else that follows her. What should I think on't?

SIR TOBY

Here's an overweening rogue!

FABIAN

O, peace! Contemplation makes a rare turkey-cock of him; how he jets under his advanced plumes!

SIR ANDREW

'Slight, I could so beat the rogue!

SIR TOBY

Peace, I say.

MALVOLIO

To be Count Malvolio.

SIR TOBY

Ah, rogue!

SIR ANDREW

Pistol him, pistol him.

SIR TOBY

Peace, peace.

MALVOLIO

There is example for't. The lady of the Strachy married the yeoman of the wardrobe.

SIR ANDREW

Fie on him, Jezebel!

FABIAN

O, peace! now he's deeply in; look how imagination blows him.

MALVOLIO

Having been three months married to her, sitting in my state—

SIR TOBY

O for a stone-bow to hit him in the eye!

MALVOLIO

Calling my officers about me, in my branched velvet gown; having come from a day-bed, where I have left Olivia sleeping.

SIR TOBY

Fire and brimstone!

FABIAN

O, peace, peace.

MALVOLIO

And then to have the humour of state; and after a demure travel of regard, telling them I know my place as I would they should do theirs, to ask for my kinsman Toby.

SIR TOBY

Bolts and shackles!

FABIAN

O, peace, peace, peace! Now, now.

MALVOLIO

Seven of my people, with an obedient start, make out for him. I frown the while, and perchance wind up my watch, or play with some rich jewel. Toby approaches; curtsies there to me—

SIR TOBY

Shall this fellow live?

FABIAN

Though our silence be drawn from us with cars, yet peace!

MALVOLIO

I extend my hand to him thus, quenching my familiar smile with an austere regard of control—

SIR TOBY

And does not Toby take you a blow o' the lips then?

MALVOLIO

Saying 'Cousin Toby, my fortunes having cast me on your niece, give me this prerogative of speech—'

SIR TOBY

What, what?

MALVOLIO

'You must amend your drunkenness.'

SIR TOBY

Out, scab!

FABIAN

Nay, patience, or we break the sinews of our plot.

MALVOLIO

'Besides, you waste the treasure of your time with a foolish knight—'

SIR ANDREW

That's me, I warrant you.

MALVOLIO

'One Sir Andrew.'

SIR ANDREW

I knew 'twas I, for many do call me fool.

MALVOLIO

[Taking up the letter.]
What employment have we here?

FABIAN

Now is the woodcock near the gin.

SIR TOBY

O, peace! And the spirit of humours intimate reading aloud to him!

MALVOLIO

By my life, this is my lady's hand: these be her very C's, her U's, and her T's, and thus makes she her great P's. It is in contempt of question, her hand.

SIR ANDREW

Her C's, her U's, and her T's. Why that?

MALVOLIO

[Reads.]
To the unknown beloved, this, and my good wishes.
Her very phrases! By your leave, wax. Soft! and the impressure her Lucrece, with which she uses to seal: 'tis my lady. To whom should this be?

FABIAN

This wins him, liver and all.

MALVOLIO

[Reads.]
Jove knows I love,
But who?
Lips, do not move,
No man must know.
'No man must know.' What follows? The numbers alter'd! 'No man must know.'—If this should be thee, Malvolio?

SIR TOBY

Marry, hang thee, brock!

MALVOLIO

I may command where I adore,
But silence, like a Lucrece knife,
With bloodless stroke my heart doth gore;
M.O.A.I. doth sway my life.

FABIAN

A fustian riddle!

SIR TOBY

Excellent wench, say I.

MALVOLIO

'M.O.A.I. doth sway my life.'—Nay, but first let me see, let me see, let me see.

FABIAN

What dish o' poison has she dressed him!

SIR TOBY

And with what wing the staniel checks at it!

MALVOLIO

'I may command where I adore.' Why, she may command me: I serve her, she is my lady. Why, this is evident to any formal capacity. There is no obstruction in this. And the end—what should that alphabetical position portend? If I could make that resemble something in me! Softly! 'M.O.A.I.'—

SIR TOBY

O, ay, make up that:—he is now at a cold scent.

FABIAN

Sowter will cry upon't for all this, though it be as rank as a fox.

MALVOLIO

'M'—Malvolio; 'M'! Why, that begins my name!

FABIAN

Did not I say he would work it out? The cur is excellent at faults.

MALVOLIO

'M'—But then there is no consonancy in the sequel; that suffers under probation: 'A' should follow, but 'O' does.

FABIAN

And 'O' shall end, I hope.

SIR TOBY

Ay, or I'll cudgel him, and make him cry 'O!'

MALVOLIO

And then 'I' comes behind.

FABIAN

Ay, and you had any eye behind you, you might see more detraction at your heels than fortunes before you.

MALVOLIO

'M.O.A.I.' This simulation is not as the former: and yet, to crush this a little, it would bow to me, for every one of these letters are in my name. Soft, here follows prose.

    [Reads.]

If this fall into thy hand, revolve. In my stars I am above thee, but be not afraid of greatness. Some are born great, some achieve greatness, and some have greatness thrust upon 'em. Thy fates open their hands, let thy blood and spirit embrace them. And, to inure thyself to what thou art like to be, cast thy humble slough and appear fresh. Be opposite with a kinsman, surly with servants. Let thy tongue tang arguments of state; put thyself into the trick of singularity. She thus advises thee that sighs for thee. Remember who commended thy yellow stockings, and wished to see thee ever cross-gartered. I say, remember. Go to, thou art made, if thou desir'st to be so. If not, let me see thee a steward still, the fellow of servants, and not worthy to touch Fortune's fingers. Farewell. She that would alter services with thee,

    The Fortunate Unhappy.

Daylight and champian discovers not more! This is open. I will be proud, I will read politic authors, I will baffle Sir Toby, I will wash off gross acquaintance, I will be point-device, the very man. I do not now fool myself, to let imagination jade me; for every reason excites to this, that my lady loves me. She did commend my yellow stockings of late, she did praise my leg being cross-gartered, and in this she manifests herself to my love, and with a kind of injunction, drives me to these habits of her liking. I thank my stars, I am happy. I will be strange, stout, in yellow stockings, and cross-gartered, even with the swiftness of putting on. Jove and my stars be praised!—Here is yet a postscript.

[Reads.]

Thou canst not choose but know who I am. If thou entertain'st my love, let it appear in thy smiling; thy smiles become thee well. Therefore in my presence still smile, dear my sweet, I prithee.

Jove, I thank thee. I will smile, I will do everything that thou wilt have me.

[Exit.]

FABIAN

I will not give my part of this sport for a pension of thousands to be paid from the Sophy.

SIR TOBY

I could marry this wench for this device.

SIR ANDREW

So could I too.

SIR TOBY

And ask no other dowry with her but such another jest.

Enter MARIA.

SIR ANDREW

Nor I neither.

FABIAN

Here comes my noble gull-catcher.

SIR TOBY

Wilt thou set thy foot o' my neck?

SIR ANDREW

Or o' mine either?

SIR TOBY

Shall I play my freedom at tray-trip, and become thy bond-slave?

SIR ANDREW

I' faith, or I either?

SIR TOBY

Why, thou hast put him in such a dream, that when the image of it leaves him he must run mad.

MARIA

Nay, but say true, does it work upon him?

SIR TOBY

Like aqua-vitae with a midwife.

MARIA

If you will then see the fruits of the sport, mark his first approach before my lady: he will come to her in yellow stockings, and 'tis a colour she abhors, and cross-gartered, a fashion she detests; and he will smile upon her, which will now be so unsuitable to her disposition, being addicted to a melancholy as she is, that it cannot but turn him into a notable contempt. If you will see it, follow me.

SIR TOBY

To the gates of Tartar, thou most excellent devil of wit!

SIR ANDREW

I'll make one too.
[Exeunt.]

ACT III

SCENE I. Olivia's garden.

Enter VIOLA and CLOWN with a tabor.

VIOLA

Save thee, friend, and thy music. Dost thou live by thy tabor?

CLOWN

No, sir, I live by the church.

VIOLA

Art thou a churchman?

CLOWN

No such matter, sir. I do live by the church, for I do live at my house, and my house doth stand by the church.

VIOLA

So thou mayst say the king lies by a beggar, if a beggar dwell near him; or the church stands by thy tabor, if thy tabor stand by the church.

CLOWN

You have said, sir. To see this age! A sentence is but a chev'ril glove to a good wit. How quickly the wrong side may be turned outward!

VIOLA

Nay, that's certain; they that dally nicely with words may quickly make them wanton.

CLOWN

I would, therefore, my sister had had no name, sir.

VIOLA

Why, man?

CLOWN

Why, sir, her name's a word; and to dally with that word might make my sister wanton. But indeed, words are very rascals, since bonds disgraced them.

VIOLA

Thy reason, man?

CLOWN

Troth, sir, I can yield you none without words, and words are grown so false, I am loath to prove reason with them.

VIOLA

I warrant thou art a merry fellow, and car'st for nothing.

CLOWN

Not so, sir, I do care for something. But in my conscience, sir, I do not care for you. If that be to care for nothing, sir, I would it would make you invisible.

VIOLA

Art not thou the Lady Olivia's fool?

CLOWN

No, indeed, sir; the Lady Olivia has no folly. She will keep no fool, sir, till she be married, and fools are as like husbands as pilchards are to herrings, the husband's the bigger. I am indeed not her fool, but her corrupter of words.

VIOLA

I saw thee late at the Count Orsino's.

CLOWN

Foolery, sir, does walk about the orb like the sun; it shines every-where. I would be sorry, sir, but the fool should be as oft with your master as with my mistress. I think I saw your wisdom there.

VIOLA

Nay, and thou pass upon me, I'll no more with thee. Hold, there's expenses for thee.

CLOWN

Now Jove, in his next commodity of hair, send thee a beard!

VIOLA

By my troth, I'll tell thee, I am almost sick for one, though I would not have it grow on my chin. Is thy lady within?

CLOWN

Would not a pair of these have bred, sir?

VIOLA

Yes, being kept together, and put to use.

CLOWN

I would play Lord Pandarus of Phrygia, sir, to bring a Cressida to this Troilus.

VIOLA

I understand you, sir; 'tis well begged.

CLOWN

The matter, I hope, is not great, sir, begging but a beggar: Cressida was a beggar. My lady is within, sir. I will conster to them whence you come; who you are and what you would are out of my welkin. I might say 'element,' but the word is overworn.

    [Exit.]

VIOLA

This fellow is wise enough to play the fool,
And to do that well, craves a kind of wit:
He must observe their mood on whom he jests,
The quality of persons, and the time,
And like the haggard, check at every feather
That comes before his eye. This is a practice
As full of labour as a wise man's art:
For folly, that he wisely shows, is fit;
But wise men, folly-fall'n, quite taint their wit.

    Enter Sir Toby and Sir Andrew.

SIR TOBY

Save you, gentleman.

VIOLA

And you, sir.

SIR ANDREW

Dieu vous garde, monsieur.

VIOLA

Et vous aussi; votre serviteur.

SIR ANDREW

I hope, sir, you are, and I am yours.

SIR TOBY

Will you encounter the house? My niece is desirous you should enter, if your trade be to her.

VIOLA

I am bound to your niece, sir, I mean, she is the list of my voyage.

SIR TOBY

Taste your legs, sir, put them to motion.

VIOLA

My legs do better understand me, sir, than I understand what you mean by bidding me taste my legs.

SIR TOBY

I mean, to go, sir, to enter.

VIOLA

I will answer you with gait and entrance: but we are prevented.
        Enter OLIVIA and MARIA.
Most excellent accomplished lady, the heavens rain odours on you!

SIR ANDREW

That youth's a rare courtier. 'Rain odours,' well.

VIOLA

My matter hath no voice, lady, but to your own most pregnant and vouchsafed car.

SIR ANDREW

'Odours,' 'pregnant,' and 'vouchsafed.'—I'll get 'em all three ready.

OLIVIA

Let the garden door be shut, and leave me to my hearing.
[Exeunt Sir Toby, Sir Andrew and Maria.]
Give me your hand, sir.

VIOLA

My duty, madam, and most humble service.

OLIVIA

What is your name?

VIOLA

Cesario is your servant's name, fair princess.

OLIVIA

My servant, sir! 'Twas never merry world,
Since lowly feigning was call'd compliment:
Y'are servant to the Count Orsino, youth.

VIOLA

And he is yours, and his must needs be yours.
Your servant's servant is your servant, madam.

OLIVIA

For him, I think not on him: for his thoughts,
Would they were blanks rather than fill'd with me!

VIOLA

Madam, I come to whet your gentle thoughts
On his behalf.

OLIVIA

O, by your leave, I pray you.
I bade you never speak again of him.
But would you undertake another suit,
I had rather hear you to solicit that
Than music from the spheres.

VIOLA

Dear lady—

OLIVIA

Give me leave, beseech you. I did send,
After the last enchantment you did here,
A ring in chase of you. So did I abuse
Myself, my servant, and, I fear me, you.
Under your hard construction must I sit;
To force that on you in a shameful cunning,
Which you knew none of yours. What might you think?
Have you not set mine honour at the stake,
And baited it with all th' unmuzzled thoughts
That tyrannous heart can think? To one of your receiving
Enough is shown. A cypress, not a bosom,
Hides my heart: so let me hear you speak.

VIOLA

I pity you.

OLIVIA

That's a degree to love.

VIOLA

No, not a grize; for 'tis a vulgar proof
That very oft we pity enemies.

OLIVIA

Why then methinks 'tis time to smile again.
O world, how apt the poor are to be proud!
If one should be a prey, how much the better
To fall before the lion than the wolf!
    [Clock strikes.]
The clock upbraids me with the waste of time.
Be not afraid, good youth, I will not have you.
And yet, when wit and youth is come to harvest,
Your wife is like to reap a proper man.
There lies your way, due west.

VIOLA

> Then westward ho!
> Grace and good disposition attend your ladyship!
> You'll nothing, madam, to my lord by me?

OLIVIA

> Stay:
> I prithee tell me what thou think'st of me.

VIOLA

> That you do think you are not what you are.

OLIVIA

> If I think so, I think the same of you.

VIOLA

> Then think you right; I am not what I am.

OLIVIA

> I would you were as I would have you be.

VIOLA

> Would it be better, madam, than I am?
> I wish it might, for now I am your fool.

OLIVIA

> O what a deal of scorn looks beautiful
> In the contempt and anger of his lip!
> A murd'rous guilt shows not itself more soon
> Than love that would seem hid. Love's night is noon.
> Cesario, by the roses of the spring,
> By maidhood, honour, truth, and everything,
> I love thee so, that maugre all thy pride,
> Nor wit nor reason can my passion hide.
> Do not extort thy reasons from this clause,
> For that I woo, thou therefore hast no cause;
> But rather reason thus with reason fetter:
> Love sought is good, but given unsought is better.

VIOLA

> By innocence I swear, and by my youth,

I have one heart, one bosom, and one truth,
And that no woman has; nor never none
Shall mistress be of it, save I alone.
And so adieu, good madam; never more
Will I my master's tears to you deplore.

OLIVIA

Yet come again: for thou perhaps mayst move
That heart, which now abhors, to like his love.
[Exeunt.]

SCENE II. A Room in Olivia's House.

Enter Sir Toby, Sir Andrew and Fabian.

SIR ANDREW

No, faith, I'll not stay a jot longer.

SIR TOBY

Thy reason, dear venom, give thy reason.

FABIAN

You must needs yield your reason, Sir Andrew.

SIR ANDREW

Marry, I saw your niece do more favours to the Count's servingman
than ever she bestowed upon me; I saw't i' th' orchard.

SIR TOBY

Did she see thee the while, old boy? Tell me that.

SIR ANDREW

As plain as I see you now.

FABIAN

This was a great argument of love in her toward you.

SIR ANDREW

'Slight! will you make an ass o' me?

FABIAN

I will prove it legitimate, sir, upon the oaths of judgment and reason.

SIR TOBY

And they have been grand-jurymen since before Noah was a sailor.

FABIAN

She did show favour to the youth in your sight only to exasperate you, to awake your dormouse valour, to put fire in your heart and brimstone in your liver. You should then have accosted her, and with some excellent jests, fire-new from the mint, you should have banged the youth into dumbness. This was looked for at your hand, and this was balked: the double gilt of this opportunity you let time wash off, and you are now sailed into the north of my lady's opinion; where you will hang like an icicle on Dutchman's beard, unless you do redeem it by some laudable attempt, either of valour or policy.

SIR ANDREW

And't be any way, it must be with valour, for policy I hate; I had as lief be a Brownist as a politician.

SIR TOBY

Why, then, build me thy fortunes upon the basis of valour. Challenge me the Count's youth to fight with him. Hurt him in eleven places; my niece shall take note of it, and assure thyself there is no love-broker in the world can more prevail in man's commendation with woman than report of valour.

FABIAN

There is no way but this, Sir Andrew.

SIR ANDREW

Will either of you bear me a challenge to him?

SIR TOBY

Go, write it in a martial hand, be curst and brief; it is no matter how witty, so it be eloquent and full of invention. Taunt him with the licence of ink. If thou 'thou'st' him some thrice, it shall not be amiss, and as many lies as will lie in thy sheet of paper, although the sheet were big enough for the bed of Ware in England, set 'em down. Go about it. Let there be gall enough in thy ink, though thou write with a goose-pen, no matter. About it.

SIR ANDREW

Where shall I find you?

SIR TOBY

We'll call thee at the cubiculo. Go.

[Exit Sir Andrew.]

FABIAN

This is a dear manikin to you, Sir Toby.

SIR TOBY

I have been dear to him, lad, some two thousand strong, or so.

FABIAN

We shall have a rare letter from him; but you'll not deliver it.

SIR TOBY

Never trust me then. And by all means stir on the youth to an answer. I think oxen and wainropes cannot hale them together. For Andrew, if he were opened and you find so much blood in his liver as will clog the foot of a flea, I'll eat the rest of th' anatomy.

FABIAN

And his opposite, the youth, bears in his visage no great presage of cruelty.

Enter Maria.

SIR TOBY

Look where the youngest wren of nine comes.

MARIA

If you desire the spleen, and will laugh yourselves into stitches, follow me. Yond gull Malvolio is turned heathen, a very renegado; for there is no Christian that means to be saved by believing rightly can ever believe such impossible passages of grossness. He's in yellow stockings.

SIR TOBY

And cross-gartered?

MARIA

Most villainously; like a pedant that keeps a school i' th' church. I have dogged him like his murderer. He does obey every point of the letter that I dropped to betray him. He does smile his face into more lines than is in the new map with the augmentation of the Indies. You have not seen such a thing as 'tis. I can hardly forbear hurling things at him. I know my lady will strike him. If she do, he'll smile and take't for a great favour.

SIR TOBY

Come, bring us, bring us where he is.
[Exeunt.]

SCENE III. A street.

Enter SEBASTIAN and ANTONIO.

SEBASTIAN

I would not by my will have troubled you,
But since you make your pleasure of your pains,
I will no further chide you.

ANTONIO

I could not stay behind you: my desire,
More sharp than filed steel, did spur me forth;
And not all love to see you, though so much,
As might have drawn one to a longer voyage,
But jealousy what might befall your travel,
Being skilless in these parts; which to a stranger,
Unguided and unfriended, often prove
Rough and unhospitable. My willing love,
The rather by these arguments of fear,
Set forth in your pursuit.

SEBASTIAN

My kind Antonio,
I can no other answer make but thanks,
And thanks, and ever thanks; and oft good turns
Are shuffled off with such uncurrent pay.
But were my worth, as is my conscience, firm,
You should find better dealing. What's to do?
Shall we go see the relics of this town?

ANTONIO

Tomorrow, sir; best first go see your lodging.

SEBASTIAN

I am not weary, and 'tis long to night;
I pray you, let us satisfy our eyes
With the memorials and the things of fame
That do renown this city.

ANTONIO

Would you'd pardon me.
I do not without danger walk these streets.
Once in a sea-fight, 'gainst the Count his galleys,
I did some service, of such note indeed,
That were I ta'en here, it would scarce be answer'd.

SEBASTIAN

Belike you slew great number of his people.

ANTONIO

Th' offence is not of such a bloody nature,
Albeit the quality of the time and quarrel
Might well have given us bloody argument.
It might have since been answered in repaying
What we took from them, which for traffic's sake,
Most of our city did. Only myself stood out,
For which, if I be lapsed in this place,
I shall pay dear.

SEBASTIAN

Do not then walk too open.

ANTONIO

It doth not fit me. Hold, sir, here's my purse.
In the south suburbs, at the Elephant,
Is best to lodge. I will bespeak our diet
Whiles you beguile the time and feed your knowledge
With viewing of the town. There shall you have me.

SEBASTIAN

Why I your purse?

ANTONIO

Haply your eye shall light upon some toy
You have desire to purchase; and your store,
I think, is not for idle markets, sir.

SEBASTIAN

I'll be your purse-bearer, and leave you for an hour.

ANTONIO

To th' Elephant.

SEBASTIAN

I do remember.
[Exeunt.]

SCENE IV. Olivia's garden.

Enter OLIVIA and MARIA.

OLIVIA

I have sent after him. He says he'll come;
How shall I feast him? What bestow of him?
For youth is bought more oft than begg'd or borrow'd.
I speak too loud.—
Where's Malvolio?—He is sad and civil,
And suits well for a servant with my fortunes;
Where is Malvolio?

MARIA

He's coming, madam:
But in very strange manner. He is sure possessed, madam.

OLIVIA

Why, what's the matter? Does he rave?

MARIA

No, madam, he does nothing but smile: your ladyship were best to have some guard about you if he come, for sure the man is tainted in 's wits.

OLIVIA

Go call him hither. I'm as mad as he,
If sad and merry madness equal be.
  Enter MALVOLIO.
How now, Malvolio?

MALVOLIO

Sweet lady, ho, ho!

OLIVIA

Smil'st thou? I sent for thee upon a sad occasion.

MALVOLIO

Sad, lady? I could be sad: this does make some obstruction in the
blood, this cross-gartering. But what of that? If it please the eye of one,
it is with me as the very true sonnet is: 'Please one and please all.'

OLIVIA

Why, how dost thou, man? What is the matter with thee?

MALVOLIO

Not black in my mind, though yellow in my legs. It did come to
his hands, and commands shall be executed. I think we do know the
sweet Roman hand.

OLIVIA

Wilt thou go to bed, Malvolio?

MALVOLIO

To bed? Ay, sweetheart, and I'll come to thee.

OLIVIA

God comfort thee! Why dost thou smile so, and kiss thy hand so
oft?

MARIA

How do you, Malvolio?

MALVOLIO

At your request? Yes, nightingales answer daws!

MARIA

Why appear you with this ridiculous boldness before my lady?

MALVOLIO

'Be not afraid of greatness.' 'Twas well writ.

OLIVIA

What mean'st thou by that, Malvolio?

MALVOLIO

'Some are born great'—

OLIVIA

Ha?

MALVOLIO

'Some achieve greatness'—

OLIVIA

What say'st thou?

MALVOLIO

'And some have greatness thrust upon them.'

OLIVIA

Heaven restore thee!

MALVOLIO

'Remember who commended thy yellow stockings'—

OLIVIA

Thy yellow stockings?

MALVOLIO

'And wished to see thee cross-gartered.'

OLIVIA

Cross-gartered?

MALVOLIO

'Go to: thou art made, if thou desir'st to be so:'—

OLIVIA

Am I made?

MALVOLIO

'If not, let me see thee a servant still.'

OLIVIA

Why, this is very midsummer madness.

Enter SERVANT.

SERVANT

Madam, the young gentleman of the Count Orsino's is returned; I could hardly entreat him back. He attends your ladyship's pleasure.

OLIVIA

I'll come to him.

[Exit SERVANT.]

Good Maria, let this fellow be looked to. Where's my cousin Toby? Let some of my people have a special care of him; I would not have him miscarry for the half of my dowry.

[Exeunt OLIVIA and MARIA.]

MALVOLIO

O ho, do you come near me now? No worse man than Sir Toby to look to me. This concurs directly with the letter: she sends him on purpose, that I may appear stubborn to him; for she incites me to that in the letter. 'Cast thy humble slough,' says she; 'be opposite with a kinsman, surly with servants, let thy tongue tang with arguments of state, put thyself into the trick of singularity,' and consequently, sets down the manner how: as, a sad face, a reverend carriage, a slow tongue, in the habit of some sir of note, and so forth. I have limed her, but it is Jove's doing, and Jove make me thankful! And when she went away now, 'Let this fellow be looked to'; 'Fellow'! not 'Malvolio,' nor after my degree, but 'fellow.' Why, everything adheres together, that no dram of a scruple, no scruple of a scruple, no obstacle, no incredulous or unsafe circumstance. What can be said? Nothing that can be can come between me and the full prospect of my hopes. Well, Jove, not I, is the doer of this, and he is to be thanked.

Enter SIR TOBY, FABIAN and MARIA.

SIR TOBY

Which way is he, in the name of sanctity? If all the devils of hell be drawn in little, and Legion himself possessed him, yet I'll speak to him.

FABIAN

Here he is, here he is. How is't with you, sir? How is't with you, man?

MALVOLIO

Go off, I discard you. Let me enjoy my private. Go off.

MARIA

Lo, how hollow the fiend speaks within him! Did not I tell you? Sir Toby, my lady prays you to have a care of him.

MALVOLIO

Ah, ha! does she so?

SIR TOBY

Go to, go to; peace, peace, we must deal gently with him. Let me alone. How do you, Malvolio? How is't with you? What, man! defy the devil! Consider, he's an enemy to mankind.

MALVOLIO

Do you know what you say?

MARIA

La you, an you speak ill of the devil, how he takes it at heart! Pray God he be not bewitched.

FABIAN

Carry his water to th' wise woman.

MARIA

Marry, and it shall be done tomorrow morning, if I live. My lady would not lose him for more than I'll say.

MALVOLIO

How now, mistress!

MARIA

O Lord!

SIR TOBY

Prithee hold thy peace, this is not the way. Do you not see you move him? Let me alone with him.

FABIAN

No way but gentleness, gently, gently. The fiend is rough, and will not be roughly used.

SIR TOBY

Why, how now, my bawcock? How dost thou, chuck?

MALVOLIO

Sir!

SIR TOBY

Ay, biddy, come with me. What, man, 'tis not for gravity to play at cherry-pit with Satan. Hang him, foul collier!

MARIA

Get him to say his prayers, good Sir Toby, get him to pray.

MALVOLIO

My prayers, minx?

MARIA

No, I warrant you, he will not hear of godliness.

MALVOLIO

Go, hang yourselves all! You are idle, shallow things. I am not of your element. You shall know more hereafter.
        [Exit.]

SIR TOBY

Is't possible?

FABIAN

If this were played upon a stage now, I could condemn it as an improbable fiction.

SIR TOBY

His very genius hath taken the infection of the device, man.

MARIA

Nay, pursue him now, lest the device take air and taint.

FABIAN

Why, we shall make him mad indeed.

MARIA

The house will be the quieter.

SIR TOBY

Come, we'll have him in a dark room and bound. My niece is already in the belief that he's mad. We may carry it thus for our pleasure, and his penance, till our very pastime, tired out of breath, prompt us to have mercy on him, at which time we will bring the device to the bar, and crown thee for a finder of madmen. But see, but see!

Enter SIR ANDREW.

FABIAN

More matter for a May morning.

SIR ANDREW

Here's the challenge, read it. I warrant there's vinegar and pepper in't.

FABIAN

Is't so saucy?

SIR ANDREW

Ay, is't, I warrant him. Do but read.

SIR TOBY

Give me.

[Reads.]

Youth, whatsoever thou art, thou art but a scurvy fellow.

FABIAN

Good, and valiant.

SIR TOBY

Wonder not, nor admire not in thy mind, why I do call thee so, for I will show thee no reason for't.

FABIAN

A good note, that keeps you from the blow of the law.

SIR TOBY

Thou comest to the Lady Olivia, and in my sight she uses thee kindly: but thou liest in thy throat; that is not the matter I challenge thee for.

FABIAN

Very brief, and to exceeding good sense—less.

SIR TOBY

I will waylay thee going home; where if it be thy chance to kill me—

FABIAN

Good.

SIR TOBY

Thou kill'st me like a rogue and a villain.

FABIAN

Still you keep o' th' windy side of the law. Good.

SIR TOBY

Fare thee well, and God have mercy upon one of our souls! He may have mercy upon mine, but my hope is better, and so look to thyself. Thy friend, as thou usest him, and thy sworn enemy,
Andrew Aguecheek.
If this letter move him not, his legs cannot. I'll give't him.

MARIA

You may have very fit occasion for't. He is now in some commerce with my lady, and will by and by depart.

SIR TOBY

Go, Sir Andrew. Scout me for him at the corner of the orchard, like a bum-baily. So soon as ever thou seest him, draw, and as thou draw'st, swear horrible, for it comes to pass oft that a terrible oath, with a swaggering accent sharply twanged off, gives manhood more approbation than ever proof itself would have earned him. Away.

SIR ANDREW

Nay, let me alone for swearing.
[Exit.]

SIR TOBY

Now will not I deliver his letter, for the behaviour of the young gentleman gives him out to be of good capacity and breeding; his employment between his lord and my niece confirms no less. Therefore this letter, being so excellently ignorant, will breed no terror in the youth. He will find it comes from a clodpole. But, sir, I will deliver his challenge by word of mouth, set upon Aguecheek notable report of valour, and drive the gentleman (as I know his youth will aptly receive it) into a most hideous opinion of his rage, skill, fury, and impetuosity. This will so fright them both that they will kill one another by the look, like cockatrices.

Enter OLIVIA and VIOLA.

FABIAN

Here he comes with your niece; give them way till he take leave, and presently after him.

SIR TOBY

I will meditate the while upon some horrid message for a challenge.
[Exeunt SIR TOBY, FABIAN and MARIA.]

OLIVIA

I have said too much unto a heart of stone,
And laid mine honour too unchary on't:
There's something in me that reproves my fault:
But such a headstrong potent fault it is,
That it but mocks reproof.

VIOLA

With the same 'haviour that your passion bears
Goes on my master's griefs.

OLIVIA

Here, wear this jewel for me, 'tis my picture.
Refuse it not, it hath no tongue to vex you.
And I beseech you come again tomorrow.
What shall you ask of me that I'll deny,
That honour sav'd, may upon asking give?

VIOLA

Nothing but this, your true love for my master.

OLIVIA

How with mine honour may I give him that
Which I have given to you?

VIOLA

I will acquit you.

OLIVIA

> Well, come again tomorrow. Fare thee well;
> A fiend like thee might bear my soul to hell.
> *[Exit.]*
> *Enter Sir Toby and Fabian.*

SIR TOBY

> Gentleman, God save thee.

VIOLA

> And you, sir.

SIR TOBY

> That defence thou hast, betake thee to't. Of what nature the wrongs are thou hast done him, I know not, but thy intercepter, full of despite, bloody as the hunter, attends thee at the orchard end. Dismount thy tuck, be yare in thy preparation, for thy assailant is quick, skilful, and deadly.

VIOLA

> You mistake, sir; I am sure no man hath any quarrel to me. My remembrance is very free and clear from any image of offence done to any man.

SIR TOBY

> You'll find it otherwise, I assure you. Therefore, if you hold your life at any price, betake you to your guard, for your opposite hath in him what youth, strength, skill, and wrath, can furnish man withal.

VIOLA

> I pray you, sir, what is he?

SIR TOBY

> He is knight, dubbed with unhatched rapier, and on carpet consideration, but he is a devil in private brawl. Souls and bodies hath he divorced three, and his incensement at this moment is so implacable that satisfaction can be none but by pangs of death and sepulchre. Hob, nob is his word; give't or take't.

VIOLA

> I will return again into the house and desire some conduct of the lady. I am no fighter. I have heard of some kind of men that put

quarrels purposely on others to taste their valour: belike this is a man of that quirk.

SIR TOBY

Sir, no. His indignation derives itself out of a very competent injury; therefore, get you on and give him his desire. Back you shall not to the house, unless you undertake that with me which with as much safety you might answer him. Therefore on, or strip your sword stark naked, for meddle you must, that's certain, or forswear to wear iron about you.

VIOLA

This is as uncivil as strange. I beseech you, do me this courteous office, as to know of the knight what my offence to him is. It is something of my negligence, nothing of my purpose.

SIR TOBY

I will do so. Signior Fabian, stay you by this gentleman till my return.

[Exit Sir Toby.]

VIOLA

Pray you, sir, do you know of this matter?

FABIAN

I know the knight is incensed against you, even to a mortal arbitrement, but nothing of the circumstance more.

VIOLA

I beseech you, what manner of man is he?

FABIAN

Nothing of that wonderful promise, to read him by his form, as you are like to find him in the proof of his valour. He is indeed, sir, the most skilful, bloody, and fatal opposite that you could possibly have found in any part of Illyria. Will you walk towards him? I will make your peace with him if I can.

VIOLA

I shall be much bound to you for't. I am one that had rather go with sir priest than sir knight: I care not who knows so much of my mettle.

[Exeunt.]

Enter Sir Toby and Sir Andrew.

SIR TOBY

Why, man, he's a very devil. I have not seen such a firago. I had a pass with him, rapier, scabbard, and all, and he gives me the stuck-in with such a mortal motion that it is inevitable; and on the answer, he pays you as surely as your feet hits the ground they step on. They say he has been fencer to the Sophy.

SIR ANDREW

Pox on't, I'll not meddle with him.

SIR TOBY

Ay, but he will not now be pacified: Fabian can scarce hold him yonder.

SIR ANDREW

Plague on't, an I thought he had been valiant, and so cunning in fence, I'd have seen him damned ere I'd have challenged him. Let him let the matter slip, and I'll give him my horse, grey Capilet.

SIR TOBY

I'll make the motion. Stand here, make a good show on't. This shall end without the perdition of souls.

[Aside.]

Marry, I'll ride your horse as well as I ride you.

Enter FABIAN and VIOLA.

[To Fabian.]

I have his horse to take up the quarrel. I have persuaded him the youth's a devil.

FABIAN

He is as horribly conceited of him, and pants and looks pale, as if a bear were at his heels.

SIR TOBY

There's no remedy, sir, he will fight with you for's oath sake. Marry, he hath better bethought him of his quarrel, and he finds that now scarce to be worth talking of. Therefore, draw for the supportance of his vow; he protests he will not hurt you.

VIOLA

[Aside.]

Pray God defend me! A little thing would make me tell them how much I lack of a man.

FABIAN

Give ground if you see him furious.

SIR TOBY

Come, Sir Andrew, there's no remedy, the gentleman will for his honour's sake have one bout with you. He cannot by the duello avoid it; but he has promised me, as he is a gentleman and a soldier, he will not hurt you. Come on: to't.

SIR ANDREW

[Draws.]
Pray God he keep his oath!
Enter ANTONIO.

VIOLA

[Draws.]
I do assure you 'tis against my will.

ANTONIO

Put up your sword. If this young gentleman
Have done offence, I take the fault on me.
If you offend him, I for him defy you.

SIR TOBY

You, sir? Why, what are you?

ANTONIO

[Draws.]
One, sir, that for his love dares yet do more
Than you have heard him brag to you he will.

SIR TOBY

[Draws.]
Nay, if you be an undertaker, I am for you.
Enter OFFICERS.

FABIAN

O good Sir Toby, hold! Here come the officers.

SIR TOBY

[To Antonio.]

I'll be with you anon.

VIOLA

[To Sir Andrew.]

Pray, sir, put your sword up, if you please.

SIR ANDREW

Marry, will I, sir; and for that I promised you, I'll be as good as my word. He will bear you easily, and reins well.

FIRST OFFICER

This is the man; do thy office.

SECOND OFFICER

Antonio, I arrest thee at the suit
Of Count Orsino.

ANTONIO

You do mistake me, sir.

FIRST OFFICER

No, sir, no jot. I know your favour well,
Though now you have no sea-cap on your head.—
Take him away, he knows I know him well.

ANTONIO

I must obey. This comes with seeking you;
But there's no remedy, I shall answer it.
What will you do? Now my necessity
Makes me to ask you for my purse. It grieves me
Much more for what I cannot do for you,
Than what befalls myself. You stand amaz'd,
But be of comfort.

SECOND OFFICER

Come, sir, away.

ANTONIO

I must entreat of you some of that money.

VIOLA

What money, sir?
For the fair kindness you have show'd me here,
And part being prompted by your present trouble,
Out of my lean and low ability
I'll lend you something. My having is not much;
I'll make division of my present with you.
Hold, there's half my coffer.

ANTONIO

Will you deny me now?
Is't possible that my deserts to you
Can lack persuasion? Do not tempt my misery,
Lest that it make me so unsound a man
As to upbraid you with those kindnesses
That I have done for you.

VIOLA

I know of none,
Nor know I you by voice or any feature.
I hate ingratitude more in a man
Than lying, vainness, babbling, drunkenness,
Or any taint of vice whose strong corruption
Inhabits our frail blood.

ANTONIO

O heavens themselves!

SECOND OFFICER

Come, sir, I pray you go.

ANTONIO

Let me speak a little. This youth that you see here
I snatch'd one half out of the jaws of death,
Reliev'd him with such sanctity of love;
And to his image, which methought did promise
Most venerable worth, did I devotion.

FIRST OFFICER

What's that to us? The time goes by. Away!

ANTONIO

But O how vile an idol proves this god!
Thou hast, Sebastian, done good feature shame.
In nature there's no blemish but the mind;
None can be call'd deform'd but the unkind.
Virtue is beauty, but the beauteous evil
Are empty trunks, o'erflourished by the devil.

FIRST OFFICER

The man grows mad, away with him. Come, come, sir.

ANTONIO

Lead me on.
[Exeunt OFFICERS *with* ANTONIO.*]*

VIOLA

Methinks his words do from such passion fly
That he believes himself; so do not I.
Prove true, imagination, O prove true,
That I, dear brother, be now ta'en for you!

SIR TOBY

Come hither, knight; come hither, Fabian. We'll whisper o'er a couplet or two of most sage saws.

VIOLA

He nam'd Sebastian. I my brother know
Yet living in my glass; even such and so
In favour was my brother, and he went
Still in this fashion, colour, ornament,
For him I imitate. O if it prove,
Tempests are kind, and salt waves fresh in love!
[Exit.]

SIR TOBY

A very dishonest paltry boy, and more a coward than a hare. His dishonesty appears in leaving his friend here in necessity, and denying him; and for his cowardship, ask Fabian.

FABIAN

A coward, a most devout coward, religious in it.

SIR ANDREW

'Slid, I'll after him again and beat him.

SIR TOBY

Do, cuff him soundly, but never draw thy sword.

SIR ANDREW

And I do not—
   [Exit.]

FABIAN

Come, let's see the event.

SIR TOBY

I dare lay any money 'twill be nothing yet.
   [Exeunt.]

ACT IV

SCENE I. The Street before Olivia's House.

Enter SEBASTIAN and CLOWN.

CLOWN

Will you make me believe that I am not sent for you?

SEBASTIAN

Go to, go to, thou art a foolish fellow.
Let me be clear of thee.

CLOWN

Well held out, i' faith! No, I do not know you, nor I am not sent
to you by my lady, to bid you come speak with her; nor your name is
not Master Cesario; nor this is not my nose neither. Nothing that is
so, is so.

SEBASTIAN

I prithee vent thy folly somewhere else,
Thou know'st not me.

CLOWN

Vent my folly! He has heard that word of some great man, and
now applies it to a fool. Vent my folly! I am afraid this great lubber,
the world, will prove a cockney. I prithee now, ungird thy strangeness,
and tell me what I shall vent to my lady. Shall I vent to her that thou
art coming?

SEBASTIAN

I prithee, foolish Greek, depart from me.
There's money for thee; if you tarry longer
I shall give worse payment.

CLOWN

By my troth, thou hast an open hand. These wise men that give fools money get themselves a good report—after fourteen years' purchase.
Enter Sir ANDREW, Sir TOBY and FABIAN.

SIR ANDREW

Now sir, have I met you again? There's for you.
[Striking Sebastian.]

SEBASTIAN

Why, there's for thee, and there, and there.
Are all the people mad?
[Beating Sir Andrew.]

SIR TOBY

Hold, sir, or I'll throw your dagger o'er the house.

CLOWN

This will I tell my lady straight. I would not be in some of your coats for twopence.
[Exit CLOWN.]

SIR TOBY

Come on, sir, hold!

SIR ANDREW

Nay, let him alone, I'll go another way to work with him. I'll have an action of battery against him, if there be any law in Illyria. Though I struck him first, yet it's no matter for that.

SEBASTIAN

Let go thy hand!

SIR TOBY

Come, sir, I will not let you go. Come, my young soldier, put up your iron: you are well fleshed. Come on.

SEBASTIAN

> I will be free from thee. What wouldst thou now?
> If thou dar'st tempt me further, draw thy sword.
> > *[Draws.]*

SIR TOBY

> What, what? Nay, then, I must have an ounce or two of this mala-
> pert blood from you.
> > *[Draws.]*
> > *Enter OLIVIA.*

OLIVIA

> Hold, Toby! On thy life I charge thee hold!

SIR TOBY

> Madam.

OLIVIA

> Will it be ever thus? Ungracious wretch,
> Fit for the mountains and the barbarous caves,
> Where manners ne'er were preach'd! Out of my sight!
> Be not offended, dear Cesario.
> Rudesby, be gone!
> > *[Exeunt SIR TOBY, SIR ANDREW and FABIAN.]*
> I prithee, gentle friend,
> Let thy fair wisdom, not thy passion, sway
> In this uncivil and unjust extent
> Against thy peace. Go with me to my house,
> And hear thou there how many fruitless pranks
> This ruffian hath botch'd up, that thou thereby
> Mayst smile at this. Thou shalt not choose but go.
> Do not deny. Beshrew his soul for me,
> He started one poor heart of mine, in thee.

SEBASTIAN

> What relish is in this? How runs the stream?
> Or I am mad, or else this is a dream.
> Let fancy still my sense in Lethe steep;
> If it be thus to dream, still let me sleep!

OLIVIA

Nay, come, I prithee. Would thou'dst be ruled by me!

SEBASTIAN

Madam, I will.

OLIVIA

O, say so, and so be!

[Exeunt.]

SCENE II. A Room in Olivia's House.

Enter MARIA and CLOWN.

MARIA

Nay, I prithee, put on this gown and this beard; make him believe thou art Sir Topas the curate. Do it quickly. I'll call Sir Toby the whilst.

[Exit MARIA.]

CLOWN

Well, I'll put it on, and I will dissemble myself in't, and I would I were the first that ever dissembled in such a gown. I am not tall enough to become the function well, nor lean enough to be thought a good student, but to be said, an honest man and a good housekeeper goes as fairly as to say, a careful man and a great scholar. The competitors enter.

Enter SIR TOBY and MARIA.

SIR TOBY

Jove bless thee, Master Parson.

CLOWN

Bonos dies, Sir Toby: for as the old hermit of Prague, that never saw pen and ink, very wittily said to a niece of King Gorboduc, 'That that is, is': so I, being Master Parson, am Master Parson; for what is 'that' but 'that'? and 'is' but 'is'?

SIR TOBY

To him, Sir Topas.

CLOWN

What ho, I say! Peace in this prison!

SIR TOBY

The knave counterfeits well. A good knave.

Malvolio within.

MALVOLIO

Who calls there?

CLOWN

Sir Topas the curate, who comes to visit Malvolio the lunatic.

MALVOLIO

Sir Topas, Sir Topas, good Sir Topas, go to my lady.

CLOWN

Out, hyperbolical fiend! how vexest thou this man? Talkest thou nothing but of ladies?

SIR TOBY

Well said, Master Parson.

MALVOLIO

Sir Topas, never was man thus wronged. Good Sir Topas, do not think I am mad. They have laid me here in hideous darkness.

CLOWN

Fie, thou dishonest Satan! I call thee by the most modest terms, for I am one of those gentle ones that will use the devil himself with courtesy. Say'st thou that house is dark?

MALVOLIO

As hell, Sir Topas.

CLOWN

Why, it hath bay windows transparent as barricadoes, and the clerestories toward the south-north are as lustrous as ebony; and yet complainest thou of obstruction?

MALVOLIO

I am not mad, Sir Topas. I say to you this house is dark.

CLOWN

Madman, thou errest. I say there is no darkness but ignorance, in which thou art more puzzled than the Egyptians in their fog.

MALVOLIO

I say this house is as dark as ignorance, though ignorance were as dark as hell; and I say there was never man thus abused. I am no more mad than you are. Make the trial of it in any constant question.

CLOWN

What is the opinion of Pythagoras concerning wildfowl?

MALVOLIO

That the soul of our grandam might haply inhabit a bird.

CLOWN

What think'st thou of his opinion?

MALVOLIO

I think nobly of the soul, and no way approve his opinion.

CLOWN

Fare thee well. Remain thou still in darkness. Thou shalt hold the opinion of Pythagoras ere I will allow of thy wits, and fear to kill a woodcock, lest thou dispossess the soul of thy grandam. Fare thee well.

MALVOLIO

Sir Topas, Sir Topas!

SIR TOBY

My most exquisite Sir Topas!

CLOWN

Nay, I am for all waters.

MARIA

Thou mightst have done this without thy beard and gown. He sees thee not.

SIR TOBY

To him in thine own voice, and bring me word how thou find'st him. I would we were well rid of this knavery. If he may be conveniently delivered, I would he were, for I am now so far in offence with my niece that I cannot pursue with any safety this sport to the upshot. Come by and by to my chamber.

    [Exeunt Sir Toby and Maria.]

CLOWN

    [Singing.]

> Hey, Robin, jolly Robin,
> Tell me how thy lady does.

MALVOLIO

    Fool!

CLOWN

> My lady is unkind, perdy.

MALVOLIO

    Fool!

CLOWN

> Alas, why is she so?

MALVOLIO

    Fool, I say!

CLOWN

> She loves another—

Who calls, ha?

MALVOLIO

    Good fool, as ever thou wilt deserve well at my hand, help me to a candle, and pen, ink, and paper. As I am a gentleman, I will live to be thankful to thee for't.

CLOWN

    Master Malvolio?

MALVOLIO

    Ay, good fool.

CLOWN

    Alas, sir, how fell you besides your five wits?

MALVOLIO

Fool, there was never man so notoriously abused. I am as well in my wits, fool, as thou art.

CLOWN

But as well? Then you are mad indeed, if you be no better in your wits than a fool.

MALVOLIO

They have here propertied me; keep me in darkness, send ministers to me, asses, and do all they can to face me out of my wits.

CLOWN

Advise you what you say: the minister is here.
[As Sir Topas]
Malvolio, Malvolio, thy wits the heavens restore. Endeavour thyself to sleep, and leave thy vain bibble-babble.

MALVOLIO

Sir Topas!

CLOWN

[As Sir Topas]
Maintain no words with him, good fellow.
[As himself]
Who, I, sir? not I, sir. God buy you, good Sir Topas.
[As Sir Topas]
Marry, amen.
[As himself]
I will sir, I will.

MALVOLIO

Fool, fool, fool, I say!

CLOWN

Alas, sir, be patient. What say you, sir? I am shent for speaking to you.

MALVOLIO

Good fool, help me to some light and some paper. I tell thee I am as well in my wits as any man in Illyria.

CLOWN

Well-a-day that you were, sir!

MALVOLIO

By this hand, I am. Good fool, some ink, paper, and light, and convey what I will set down to my lady. It shall advantage thee more than ever the bearing of letter did.

CLOWN

I will help you to't. But tell me true, are you not mad indeed? or do you but counterfeit?

MALVOLIO

Believe me, I am not. I tell thee true.

CLOWN

Nay, I'll ne'er believe a madman till I see his brains. I will fetch you light, and paper, and ink.

MALVOLIO

Fool, I'll requite it in the highest degree: I prithee be gone.

CLOWN

[Singing.]

I am gone, sir, and anon, sir,
I'll be with you again,
In a trice, like to the old Vice,
Your need to sustain;
Who with dagger of lath, in his rage and his wrath,
Cries 'ah, ha!' to the devil:
Like a mad lad, 'Pare thy nails, dad.
Adieu, goodman devil.'

[Exit.]

SCENE III. Olivia's Garden.

Enter SEBASTIAN.

SEBASTIAN

This is the air; that is the glorious sun,
This pearl she gave me, I do feel't and see't,
And though 'tis wonder that enwraps me thus,
Yet 'tis not madness. Where's Antonio, then?

I could not find him at the Elephant,
Yet there he was, and there I found this credit,
That he did range the town to seek me out.
His counsel now might do me golden service.
For though my soul disputes well with my sense
That this may be some error, but no madness,
Yet doth this accident and flood of fortune
So far exceed all instance, all discourse,
That I am ready to distrust mine eyes
And wrangle with my reason that persuades me
To any other trust but that I am mad,
Or else the lady's mad; yet if 'twere so,
She could not sway her house, command her followers,
Take and give back affairs and their dispatch,
With such a smooth, discreet, and stable bearing
As I perceive she does. There's something in't
That is deceivable. But here the lady comes.
        Enter OLIVIA and a PRIEST.

OLIVIA

Blame not this haste of mine. If you mean well,
Now go with me and with this holy man
Into the chantry by: there, before him
And underneath that consecrated roof,
Plight me the full assurance of your faith,
That my most jealous and too doubtful soul
May live at peace. He shall conceal it
Whiles you are willing it shall come to note,
What time we will our celebration keep
According to my birth. What do you say?

SEBASTIAN

I'll follow this good man, and go with you,
And having sworn truth, ever will be true.

OLIVIA

Then lead the way, good father, and heavens so shine,
That they may fairly note this act of mine!
        [Exeunt.]

ACT V

SCENE I. The Street before Olivia's House.

Enter CLOWN and FABIAN.

FABIAN

Now, as thou lov'st me, let me see his letter.

CLOWN

Good Master Fabian, grant me another request.

FABIAN

Anything.

CLOWN

Do not desire to see this letter.

FABIAN

This is to give a dog, and in recompense desire my dog again.
Enter DUKE, VIOLA, CURIO and LORDS.

DUKE

Belong you to the Lady Olivia, friends?

CLOWN

Ay, sir, we are some of her trappings.

DUKE

I know thee well. How dost thou, my good fellow?

CLOWN

Truly, sir, the better for my foes, and the worse for my friends.

DUKE

Just the contrary; the better for thy friends.

CLOWN

No, sir, the worse.

DUKE

How can that be?

CLOWN

Marry, sir, they praise me, and make an ass of me. Now my foes tell me plainly I am an ass: so that by my foes, sir, I profit in the knowledge of myself, and by my friends I am abused. So that, conclusions to be as kisses, if your four negatives make your two affirmatives, why then, the worse for my friends, and the better for my foes.

DUKE

Why, this is excellent.

CLOWN

By my troth, sir, no; though it please you to be one of my friends.

DUKE

Thou shalt not be the worse for me; there's gold.

CLOWN

But that it would be double-dealing, sir, I would you could make it another.

DUKE

O, you give me ill counsel.

CLOWN

Put your grace in your pocket, sir, for this once, and let your flesh and blood obey it.

DUKE

Well, I will be so much a sinner to be a double-dealer: there's another.

CLOWN

Primo, secundo, tertio, is a good play, and the old saying is, the third pays for all; the triplex, sir, is a good tripping measure; or the bells of Saint Bennet, sir, may put you in mind—one, two, three.

DUKE

You can fool no more money out of me at this throw. If you will let your lady know I am here to speak with her, and bring her along with you, it may awake my bounty further.

CLOWN

Marry, sir, lullaby to your bounty till I come again. I go, sir, but I would not have you to think that my desire of having is the sin of covetousness: but as you say, sir, let your bounty take a nap, I will awake it anon.

　　　[Exit CLOWN.]
　　　Enter ANTONIO and OFFICERS.

VIOLA

Here comes the man, sir, that did rescue me.

DUKE

That face of his I do remember well.
Yet when I saw it last it was besmear'd
As black as Vulcan, in the smoke of war.
A baubling vessel was he captain of,
For shallow draught and bulk unprizable,
With which such scathful grapple did he make
With the most noble bottom of our fleet,
That very envy and the tongue of loss
Cried fame and honour on him. What's the matter?

FIRST OFFICER

Orsino, this is that Antonio
That took the *Phoenix* and her fraught from Candy,
And this is he that did the *Tiger* board
When your young nephew Titus lost his leg.
Here in the streets, desperate of shame and state,
In private brabble did we apprehend him.

VIOLA

> He did me kindness, sir; drew on my side,
> But in conclusion, put strange speech upon me.
> I know not what 'twas, but distraction.

DUKE

> Notable pirate, thou salt-water thief,
> What foolish boldness brought thee to their mercies,
> Whom thou, in terms so bloody and so dear,
> Hast made thine enemies?

ANTONIO

> Orsino, noble sir,
> Be pleased that I shake off these names you give me:
> Antonio never yet was thief or pirate,
> Though, I confess, on base and ground enough,
> Orsino's enemy. A witchcraft drew me hither:
> That most ingrateful boy there by your side
> From the rude sea's enraged and foamy mouth
> Did I redeem; a wreck past hope he was.
> His life I gave him, and did thereto add
> My love, without retention or restraint,
> All his in dedication. For his sake
> Did I expose myself, pure for his love,
> Into the danger of this adverse town;
> Drew to defend him when he was beset;
> Where being apprehended, his false cunning
> (Not meaning to partake with me in danger)
> Taught him to face me out of his acquaintance,
> And grew a twenty years' removed thing
> While one would wink; denied me mine own purse,
> Which I had recommended to his use
> Not half an hour before.

VIOLA

> How can this be?

DUKE

> When came he to this town?

ANTONIO

> Today, my lord; and for three months before,
> No int'rim, not a minute's vacancy,
> Both day and night did we keep company.
> *Enter OLIVIA and ATTENDANTS.*

DUKE

> Here comes the Countess, now heaven walks on earth.
> But for thee, fellow, fellow, thy words are madness.
> Three months this youth hath tended upon me;
> But more of that anon. Take him aside.

OLIVIA

> What would my lord, but that he may not have,
> Wherein Olivia may seem serviceable?
> Cesario, you do not keep promise with me.

VIOLA

> Madam?

DUKE

> Gracious Olivia—

OLIVIA

> What do you say, Cesario? Good my lord—

VIOLA

> My lord would speak, my duty hushes me.

OLIVIA

> If it be aught to the old tune, my lord,
> It is as fat and fulsome to mine ear
> As howling after music.

DUKE

> Still so cruel?

OLIVIA

> Still so constant, lord.

DUKE

> What, to perverseness? You uncivil lady,

To whose ingrate and unauspicious altars
My soul the faithfull'st off'rings hath breathed out
That e'er devotion tender'd! What shall I do?

OLIVIA

Even what it please my lord that shall become him.

DUKE

Why should I not, had I the heart to do it,
Like to the Egyptian thief at point of death,
Kill what I love?—a savage jealousy
That sometime savours nobly. But hear me this:
Since you to non-regardance cast my faith,
And that I partly know the instrument
That screws me from my true place in your favour,
Live you the marble-breasted tyrant still.
But this your minion, whom I know you love,
And whom, by heaven I swear, I tender dearly,
Him will I tear out of that cruel eye
Where he sits crowned in his master's spite.—
Come, boy, with me; my thoughts are ripe in mischief:
I'll sacrifice the lamb that I do love,
To spite a raven's heart within a dove.

VIOLA

And I, most jocund, apt, and willingly,
To do you rest, a thousand deaths would die.

OLIVIA

Where goes Cesario?

VIOLA

After him I love
More than I love these eyes, more than my life,
More, by all mores, than e'er I shall love wife.
If I do feign, you witnesses above
Punish my life for tainting of my love.

OLIVIA

Ah me, detested! how am I beguil'd!

VIOLA

Who does beguile you? Who does do you wrong?

OLIVIA

Hast thou forgot thyself? Is it so long?
Call forth the holy father.
[Exit an Attendant.]

DUKE

[To VIOLA.]
Come, away!

OLIVIA

Whither, my lord? Cesario, husband, stay.

DUKE

Husband?

OLIVIA

Ay, husband. Can he that deny?

DUKE

Her husband, sirrah?

VIOLA

No, my lord, not I.

OLIVIA

Alas, it is the baseness of thy fear
That makes thee strangle thy propriety.
Fear not, Cesario, take thy fortunes up.
Be that thou know'st thou art, and then thou art
As great as that thou fear'st.
Enter PRIEST.
O, welcome, father!
Father, I charge thee, by thy reverence
Here to unfold—though lately we intended
To keep in darkness what occasion now
Reveals before 'tis ripe—what thou dost know
Hath newly passed between this youth and me.

PRIEST

A contract of eternal bond of love,
Confirmed by mutual joinder of your hands,
Attested by the holy close of lips,
Strengthen'd by interchangement of your rings,
And all the ceremony of this compact
Sealed in my function, by my testimony;
Since when, my watch hath told me, toward my grave,
I have travelled but two hours.

DUKE

O thou dissembling cub! What wilt thou be
When time hath sowed a grizzle on thy case?
Or will not else thy craft so quickly grow
That thine own trip shall be thine overthrow?
Farewell, and take her; but direct thy feet
Where thou and I henceforth may never meet.

VIOLA

My lord, I do protest—

OLIVIA

O, do not swear.
Hold little faith, though thou has too much fear.
Enter Sir Andrew.

SIR ANDREW

For the love of God, a surgeon! Send one presently to Sir Toby.

OLIVIA

What's the matter?

SIR ANDREW

'Has broke my head across, and has given Sir Toby a bloody cox-comb too. For the love of God, your help! I had rather than forty pound I were at home.

OLIVIA

Who has done this, Sir Andrew?

SIR ANDREW

The Count's gentleman, one Cesario. We took him for a coward, but he's the very devil incardinate.

DUKE

My gentleman, Cesario?

SIR ANDREW

'Od's lifelings, here he is!—You broke my head for nothing; and that that I did, I was set on to do't by Sir Toby.

VIOLA

Why do you speak to me? I never hurt you:
You drew your sword upon me without cause,
But I bespake you fair and hurt you not.
Enter SIR TOBY, drunk, led by the CLOWN.

SIR ANDREW

If a bloody coxcomb be a hurt, you have hurt me. I think you set nothing by a bloody coxcomb. Here comes Sir Toby halting, you shall hear more: but if he had not been in drink, he would have tickled you othergates than he did.

DUKE

How now, gentleman? How is't with you?

SIR TOBY

That's all one; 'has hurt me, and there's th' end on't. Sot, didst see Dick Surgeon, sot?

CLOWN

O, he's drunk, Sir Toby, an hour agone; his eyes were set at eight i' th' morning.

SIR TOBY

Then he's a rogue, and a passy measures pavin. I hate a drunken rogue.

OLIVIA

Away with him. Who hath made this havoc with them?

SIR ANDREW

I'll help you, Sir Toby, because we'll be dressed together.

SIR TOBY

Will you help? An ass-head, and a coxcomb, and a knave, a thin-faced knave, a gull?

OLIVIA

Get him to bed, and let his hurt be looked to.
[Exeunt CLOWN, FABIAN, SIR TOBY and SIR ANDREW.]
Enter SEBASTIAN.

SEBASTIAN

I am sorry, madam, I have hurt your kinsman;
But had it been the brother of my blood,
I must have done no less with wit and safety.
You throw a strange regard upon me, and by that
I do perceive it hath offended you.
Pardon me, sweet one, even for the vows
We made each other but so late ago.

DUKE

One face, one voice, one habit, and two persons!
A natural perspective, that is, and is not!

SEBASTIAN

Antonio, O my dear Antonio!
How have the hours rack'd and tortur'd me
Since I have lost thee.

ANTONIO

Sebastian are you?

SEBASTIAN

Fear'st thou that, Antonio?

ANTONIO

How have you made division of yourself?
An apple cleft in two is not more twin
Than these two creatures. Which is Sebastian?

OLIVIA

> Most wonderful!

SEBASTIAN

> Do I stand there? I never had a brother:
> Nor can there be that deity in my nature
> Of here and everywhere. I had a sister,
> Whom the blind waves and surges have devoured.
> Of charity, what kin are you to me?
> What countryman? What name? What parentage?

VIOLA

> Of Messaline: Sebastian was my father;
> Such a Sebastian was my brother too:
> So went he suited to his watery tomb.
> If spirits can assume both form and suit,
> You come to fright us.

SEBASTIAN

> A spirit I am indeed,
> But am in that dimension grossly clad,
> Which from the womb I did participate.
> Were you a woman, as the rest goes even,
> I should my tears let fall upon your cheek,
> And say, 'Thrice welcome, drowned Viola.'

VIOLA

> My father had a mole upon his brow.

SEBASTIAN

> And so had mine.

VIOLA

> And died that day when Viola from her birth
> Had numbered thirteen years.

SEBASTIAN

> O, that record is lively in my soul!
> He finished indeed his mortal act
> That day that made my sister thirteen years.

VIOLA

    If nothing lets to make us happy both
    But this my masculine usurp'd attire,
    Do not embrace me till each circumstance
    Of place, time, fortune, do cohere and jump
    That I am Viola; which to confirm,
    I'll bring you to a captain in this town,
    Where lie my maiden weeds; by whose gentle help
    I was preserv'd to serve this noble count.
    All the occurrence of my fortune since
    Hath been between this lady and this lord.

SEBASTIAN

    [To Olivia.]
    So comes it, lady, you have been mistook.
    But nature to her bias drew in that.
    You would have been contracted to a maid;
    Nor are you therein, by my life, deceived:
    You are betroth'd both to a maid and man.

DUKE

    Be not amazed; right noble is his blood.
    If this be so, as yet the glass seems true,
    I shall have share in this most happy wreck.
    [To Viola.]
    Boy, thou hast said to me a thousand times
    Thou never shouldst love woman like to me.

VIOLA

    And all those sayings will I over-swear,
    And all those swearings keep as true in soul
    As doth that orbed continent the fire
    That severs day from night.

DUKE

    Give me thy hand,
    And let me see thee in thy woman's weeds.

VIOLA

    The captain that did bring me first on shore

Hath my maid's garments. He, upon some action,
Is now in durance, at Malvolio's suit,
A gentleman and follower of my lady's.

OLIVIA

He shall enlarge him. Fetch Malvolio hither.
And yet, alas, now I remember me,
They say, poor gentleman, he's much distract.
Enter CLOWN, with a letter, and FABIAN.
A most extracting frenzy of mine own
From my remembrance clearly banished his.
How does he, sirrah?

CLOWN

Truly, madam, he holds Belzebub at the stave's end as well as a man in his case may do. Has here writ a letter to you. I should have given it you today morning, but as a madman's epistles are no gospels, so it skills not much when they are delivered.

OLIVIA

Open't, and read it.

CLOWN

Look then to be well edified, when the fool delivers the madman. *By the Lord, madam,—*

OLIVIA

How now, art thou mad?

CLOWN

No, madam, I do but read madness: an your ladyship will have it as it ought to be, you must allow *vox.*

OLIVIA

Prithee, read i' thy right wits.

CLOWN

So I do, madonna. But to read his right wits is to read thus; therefore perpend, my princess, and give ear.

OLIVIA

[To Fabian.]
Read it you, sirrah.

FABIAN

> *[Reads.]*
>
> *By the Lord, madam, you wrong me, and the world shall know it. Though you have put me into darkness and given your drunken cousin rule over me, yet have I the benefit of my senses as well as your ladyship. I have your own letter that induced me to the semblance I put on; with the which I doubt not but to do myself much right or you much shame. Think of me as you please. I leave my duty a little unthought of, and speak out of my injury.*
>
> *The madly-used Malvolio.*

OLIVIA

> Did he write this?

CLOWN

> Ay, madam.

DUKE

> This savours not much of distraction.

OLIVIA

> See him delivered, Fabian, bring him hither.
>> *[Exit FABIAN.]*
>
> My lord, so please you, these things further thought on,
> To think me as well a sister, as a wife,
> One day shall crown th' alliance on't, so please you,
> Here at my house, and at my proper cost.

DUKE

> Madam, I am most apt t' embrace your offer.
>> *[To Viola.]*
>
> Your master quits you; and for your service done him,
> So much against the mettle of your sex,
> So far beneath your soft and tender breeding,
> And since you call'd me master for so long,
> Here is my hand; you shall from this time be
> You master's mistress.

OLIVIA

> A sister? You are she.
>> *Enter FABIAN and MALVOLIO.*

DUKE

> Is this the madman?

OLIVIA

> Ay, my lord, this same.
> How now, Malvolio?

MALVOLIO

> Madam, you have done me wrong,
> Notorious wrong.

OLIVIA

> Have I, Malvolio? No.

MALVOLIO

> Lady, you have. Pray you peruse that letter.
> You must not now deny it is your hand,
> Write from it, if you can, in hand, or phrase,
> Or say 'tis not your seal, not your invention:
> You can say none of this. Well, grant it then,
> And tell me, in the modesty of honour,
> Why you have given me such clear lights of favour,
> Bade me come smiling and cross-garter'd to you,
> To put on yellow stockings, and to frown
> Upon Sir Toby, and the lighter people;
> And acting this in an obedient hope,
> Why have you suffer'd me to be imprison'd,
> Kept in a dark house, visited by the priest,
> And made the most notorious geck and gull
> That e'er invention played on? Tell me why?

OLIVIA

> Alas, Malvolio, this is not my writing,
> Though I confess, much like the character:
> But out of question, 'tis Maria's hand.
> And now I do bethink me, it was she
> First told me thou wast mad; then cam'st in smiling,
> And in such forms which here were presuppos'd
> Upon thee in the letter. Prithee, be content.
> This practice hath most shrewdly pass'd upon thee.

But when we know the grounds and authors of it,
Thou shalt be both the plaintiff and the judge
Of thine own cause.

FABIAN

Good madam, hear me speak,
And let no quarrel, nor no brawl to come,
Taint the condition of this present hour,
Which I have wonder'd at. In hope it shall not,
Most freely I confess, myself and Toby
Set this device against Malvolio here,
Upon some stubborn and uncourteous parts
We had conceiv'd against him. Maria writ
The letter, at Sir Toby's great importance,
In recompense whereof he hath married her.
How with a sportful malice it was follow'd
May rather pluck on laughter than revenge,
If that the injuries be justly weigh'd
That have on both sides passed.

OLIVIA

Alas, poor fool, how have they baffled thee!

CLOWN

Why, 'some are born great, some achieve greatness, and some have greatness thrown upon them.' I was one, sir, in this interlude, one Sir Topas, sir, but that's all one. 'By the Lord, fool, I am not mad.' But do you remember? 'Madam, why laugh you at such a barren rascal? And you smile not, he's gagged'? And thus the whirligig of time brings in his revenges.

MALVOLIO

I'll be revenged on the whole pack of you.
[Exit.]

OLIVIA

He hath been most notoriously abus'd.

DUKE

Pursue him, and entreat him to a peace:

He hath not told us of the captain yet.
When that is known, and golden time convents,
A solemn combination shall be made
Of our dear souls.—Meantime, sweet sister,
We will not part from hence.—Cesario, come:
For so you shall be while you are a man;
But when in other habits you are seen,
Orsino's mistress, and his fancy's queen.
> *[Exeunt.]*
> *[Clown sings.]*

     When that I was and a little tiny boy,
       With hey, ho, the wind and the rain,
         A foolish thing was but a toy,
       For the rain it raineth every day.
      But when I came to man's estate,
       With hey, ho, the wind and the rain,
'Gainst knaves and thieves men shut their gate,
       For the rain it raineth every day.
      But when I came, alas, to wive,
       With hey, ho, the wind and the rain,
      By swaggering could I never thrive,
       For the rain it raineth every day.
      But when I came unto my beds,
       With hey, ho, the wind and the rain,
     With toss-pots still had drunken heads,
       For the rain it raineth every day.
      A great while ago the world begun,
       With hey, ho, the wind and the rain,
      But that's all one, our play is done,
    And we'll strive to please you every day.
> *[Exit.]*

THE SONNETS

1

From fairest creatures we desire increase,
That thereby beauty's rose might never die,
But as the riper should by time decease,
His tender heir might bear his memory:
But thou contracted to thine own bright eyes,
Feed'st thy light's flame with self-substantial fuel,
Making a famine where abundance lies,
Thy self thy foe, to thy sweet self too cruel:
Thou that art now the world's fresh ornament,
And only herald to the gaudy spring,
Within thine own bud buriest thy content,
And, tender churl, mak'st waste in niggarding:
Pity the world, or else this glutton be,
To eat the world's due, by the grave and thee.

2

When forty winters shall besiege thy brow,
And dig deep trenches in thy beauty's field,
Thy youth's proud livery so gazed on now,
Will be a tattered weed of small worth held:
Then being asked, where all thy beauty lies,
Where all the treasure of thy lusty days;
To say, within thine own deep sunken eyes,
Were an all-eating shame, and thriftless praise.
How much more praise deserv'd thy beauty's use,
If thou couldst answer 'This fair child of mine
Shall sum my count, and make my old excuse,'
Proving his beauty by succession thine.
This were to be new made when thou art old,
And see thy blood warm when thou feel'st it cold.

3

Look in thy glass and tell the face thou viewest,
Now is the time that face should form another,
Whose fresh repair if now thou not renewest,
Thou dost beguile the world, unbless some mother.
For where is she so fair whose uneared womb
Disdains the tillage of thy husbandry?
Or who is he so fond will be the tomb
Of his self-love to stop posterity?
Thou art thy mother's glass and she in thee

Calls back the lovely April of her prime,
So thou through windows of thine age shalt see,
Despite of wrinkles this thy golden time.
But if thou live remembered not to be,
Die single and thine image dies with thee.

4

Unthrifty loveliness why dost thou spend,
Upon thy self thy beauty's legacy?
Nature's bequest gives nothing but doth lend,
And being frank she lends to those are free:
Then beauteous niggard why dost thou abuse,
The bounteous largess given thee to give?
Profitless usurer why dost thou use
So great a sum of sums yet canst not live?
For having traffic with thy self alone,
Thou of thy self thy sweet self dost deceive,
Then how when nature calls thee to be gone,
What acceptable audit canst thou leave?
Thy unused beauty must be tombed with thee,
Which used lives th' executor to be.

5

Those hours that with gentle work did frame
The lovely gaze where every eye doth dwell
Will play the tyrants to the very same,
And that unfair which fairly doth excel:
For never-resting time leads summer on
To hideous winter and confounds him there,
Sap checked with frost and lusty leaves quite gone,
Beauty o'er-snowed and bareness every where:
Then were not summer's distillation left
A liquid prisoner pent in walls of glass,
Beauty's effect with beauty were bereft,
Nor it nor no remembrance what it was.
But flowers distilled though they with winter meet,
Leese but their show, their substance still lives sweet.

6

Then let not winter's ragged hand deface,
In thee thy summer ere thou be distilled:
Make sweet some vial; treasure thou some place,

With beauty's treasure ere it be self-killed:
That use is not forbidden usury,
Which happies those that pay the willing loan;
That's for thy self to breed another thee,
Or ten times happier be it ten for one,
Ten times thy self were happier than thou art,
If ten of thine ten times refigured thee:
Then what could death do if thou shouldst depart,
Leaving thee living in posterity?
Be not self-willed for thou art much too fair,
To be death's conquest and make worms thine heir.

7

Lo in the orient when the gracious light
Lifts up his burning head, each under eye
Doth homage to his new-appearing sight,
Serving with looks his sacred majesty,
And having climbed the steep-up heavenly hill,
Resembling strong youth in his middle age,
Yet mortal looks adore his beauty still,
Attending on his golden pilgrimage:
But when from highmost pitch with weary car,
Like feeble age he reeleth from the day,
The eyes (fore duteous) now converted are
From his low tract and look another way:
So thou, thy self out-going in thy noon:
Unlooked on diest unless thou get a son.

8

Music to hear, why hear'st thou music sadly?
Sweets with sweets war not, joy delights in joy:
Why lov'st thou that which thou receiv'st not gladly,
Or else receiv'st with pleasure thine annoy?
If the true concord of well-tuned sounds,
By unions married do offend thine ear,
They do but sweetly chide thee, who confounds
In singleness the parts that thou shouldst bear:
Mark how one string sweet husband to another,
Strikes each in each by mutual ordering;
Resembling sire, and child, and happy mother,
Who all in one, one pleasing note do sing:

Whose speechless song being many, seeming one,
Sings this to thee, 'Thou single wilt prove none.'

9

Is it for fear to wet a widow's eye,
That thou consum'st thy self in single life?
Ah, if thou issueless shalt hap to die,
The world will wail thee like a makeless wife,
The world will be thy widow and still weep,
That thou no form of thee hast left behind,
When every private widow well may keep,
By children's eyes, her husband's shape in mind:
Look what an unthrift in the world doth spend
Shifts but his place, for still the world enjoys it;
But beauty's waste hath in the world an end,
And kept unused the user so destroys it:
No love toward others in that bosom sits
That on himself such murd'rous shame commits.

10

For shame deny that thou bear'st love to any
Who for thy self art so unprovident.
Grant if thou wilt, thou art beloved of many,
But that thou none lov'st is most evident:
For thou art so possessed with murd'rous hate,
That 'gainst thy self thou stick'st not to conspire,
Seeking that beauteous roof to ruinate
Which to repair should be thy chief desire:
O change thy thought, that I may change my mind,
Shall hate be fairer lodged than gentle love?
Be as thy presence is gracious and kind,
Or to thy self at least kind-hearted prove,
Make thee another self for love of me,
That beauty still may live in thine or thee.

11

As fast as thou shalt wane so fast thou grow'st,
In one of thine, from that which thou departest,
And that fresh blood which youngly thou bestow'st,
Thou mayst call thine, when thou from youth convertest,
Herein lives wisdom, beauty, and increase,
Without this folly, age, and cold decay,

If all were minded so, the times should cease,
And threescore year would make the world away:
Let those whom nature hath not made for store,
Harsh, featureless, and rude, barrenly perish:
Look whom she best endowed, she gave thee more;
Which bounteous gift thou shouldst in bounty cherish:
She carved thee for her seal, and meant thereby,
Thou shouldst print more, not let that copy die.

12

When I do count the clock that tells the time,
And see the brave day sunk in hideous night,
When I behold the violet past prime,
And sable curls all silvered o'er with white:
When lofty trees I see barren of leaves,
Which erst from heat did canopy the herd
And summer's green all girded up in sheaves
Borne on the bier with white and bristly beard:
Then of thy beauty do I question make
That thou among the wastes of time must go,
Since sweets and beauties do themselves forsake,
And die as fast as they see others grow,
And nothing 'gainst Time's scythe can make defence
Save breed to brave him, when he takes thee hence.

13

O that you were your self, but love you are
No longer yours, than you your self here live,
Against this coming end you should prepare,
And your sweet semblance to some other give.
So should that beauty which you hold in lease
Find no determination, then you were
Your self again after your self's decease,
When your sweet issue your sweet form should bear.
Who lets so fair a house fall to decay,
Which husbandry in honour might uphold,
Against the stormy gusts of winter's day
And barren rage of death's eternal cold?
O none but unthrifts, dear my love you know,
You had a father, let your son say so.

When I do count the clock that tells the time,

And see the brave day sunk in hideous night,

When I behold the violet past prime,

And sable curls all silvered o'er with white:

When lofty trees I see barren of leaves,

Which erst from heat did canopy the herd

And summer's green all girded up in sheaves

Borne on the bier with white and bristly beard:

Then of thy beauty do I question make

That thou among the wastes of time must go,

Since sweets and beauties do themselves forsake,

And die as fast as they see others grow,

And nothing 'gainst Time's scythe can make defence

Save breed to brave him, when he takes thee hence.

—SONNET 12

14

Not from the stars do I my judgement pluck,
And yet methinks I have astronomy,
But not to tell of good, or evil luck,
Of plagues, of dearths, or seasons' quality,
Nor can I fortune to brief minutes tell;
Pointing to each his thunder, rain and wind,
Or say with princes if it shall go well
By oft predict that I in heaven find.
But from thine eyes my knowledge I derive,
And constant stars in them I read such art
As truth and beauty shall together thrive
If from thy self, to store thou wouldst convert:
Or else of thee this I prognosticate,
Thy end is truth's and beauty's doom and date.

15

When I consider every thing that grows
Holds in perfection but a little moment.
That this huge stage presenteth nought but shows
Whereon the stars in secret influence comment.
When I perceive that men as plants increase,
Cheered and checked even by the self-same sky:
Vaunt in their youthful sap, at height decrease,
And wear their brave state out of memory.
Then the conceit of this inconstant stay,
Sets you most rich in youth before my sight,
Where wasteful time debateth with decay
To change your day of youth to sullied night,
And all in war with Time for love of you,
As he takes from you, I engraft you new.

16

But wherefore do not you a mightier way
Make war upon this bloody tyrant Time?
And fortify your self in your decay
With means more blessed than my barren rhyme?
Now stand you on the top of happy hours,
And many maiden gardens yet unset,
With virtuous wish would bear you living flowers,
Much liker than your painted counterfeit:

So should the lines of life that life repair
Which this (Time's pencil) or my pupil pen
Neither in inward worth nor outward fair
Can make you live your self in eyes of men.
To give away your self, keeps your self still,
And you must live drawn by your own sweet skill.

17

Who will believe my verse in time to come
If it were filled with your most high deserts?
Though yet heaven knows it is but as a tomb
Which hides your life, and shows not half your parts:
If I could write the beauty of your eyes,
And in fresh numbers number all your graces,
The age to come would say this poet lies,
Such heavenly touches ne'er touched earthly faces.
So should my papers (yellowed with their age)
Be scorned, like old men of less truth than tongue,
And your true rights be termed a poet's rage,
And stretched metre of an antique song.
But were some child of yours alive that time,
You should live twice in it, and in my rhyme.

18

Shall I compare thee to a summer's day?
Thou art more lovely and more temperate:
Rough winds do shake the darling buds of May,
And summer's lease hath all too short a date:
Sometime too hot the eye of heaven shines,
And often is his gold complexion dimmed,
And every fair from fair sometime declines,
By chance, or nature's changing course untrimmed:
But thy eternal summer shall not fade,
Nor lose possession of that fair thou ow'st,
Nor shall death brag thou wand'rest in his shade,
When in eternal lines to time thou grow'st,
So long as men can breathe or eyes can see,
So long lives this, and this gives life to thee.

19

Devouring Time blunt thou the lion's paws,
And make the earth devour her own sweet brood,

Pluck the keen teeth from the fierce tiger's jaws,
And burn the long-lived phoenix, in her blood,
Make glad and sorry seasons as thou fleet'st,
And do whate'er thou wilt swift-footed Time
To the wide world and all her fading sweets:
But I forbid thee one most heinous crime,
O carve not with thy hours my love's fair brow,
Nor draw no lines there with thine antique pen,
Him in thy course untainted do allow,
For beauty's pattern to succeeding men.
Yet do thy worst old Time: despite thy wrong,
My love shall in my verse ever live young.

20

A woman's face with nature's own hand painted,
Hast thou the master mistress of my passion,
A woman's gentle heart but not acquainted
With shifting change as is false women's fashion,
An eye more bright than theirs, less false in rolling:
Gilding the object whereupon it gazeth,
A man in hue all hues in his controlling,
Which steals men's eyes and women's souls amazeth.
And for a woman wert thou first created,
Till nature as she wrought thee fell a-doting,
And by addition me of thee defeated,
By adding one thing to my purpose nothing.
But since she pricked thee out for women's pleasure,
Mine be thy love and thy love's use their treasure.

21

So is it not with me as with that muse,
Stirred by a painted beauty to his verse,
Who heaven it self for ornament doth use,
And every fair with his fair doth rehearse,
Making a couplement of proud compare
With sun and moon, with earth and sea's rich gems:
With April's first-born flowers and all things rare,
That heaven's air in this huge rondure hems.
O let me true in love but truly write,
And then believe me, my love is as fair,
As any mother's child, though not so bright

As those gold candles fixed in heaven's air:
Let them say more that like of hearsay well,
I will not praise that purpose not to sell.

22

My glass shall not persuade me I am old,
So long as youth and thou are of one date,
But when in thee time's furrows I behold,
Then look I death my days should expiate.
For all that beauty that doth cover thee,
Is but the seemly raiment of my heart,
Which in thy breast doth live, as thine in me,
How can I then be elder than thou art?
O therefore love be of thyself so wary,
As I not for my self, but for thee will,
Bearing thy heart which I will keep so chary
As tender nurse her babe from faring ill.
Presume not on thy heart when mine is slain,
Thou gav'st me thine not to give back again.

23

As an unperfect actor on the stage,
Who with his fear is put beside his part,
Or some fierce thing replete with too much rage,
Whose strength's abundance weakens his own heart;
So I for fear of trust, forget to say,
The perfect ceremony of love's rite,
And in mine own love's strength seem to decay,
O'ercharged with burthen of mine own love's might:
O let my looks be then the eloquence,
And dumb presagers of my speaking breast,
Who plead for love, and look for recompense,
More than that tongue that more hath more expressed.
O learn to read what silent love hath writ,
To hear with eyes belongs to love's fine wit.

24

Mine eye hath played the painter and hath stelled,
Thy beauty's form in table of my heart,
My body is the frame wherein 'tis held,
And perspective it is best painter's art.
For through the painter must you see his skill,

To find where your true image pictured lies,
Which in my bosom's shop is hanging still,
That hath his windows glazed with thine eyes:
Now see what good turns eyes for eyes have done,
Mine eyes have drawn thy shape, and thine for me
Are windows to my breast, where-through the sun
Delights to peep, to gaze therein on thee;
Yet eyes this cunning want to grace their art,
They draw but what they see, know not the heart.

25

Let those who are in favour with their stars,
Of public honour and proud titles boast,
Whilst I whom fortune of such triumph bars
Unlooked for joy in that I honour most;
Great princes' favourites their fair leaves spread,
But as the marigold at the sun's eye,
And in themselves their pride lies buried,
For at a frown they in their glory die.
The painful warrior famoused for fight,
After a thousand victories once foiled,
Is from the book of honour razed quite,
And all the rest forgot for which he toiled:
Then happy I that love and am beloved
Where I may not remove nor be removed.

26

Lord of my love, to whom in vassalage
Thy merit hath my duty strongly knit;
To thee I send this written embassage
To witness duty, not to show my wit.
Duty so great, which wit so poor as mine
May make seem bare, in wanting words to show it;
But that I hope some good conceit of thine
In thy soul's thought (all naked) will bestow it:
Till whatsoever star that guides my moving,
Points on me graciously with fair aspect,
And puts apparel on my tattered loving,
To show me worthy of thy sweet respect,
Then may I dare to boast how I do love thee,
Till then, not show my head where thou mayst prove me.

27

Weary with toil, I haste me to my bed,
The dear respose for limbs with travel tired,
But then begins a journey in my head
To work my mind, when body's work's expired.
For then my thoughts (from far where I abide)
Intend a zealous pilgrimage to thee,
And keep my drooping eyelids open wide,
Looking on darkness which the blind do see.
Save that my soul's imaginary sight
Presents thy shadow to my sightless view,
Which like a jewel (hung in ghastly night)
Makes black night beauteous, and her old face new.
Lo thus by day my limbs, by night my mind,
For thee, and for my self, no quiet find.

28

How can I then return in happy plight
That am debarred the benefit of rest?
When day's oppression is not eased by night,
But day by night and night by day oppressed.
And each (though enemies to either's reign)
Do in consent shake hands to torture me,
The one by toil, the other to complain
How far I toil, still farther off from thee.
I tell the day to please him thou art bright,
And dost him grace when clouds do blot the heaven:
So flatter I the swart-complexioned night,
When sparkling stars twire not thou gild'st the even.
But day doth daily draw my sorrows longer,
And night doth nightly make grief's length seem stronger

29

When in disgrace with Fortune and men's eyes,
I all alone beweep my outcast state,
And trouble deaf heaven with my bootless cries,
And look upon my self and curse my fate,
Wishing me like to one more rich in hope,
Featured like him, like him with friends possessed,
Desiring this man's art, and that man's scope,
With what I most enjoy contented least,

Yet in these thoughts my self almost despising,
Haply I think on thee, and then my state,
(Like to the lark at break of day arising
From sullen earth) sings hymns at heaven's gate,
For thy sweet love remembered such wealth brings,
That then I scorn to change my state with kings.

30

When to the sessions of sweet silent thought,
I summon up remembrance of things past,
I sigh the lack of many a thing I sought,
And with old woes new wail my dear time's waste:
Then can I drown an eye (unused to flow)
For precious friends hid in death's dateless night,
And weep afresh love's long since cancelled woe,
And moan th' expense of many a vanished sight.
Then can I grieve at grievances foregone,
And heavily from woe to woe tell o'er
The sad account of fore-bemoaned moan,
Which I new pay as if not paid before.
But if the while I think on thee (dear friend)
All losses are restored, and sorrows end.

31

Thy bosom is endeared with all hearts,
Which I by lacking have supposed dead,
And there reigns love and all love's loving parts,
And all those friends which I thought buried.
How many a holy and obsequious tear
Hath dear religious love stol'n from mine eye,
As interest of the dead, which now appear,
But things removed that hidden in thee lie.
Thou art the grave where buried love doth live,
Hung with the trophies of my lovers gone,
Who all their parts of me to thee did give,
That due of many, now is thine alone.
Their images I loved, I view in thee,
And thou (all they) hast all the all of me.

32

If thou survive my well-contented day,
When that churl death my bones with dust shall cover

And shalt by fortune once more re-survey
These poor rude lines of thy deceased lover:
Compare them with the bett'ring of the time,
And though they be outstripped by every pen,
Reserve them for my love, not for their rhyme,
Exceeded by the height of happier men.
O then vouchsafe me but this loving thought,
'Had my friend's Muse grown with this growing age,
A dearer birth than this his love had brought
To march in ranks of better equipage:
But since he died and poets better prove,
Theirs for their style I'll read, his for his love.'

33

Full many a glorious morning have I seen,
Flatter the mountain tops with sovereign eye,
Kissing with golden face the meadows green;
Gilding pale streams with heavenly alchemy:
Anon permit the basest clouds to ride,
With ugly rack on his celestial face,
And from the forlorn world his visage hide
Stealing unseen to west with this disgrace:
Even so my sun one early morn did shine,
With all triumphant splendour on my brow,
But out alack, he was but one hour mine,
The region cloud hath masked him from me now.
Yet him for this, my love no whit disdaineth,
Suns of the world may stain, when heaven's sun staineth.

34

Why didst thou promise such a beauteous day,
And make me travel forth without my cloak,
To let base clouds o'ertake me in my way,
Hiding thy brav'ry in their rotten smoke?
'Tis not enough that through the cloud thou break,
To dry the rain on my storm-beaten face,
For no man well of such a salve can speak,
That heals the wound, and cures not the disgrace:
Nor can thy shame give physic to my grief,
Though thou repent, yet I have still the loss,
Th' offender's sorrow lends but weak relief

To him that bears the strong offence's cross.
Ah but those tears are pearl which thy love sheds,
And they are rich, and ransom all ill deeds.

35

No more be grieved at that which thou hast done,
Roses have thorns, and silver fountains mud,
Clouds and eclipses stain both moon and sun,
And loathsome canker lives in sweetest bud.
All men make faults, and even I in this,
Authorizing thy trespass with compare,
My self corrupting salving thy amiss,
Excusing thy sins more than thy sins are:
For to thy sensual fault I bring in sense,
Thy adverse party is thy advocate,
And 'gainst my self a lawful plea commence:
Such civil war is in my love and hate,
That I an accessary needs must be,
To that sweet thief which sourly robs from me.

36

Let me confess that we two must be twain,
Although our undivided loves are one:
So shall those blots that do with me remain,
Without thy help, by me be borne alone.
In our two loves there is but one respect,
Though in our lives a separable spite,
Which though it alter not love's sole effect,
Yet doth it steal sweet hours from love's delight.
I may not evermore acknowledge thee,
Lest my bewailed guilt should do thee shame,
Nor thou with public kindness honour me,
Unless thou take that honour from thy name:
But do not so, I love thee in such sort,
As thou being mine, mine is thy good report.

37

As a decrepit father takes delight,
To see his active child do deeds of youth,
So I, made lame by Fortune's dearest spite
Take all my comfort of thy worth and truth.
For whether beauty, birth, or wealth, or wit,

Or any of these all, or all, or more
Entitled in thy parts, do crowned sit,
I make my love engrafted to this store:
So then I am not lame, poor, nor despised,
Whilst that this shadow doth such substance give,
That I in thy abundance am sufficed,
And by a part of all thy glory live:
Look what is best, that best I wish in thee,
This wish I have, then ten times happy me.

38

How can my muse want subject to invent
While thou dost breathe that pour'st into my verse,
Thine own sweet argument, too excellent,
For every vulgar paper to rehearse?
O give thy self the thanks if aught in me,
Worthy perusal stand against thy sight,
For who's so dumb that cannot write to thee,
When thou thy self dost give invention light?
Be thou the tenth Muse, ten times more in worth
Than those old nine which rhymers invocate,
And he that calls on thee, let him bring forth
Eternal numbers to outlive long date.
If my slight muse do please these curious days,
The pain be mine, but thine shall be the praise.

39

O how thy worth with manners may I sing,
When thou art all the better part of me?
What can mine own praise to mine own self bring:
And what is't but mine own when I praise thee?
Even for this, let us divided live,
And our dear love lose name of single one,
That by this separation I may give:
That due to thee which thou deserv'st alone:
O absence what a torment wouldst thou prove,
Were it not thy sour leisure gave sweet leave,
To entertain the time with thoughts of love,
Which time and thoughts so sweetly doth deceive.
And that thou teachest how to make one twain,
By praising him here who doth hence remain.

40

Take all my loves, my love, yea take them all,
What hast thou then more than thou hadst before?
No love, my love, that thou mayst true love call,
All mine was thine, before thou hadst this more:
Then if for my love, thou my love receivest,
I cannot blame thee, for my love thou usest,
But yet be blamed, if thou thy self deceivest
By wilful taste of what thy self refusest.
I do forgive thy robbery gentle thief
Although thou steal thee all my poverty:
And yet love knows it is a greater grief
To bear greater wrong, than hate's known injury.
Lascivious grace, in whom all ill well shows,
Kill me with spites yet we must not be foes.

41

Those pretty wrongs that liberty commits,
When I am sometime absent from thy heart,
Thy beauty, and thy years full well befits,
For still temptation follows where thou art.
Gentle thou art, and therefore to be won,
Beauteous thou art, therefore to be assailed.
And when a woman woos, what woman's son,
Will sourly leave her till he have prevailed?
Ay me, but yet thou mightst my seat forbear,
And chide thy beauty, and thy straying youth,
Who lead thee in their riot even there
Where thou art forced to break a twofold truth:
Hers by thy beauty tempting her to thee,
Thine by thy beauty being false to me.

42

That thou hast her it is not all my grief,
And yet it may be said I loved her dearly,
That she hath thee is of my wailing chief,
A loss in love that touches me more nearly.
Loving offenders thus I will excuse ye,
Thou dost love her, because thou know'st I love her,
And for my sake even so doth she abuse me,
Suff'ring my friend for my sake to approve her.

If I lose thee, my loss is my love's gain,
And losing her, my friend hath found that loss,
Both find each other, and I lose both twain,
And both for my sake lay on me this cross,
But here's the joy, my friend and I are one,
Sweet flattery, then she loves but me alone.

43

When most I wink then do mine eyes best see,
For all the day they view things unrespected,
But when I sleep, in dreams they look on thee,
And darkly bright, are bright in dark directed.
Then thou whose shadow shadows doth make bright
How would thy shadow's form, form happy show,
To the clear day with thy much clearer light,
When to unseeing eyes thy shade shines so!
How would (I say) mine eyes be blessed made,
By looking on thee in the living day,
When in dead night thy fair imperfect shade,
Through heavy sleep on sightless eyes doth stay!
All days are nights to see till I see thee,
And nights bright days when dreams do show thee me.

44

If the dull substance of my flesh were thought,
Injurious distance should not stop my way,
For then despite of space I would be brought,
From limits far remote, where thou dost stay,
No matter then although my foot did stand
Upon the farthest earth removed from thee,
For nimble thought can jump both sea and land,
As soon as think the place where he would be.
But ah, thought kills me that I am not thought
To leap large lengths of miles when thou art gone,
But that so much of earth and water wrought,
I must attend, time's leisure with my moan.
Receiving nought by elements so slow,
But heavy tears, badges of either's woe.

45

The other two, slight air, and purging fire,
Are both with thee, wherever I abide,

The first my thought, the other my desire,
These present-absent with swift motion slide.
For when these quicker elements are gone
In tender embassy of love to thee,
My life being made of four, with two alone,
Sinks down to death, oppressed with melancholy.
Until life's composition be recured,
By those swift messengers returned from thee,
Who even but now come back again assured,
Of thy fair health, recounting it to me.
This told, I joy, but then no longer glad,
I send them back again and straight grow sad.

46

Mine eye and heart are at a mortal war,
How to divide the conquest of thy sight,
Mine eye, my heart thy picture's sight would bar,
My heart, mine eye the freedom of that right,
My heart doth plead that thou in him dost lie,
(A closet never pierced with crystal eyes)
But the defendant doth that plea deny,
And says in him thy fair appearance lies.
To side this title is impanelled
A quest of thoughts, all tenants to the heart,
And by their verdict is determined
The clear eye's moiety, and the dear heart's part.
As thus, mine eye's due is thy outward part,
And my heart's right, thy inward love of heart.

47

Betwixt mine eye and heart a league is took,
And each doth good turns now unto the other,
When that mine eye is famished for a look,
Or heart in love with sighs himself doth smother;
With my love's picture then my eye doth feast,
And to the painted banquet bids my heart:
Another time mine eye is my heart's guest,
And in his thoughts of love doth share a part.
So either by thy picture or my love,
Thy self away, art present still with me,
For thou not farther than my thoughts canst move,

And I am still with them, and they with thee.
Or if they sleep, thy picture in my sight
Awakes my heart, to heart's and eye's delight.

48

How careful was I when I took my way,
Each trifle under truest bars to thrust,
That to my use it might unused stay
From hands of falsehood, in sure wards of trust!
But thou, to whom my jewels trifles are,
Most worthy comfort, now my greatest grief,
Thou best of dearest, and mine only care,
Art left the prey of every vulgar thief.
Thee have I not locked up in any chest,
Save where thou art not, though I feel thou art,
Within the gentle closure of my breast,
From whence at pleasure thou mayst come and part,
And even thence thou wilt be stol'n I fear,
For truth proves thievish for a prize so dear.

49

Against that time (if ever that time come)
When I shall see thee frown on my defects,
When as thy love hath cast his utmost sum,
Called to that audit by advised respects,
Against that time when thou shalt strangely pass,
And scarcely greet me with that sun thine eye,
When love converted from the thing it was
Shall reasons find of settled gravity;
Against that time do I ensconce me here
Within the knowledge of mine own desert,
And this my hand, against my self uprear,
To guard the lawful reasons on thy part,
To leave poor me, thou hast the strength of laws,
Since why to love, I can allege no cause.

50

How heavy do I journey on the way,
When what I seek (my weary travel's end)
Doth teach that case and that repose to say
'Thus far the miles are measured from thy friend.'
The beast that bears me, tired with my woe,

Plods dully on, to bear that weight in me,
As if by some instinct the wretch did know
His rider loved not speed being made from thee:
The bloody spur cannot provoke him on,
That sometimes anger thrusts into his hide,
Which heavily he answers with a groan,
More sharp to me than spurring to his side,
For that same groan doth put this in my mind,
My grief lies onward and my joy behind.

51

Thus can my love excuse the slow offence,
Of my dull bearer, when from thee I speed,
From where thou art, why should I haste me thence?
Till I return of posting is no need.
O what excuse will my poor beast then find,
When swift extremity can seem but slow?
Then should I spur though mounted on the wind,
In winged speed no motion shall I know,
Then can no horse with my desire keep pace,
Therefore desire (of perfect'st love being made)
Shall neigh (no dull flesh) in his fiery race,
But love, for love, thus shall excuse my jade,
Since from thee going, he went wilful-slow,
Towards thee I'll run, and give him leave to go.

52

So am I as the rich whose blessed key,
Can bring him to his sweet up-locked treasure,
The which he will not every hour survey,
For blunting the fine point of seldom pleasure.
Therefore are feasts so solemn and so rare,
Since seldom coming in that long year set,
Like stones of worth they thinly placed are,
Or captain jewels in the carcanet.
So is the time that keeps you as my chest
Or as the wardrobe which the robe doth hide,
To make some special instant special-blest,
By new unfolding his imprisoned pride.
Blessed are you whose worthiness gives scope,
Being had to triumph, being lacked to hope.

53

What is your substance, whereof are you made,
That millions of strange shadows on you tend?
Since every one, hath every one, one shade,
And you but one, can every shadow lend:
Describe Adonis and the counterfeit,
Is poorly imitated after you,
On Helen's cheek all art of beauty set,
And you in Grecian tires are painted new:
Speak of the spring, and foison of the year,
The one doth shadow of your beauty show,
The other as your bounty doth appear,
And you in every blessed shape we know.
In all external grace you have some part,
But you like none, none you for constant heart.

54

O how much more doth beauty beauteous seem,
By that sweet ornament which truth doth give!
The rose looks fair, but fairer we it deem
For that sweet odour, which doth in it live:
The canker blooms have full as deep a dye,
As the perfumed tincture of the roses,
Hang on such thorns, and play as wantonly,
When summer's breath their masked buds discloses:
But for their virtue only is their show,
They live unwooed, and unrespected fade,
Die to themselves. Sweet roses do not so,
Of their sweet deaths, are sweetest odours made:
And so of you, beauteous and lovely youth,
When that shall fade, my verse distills your truth.

55

Not marble, nor the gilded monuments
Of princes shall outlive this powerful rhyme,
But you shall shine more bright in these contents
Than unswept stone, besmeared with sluttish time.
When wasteful war shall statues overturn,
And broils root out the work of masonry,
Nor Mars his sword, nor war's quick fire shall burn:
The living record of your memory.
'Gainst death, and all-oblivious enmity

Shall you pace forth, your praise shall still find room,
Even in the eyes of all posterity
That wear this world out to the ending doom.
So till the judgment that your self arise,
You live in this, and dwell in lovers' eyes.

56

Sweet love renew thy force, be it not said
Thy edge should blunter be than appetite,
Which but to-day by feeding is allayed,
To-morrow sharpened in his former might.
So love be thou, although to-day thou fill
Thy hungry eyes, even till they wink with fulness,
To-morrow see again, and do not kill
The spirit of love, with a perpetual dulness:
Let this sad interim like the ocean be
Which parts the shore, where two contracted new,
Come daily to the banks, that when they see:
Return of love, more blest may be the view.
Or call it winter, which being full of care,
Makes summer's welcome, thrice more wished, more rare.

57

Being your slave what should I do but tend,
Upon the hours, and times of your desire?
I have no precious time at all to spend;
Nor services to do till you require.
Nor dare I chide the world-without-end hour,
Whilst I (my sovereign) watch the clock for you,
Nor think the bitterness of absence sour,
When you have bid your servant once adieu.
Nor dare I question with my jealous thought,
Where you may be, or your affairs suppose,
But like a sad slave stay and think of nought
Save where you are, how happy you make those.
So true a fool is love, that in your will,
(Though you do any thing) he thinks no ill.

58

That god forbid, that made me first your slave,
I should in thought control your times of pleasure,
Or at your hand th' account of hours to crave,

Being your vassal bound to stay your leisure.
O let me suffer (being at your beck)
Th' imprisoned absence of your liberty,
And patience tame to sufferance bide each check,
Without accusing you of injury.
Be where you list, your charter is so strong,
That you your self may privilage your time
To what you will, to you it doth belong,
Your self to pardon of self-doing crime.
I am to wait, though waiting so be hell,
Not blame your pleasure be it ill or well.

59

If there be nothing new, but that which is,
Hath been before, how are our brains beguiled,
Which labouring for invention bear amis
The second burthen of a former child!
O that record could with a backward look,
Even of five hundred courses of the sun,
Show me your image in some antique book,
Since mind at first in character was done.
That I might see what the old world could say,
To this composed wonder of your frame,
Whether we are mended, or whether better they,
Or whether revolution be the same.
O sure I am the wits of former days,
To subjects worse have given admiring praise.

60

Like as the waves make towards the pebbled shore,
So do our minutes hasten to their end,
Each changing place with that which goes before,
In sequent toil all forwards do contend.
Nativity once in the main of light,
Crawls to maturity, wherewith being crowned,
Crooked eclipses 'gainst his glory fight,
And Time that gave, doth now his gift confound.
Time doth transfix the flourish set on youth,
And delves the parallels in beauty's brow,
Feeds on the rarities of nature's truth,
And nothing stands but for his scythe to mow.

And yet to times in hope, my verse shall stand
Praising thy worth, despite his cruel hand.

61

Is it thy will, thy image should keep open
My heavy eyelids to the weary night?
Dost thou desire my slumbers should be broken,
While shadows like to thee do mock my sight?
Is it thy spirit that thou send'st from thee
So far from home into my deeds to pry,
To find out shames and idle hours in me,
The scope and tenure of thy jealousy?
O no, thy love though much, is not so great,
It is my love that keeps mine eye awake,
Mine own true love that doth my rest defeat,
To play the watchman ever for thy sake.
For thee watch I, whilst thou dost wake elsewhere,
From me far off, with others all too near.

62

Sin of self-love possesseth all mine eye,
And all my soul, and all my every part;
And for this sin there is no remedy,
It is so grounded inward in my heart.
Methinks no face so gracious is as mine,
No shape so true, no truth of such account,
And for my self mine own worth do define,
As I all other in all worths surmount.
But when my glass shows me my self indeed
beated and chopt with tanned antiquity,
Mine own self-love quite contrary I read:
Self, so self-loving were iniquity.
'Tis thee (my self) that for my self I praise,
Painting my age with beauty of thy days.

63

Against my love shall be as I am now
With Time's injurious hand crushed and o'erworn,
When hours have drained his blood and filled his brow
With lines and wrinkles, when his youthful morn
Hath travelled on to age's steepy night,
And all those beauties whereof now he's king

Are vanishing, or vanished out of sight,
Stealing away the treasure of his spring:
For such a time do I now fortify
Against confounding age's cruel knife,
That he shall never cut from memory
My sweet love's beauty, though my lover's life.
His beauty shall in these black lines be seen,
And they shall live, and he in them still green.

64

When I have seen by Time's fell hand defaced
The rich-proud cost of outworn buried age,
When sometime lofty towers I see down-rased,
And brass eternal slave to mortal rage.
When I have seen the hungry ocean gain
Advantage on the kingdom of the shore,
And the firm soil win of the watery main,
Increasing store with loss, and loss with store.
When I have seen such interchange of State,
Or state it self confounded, to decay,
Ruin hath taught me thus to ruminate
That Time will come and take my love away.
This thought is as a death which cannot choose
But weep to have, that which it fears to lose.

65

Since brass, nor stone, nor earth, nor boundless sea,
But sad mortality o'ersways their power,
How with this rage shall beauty hold a plea,
Whose action is no stronger than a flower?
O how shall summer's honey breath hold out,
Against the wrackful siege of batt'ring days,
When rocks impregnable are not so stout,
Nor gates of steel so strong but time decays?
O fearful meditation, where alack,
Shall Time's best jewel from Time's chest lie hid?
Or what strong hand can hold his swift foot back,
Or who his spoil of beauty can forbid?
O none, unless this miracle have might,
That in black ink my love may still shine bright.

66

Tired with all these for restful death I cry,
As to behold desert a beggar born,
And needy nothing trimmed in jollity,
And purest faith unhappily forsworn,
And gilded honour shamefully misplaced,
And maiden virtue rudely strumpeted,
And right perfection wrongfully disgraced,
And strength by limping sway disabled
And art made tongue-tied by authority,
And folly (doctor-like) controlling skill,
And simple truth miscalled simplicity,
And captive good attending captain ill.
Tired with all these, from these would I be gone,
Save that to die, I leave my love alone.

67

Ah wherefore with infection should he live,
And with his presence grace impiety,
That sin by him advantage should achieve,
And lace it self with his society?
Why should false painting imitate his cheek,
And steal dead seeming of his living hue?
Why should poor beauty indirectly seek,
Roses of shadow, since his rose is true?
Why should he live, now nature bankrupt is,
Beggared of blood to blush through lively veins,
For she hath no exchequer now but his,
And proud of many, lives upon his gains?
O him she stores, to show what wealth she had,
In days long since, before these last so bad.

68

Thus is his cheek the map of days outworn,
When beauty lived and died as flowers do now,
Before these bastard signs of fair were born,
Or durst inhabit on a living brow:
Before the golden tresses of the dead,
The right of sepulchres, were shorn away,
To live a second life on second head,
Ere beauty's dead fleece made another gay:

In him those holy antique hours are seen,
Without all ornament, it self and true,
Making no summer of another's green,
Robbing no old to dress his beauty new,
And him as for a map doth Nature store,
To show false Art what beauty was of yore.

69

Those parts of thee that the world's eye doth view,
Want nothing that the thought of hearts can mend:
All tongues (the voice of souls) give thee that due,
Uttering bare truth, even so as foes commend.
Thy outward thus with outward praise is crowned,
But those same tongues that give thee so thine own,
In other accents do this praise confound
By seeing farther than the eye hath shown.
They look into the beauty of thy mind,
And that in guess they measure by thy deeds,
Then churls their thoughts (although their eyes were kind)
To thy fair flower add the rank smell of weeds:
But why thy odour matcheth not thy show,
The soil is this, that thou dost common grow.

70

That thou art blamed shall not be thy defect,
For slander's mark was ever yet the fair,
The ornament of beauty is suspect,
A crow that flies in heaven's sweetest air.
So thou be good, slander doth but approve,
Thy worth the greater being wooed of time,
For canker vice the sweetest buds doth love,
And thou present'st a pure unstained prime.
Thou hast passed by the ambush of young days,
Either not assailed, or victor being charged,
Yet this thy praise cannot be so thy praise,
To tie up envy, evermore enlarged,
If some suspect of ill masked not thy show,
Then thou alone kingdoms of hearts shouldst owe.

71

No longer mourn for me when I am dead,
Than you shall hear the surly sullen bell

Give warning to the world that I am fled
From this vile world with vilest worms to dwell:
Nay if you read this line, remember not,
The hand that writ it, for I love you so,
That I in your sweet thoughts would be forgot,
If thinking on me then should make you woe.
O if (I say) you look upon this verse,
When I (perhaps) compounded am with clay,
Do not so much as my poor name rehearse;
But let your love even with my life decay.
Lest the wise world should look into your moan,
And mock you with me after I am gone.

72

O lest the world should task you to recite,
What merit lived in me that you should love
After my death (dear love) forget me quite,
For you in me can nothing worthy prove.
Unless you would devise some virtuous lie,
To do more for me than mine own desert,
And hang more praise upon deceased I,
Than niggard truth would willingly impart:
O lest your true love may seem false in this,
That you for love speak well of me untrue,
My name be buried where my body is,
And live no more to shame nor me, nor you.
For I am shamed by that which I bring forth,
And so should you, to love things nothing worth.

73

That time of year thou mayst in me behold,
When yellow leaves, or none, or few do hang
Upon those boughs which shake against the cold,
Bare ruined choirs, where late the sweet birds sang.
In me thou seest the twilight of such day,
As after sunset fadeth in the west,
Which by and by black night doth take away,
Death's second self that seals up all in rest.
In me thou seest the glowing of such fire,
That on the ashes of his youth doth lie,
As the death-bed, whereon it must expire,

Consumed with that which it was nourished by.
This thou perceiv'st, which makes thy love more strong,
To love that well, which thou must leave ere long.

74

But be contented when that fell arrest,
Without all bail shall carry me away,
My life hath in this line some interest,
Which for memorial still with thee shall stay.
When thou reviewest this, thou dost review,
The very part was consecrate to thee,
The earth can have but earth, which is his due,
My spirit is thine the better part of me,
So then thou hast but lost the dregs of life,
The prey of worms, my body being dead,
The coward conquest of a wretch's knife,
Too base of thee to be remembered,
The worth of that, is that which it contains,
And that is this, and this with thee remains.

75

So are you to my thoughts as food to life,
Or as sweet-seasoned showers are to the ground;
And for the peace of you I hold such strife
As 'twixt a miser and his wealth is found.
Now proud as an enjoyer, and anon
Doubting the filching age will steal his treasure,
Now counting best to be with you alone,
Then bettered that the world may see my pleasure,
Sometime all full with feasting on your sight,
And by and by clean starved for a look,
Possessing or pursuing no delight
Save what is had, or must from you be took.
Thus do I pine and surfeit day by day,
Or gluttoning on all, or all away.

76

Why is my verse so barren of new pride?
So far from variation or quick change?
Why with the time do I not glance aside
To new-found methods, and to compounds strange?
Why write I still all one, ever the same,

And keep invention in a noted weed,
That every word doth almost tell my name,
Showing their birth, and where they did proceed?
O know sweet love I always write of you,
And you and love are still my argument:
So all my best is dressing old words new,
Spending again what is already spent:
For as the sun is daily new and old,
So is my love still telling what is told.

77

Thy glass will show thee how thy beauties wear,
Thy dial how thy precious minutes waste,
These vacant leaves thy mind's imprint will bear,
And of this book, this learning mayst thou taste.
The wrinkles which thy glass will truly show,
Of mouthed graves will give thee memory,
Thou by thy dial's shady stealth mayst know,
Time's thievish progress to eternity.
Look what thy memory cannot contain,
Commit to these waste blanks, and thou shalt find
Those children nursed, delivered from thy brain,
To take a new acquaintance of thy mind.
These offices, so oft as thou wilt look,
Shall profit thee, and much enrich thy book.

78

So oft have I invoked thee for my muse,
And found such fair assistance in my verse,
As every alien pen hath got my use,
And under thee their poesy disperse.
Thine eyes, that taught the dumb on high to sing,
And heavy ignorance aloft to fly,
Have added feathers to the learned's wing,
And given grace a double majesty.
Yet be most proud of that which I compile,
Whose influence is thine, and born of thee,
In others' works thou dost but mend the style,
And arts with thy sweet graces graced be.
But thou art all my art, and dost advance
As high as learning, my rude ignorance.

79

Whilst I alone did call upon thy aid,
My verse alone had all thy gentle grace,
But now my gracious numbers are decayed,
And my sick muse doth give an other place.
I grant (sweet love) thy lovely argument
Deserves the travail of a worthier pen,
Yet what of thee thy poet doth invent,
He robs thee of, and pays it thee again,
He lends thee virtue, and he stole that word,
From thy behaviour, beauty doth he give
And found it in thy cheek: he can afford
No praise to thee, but what in thee doth live.
Then thank him not for that which he doth say,
Since what he owes thee, thou thy self dost pay.

80

O how I faint when I of you do write,
Knowing a better spirit doth use your name,
And in the praise thereof spends all his might,
To make me tongue-tied speaking of your fame.
But since your worth (wide as the ocean is)
The humble as the proudest sail doth bear,
My saucy bark (inferior far to his)
On your broad main doth wilfully appear.
Your shallowest help will hold me up afloat,
Whilst he upon your soundless deep doth ride,
Or (being wrecked) I am a worthless boat,
He of tall building, and of goodly pride.
Then if he thrive and I be cast away,
The worst was this, my love was my decay.

81

Or I shall live your epitaph to make,
Or you survive when I in earth am rotten,
From hence your memory death cannot take,
Although in me each part will be forgotten.
Your name from hence immortal life shall have,
Though I (once gone) to all the world must die,
The earth can yield me but a common grave,
When you entombed in men's eyes shall lie,
Your monument shall be my gentle verse,

Which eyes not yet created shall o'er-read,
And tongues to be, your being shall rehearse,
When all the breathers of this world are dead,
You still shall live (such virtue hath my pen)
Where breath most breathes, even in the mouths of men.

82

I grant thou wert not married to my muse,
And therefore mayst without attaint o'erlook
The dedicated words which writers use
Of their fair subject, blessing every book.
Thou art as fair in knowledge as in hue,
Finding thy worth a limit past my praise,
And therefore art enforced to seek anew,
Some fresher stamp of the time-bettering days.
And do so love, yet when they have devised,
What strained touches rhetoric can lend,
Thou truly fair, wert truly sympathized,
In true plain words, by thy true-telling friend.
And their gross painting might be better used,
Where cheeks need blood, in thee it is abused.

83

I never saw that you did painting need,
And therefore to your fair no painting set,
I found (or thought I found) you did exceed,
That barren tender of a poet's debt:
And therefore have I slept in your report,
That you your self being extant well might show,
How far a modern quill doth come too short,
Speaking of worth, what worth in you doth grow.
This silence for my sin you did impute,
Which shall be most my glory being dumb,
For I impair not beauty being mute,
When others would give life, and bring a tomb.
There lives more life in one of your fair eyes,
Than both your poets can in praise devise.

84

Who is it that says most, which can say more,
Than this rich praise, that you alone, are you?
In whose confine immured is the store,

Which should example where your equal grew.
Lean penury within that pen doth dwell,
That to his subject lends not some small glory,
But he that writes of you, if he can tell,
That you are you, so dignifies his story.
Let him but copy what in you is writ,
Not making worse what nature made so clear,
And such a counterpart shall fame his wit,
Making his style admired every where.
You to your beauteous blessings add a curse,
Being fond on praise, which makes your praises worse.

85

My tongue-tied muse in manners holds her still,
While comments of your praise richly compiled,
Reserve their character with golden quill,
And precious phrase by all the Muses filed.
I think good thoughts, whilst other write good words,
And like unlettered clerk still cry Amen,
To every hymn that able spirit affords,
In polished form of well refined pen.
Hearing you praised, I say 'tis so, 'tis true,
And to the most of praise add something more,
But that is in my thought, whose love to you
(Though words come hindmost) holds his rank before,
Then others, for the breath of words respect,
Me for my dumb thoughts, speaking in effect.

86

Was it the proud full sail of his great verse,
Bound for the prize of (all too precious) you,
That did my ripe thoughts in my brain inhearse,
Making their tomb the womb wherein they grew?
Was it his spirit, by spirits taught to write,
Above a mortal pitch, that struck me dead?
No, neither he, nor his compeers by night
Giving him aid, my verse astonished.
He nor that affable familiar ghost
Which nightly gulls him with intelligence,
As victors of my silence cannot boast,
I was not sick of any fear from thence.

But when your countenance filled up his line,
Then lacked I matter, that enfeebled mine.

87

Farewell! thou art too dear for my possessing,
And like enough thou know'st thy estimate,
The charter of thy worth gives thee releasing:
My bonds in thee are all determinate.
For how do I hold thee but by thy granting,
And for that riches where is my deserving?
The cause of this fair gift in me is wanting,
And so my patent back again is swerving.
Thy self thou gav'st, thy own worth then not knowing,
Or me to whom thou gav'st it, else mistaking,
So thy great gift upon misprision growing,
Comes home again, on better judgement making.
Thus have I had thee as a dream doth flatter,
In sleep a king, but waking no such matter.

88

When thou shalt be disposed to set me light,
And place my merit in the eye of scorn,
Upon thy side, against my self I'll fight,
And prove thee virtuous, though thou art forsworn:
With mine own weakness being best acquainted,
Upon thy part I can set down a story
Of faults concealed, wherein I am attainted:
That thou in losing me, shalt win much glory:
And I by this will be a gainer too,
For bending all my loving thoughts on thee,
The injuries that to my self I do,
Doing thee vantage, double-vantage me.
Such is my love, to thee I so belong,
That for thy right, my self will bear all wrong.

89

Say that thou didst forsake me for some fault,
And I will comment upon that offence,
Speak of my lameness, and I straight will halt:
Against thy reasons making no defence.
Thou canst not (love) disgrace me half so ill,

To set a form upon desired change,
As I'll my self disgrace, knowing thy will,
I will acquaintance strangle and look strange:
Be absent from thy walks and in my tongue,
Thy sweet beloved name no more shall dwell,
Lest I (too much profane) should do it wronk:
And haply of our old acquaintance tell.
For thee, against my self I'll vow debate,
For I must ne'er love him whom thou dost hate.

90

Then hate me when thou wilt, if ever, now,
Now while the world is bent my deeds to cross,
join with the spite of fortune, make me bow,
And do not drop in for an after-loss:
Ah do not, when my heart hath 'scaped this sorrow,
Come in the rearward of a conquered woe,
Give not a windy night a rainy morrow,
To linger out a purposed overthrow.
If thou wilt leave me, do not leave me last,
When other petty griefs have done their spite,
But in the onset come, so shall I taste
At first the very worst of fortune's might.
And other strains of woe, which now seem woe,
Compared with loss of thee, will not seem so.

91

Some glory in their birth, some in their skill,
Some in their wealth, some in their body's force,
Some in their garments though new-fangled ill:
Some in their hawks and hounds, some in their horse.
And every humour hath his adjunct pleasure,
Wherein it finds a joy above the rest,
But these particulars are not my measure,
All these I better in one general best.
Thy love is better than high birth to me,
Richer than wealth, prouder than garments' costs,
Of more delight than hawks and horses be:
And having thee, of all men's pride I boast.
Wretched in this alone, that thou mayst take,
All this away, and me most wretchcd make.

92

But do thy worst to steal thy self away,
For term of life thou art assured mine,
And life no longer than thy love will stay,
For it depends upon that love of thine.
Then need I not to fear the worst of wrongs,
When in the least of them my life hath end,
I see, a better state to me belongs
Than that, which on thy humour doth depend.
Thou canst not vex me with inconstant mind,
Since that my life on thy revolt doth lie,
O what a happy title do I find,
Happy to have thy love, happy to die!
But what's so blessed-fair that fears no blot?
Thou mayst be false, and yet I know it not.

93

So shall I live, supposing thou art true,
Like a deceived husband, so love's face,
May still seem love to me, though altered new:
Thy looks with me, thy heart in other place.
For there can live no hatred in thine eye,
Therefore in that I cannot know thy change,
In many's looks, the false heart's history
Is writ in moods and frowns and wrinkles strange.
But heaven in thy creation did decree,
That in thy face sweet love should ever dwell,
Whate'er thy thoughts, or thy heart's workings be,
Thy looks should nothing thence, but sweetness tell.
How like Eve's apple doth thy beauty grow,
If thy sweet virtue answer not thy show.

94

They that have power to hurt, and will do none,
That do not do the thing, they most do show,
Who moving others, are themselves as stone,
Unmoved, cold, and to temptation slow:
They rightly do inherit heaven's graces,
And husband nature's riches from expense,
Tibey are the lords and owners of their faces,
Others, but stewards of their excellence:

The summer's flower is to the summer sweet,
Though to it self, it only live and die,
But if that flower with base infection meet,
The basest weed outbraves his dignity:
For sweetest things turn sourest by their deeds,
Lilies that fester, smell far worse than weeds.

95

How sweet and lovely dost thou make the shame,
Which like a canker in the fragrant rose,
Doth spot the beauty of thy budding name!
O in what sweets dost thou thy sins enclose!
That tongue that tells the story of thy days,
(Making lascivious comments on thy sport)
Cannot dispraise, but in a kind of praise,
Naming thy name, blesses an ill report.
O what a mansion have those vices got,
Which for their habitation chose out thee,
Where beauty's veil doth cover every blot,
And all things turns to fair, that eyes can see!
Take heed (dear heart) of this large privilege,
The hardest knife ill-used doth lose his edge.

96

Some say thy fault is youth, some wantonness,
Some say thy grace is youth and gentle sport,
Both grace and faults are loved of more and less:
Thou mak'st faults graces, that to thee resort:
As on the finger of a throned queen,
The basest jewel will be well esteemed:
So are those errors that in thee are seen,
To truths translated, and for true things deemed.
How many lambs might the stern wolf betray,
If like a lamb he could his looks translate!
How many gazers mightst thou lead away,
if thou wouldst use the strength of all thy state!
But do not so, I love thee in such sort,
As thou being mine, mine is thy good report.

97

How like a winter hath my absence been
From thee, the pleasure of the fleeting year!

What freezings have I felt, what dark days seen!
What old December's bareness everywhere!
And yet this time removed was summer's time,
The teeming autumn big with rich increase,
Bearing the wanton burden of the prime,
Like widowed wombs after their lords' decease:
Yet this abundant issue seemed to me
But hope of orphans, and unfathered fruit,
For summer and his pleasures wait on thee,
And thou away, the very birds are mute.
Or if they sing, 'tis with so dull a cheer,
That leaves look pale, dreading the winter's near.

98

From you have I been absent in the spring,
When proud-pied April (dressed in all his trim)
Hath put a spirit of youth in every thing:
That heavy Saturn laughed and leaped with him.
Yet nor the lays of birds, nor the sweet smell
Of different flowers in odour and in hue,
Could make me any summer's story tell:
Or from their proud lap pluck them where they grew:
Nor did I wonder at the lily's white,
Nor praise the deep vermilion in the rose,
They were but sweet, but figures of delight:
Drawn after you, you pattern of all those.
Yet seemed it winter still, and you away,
As with your shadow I with these did play.

99

The forward violet thus did I chide,
Sweet thief, whence didst thou steal thy sweet that smells,
If not from my love's breath? The purple pride
Which on thy soft check for complexion dwells,
In my love's veins thou hast too grossly dyed.
The lily I condemned for thy hand,
And buds of marjoram had stol'n thy hair,
The roses fearfully on thorns did stand,
One blushing shame, another white despair:
A third nor red, nor white, had stol'n of both,
And to his robbery had annexed thy breath,

But for his theft in pride of all his growth
A vengeful canker eat him up to death.
More flowers I noted, yet I none could see,
But sweet, or colour it had stol'n from thee.

100

Where art thou Muse that thou forget'st so long,
To speak of that which gives thee all thy might?
Spend'st thou thy fury on some worthless song,
Darkening thy power to lend base subjects light?
Return forgetful Muse, and straight redeem,
In gentle numbers time so idly spent,
Sing to the ear that doth thy lays esteem,
And gives thy pen both skill and argument.
Rise resty Muse, my love's sweet face survey,
If time have any wrinkle graven there,
If any, be a satire to decay,
And make time's spoils despised everywhere.
Give my love fame faster than Time wastes life,
So thou prevent'st his scythe, and crooked knife.

101

O truant Muse what shall be thy amends,
For thy neglect of truth in beauty dyed?
Both truth and beauty on my love depends:
So dost thou too, and therein dignified:
Make answer Muse, wilt thou not haply say,
'Truth needs no colour with his colour fixed,
Beauty no pencil, beauty's truth to lay:
But best is best, if never intermixed'?
Because he needs no praise, wilt thou be dumb?
Excuse not silence so, for't lies in thee,
To make him much outlive a gilded tomb:
And to be praised of ages yet to be.
Then do thy office Muse, I teach thee how,
To make him seem long hence, as he shows now.

102

My love is strengthened though more weak in seeming,
I love not less, though less the show appear,
That love is merchandized, whose rich esteeming,
The owner's tongue doth publish every where.

Our love was new, and then but in the spring,
When I was wont to greet it with my lays,
As Philomel in summer's front doth sing,
And stops her pipe in growth of riper days:
Not that the summer is less pleasant now
Than when her mournful hymns did hush the night,
But that wild music burthens every bough,
And sweets grown common lose their dear delight.
Therefore like her, I sometime hold my tongue:
Because I would not dull you with my song.

103

Alack what poverty my muse brings forth,
That having such a scope to show her pride,
The argument all bare is of more worth
Than when it hath my added praise beside.
O blame me not if I no more can write!
Look in your glass and there appears a face,
That over-goes my blunt invention quite,
Dulling my lines, and doing me disgrace.
Were it not sinful then striving to mend,
To mar the subject that before was well?
For to no other pass my verses tend,
Than of your graces and your gifts to tell.
And more, much more than in my verse can sit,
Your own glass shows you, when you look in it.

104

To me fair friend you never can be old,
For as you were when first your eye I eyed,
Such seems your beauty still: three winters cold,
Have from the forests shook three summers' pride,
Three beauteous springs to yellow autumn turned,
In process of the seasons have I seen,
Three April perfumes in three hot Junes burned,
Since first I saw you fresh which yet are green.
Ah yet doth beauty like a dial hand,
Steal from his figure, and no pace perceived,
So your sweet hue, which methinks still doth stand
Hath motion, and mine eye may be deceived.
For fear of which, hear this thou age unbred,
Ere you were born was beauty's summer dead.

105

Let not my love be called idolatry,
Nor my beloved as an idol show,
Since all alike my songs and praises be
To one, of one, still such, and ever so.
Kind is my love to-day, to-morrow kind,
Still constant in a wondrous excellence,
Therefore my verse to constancy confined,
One thing expressing, leaves out difference.
Fair, kind, and true, is all my argument,
Fair, kind, and true, varying to other words,
And in this change is my invention spent,
Three themes in one, which wondrous scope affords.
Fair, kind, and true, have often lived alone.
Which three till now, never kept seat in one.

106

When in the chronicle of wasted time,
I see descriptions of the fairest wights,
And beauty making beautiful old rhyme,
In praise of ladies dead, and lovely knights,
Then in the blazon of sweet beauty's best,
Of hand, of foot, of lip, of eye, of brow,
I see their antique pen would have expressed,
Even such a beauty as you master now.
So all their praises are but prophecies
Of this our time, all you prefiguring,
And for they looked but with divining eyes,
They had not skill enough your worth to sing:
For we which now behold these present days,
Have eyes to wonder, but lack tongues to praise.

107

Not mine own fears, nor the prophetic soul,
Of the wide world, dreaming on things to come,
Can yet the lease of my true love control,
Supposed as forfeit to a confined doom.
The mortal moon hath her eclipse endured,
And the sad augurs mock their own presage,
Incertainties now crown themselves assured,
And peace proclaims olives of endless age.
Now with the drops of this most balmy time,

My love looks fresh, and death to me subscribes,
Since spite of him I'll live in this poor rhyme,
While he insults o'er dull and speechless tribes.
And thou in this shalt find thy monument,
When tyrants' crests and tombs of brass are spent.

108

What's in the brain that ink may character,
Which hath not figured to thee my true spirit,
What's new to speak, what now to register,
That may express my love, or thy dear merit?
Nothing, sweet boy, but yet like prayers divine,
I must each day say o'er the very same,
Counting no old thing old, thou mine, I thine,
Even as when first I hallowed thy fair name.
So that eternal love in love's fresh case,
Weighs not the dust and injury of age,
Nor gives to necessary wrinkles place,
But makes antiquity for aye his page,
Finding the first conceit of love there bred,
Where time and outward form would show it dead.

109

O never say that I was false of heart,
Though absence seemed my flame to qualify,
As easy might I from my self depart,
As from my soul which in thy breast doth lie:
That is my home of love, if I have ranged,
Like him that travels I return again,
Just to the time, not with the time exchanged,
So that my self bring water for my stain,
Never believe though in my nature reigned,
All frailties that besiege all kinds of blood,
That it could so preposterously be stained,
To leave for nothing all thy sum of good:
For nothing this wide universe I call,
Save thou my rose, in it thou art my all.

110

Alas 'tis true, I have gone here and there,
And made my self a motley to the view,
Gored mine own thoughts, sold cheap what is most dear,

Made old offences of affections new.
Most true it is, that I have looked on truth
Askance and strangely: but by all above,
These blenches gave my heart another youth,
And worse essays proved thee my best of love.
Now all is done, have what shall have no end,
Mine appetite I never more will grind
On newer proof, to try an older friend,
A god in love, to whom I am confined.
Then give me welcome, next my heaven the best,
Even to thy pure and most most loving breast.

111

O for my sake do you with Fortune chide,
The guilty goddess of my harmful deeds,
That did not better for my life provide,
Than public means which public manners breeds.
Thence comes it that my name receives a brand,
And almost thence my nature is subdued
To what it works in, like the dyer's hand:
Pity me then, and wish I were renewed,
Whilst like a willing patient I will drink,
Potions of eisel 'gainst my strong infection,
No bitterness that I will bitter think,
Nor double penance to correct correction.
Pity me then dear friend, and I assure ye,
Even that your pity is enough to cure me.

112

Your love and pity doth th' impression fill,
Which vulgar scandal stamped upon my brow,
For what care I who calls me well or ill,
So you o'er-green my bad, my good allow?
You are my all the world, and I must strive,
To know my shames and praises from your tongue,
None else to me, nor I to none alive,
That my steeled sense or changes right or wrong.
In so profound abysm I throw all care
Of others' voices, that my adder's sense,
To critic and to flatterer stopped are:
Mark how with my neglect I do dispense.

You are so strongly in my purpose bred,
That all the world besides methinks are dead.

113

Since I left you, mine eye is in my mind,
And that which governs me to go about,
Doth part his function, and is partly blind,
Seems seeing, but effectually is out:
For it no form delivers to the heart
Of bird, of flower, or shape which it doth latch,
Of his quick objects hath the mind no part,
Nor his own vision holds what it doth catch:
For if it see the rud'st or gentlest sight,
The most sweet favour or deformed'st creature,
The mountain, or the sea, the day, or night:
The crow, or dove, it shapes them to your feature.
Incapable of more, replete with you,
My most true mind thus maketh mine untrue.

114

Or whether doth my mind being crowned with you
Drink up the monarch's plague this flattery?
Or whether shall I say mine eye saith true,
And that your love taught it this alchemy?
To make of monsters, and things indigest,
Such cherubins as your sweet self resemble,
Creating every bad a perfect best
As fast as objects to his beams assemble:
O 'tis the first, 'tis flattery in my seeing,
And my great mind most kingly drinks it up,
Mine eye well knows what with his gust is 'greeing,
And to his palate doth prepare the cup.
If it be poisoned, 'tis the lesser sin,
That mine eye loves it and doth first begin.

115

Those lines that I before have writ do lie,
Even those that said I could not love you dearer,
Yet then my judgment knew no reason why,
My most full flame should afterwards burn clearer,
But reckoning time, whose millioned accidents

Creep in 'twixt vows, and change decrees of kings,
Tan sacred beauty, blunt the sharp'st intents,
Divert strong minds to the course of alt'ring things:
Alas why fearing of time's tyranny,
Might I not then say 'Now I love you best,'
When I was certain o'er incertainty,
Crowning the present, doubting of the rest?
Love is a babe, then might I not say so
To give full growth to that which still doth grow.

116

Let me not to the marriage of true minds
Admit impediments, love is not love
Which alters when it alteration finds,
Or bends with the remover to remove.
O no, it is an ever-fixed mark
That looks on tempests and is never shaken;
It is the star to every wand'ring bark,
Whose worth's unknown, although his height be taken.
Love's not Time's fool, though rosy lips and cheeks
Within his bending sickle's compass come,
Love alters not with his brief hours and weeks,
But bears it out even to the edge of doom:
If this be error and upon me proved,
I never writ, nor no man ever loved.

117

Accuse me thus, that I have scanted all,
Wherein I should your great deserts repay,
Forgot upon your dearest love to call,
Whereto all bonds do tie me day by day,
That I have frequent been with unknown minds,
And given to time your own dear-purchased right,
That I have hoisted sail to all the winds
Which should transport me farthest from your sight.
Book both my wilfulness and errors down,
And on just proof surmise, accumulate,
Bring me within the level of your frown,
But shoot not at me in your wakened hate:
Since my appeal says I did strive to prove
The constancy and virtue of your love.

118

Like as to make our appetite more keen
With eager compounds we our palate urge,
As to prevent our maladies unseen,
We sicken to shun sickness when we purge.
Even so being full of your ne'er-cloying sweetness,
To bitter sauces did I frame my feeding;
And sick of welfare found a kind of meetness,
To be diseased ere that there was true needing.
Thus policy in love t' anticipate
The ills that were not, grew to faults assured,
And brought to medicine a healthful state
Which rank of goodness would by ill be cured.
But thence I learn and find the lesson true,
Drugs poison him that so feil sick of you.

119

What potions have I drunk of Siren tears
Distilled from limbecks foul as hell within,
Applying fears to hopes, and hopes to fears,
Still losing when I saw my self to win!
What wretched errors hath my heart committed,
Whilst it hath thought it self so blessed never!
How have mine eyes out of their spheres been fitted
In the distraction of this madding fever!
O benefit of ill, now I find true
That better is, by evil still made better.
And ruined love when it is built anew
Grows fairer than at first, more strong, far greater.
So I return rebuked to my content,
And gain by ills thrice more than I have spent.

120

That you were once unkind befriends me now,
And for that sorrow, which I then did feel,
Needs must I under my transgression bow,
Unless my nerves were brass or hammered steel.
For if you were by my unkindness shaken
As I by yours, y'have passed a hell of time,
And I a tyrant have no leisure taken
To weigh how once I suffered in your crime.

O that our night of woe might have remembered
My deepest sense, how hard true sorrow hits,
And soon to you, as you to me then tendered
The humble salve, which wounded bosoms fits!
But that your trespass now becomes a fee,
Mine ransoms yours, and yours must ransom me.

121

'Tis better to be vile than vile esteemed,
When not to be, receives reproach of being,
And the just pleasure lost, which is so deemed,
Not by our feeling, but by others' seeing.
For why should others' false adulterate eyes
Give salutation to my sportive blood?
Or on my frailties why are frailer spies,
Which in their wills count bad what I think good?
No, I am that I am, and they that level
At my abuses, reckon up their own,
I may be straight though they themselves be bevel;
By their rank thoughts, my deeds must not be shown
Unless this general evil they maintain,
All men are bad and in their badness reign.

122

Thy gift, thy tables, are within my brain
Full charactered with lasting memory,
Which shall above that idle rank remain
Beyond all date even to eternity.
Or at the least, so long as brain and heart
Have faculty by nature to subsist,
Till each to razed oblivion yield his part
Of thee, thy record never can be missed:
That poor retention could not so much hold,
Nor need I tallies thy dear love to score,
Therefore to give them from me was I bold,
To trust those tables that receive thee more:
To keep an adjunct to remember thee
Were to import forgetfulness in me.

123

No! Time, thou shalt not boast that I do change,
Thy pyramids built up with newer might

To me are nothing novel, nothing strange,
They are but dressings of a former sight:
Our dates are brief, and therefore we admire,
What thou dost foist upon us that is old,
And rather make them born to our desire,
Than think that we before have heard them told:
Thy registers and thee I both defy,
Not wond'ring at the present, nor the past,
For thy records, and what we see doth lie,
Made more or less by thy continual haste:
This I do vow and this shall ever be,
I will be true despite thy scythe and thee.

124

If my dear love were but the child of state,
It might for Fortune's bastard be unfathered,
As subject to time's love or to time's hate,
Weeds among weeds, or flowers with flowers gathered.
No it was builded far from accident,
It suffers not in smiling pomp, nor falls
Under the blow of thralled discontent,
Whereto th' inviting time our fashion calls:
It fears not policy that heretic,
Which works on leases of short-numbered hours,
But all alone stands hugely politic,
That it nor grows with heat, nor drowns with showers.
To this I witness call the fools of time,
Which die for goodness, who have lived for crime.

125

Were't aught to me I bore the canopy,
With my extern the outward honouring,
Or laid great bases for eternity,
Which proves more short than waste or ruining?
Have I not seen dwellers on form and favour
Lose all, and more by paying too much rent
For compound sweet; forgoing simple savour,
Pitiful thrivers in their gazing spent?
No, let me be obsequious in thy heart,
And take thou my oblation, poor but free,
Which is not mixed with seconds, knows no art,

But mutual render, only me for thee.
Hence, thou suborned informer, a true soul
When most impeached, stands least in thy control.

126

O thou my lovely boy who in thy power,
Dost hold Time's fickle glass his fickle hour:
Who hast by waning grown, and therein show'st,
Thy lovers withering, as thy sweet self grow'st.
If Nature (sovereign mistress over wrack)
As thou goest onwards still will pluck thee back,
She keeps thee to this purpose, that her skill
May time disgrace, and wretched minutes kill.
Yet fear her O thou minion of her pleasure,
She may detain, but not still keep her treasure!
Her audit (though delayed) answered must be,
And her quietus is to render thee.

127

In the old age black was not counted fair,
Or if it were it bore not beauty's name:
But now is black beauty's successive heir,
And beauty slandered with a bastard shame,
For since each hand hath put on nature's power,
Fairing the foul with art's false borrowed face,
Sweet beauty hath no name no holy bower,
But is profaned, if not lives in disgrace.
Therefore my mistress' eyes are raven black,
Her eyes so suited, and they mourners seem,
At such who not born fair no beauty lack,
Slandering creation with a false esteem,
Yet so they mourn becoming of their woe,
That every tongue says beauty should look so.

128

How oft when thou, my music, music play'st,
Upon that blessed wood whose motion sounds
With thy sweet fingers when thou gently sway'st
The wiry concord that mine ear confounds,
Do I envy those jacks that nimble leap,
To kiss the tender inward of thy hand,

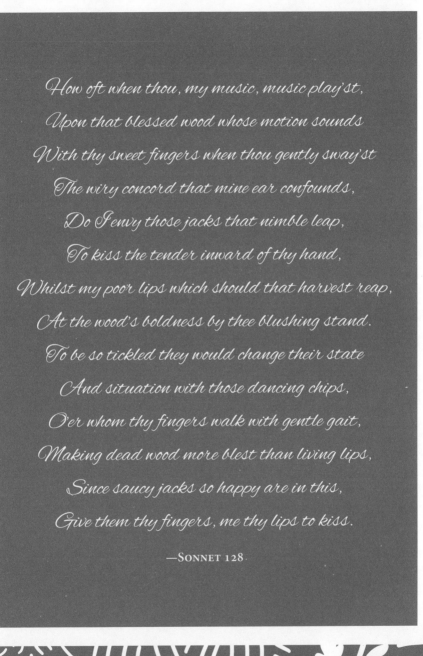

How oft when thou, my music, music play'st,

Upon that blessed wood whose motion sounds

With thy sweet fingers when thou gently sway'st

The wiry concord that mine ear confounds,

Do I envy those jacks that nimble leap,

To kiss the tender inward of thy hand,

Whilst my poor lips which should that harvest reap,

At the wood's boldness by thee blushing stand.

To be so tickled they would change their state

And situation with those dancing chips,

O'er whom thy fingers walk with gentle gait,

Making dead wood more blest than living lips,

Since saucy jacks so happy are in this,

Give them thy fingers, me thy lips to kiss.

—SONNET 128

Whilst my poor lips which should that harvest reap,
At the wood's boldness by thee blushing stand.
To be so tickled they would change their state
And situation with those dancing chips,
O'er whom thy fingers walk with gentle gait,
Making dead wood more blest than living lips,
Since saucy jacks so happy are in this,
Give them thy fingers, me thy lips to kiss.

129

Th' expense of spirit in a waste of shame
Is lust in action, and till action, lust
Is perjured, murd'rous, bloody full of blame,
Savage, extreme, rude, cruel, not to trust,
Enjoyed no sooner but despised straight,
Past reason hunted, and no sooner had
Past reason hated as a swallowed bait,
On purpose laid to make the taker mad.
Mad in pursuit and in possession so,
Had, having, and in quest, to have extreme,
A bliss in proof and proved, a very woe,
Before a joy proposed behind a dream.
All this the world well knows yet none knows well,
To shun the heaven that leads men to this hell.

130

My mistress' eyes are nothing like the sun,
Coral is far more red, than her lips red,
If snow be white, why then her breasts are dun:
If hairs be wires, black wires grow on her head:
I have seen roses damasked, red and white,
But no such roses see I in her cheeks,
And in some perfumes is there more delight,
Than in the breath that from my mistress reeks.
I love to hear her speak, yet well I know,
That music hath a far more pleasing sound:
I grant I never saw a goddess go,
My mistress when she walks treads on the ground.
And yet by heaven I think my love as rare,
As any she belied with false compare.

Thou art as tyrannous, so as thou art,
As those whose beauties proudly make them cruel;
For well thou know'st to my dear doting heart
Thou art the fairest and most precious jewel.
Yet in good faith some say that thee behold,
Thy face hath not the power to make love groan;
To say they err, I dare not be so bold,
Although I swear it to my self alone.
And to be sure that is not false I swear,
A thousand groans but thinking on thy face,
One on another's neck do witness bear
Thy black is fairest in my judgment's place.
In nothing art thou black save in thy deeds,
And thence this slander as I think proceeds.

132

Thine eyes I love, and they as pitying me,
Knowing thy heart torment me with disdain,
Have put on black, and loving mourners be,
Looking with pretty ruth upon my pain.
And truly not the morning sun of heaven
Better becomes the grey cheeks of the east,
Nor that full star that ushers in the even
Doth half that glory to the sober west
As those two mourning eyes become thy face:
O let it then as well beseem thy heart
To mourn for me since mourning doth thee grace,
And suit thy pity like in every part.
Then will I swear beauty herself is black,
And all they foul that thy complexion lack.

133

Beshrew that heart that makes my heart to groan
For that deep wound it gives my friend and me;
Is't not enough to torture me alone,
But slave to slavery my sweet'st friend must be?
Me from my self thy cruel eye hath taken,
And my next self thou harder hast engrossed,
Of him, my self, and thee I am forsaken,
A torment thrice three-fold thus to be crossed:
Prison my heart in thy steel bosom's ward,

But then my friend's heart let my poor heart bail,
Whoe'er keeps me, let my heart be his guard,
Thou canst not then use rigour in my gaol.
And yet thou wilt, for I being pent in thee,
Perforce am thine and all that is in me.

134

So now I have confessed that he is thine,
And I my self am mortgaged to thy will,
My self I'll forfeit, so that other mine,
Thou wilt restore to be my comfort still:
But thou wilt not, nor he will not be free,
For thou art covetous, and he is kind,
He learned but surety-like to write for me,
Under that bond that him as fist doth bind.
The statute of thy beauty thou wilt take,
Thou usurer that put'st forth all to use,
And sue a friend, came debtor for my sake,
So him I lose through my unkind abuse.
Him have I lost, thou hast both him and me,
He pays the whole, and yet am I not free.

135

Whoever hath her wish, thou hast thy will,
And Will to boot, and Will in overplus,
More than enough am I that vex thee still,
To thy sweet will making addition thus.
Wilt thou whose will is large and spacious,
Not once vouchsafe to hide my will in thine?
Shall will in others seem right gracious,
And in my will no fair acceptance shine?
The sea all water, yet receives rain still,
And in abundance addeth to his store,
So thou being rich in will add to thy will
One will of mine to make thy large will more.
Let no unkind, no fair beseechers kill,
Think all but one, and me in that one Will.

136

If thy soul check thee that I come so near,
Swear to thy blind soul that I was thy Will,
And will thy soul knows is admitted there,

Thus far for love, my love-suit sweet fulfil.
Will will fulfil the treasure of thy love,
Ay, fill it full with wills, and my will one,
In things of great receipt with case we prove,
Among a number one is reckoned none.
Then in the number let me pass untold,
Though in thy store's account I one must be,
For nothing hold me, so it please thee hold,
That nothing me, a something sweet to thee.
Make but my name thy love, and love that still,
And then thou lov'st me for my name is Will.

137

Thou blind fool Love, what dost thou to mine eyes,
That they behold and see not what they see?
They know what beauty is, see where it lies,
Yet what the best is, take the worst to be.
If eyes corrupt by over-partial looks,
Be anchored in the bay where all men ride,
Why of eyes' falsehood hast thou forged hooks,
Whereto the judgment of my heart is tied?
Why should my heart think that a several plot,
Which my heart knows the wide world's common place?
Or mine eyes seeing this, say this is not
To put fair truth upon so foul a face?
In things right true my heart and eyes have erred,
And to this false plague are they now transferred.

138

When my love swears that she is made of truth,
I do believe her though I know she lies,
That she might think me some untutored youth,
Unlearned in the world's false subtleties.
Thus vainly thinking that she thinks me young,
Although she knows my days are past the best,
Simply I credit her false-speaking tongue,
On both sides thus is simple truth suppressed:
But wherefore says she not she is unjust?
And wherefore say not I that I am old?
O love's best habit is in seeming trust,
And age in love, loves not to have years told.

Therefore I lie with her, and she with me,
And in our faults by lies we flattered be.

139

O call not me to justify the wrong,
That thy unkindness lays upon my heart,
Wound me not with thine eye but with thy tongue,
Use power with power, and slay me not by art,
Tell me thou lov'st elsewhere; but in my sight,
Dear heart forbear to glance thine eye aside,
What need'st thou wound with cunning when thy might
Is more than my o'erpressed defence can bide?
Let me excuse thee, ah my love well knows,
Her pretty looks have been mine enemies,
And therefore from my face she turns my foes,
That they elsewhere might dart their injuries:
Yet do not so, but since I am near slain,
Kill me outright with looks, and rid my pain.

140

Be wise as thou art cruel, do not press
My tongue-tied patience with too much disdain:
Lest sorrow lend me words and words express,
The manner of my pity-wanting pain.
If I might teach thee wit better it were,
Though not to love, yet love to tell me so,
As testy sick men when their deaths be near,
No news but health from their physicians know.
For if I should despair I should grow mad,
And in my madness might speak ill of thee,
Now this ill-wresting world is grown so bad,
Mad slanderers by mad ears believed be.
That I may not be so, nor thou belied,
Bear thine eyes straight, though thy proud heart go wide.

141

In faith I do not love thee with mine eyes,
For they in thee a thousand errors note,
But 'tis my heart that loves what they despise,
Who in despite of view is pleased to dote.
Nor are mine ears with thy tongue's tune delighted,

Nor tender feeling to base touches prone,
Nor taste, nor smell, desire to be invited
To any sensual feast with thee alone:
But my five wits, nor my five senses can
Dissuade one foolish heart from serving thee,
Who leaves unswayed the likeness of a man,
Thy proud heart's slave and vassal wretch to be:
Only my plague thus far I count my gain,
That she that makes me sin, awards me pain.

142

Love is my sin, and thy dear virtue hate,
Hate of my sin, grounded on sinful loving,
O but with mine, compare thou thine own state,
And thou shalt find it merits not reproving,
Or if it do, not from those lips of thine,
That have profaned their scarlet ornaments,
And sealed false bonds of love as oft as mine,
Robbed others' beds' revenues of their rents.
Be it lawful I love thee as thou lov'st those,
Whom thine eyes woo as mine importune thee,
Root pity in thy heart that when it grows,
Thy pity may deserve to pitied be.
If thou dost seek to have what thou dost hide,
By self-example mayst thou be denied.

143

Lo as a careful huswife runs to catch,
One of her feathered creatures broke away,
Sets down her babe and makes all swift dispatch
In pursuit of the thing she would have stay:
Whilst her neglected child holds her in chase,
Cries to catch her whose busy care is bent,
To follow that which flies before her face:
Not prizing her poor infant's discontent;
So run'st thou after that which flies from thee,
Whilst I thy babe chase thee afar behind,
But if thou catch thy hope turn back to me:
And play the mother's part, kiss me, be kind.
So will I pray that thou mayst have thy Will,
If thou turn back and my loud crying still.

144

Two loves I have of comfort and despair,
Which like two spirits do suggest me still,
The better angel is a man right fair:
The worser spirit a woman coloured ill.
To win me soon to hell my female evil,
Tempteth my better angel from my side,
And would corrupt my saint to be a devil:
Wooing his purity with her foul pride.
And whether that my angel be turned fiend,
Suspect I may, yet not directly tell,
But being both from me both to each friend,
I guess one angel in another's hell.
Yet this shall I ne'er know but live in doubt,
Till my bad angel fire my good one out.

145

Those lips that Love's own hand did make,
Breathed forth the sound that said 'I hate,'
To me that languished for her sake:
But when she saw my woeful state,
Straight in her heart did mercy come,
Chiding that tongue that ever sweet,
Was used in giving gentle doom:
And taught it thus anew to greet:
'I hate' she altered with an end,
That followed it as gentle day,
Doth follow night who like a fiend
From heaven to hell is flown away.
'I hate,' from hate away she threw,
And saved my life saying 'not you.'

146

Poor soul the centre of my sinful earth,
My sinful earth these rebel powers array,
Why dost thou pine within and suffer dearth
Painting thy outward walls so costly gay?
Why so large cost having so short a lease,
Dost thou upon thy fading mansion spend?
Shall worms inheritors of this excess
Eat up thy charge? is this thy body's end?

Then soul live thou upon thy servant's loss,
And let that pine to aggravate thy store;
Buy terms divine in selling hours of dross;
Within be fed, without be rich no more,
So shall thou feed on death, that feeds on men,
And death once dead, there's no more dying then.

147

My love is as a fever longing still,
For that which longer nurseth the disease,
Feeding on that which doth preserve the ill,
Th' uncertain sickly appetite to please:
My reason the physician to my love,
Angry that his prescriptions are not kept
Hath left me, and I desperate now approve,
Desire is death, which physic did except.
Past cure I am, now reason is past care,
And frantic-mad with evermore unrest,
My thoughts and my discourse as mad men's are,
At random from the truth vainly expressed.
For I have sworn thee fair, and thought thee bright,
Who art as black as hell, as dark as night.

148

O me! what eyes hath love put in my head,
Which have no correspondence with true sight,
Or if they have, where is my judgment fled,
That censures falsely what they see aright?
If that be fair whereon my false eyes dote,
What means the world to say it is not so?
If it be not, then love doth well denote,
Love's eye is not so true as all men's: no,
How can it? O how can love's eye be true,
That is so vexed with watching and with tears?
No marvel then though I mistake my view,
The sun it self sees not, till heaven clears.
O cunning love, with tears thou keep'st me blind,
Lest eyes well-seeing thy foul faults should find.

149

Canst thou O cruel, say I love thee not,
When I against my self with thee partake?

Do I not think on thee when I forgot
Am of my self, all-tyrant, for thy sake?
Who hateth thee that I do call my friend,
On whom frown'st thou that I do fawn upon,
Nay if thou lour'st on me do I not spend
Revenge upon my self with present moan?
What merit do I in my self respect,
That is so proud thy service to despise,
When all my best doth worship thy defect,
Commanded by the motion of thine eyes?
But love hate on for now I know thy mind,
Those that can see thou lov'st, and I am blind.

150

O from what power hast thou this powerful might,
With insufficiency my heart to sway,
To make me give the lie to my true sight,
And swear that brightness doth not grace the day?
Whence hast thou this becoming of things ill,
That in the very refuse of thy deeds,
There is such strength and warrantise of skill,
That in my mind thy worst all best exceeds?
Who taught thee how to make me love thee more,
The more I hear and see just cause of hate?
O though I love what others do abhor,
With others thou shouldst not abhor my state.
If thy unworthiness raised love in me,
More worthy I to be beloved of thee.

151

Love is too young to know what conscience is,
Yet who knows not conscience is born of love?
Then gentle cheater urge not my amiss,
Lest guilty of my faults thy sweet self prove.
For thou betraying me, I do betray
My nobler part to my gross body's treason,
My soul doth tell my body that he may,
Triumph in love, flesh stays no farther reason,
But rising at thy name doth point out thee,
As his triumphant prize, proud of this pride,
He is contented thy poor drudge to be,

To stand in thy affairs, fall by thy side.
No want of conscience hold it that I call,
Her love, for whose dear love I rise and fall.

152

In loving thee thou know'st I am forsworn,
But thou art twice forsworn to me love swearing,
In act thy bed-vow broke and new faith torn,
In vowing new hate after new love bearing:
But why of two oaths' breach do I accuse thee,
When I break twenty? I am perjured most,
For all my vows are oaths but to misuse thee:
And all my honest faith in thee is lost.
For I have sworn deep oaths of thy deep kindness:
Oaths of thy love, thy truth, thy constancy,
And to enlighten thee gave eyes to blindness,
Or made them swear against the thing they see.
For I have sworn thee fair: more perjured I,
To swear against the truth so foul a be.

153

Cupid laid by his brand and fell asleep,
A maid of Dian's this advantage found,
And his love-kindling fire did quickly steep
In a cold valley-fountain of that ground:
Which borrowed from this holy fire of Love,
A dateless lively heat still to endure,
And grew a seeting bath which yet men prove,
Against strange maladies a sovereign cure:
But at my mistress' eye Love's brand new-fired,
The boy for trial needs would touch my breast,
I sick withal the help of bath desired,
And thither hied a sad distempered guest.
But found no cure, the bath for my help lies,
Where Cupid got new fire; my mistress' eyes.

154

The little Love-god lying once asleep,
Laid by his side his heart-inflaming brand,
Whilst many nymphs that vowed chaste life to keep,
Came tripping by, but in her maiden hand,

The fairest votary took up that fire,
Which many legions of true hearts had warmed,
And so the general of hot desire,
Was sleeping by a virgin hand disarmed.
This brand she quenched in a cool well by,
Which from Love's fire took heat perpetual,
Growing a bath and healthful remedy,
For men discased, but I my mistress' thrall,
Came there for cure and this by that I prove,
Love's fire heats water, water cools not love.

THE END

TITLES IN THE
SEASONS EDITION—FALL
COLLECTION

Anne of Green Gables

Dracula

Sense and Sensibility

Shakespeare in Autumn:
Select Plays and the Complete Sonnets